Praise for *Death in a Read Canvas Chair*

"... *Death in a Red Canvas Chair* is a fun read. The quaint little town of Pequod, Maine is a hotbed of iniquity - they've got co-eds behaving badly, gangsters lurking in the shadows, and dead bodies turning up on soccer fields. I could not put the book down." Elizabeth Hein, author of *Climbing the Eiffel Tower*

"Meet Rhe Brewster. She's an ER nurse who is catapulted into the world of murder. Rhe is funny, brave and smart and you'll enjoy every moment of watching her take on the bad guys (and sometimes the powers-that-be). Try this book, it's a damn good read and I, for one, am looking forward to the next one." R.M. Byrd, author of *The Fur, Fish, Flea and Beagle Club*

"*Death in a Red Canvas Chair* is an enjoyable murder mystery, including elements of suspense, and featuring the work of forensic experts. I was drawn into the novel immediately... it was a pleasure to read, due to the well-written, vivid, and flowing language. Rhe is an unlikely and loveable heroine. Although she is highly regarded professionally, on a personal level, she struggles with important issues, and there are plenty of exciting moments to keep you on the edge of your seat, in a plot which is carefully woven with plenty of twists and turns!" Luccia Gray, author of *All Hallows at Eyre Hall*

"There is a new sleuth on the scene. Rhe Brewster can't help herself. A wife, mother, ER nurse, a full life she is content with, still she loves solving crimes. Author N.A. Granger brings her medical background to the writing, her firsthand knowledge of the setting, and a skill set that includes sailing, all of which add to the richness of the story. As the Rhe Brewster series evolves, I expect my admiration for this particular 'world' will grow. I have a lot to look forward to. There is nothing better than a good mystery." Stepheny Forgue Houghtlin, author of *Greening of the Heart*

Death in a Dacron Sail

A Rhe Brewster Mystery

by
N. A. Granger

ISBN: 0578149532
ISBN 13: 9780578149530
Library of Congress Control Number: 2014915721
N. A. Granger, Chapel Hill, NC

Dedication

This book is dedicated to the two strong women who shaped my life: my maternal grandmother, Julia Paderewski LaCourse, and my mother, Audrey LaCourse Parsons.

1

The lobster boat rocked violently against the pier as I backed down the ladder and extended my foot onto its heaving deck. It was a typical February day on the Maine coast, bitter cold, a biting wind and spitting snow – the type of day only a hardy lobsterman could love. The usual crabbing contingent of sea gulls, which normally accompanied the lobster boat fleet, was perched here and there on the dock. They added swatches of white and gray to the dock's piles of yellow, green and black lobster traps and sat facing into the wind, looking cold and hungry. My brother-in-law, Sam Brewster, the Pequod Chief of Police, was already on board and grabbed me to steady my landing.

"You should have stayed on the dock, Rhe. You could get thrown against something down here," he cautioned.

"Oh, fiddle-dee-dee," I replied with my best Scarlett O'Hara accent. "I'm pregnant, not paralyzed!" True, my baby bump was just beginning to show under my fitted wool coat and balancing was a little more of a challenge than it might have been a few months ago, but what the boat's owner had found was too intriguing not to see in situ.

The *Alice Anne* was an older commercial lobster boat, the "pickup trucks" of the Maine coast. This one had the typical beamier aft, or rear, section and a semi-enclosed bridge cabin, housing its electronic gear. I widened my stance to accommodate the rocking. "Where's that lobster trap, Sam?"

Sam pointed towards the stern of the *Alice Anne*, where Marsh Adams, Sturdevant Hospital's pathologist and the county coroner, was trying to stay upright next to a stack of traps. Marsh was of only medium height but worked out furiously and his muscles stretched everything he wore. Today, in a white parka, he looked like the Michelin Man.

"Just waiting on you, Rhe," he said, indicating one of the traps sitting on the freeboard deck at the stern of the boat. The box-like trap was made of woven metal wire, plastic-coated in a bright yellow, with an opening on either side, leading into mesh sleeves that narrowed towards the interior. The finger was caught in one of the mesh sleeves. "It's definitely a finger, I think a child's."

I leaned over to get a good look at the appendage and shuddered.

"Where did you haul this in, Pete?" Sam asked, turning to the owner of the boat.

Peter Barnes was tall, blonde, grizzled with a light beard, and despite being only in his mid-thirties, was just as weather-beaten and spare as his boat. He reminded me of a Viking. We'd all grown up together, Sam, Pete and I, sailing and swimming each summer, but I hadn't crossed paths with Pete since high school.

"This is the last trap in my string closest to the harbor, Sheriff. Most of my traps are pretty deep, water temp is more constant there in winter. But this one wasn't that far out. It didn't have no lobsters in it when I hauled it out, but it did have *that* and I figured I'd better call you right away."

"Do you know anything about the currents where this trap was located?" I asked.

"Yes, ma'am."

"Pete, it's still Rhe… unless you think I look old enough for a ma'am?" I offered him the warmest smile I could muster with a cold-stiff face.

Pete gave me a shy smile. "Um, sorry, Rhe. The tides here in the harbor are the main current, run about seven to nine feet, but this time of year, there's a weak current running north to south along the coast. Does that help?"

Sam tried jotting something down in his ever-present notebook, but had to give up with the rocking of the boat. "Well, that gives us a place to start, thinking about where the finger may have come from," he said, closing the notebook and jamming it back in his pocket. "Thanks, I'll be in touch. Do you think you can keep this quiet for the time being?"

"I'll try," Pete replied, but he shrugged his shoulders at the same time.

I wouldn't bet on it. I looked at Marsh and Sam. "You think we could go someplace warm now?" My question hid an ulterior motive. The rocking of the boat was making me nauseated, and although the worst of my morning sickness was over, there were still times when I headed for the saltines and ginger ale.

They both nodded in unison, rather vigorously. Marsh had apparently already taken pictures, because he exchanged one fur-lined glove for Latex and reached into the lobster trap, removed the finger and placed it in an evidence bag. The bag went into a cooler at his feet.

I duck-walked back to the dock ladder, and as I did, noticed there was another person on board, standing quietly in the bridge cabin. I walked beyond the ladder to introduce myself. "Hi, I'm Rhe Brewster." I held out my gloved hand and smiled.

"James Barnes, Pete's brother. I'm his stern man," he replied, taking my hand in a strong grip. "Nice to meet you." James was taller and bulkier than Pete and I could see why he'd make a good stern man, the crew member responsible for hauling, emptying and re-baiting the lobster traps. He was dark, compared to Pete's blonde looks, with a three-day stubble of beard, and he didn't smile, his face fixed in a chiseled block. I couldn't help but notice his eyes, dark brown, almost black, making him look like he had huge pupils.

"So you're the person who actually found the finger, right?"

"No, it was Pete. He offered to haul the traps today and let me run the boat." Still no smile.

"Well, nice to meet you," I replied and turned back to the dock ladder. Calling thanks to Pete, I began the climb back up to the dock, with Sam following behind me, to keep me from falling, or so he said. I really think he wanted an opportunity to make a comment on how big my rear had gotten. Lucky for him, he didn't. Pete shoved the yellow trap up onto the dock for Marsh, who had gone ahead with the cooler, and once on solid ground, Sam and I walked to the graveled lot where our cars were parked. "Wanna chat?" he asked, indicating his ten-year-old Jeep Wrangler.

I nodded yes, but pointed to my vehicle, saying, "Warmer." Sam just kept walking towards his Jeep, so I followed, but not happily.

Sam headed up the police force in Pequod, which consisted of two deputy-investigators and four beat cops. I had become involved with the police in solving a murder the previous fall, and a robbery before that, mainly because I had a knack for investigating. Which was a polite way of saying that I was nosey and effective, plus I also got a kick out of it. Because this was a small town and police resources were limited, Sam had decided to make me official, as a paid, part-time consultant. I even had a badge to prove it.

Sam gave me a hand as I hoisted myself into his passenger seat, then got in on his side, started the Jeep and set the heat on high. I wrapped my scarf more tightly around my neck and shivered. Even with the Plexiglas side curtains up and the heat on full blast, I could still see my breath in the air. "Why on earth can't you drive an enclosed car like everyone else?"

"Well, it's wicked nice in the summer and it's got a light bar, a new radio and mobile data terminal. What more could I need?"

"How about a little leg room and some heat for a start?"

"Do you know how much it would cost to fix up a newer model?"

"I wasn't implying a new Wrangler, Sam. I was thinking something altogether different, like maybe a real police cruiser."

"You know I'd never drive around in one of those sissy cars."

I harrumphed in frustration. "So John and Phil drive sissy cars?" John Smith and Phil Pearce were his deputy-investigators.

"Don't look sissy on them."

"Well, at least consider that it'd be harder to steal your fancy electronics."

"Not likely. Everyone knows this Jeep belongs to the Chief."

I shook my head and smiled at his stubbornness. Sam, all six foot five inches of him, did seem to fit comfortably in the Jeep, even with his increasing girth wedged behind the wheel. He'd wanted to be a cowboy for all the years I'd known him; a cowboy hat with a star affixed, string tie, and Jeep were how he managed it on the coast of Maine. And after his brother — my husband, Will — he was my favorite person.

"I'll ask Phil to check with local hospitals to see if any kid's come in with a missing finger. Maybe some kid helping his dad got his finger caught in the trap. If not, he can follow up on missing children," Sam outlined. Phil was Sam's second deputy and a computer geek, in my opinion. "You want to run interference for me with Marsh?"

"No problem. I'll check and see what he's got on the finger tomorrow morning. Call me crazy, and I know you do, but maybe the finger's from a body that got dumped. After what Pete told us about the currents, I'd like to take a look at some coastal charts. Mind if I do a search myself?"

"As if I could stop you."

"I hate even thinking about this. What if it *is* from a missing child? Imagine the pain of the parents."

"Do you want to touch base with Phil? How about some coffee at the station?" he asked.

"Not today, sorry. I need to get home, put my feet up and relieve my pregnant bladder. I'm working the midnight to eight shift tonight." My other job was as an emergency room nurse at our regional hospital, and although I was getting some money as a consultant to Sam's department, my job at the hospital was what helped pay the bills.

"Sure thing, sugar. I'll call you if we find anything. You take care of yourself." He touched the brim of his hat, in full John Wayne mode.

☙❧

When I got home, I parked my own ancient Jeep – they run in the family and mine was an eleven-year-old green, dented Cherokee I called Miss Daisy – in the garage, closed the door and hurried into the house. The welcome warmth enveloped me and, as quickly as possible, I divested myself of my typical winter uniform, peeling layers like an onion: fur-lined gloves, warm knitted scarf, wool hat that could be rolled down over my ears, long navy wool coat, heavy fisherman's sweater, and knee-high, wool-lined rubber boots.

It took almost as long to get out of the outfit as into it, and I thought how much I hated winters by the time February rolled around. *I'm a summer girl*, I thought, *but I'm not looking too girlish now.* I peered down at the turtleneck that stretched a little over my stomach. I was just over three months along, and Will had not been a happy camper when I told him of the pregnancy the previous November. He'd only wanted one child. Last year, cushioned by six years of contraception, we'd foolishly decided not to use birth control any more. Well, I guess the decision had been more mine. Why should we, when it had taken us three years and a round of *in vitro* fertilization to get pregnant with my son Jack, now seven? I'd figured that at thirty-five, I was unlikely to get pregnant again, and I was tired of additional hormones. Big mistake. *Big* mistake. But I was happy. I liked the feeling of a new life growing inside me.

As soon as I'd peeled, I made myself a cup of decaf coffee and sat down with my laptop in our kitchen, warming my hands around the cup while I waited for the aging computer to boot up. I knew Sam would have Phil Pearce searching for missing children, but I just couldn't wait. My antennae were twitching. Forget the coastal charts.

Tux, our five month old black and white cat, appeared from the family room and stropped against my legs, begging for attention, so I absentmindedly petted him while thinking of where to start. I skipped our town's newspaper, the Pequod Post and Sentinel, because that rag would have thrashed a missing child story to pulp over the course of several weeks, and I wouldn't have forgotten it. Chancing that this child had come from somewhere nearby, I searched the archives of other coastal newspapers: the Bar Harbor Times, the Harpswell Anchor and the Lincoln County News. After an hour of squinting at small print, I felt a dull pain beginning behind my eyes, and with no results, I decided to hit the big cheese, the Portland Press. Something popped up in an issue from the previous March, demonstrating that my bias of sticking to coastal communities had cost me a headache. Savannah Engstrom, age eleven, had gone missing from Camden a year ago.

Wondering if Phil had found anything more with the sites he had access to, I called his number at the station. Before he could speak, I said, "Hi, Phil, it's Rhe. Found anything yet?"

"Good grief, Rhe, Sam just told me! Give me a break here."

"Did you check the hospitals?"

"That I did do – no kids with missing fingers."

"Well, I found something, or rather someone. Do you want to pop this name into the National Registry of Missing and Exploited Children? It's Savannah Engstrom."

"Interesting name."

I could hear his fingers clicking on his computer keys. Impatiently I asked, "Did something come up?"

"Mmmm...not much. Seems Maine's not prime ground for missing children, which is definitely a good thing. I've only got four names. The latest is Savannah Engstrom, age eleven, your find. A year before her, there's another,

Jane Alderson, age ten. Three years ago, Rachel Vance, also eleven. Strange, almost a year apart in each case."

"What about the fourth?"

"This is an old one, from more than twenty-five years ago."

With those words, a guilty memory I'd repressed for years came to the surface, and I found myself engulfed in the anxiety and sick fear of a twelve-year-old again. "It's Deirdre Dunn, isn't it?" My voice quavered.

"Did you know her?"

I took a deep breath and fought the memory. "She was my best friend."

"This search is going to drag up a lot of old feelings for you, Rhe. You sure you're up to it?

"More than ever. I have to help the parents of these missing girls. I can see the agony of Deirdre's relatives as if it were yesterday. See what you can find on each, and include Deirdre too, will you? I'll keep searching for information at my end when I have time."

"You bet."

"Oh, and Phil, let Sam know what we've found as soon as you see him."

"We?" He chuckled. "Okay, will do."

I'd just hung up the phone when I heard the garage door open and close, and a few minutes later Will and Jack came in, Jack's cheeks a rosy red and his face full of excitement. "I scored two points, Mom!"

"Did you now? How did the team do?"

"Both teams won!" Will exclaimed loudly, then whispered to me, "They lost twelve to ten, but that hasn't dampened his enthusiasm." His glasses had fogged up and he took them off before putting Jack's gym bag and basketball on the floor and removing his parka and boots. Jack was already sitting on the floor, peeling layers as fast as he could, and when he was down to his jeans and shirt, started towards the family room.

"Not so fast, young man. Haven't you forgotten something?"

"Ah, geez, Mom, it's time for Nickelodeon."

"What's still sitting on the floor?"

"My coat 'n hat. And maybe my gloves," he answered, hanging his head. Water had pooled under his boots on the kitchen floor.

"You know what to do and please put your boots on the mat." Jack shuffled back to the kitchen, hung up his coat and scarf on a child-height peg on the wall, placed his boots on the rubber mat and then raced to turn on the TV. It was Friday night, so no homework. We all loved Fridays.

"So what did you do today?" Will asked, sitting down at the kitchen table while I poured him a cup of coffee. He made a face after his first sip. "Yuck. How can you drink this stuff? And how long has it been sitting?" He pushed the cup away. In my opinion, decaf was a dishwater substitute for the real thing but had the benefit of not stimulating 'little It.' We'd been calling the baby 'little It' since our decision to wait until he or she was born to find out the sex. But I also had an affection for Addams Family cartoons.

"You know it's decaf or nothing for me, and don't you think for one minute that I wouldn't give my left arm for real coffee," I countered with a smile. "As to what I did today, it'll have to wait 'til after supper."

"Something for the police?" he asked gruffly. Will was not happy with my being a consultant for Sam. We'd nearly come to blows over my role in the previous murder investigation, but since then he'd calmed down, probably thinking that my pregnancy solved our problem. *Little did he know.* However, my part-time gig was bringing in some extra money, which helped with Jack's weekly session with an ADHD specialist, so it wasn't all bad.

੨੦੶੶

After supper, Jack's bath, more cartoons, and finally getting him into bed, Will and I sat at the kitchen table, drinking fresh decaf. "So what happened today?" he asked, tilting back in his chair.

"Peter Barnes, remember him? He's a lobsterman now, and he found a human finger in one of his traps."

"A finger?" Even Will seemed surprised at that.

"Yup. Pete called Sam and we met with Marsh on Pete's boat, the *Alice Anne*. And there it was, caught in the netting. Marsh says it's probably from a child."

"Oh no," groaned Will. "Tell me you're not involved in this!"

"Already with the 'no involvement'? Come on, Will. It was just a finger and it's my job. I did a little computer search for missing children this afternoon and found three girls who've disappeared in the last few years. Marsh can get a DNA analysis done and maybe it'll match one of them. If you were their parents, wouldn't you want to know? Get closure?"

He finished his coffee, glared at me with the wrinkle between his eyebrows that indicated displeasure, but ultimately sighed and agreed. "Okay, I see your point. If Jack were to go missing, I'd be nuts with worry. But I'm not happy about this." He stood up, still frowning, and put his mug in the sink.

"Would you mind cleaning up for me tonight, hon? I'd like to put my feet up before going to work." Lately he'd helped out less and less around the house, but I still hated asking.

"Okay."

I could tell he really didn't want to do it.

I reclined in the softest chair in the family room and listened to the sounds of running water and the occasional clash of a pan, thinking of the missing girls. *I need to check with Marsh when I get off work tomorrow. Wonder if it's one of those girls? And whatever happened to Deirdre...?*

2

The midnight shift in the ER at Sturdevant was normally quiet, but it was a Friday night and a full moon, which meant a lot of loonies would be out. And they were: students from Pequod College with alcohol poisoning, the occasional victim of a bar fight with broken bones and slash wounds, and a multivehicle accident which had EMS trucks lined up at the dock. By eight the next morning, I was dead on my feet, but was determined to see Marsh about that finger before I left.

Marsh's work space was in the basement of the hospital. Even though it was Saturday, I knew he'd be around, workaholic that he was. I had to pass by his office anyway, on my way to the employees' parking lot in back, and seeing his light was on through the frosted glass of his door, I knocked. A muffled response resembling 'come in' gave me permission to enter. Marsh was ensconced at his desk, feet up, reading from one of many files that littered its surface. The steam from his coffee rose in a slow coil, the powdered sugar on his shirt telling me he'd just finished eating a doughnut.

"Were those lemon-filled, Marsh?" I asked, knowing full well those were his favorite.

He looked up, startled, and said, "Sorry, what did you say, Rhe?" I pointed at his powdered shirt and he guessed my question. "Yup, lemon-filled. You here about the finger?"

"Yeah, what've you got? You wouldn't happen to have another doughnut you might want to part with, would you? I'm starving!"

Marsh reached down and picked up a paper bag emblazoned with a Hole in One logo from the floor beside his chair. "One left, and I'd only give it to you," he said handing me the bag with a smile.

I grabbed the bag, pulled out the doughnut and crammed a large bite into my mouth, while mumbling, "So, what about the finger?" *Lemon nirvana.*

"First off, it's the middle finger. Figured that out from the muscles. X-rayed it and got an approximate age of the victim. Wanna see?" He got up and led me across the hallway to one of the morgue bays, but not before I jammed the rest of the doughnut into my mouth. No food was allowed in autopsy, but I wasn't going to let that doughnut go. In the bay, he slapped an X-ray up on a light box and I could see the three bones of the finger clearly.

"See here, Rhe," Marsh tapped the middle one of the three bones with his finger. "I'm pretty sure you remember these three phalanges start out as cartilage and then become ossified from two centers in each bone. The two centers become united in all the phalanges between ages eighteen and twenty. You can see that this hasn't happened yet in this finger, so the victim is younger than eighteen. Take a look at this middle phalanx. This bone is fully ossified by age eleven in girls or fourteen in boys. So this is a pre-pubertal girl or a pubertal boy. I'm pretty sure a girl."

"Why would you say that?"

"Well, the finger is small, but mainly because I found some pink nail polish in the crease between the edge of the nail and the surrounding skin."

"Was there enough for an analysis to figure out the kind of nail polish?"

"Not sure, but I sent off the sample anyway. You never know."

"Do you have any idea how long the finger had been in the water?"

"Since the skin was not entirely sloughed off, just some of the epidermis, I'd say less than five days. It's hard to determine because of the water temperature. I managed to get a fingerprint from the dermis."

"How'd you do that?" I asked. "I didn't think it'd have the same whorls as the epidermis."

Marsh gave me a gotcha smile and said, "Ah, but it does! Not quite as clear as the epidermal ridges, but good enough. Oh, and I took a sample for DNA analysis, but neither the fingerprint nor the DNA are going to be any help if we don't have exemplars to compare them to. Have any leads?"

"Phil and I searched yesterday and found three girls missing over the last three to four years." I didn't mention Deirdre; this wasn't her. "The latest was Savannah Engstrom from Camden. Were you involved in that case?"

"No, but I'm pretty sure the FBI was. Maybe Sam can request a DNA profile or fingerprints."

One more thought occurred to me. "Marsh, can you tell if the finger was dislocated, sawn off, or eaten off by sea creatures?"

"There are no saw marks on the first phalanx. The bone isn't broken, so maybe the ligaments were nibbled to the point of disconnection from the meta-carpal. The skin was pretty macerated at the proximal end."

"Phil Pearce told me none of the local hospitals had records of a child with a missing finger. Maybe the rest of the body is still in the water somewhere," I mused. All of a sudden, I felt profoundly tired and must have wobbled a bit, because Marsh took me by the arm and led me back to his office. He sat me down, saying, "Sit there a minute, Rhe, then get yourself home and to bed. We've got a dead victim, and she's not going anywhere." He waited until he was satisfied I was steady again, then walked me out to my car.

☙ ❧

When I got home and peeled my layers, I glanced around the kitchen, hoping for a note from Will. Over the years, he'd had a habit of making me a pot of coffee and a sandwich and leaving a note for me when I came home from an overnight shift. But for the last few months, he hadn't been doing that. Little touches of kindness and remembrance seemed to be slipping from our marriage and I wondered if this was how all marriages went after a number of years. I had no idea what to do about it, except keep up my end. It was Saturday morning, and I wondered what he and Jack were up to. *He could have at least left me word where they were going*, I thought with irritation, opening the refrigerator door. Largely empty shelves greeted me, and I sighed, remembering I'd have to go to the grocery store after my nap. I slapped together a cheese sandwich with mus-tard and mayo, drank some milk and lay down on the sofa in the family room, shutting down as soon as my eyes closed.

Sometime later, I gradually became aware of a child's excited piping, then a not-so-gentle shake roused me from the depths. "Mom, Mom, are you sleeping?"

Ah, Jack, master of the obvious. I groaned and opened my eyes.

"She's awake, Dad! Come and see what we got, Mom. Dad and I went shopping." I sat up, rubbing my face with my hand, yawning and trying to shake the cobwebs. Jack took my hand, pulled me up and dragged me into the kitchen. Grocery bags covered every surface. "See, Mom? Dad and I did the grocery shopping!"

Oh man, a real gift! I smiled and bent down to envelope my son in a hug. *Not so far to bend now*, I thought. *He's growing fast.* I rose and hugged Will, too, who looked pleased with himself. I'd always done the shopping, either alone or with them, and all the irritation at the cheese sandwich flew out the window. "So what did you guys decide we should have for supper?"

"Spaghetti, of course," answered Jack, "and we even got the turkey meatballs." I couldn't have been happier, still tired, but definitely happier.

"Oh, by the way," and here Will hesitated a beat, "Phil called this morning before we left for the store." I could tell he was working hard not to be irritable about it.

"Did he tell you what he wanted?" I tried not to sound interested.

"Yeah, he wanted to know if you could stop by the police station. He said he had some case files for you to look at. I told him you needed the weekend to get some rest. He said he'd see you Monday morning."

A frisson of irritation ran through me. I was eager to see those files and Will knew it. He just *had* to exert control over my work for the police department, and now he could use my pregnancy as an excuse. For the sake of maintaining the peace, I continued the pretense of disinterest. "Okay, I'll see him Monday then." But it still rankled.

❦

Monday I dropped Jack off at school and drove into town to the two-story, 1960s bland-as-a-box brick building that was our local police station. It didn't help that it occupied the space between a neoclassic court house and some charming turn-of-the-century buildings, whose foundations dated from the late

1600s. As a result, the station and its pot-holed parking lot stood out like a sore thumb. When anyone entered the station's street door, they had to pass by a huge front desk, which dwarfed the woman who'd sat there for going on thirty years. Ruthie Hersh had been my friend for at least ten of those years and was a renowned local busy-body.

"So, you found another body, huh?" she asked as soon as I was in the door. She was referring to the body I had found on my son's soccer field in October.

"Just a body part this time, Ruthie. A small part, just a finger."

"You going to be investigating it?"

"I hope so...unless Will makes a federal case out of it."

She shook her head at my words, jostling her bun of reddish gray hair from which a fringe of loose ends hung out. "Phil's in his office." She indicated the corridor on the left with a nod of her head. *How did she know I was coming to see Phil? I wouldn't put it past her to listen in on phone calls.*

I knocked on Phil's door, which was open, came in without waiting and plopped down on the utilitarian metal chair beside his desk. "Sorry I couldn't get here Saturday," I said with a frown.

"No problem. These're the unsolved cases of child disappearances," he said, tapping a pile on the corner of his desk. "They're yours, but Sam wants to talk to you about the finger before you go." He gave me a closed lip, straight line smile and tilted his head sympathetically. It occurred to me he knew about Will.

"Can I take these files with me or do I need to read them here? I can't stay long."

"I'll get them Xeroxed for you. You can pick them up at Ruthie's desk on your way out."

"Did you include Deirdre Dunn's?"

"I did. Talk to Sam about that one. I think he wants new eyes on it, as long as you're looking at the other unsolveds. You know he went to high school with her brother?"

"I didn't, but thanks." *Maybe Sam knows something I didn't, all these years?* I got up and bent over to give him a half hug. Maybe not the professional thing to do, but he was a generous, sweet, intelligent man. If it weren't for his face – homely with a ski slope nose and jug handle ears – he'd be attractive to women. I'd more than once sensed an underlying loneliness. His face lit up with the hug, as I knew it would.

Sam's office was further down the hallway, and as I looked through the glass window in his door, I noted that, as usual, the place was a mess. There were files and papers everywhere – mounded on his desk, a chair, and the top of the filing cabinet, and spilling off the bookcase behind him. The only thing that had changed from my last visit was the absence of the dead Christmas cactus. *Maybe Ruthie got tired of looking at it and snatched it when he wasn't looking? Not that he would notice.* Sam looked up, smiled and motioned me in.

"You've seen Phil?"

"And good morning to you, too." We had a habit of picking up conversations where we had left off previously, foregoing the usual civilities.

"Have a seat, Rhe. Take the extra load off."

I gave him a face and picked up the pile of papers on the chair, handing them to him. "You really need a housekeeper, Sam. This place is a pigsty."

"Yes, but it's my pigsty and I know where everything is."

"I know you do, and yes, I saw Phil. He's going to copy the files on the missing girls for me. Did you get the autopsy report on the finger from Marsh?"

"I did, and I know there's no local kid walking around with a missing finger. But if it does belong to a dead girl, she must have been killed recently. She wouldn't be one of the girls on file."

"Unless she was kidnapped and held for a year."

"True."

"Are there fingerprints and a DNA analysis on file for each of the girls?" I asked.

"There are, but we have to get them from the FBI. I called, and what with Marsh being an assistant state ME, they're willing to send them along. Better than sending them the finger."

"How soon do you think they'll get here?"

"Maybe today if they get around to faxing them. I know Marsh asked for an expedited analysis of the DNA in his report, so maybe we'll even have that by the end of the week. At the very least we can compare fingerprints."

"What would you like me to do?"

"For starters, go over those files. Maybe a fresh set of eyes will find something we've missed or at least generate some new questions. Then if the DNA or prints match anything on file, well, then we'll have to think about notifying the parents. I'm trying to keep a lid on this, although that cock-eyed editor friend of yours was here on Saturday asking questions. How in hell did he find out about the finger?"

That cock-eyed editor was Bob Morgan, an old high school flame of mine and the editor-in-chief and owner of the Pequod Post and Sentinel. The locals considered it good reading for gossip and innuendo, but not much for news. Bob had figured tangentially in the case I had previously solved and had hounded me for weeks for a story, which he'd finally gotten when Sam gave me the go-ahead.

"I'll bet lobstermen gossip, and Pete would be hot to talk about this with his friends. Did you manage to deflect Bob, or will his reporters be stalking me again?"

"I told him that we'd found a body part but there was nothing else to tell, because there isn't."

"I'm sure he'll have done the digging Phil and I did. Have you seen the newspaper today? Betcha it's front page, above the fold. The parents of those missing girls will be calling you."

"I wouldn't take that bet, Rhe. Before you go, I want to talk to you about Deirdre."

"Yeah, Phil told me."

"Are you okay looking at her file? I know you were pretty close to her."

"I was." Hearing her name again opened up feelings I thought I'd walled off, and my breath hitched as some memories of my best friend came back without warning. Summers wandering together in the tide pools, weaving dreams of the future in the meanderings of the salt marsh behind the beach. Eating grape pop-sicles on a hot day, playing hopscotch on the sidewalk in front of her house. I shook them off, bore back down on the here and now. "I won't be able to look at the file impartially, Sam, but I can handle it. What do you know that's not in the file?"

"I went to high school with her brother."

"Yeah, Phil told me that too. What about him?"

"Artie and I were both on the basketball team for three years – small guy but quick, really muscular. Solid point guard." Sam paused and I could see that he too had his memories, maybe back in the gym playing basketball. After a few seconds, he added, "Artie didn't act normal after Deirdre disappeared. He didn't seem worried or anxious, just matter of fact, got on with his life, never seemed to mourn. Once he said to me 'My sister's gone. I'll bet they don't find her.'"

Sam rubbed his semi-bald head with one hand, then rubbed his face and ended with stroking his chin. "At the time I thought it was strange, but never thought anything more about it." Then he smiled. "I was just a testosterone-driven teenager and more interested in girls than what Artie might have meant by that."

"I seem to remember you making a play for one of the cheerleaders. Candy, right? The blonde with the long legs."

"Yeah," he replied dreamily. "Really nice legs."

I reached over and swatted him on the arm. "You should see her now. At least thirty pounds overweight and three teenage kids with acne and no manners. Really, Sam."

"I can always dream. Back to business. Could you do some digging on Artie? Maybe you can find him. I haven't seen him in years."

"Will do. Call me when the DNA results come in. How about dinner with us sometime this week?"

"You know I can never resist a home-cooked meal. Let's see how the week plays out."

"Any special requests?"

"Just something edible."

I couldn't help it – my inner child took over and I stuck out my tongue at him. My cooking had always been a source of great humor at the police station, courtesy of Sam, because of my general ineptitude in the kitchen. Lately, however, with the help of Paulette McGillivray, a gourmet cook who just happened to be my best friend, my offerings to guests had improved. "I can only promise not to burn it," I replied primly as I headed out the door.

I picked up a newspaper on my way to my shift at the hospital. Sure enough, the story was on the front page, above the fold with a blaring headline: 'Local Man Finds Finger in Lobster Trap.'

3

Bob Morgan proved as pesky as ever, and I had three messages on my cell phone, all from him, when I finished my shift at the hospital around 8 PM. As I prepared to leave, the charge nurse gave me a pink message slip. 'You have a meeting with Dr. Manning at 9 AM Tuesday,' it read. *Oh joy.* James Manning was the CEO of the hospital and a surgeon, stuffy and full of crap, to be blunt. Right now, he was knee deep in the legal fall-out from transplants done at the hospital using non-regulated tissues from a funeral home. He'd had to fire the surgeon who had done those transplants, a man he'd hired to create a new center for Sturdevant. Since I was the one who had discovered the source of those tissues, my infrequent interactions with Manning had become downright icy. I mulled over what he might want as I walked to my car. *Whatever it is*, I concluded, *it's probably going to involve shooting the former messenger.* I decided to answer Bob's calls before I drove home, to avoid having him sic a reporter on me. I noted it was his personal phone number, not the newspaper's. Despite the hour, he picked up.

"Hi, Bob. It's Rhe. I can't tell you anything."

"Hello to you, too. And how do you know what I want?"

"I saw today's paper. What else could it be?"

"Aaah, Rhe, I know you're smack dab in the middle of finding out who belongs to that finger. Is it a kid?"

"Sorry, can't comment."

"It's Savannah Engstrom, isn't it?"

"Why would you think that? Who told you about the finger?"

"Sorry, can't comment," he replied, mimicking me. "What *can* you tell me?"

"Nothing, until the remains have been identified. Then Sam will have a statement for the press."

"You're a hard nose, you know that?"

"Just with you, Bob. Just with you. See ya!" I hung up.

☙❧

After a late dinner of reheated pizza and a glass of milk, followed by the usual struggle to get Jack to finish his homework, I tucked him in for the night and went back to the kitchen. Will had gone to his study to grade papers from the Psych 101 class he taught at Pequod College. We'd married the year he'd been appointed an assistant professor, and now that he had tenure, he seemed even more dedicated to his academic career. We hadn't had a lot of time together recently.

After returning Jack to bed following several appearances in the kitchen with requests for water, I could finally dig into the girls' files. They'd been burning a hole in my bag since I got them. I took out my laptop and sat down at the kitchen table with another cup of decaf, which was more for the comfort of seeing a mug of coffee and smelling the aroma than actually drinking the stuff. I set Deirdre Dunn's file aside, then put the other three in reverse chronological order, starting with the most recently missing girl, Savannah Engstrom, age eleven. *Romantic first name, coupled with that Swedish last name,* I thought idly. Savannah was from Camden, a picturesque seaside tourist town that sat where the Megunticook River met the Atlantic, not far from Pequod as the crow flies. So the Engstroms were local and probably not summer residents I surmised, as I looked at the abduction date: January 30th the previous year.

Savannah had been walking home from school, which was about a quarter of a mile from her home, said good-by to a friend at the corner of her street and vanished. *Same as Deirdre.* I shuddered, but read on. Her parents didn't miss her until around five, called all her friends, went to the school to see if she had stayed for a basketball game, and then called the police in a frenzy of anxiety. She'd been wearing a blue parka, jeans, brown Uggs, and a red wool hat, scarf and mittens. Phil had Xeroxed her picture: a pretty girl with straight blond hair, fine, delicate facial features, a big smile and braces. *Did she wear pink nail polish?* I made a note on my laptop to ask the parents of the missing girls.

I continued reading – interviews with her parents, her friends, her teachers. She was an indifferent student with a high IQ, more interested in social activities than homework. Her parents had said she was too young to have a boyfriend, but one of her friends mentioned a classmate named Josh Henson. According to her computer records, he and Savannah had been having online conversations for a couple of weeks. He was interviewed but was playing basketball when she disappeared. Only her homeroom teacher had mentioned anything out of the ordinary. He'd seen Savannah with a man just after school, about a week prior to her disappearance. He'd thought it might have been her father, but her father had been working at the time. His description was vague because of the layers of dark winter clothing: tall, over six feet, couldn't see his face, nothing to follow up on, although the police interviewed half the school and the school's neighbors, asking about the unknown man. And there was nothing else on Savannah's computer. *Where to start with this case?*

I was about to pick up the second folder when my cell phone rang. I hoisted myself out of the chair and walked over to the counter where I'd left it. It was Sam.

"Hi, Sam. What's up?"

"Sorry to call, I know it's late, but I wanted you to know that someone thinks they saw a body on the shore in Dornish Cove.

"A child?" My hand went to my stomach automatically.

"I'm not even sure it *is* a body. Might be a wild goose chase but I gotta follow up. The guy's a lobsterman, name of Wellman. He put a few pots near the rocks at the edge of the cove and was hauling them in when he noticed something wrapped in what he *thinks* is a sail, beached on the little sandy area. He got as close as he could to take a look and snapped a picture with his cell phone. We didn't find out about it until a while ago, because he waited to report it until he came in."

"What do you think?"

"The picture is blurry because his boat was bobbing, so I can't tell. I figure it's worth a look, but we're going to have to wait until morning. That site's difficult to get to in daylight, let alone when it's pitch black."

"What about the tide? Won't that dislodge the body?"

"Tide's going out, so we should be okay to wait."

"How are you going to get to the beach?"

"I'm thinking we'll have to come down the cliff."

"Why wouldn't you go in by boat? That seems a bit easier."

"Winds'll be up tomorrow and the waves are going to run five to six feet, just like today. We couldn't get close in with the police boat. We'd have to go over the side and come in by dinghy. I called the Fire Department, and turns out they've got a guy trained in mountain rescue who can rappel down."

"Who's going down to do the examination?"

"Probably Marsh. I called him right after I got Wellman's picture. We're all meeting on the road above the cliff tomorrow morning, early, maybe eight o'clock. Do you want to be there?"

"Do you need to ask?"

"You working tomorrow?"

"No...I just have to drop Jack off at school. I'll call you right after that, okay?"

"Talk to you then."

⇚⇛

At 7:55 AM the next morning, while idling in the drop off lane at Jack's school, I called Sam and found out everyone had already gathered on the cliff road above the cove. As I drove away from the school, I suddenly remembered my appointment with Dr. Manning, pulled over and called his secretary, dreading the impending interaction.

"Dolores, this is Rhe Brewster. I'm so sorry, but something's come up and I can't meet with Dr. Manning this morning." I heard a huff at the other end of the line. Dolores Richmond was the Queen of Administration, an insufferable shrew who ruled her boss's schedule with an iron fist.

"Ms. Brewster, may I remind you that Dr. Manning's time is very valuable. Why didn't you notify me yesterday?"

"This just came up and it's important. I would have called you had I known, believe me. I'm truly sorry." *Time to grovel.*

"This is going to throw off his entire day's schedule."

"Thank you so much. Again, I'm really sorry to have caused you such trouble." At this point, I had to stop myself from laughing. "Why don't you just cancel his daily three hour lunch?" I muttered under my breath as I hung up.

The drive to the cove seemed to take forever. Although I'd sailed there with a bunch of my high school friends for picnics many years before, I had no clue how to reach it by road. Persephone, as I had named my British-accented Garmin voice, took me by some roundabout route over every two lane country road in the county, and as a result it was 8:30 when I finally got there.

I knew I'd found the right place when I saw a viewpoint sign with an arrow directing me off to the right and a parking lot clogged with a fire truck, the medical examiner's van, a police car and Sam's jeep. I parked next to Sam, zippered up my parka, pulled my hat down over my ears and tugged on my lined gloves before getting out of the car. Ambient temperature was a balmy 19 degrees, but as Sam had predicted, there was a stiff ocean breeze which burned my cheeks. Sam was standing at a rock wall that formed a curve around the parking lot. Huge signs said 'Don't climb on the wall' and 'Danger! Steep cliff,' and I wondered why the DOT had created an overlook here if it was so dangerous. Next to Sam stood Marsh, who was shaking his head vigorously.

"Hi folks, what's going on?" I asked.

"A fire fighter's already down there," Sam replied. I peered over the edge of the wall and saw a steep cliff, lined with sharp rocks, ending at a post-age stamp-sized patch of sand where I could see the small figure of a man in black weather gear. Something off-white lay on the sand, but I couldn't see it clearly from where I stood. "There *is* a body and it's wrapped in a sail, just what Wellman thought. The ME needs to go down for an initial inspection and some picture-taking," he said, looking pointedly at Marsh.

"I can't do it, Sam," Marsh said, backing away from the wall. "I just can't. I've had acrophobia my whole life. Even standing on a step ladder gives me vertigo. I could never go down there. Send me around by boat, *please*."

"No can do, Marsh. Tide's coming in, and it will be higher than usual with the onshore wind. We don't want the body to wash away or lose evidence. You should understand that," Sam replied testily. "How about your assistant?" He turned to a small, round Asian woman completely enveloped in a knee length, red down coat, with a heavy wool stocking cap pulled down to her eyebrows and a matching green scarf wrapped several times around her neck. She looked like a Christmas tree ornament.

"Chief," she piped her tiny voice, "I've only been with Dr. Adams for two months and I've never done anything like this."

"That's right," said Marsh. "Midori's straight from a community college forensic tech program and in the two months she's been with me, we haven't had to process a single crime scene. What medical knowledge she has, I've taught her as we've gone along."

Sam radioed the fireman who was down on the beach. "Matt, we need you to do the investigation of the crime scene and also the preliminary medical examination. Dr. Adams can give you directions on what to do."

I couldn't see his reaction but Matt's response sounded desperate. "No, sir, I can't do that. I've never had anything to do with a crime scene. And what little I've seen makes me want to puke. I can't do that..."

Leaving all this back and forth, I walked over to the rappelling gear and motioned to the other fireman to help me put it on, strapping myself into the harness. I adjusted the harness to fit around my waist and legs, and clamped a helmet on my head over my hat.

At that point, Sam realized that I was no longer in his discussion group and noticed me getting into the gear. "What the hell do you think you're doing, Rhe?" he bellowed at me while charging over to the fire truck. "Are you nuts? You're pregnant."

"And you're getting bald," I snapped back. "Look, Sam, I'm the logical one to do this. I got into rock climbing in college and spent one summer in the Rockies, where I did a lot of rappelling and belaying. This is a cake walk."

"We can just bring the body up wrapped in the sail and..."

I cut him off. "And just dismiss or trample on any evidence around it? And who else here has the medical expertise to evaluate the body in situ? You know I can communicate with Marsh by radio."

Marsh joined Sam and both of them looked at me and shook their heads. "Really, what other choice do you have?" I insisted.

"Maybe we could get someone here from the state ME's office. Let me make a call." Sam took out his phone to make the call and walked away from us, pacing back and forth. Finally, shaking his head, he took off his cowboy hat, slapped it on his thigh and hung up. As he came back toward me, I noticed his ears were bright red from the cold. "Doggone it, Rhe! Will's going to have my head for doing this. What if something happens?"

I took that as meaning I was the only one available, at least before the tide came in. "It's my choice, and it's not Mount Everest, for heaven's sake!" I straightened my shoulders and tried to look defiant.

Ten minutes later, I was attached to a line running from an electric winch, which was attached to the fire truck by a winch plate. The line ran through a three-legged portable anchor system the firemen had borrowed from a mountain rescue group. I was also attached to a belaying line as a safety backup, one end of which was held by Matt down on the beach and the other by a beefy fireman up top. As the winch unwound the low-stretch rope, I sat at the edge of the cliff, turned around, and placed my feet on the sheer wall below it. Leaning back and standing with extended legs, I started to walk backward down the cliff, the rope being slowly let out by a fireman stationed at the winch. He was taking orders from Sam, who was leaning over the edge, observing my progress. With the wind whipping around me and the amazing view, I remembered why I loved climbing... and lost my concentration. My boot slipped and I came face to face with the rocks of the wall before regaining my footing.

"What happened?" I heard Sam yell.

"Nothing, foot slipped, I'm fine!" I thought of all the times I had slipped at far greater heights in the Rockies and almost laughed. But I still had to accomplish this rappel without drama or I'd never hear the end of it. *Concentrate, Rhe. Just get down to the beach. Don't think about what Will will say when he finds out.*

"You need to speed it up, Mrs. Brewster," I heard Matt call nervously from below.

I reached the beach without further problems, then detached the ropes. Matt helped me out of the harness. I took off the helmet, pocketed my gloves, and retrieved the camera that was latched to the harness. Speaking into the lapel microphone attached to my collar, I said, "I'm down, Marsh. How do you want me to photograph?"

His voice came back to me through an ear bud. "Before you start, give me a general description of what you see. Then circle into the body in a spiral pattern, taking pictures from all angles, even from the water. Photograph the surroundings – sand, detritus, anything interesting. Matt can collect samples for you. I sent down evidence bags, markers, and gloves earlier." Sure enough,

Matt was already gloved and, after I'd done the same, I moved in a tightening spiral around the rolled sail, snapping pictures. We found cigarette butts, bottle caps, some broken bottles and other waste, and all were carefully marked, photographed, collected and labeled. I contacted Marsh again when I finally reached the sail.

"Tell me what you see." His voice was loud in my ear.

"A sail, probably a foresail or jib because it's smallish, and there appears to be a body rolled up in it. I can see the foot. Body is small. The sail is tied up with what looks like marine braid rope, and there are some marks on it. I'll take some close-ups, so maybe you can figure out what they are." I snapped some pictures. "Do you want me to unroll the body or leave it in the sail?"

"Go ahead and unroll it, Rhe, but carefully. I don't want any body parts detaching until we can get photographs."

"Okay, I'll have Matt take photographs while I collect anything from inside the sail."

I handed Matt the camera and gently unrolled the sail. When I finally saw the body clearly, I had to stop and take more than a few deep breaths. I felt like retching; this was a mother's nightmare. After a minute, during which I noticed Matt had also looked away, breathing deeply, I told him to start taking pictures, first a full shot, then as I directed. More deep breaths, and I knelt over the body.

"It's a young person, Marsh, maybe a preteen. She's stick thin. From the length of the hair it could be a girl. Hair is blond; she's wearing jeans and a blue shirt." *Funny, both seem more than a size too small.* I immediately looked at the fingers; several were missing, including the one middle finger. "Middle finger of the right hand is missing, Marsh. No shoes or socks." I gingerly undid the top three buttons of the shirt and peered at the chest. "It's definitely a girl. She has breast buds, Tanner stage 2."

I paused and took another deep breath before continuing. "The remains are not skeletonized. I think the cold water has impeded decomposition because the abdomen is only just starting to distend." I applied a little pressure to the abdomen, and it felt like a balloon. "The exposed parts of the body have been scavenged: the nose, ears and one eye are missing. Some fingers and toes are gone, too, and the skin is sloughing. Looks like some bruising around the neck." I examined one of the remaining fingers more closely. *Pink nail polish. This has to be the owner of the finger in the lobster trap.*

"Can you roll the body over?"

I gently rolled the body on its side, but there was nothing underneath but some sand. Rising and stepping back, I thought, *Dear heavens, I hope the parents don't have to try to identify this poor thing.* Marsh's voice sounded in my ear. "They're sending down a body board. Can you and Matt rewrap the body and roll it onto the board? Make sure that nothing falls out, like the head or hands or feet."

Thirty minutes later both the body and I had been winched up to the parking lot. Marsh was busy overseeing the transfer of everything into his van. From somewhere, one of Sam's men had found everyone hot coffee and chocolate, and sitting in my Jeep with Sam, I gratefully wrapped my fingers around the warmth of the cup and sipped. I had the heater on high and had taken off my hat, but my cheeks still burned from the cold.

"You actually look like you enjoyed that," Sam said, taking a deep drag of his coffee and regarding me with interest.

"Enjoyed? You've got to be kidding. Well, the rappelling was fun, but definitely not what I saw on the beach."

"Was a middle finger missing?"

"Yes, and one of the remaining ones had pink nail polish, maybe the same as on the finger Pete found."

Sam took another drag of coffee. His breath was still visible in the air and I turned the blower up another notch. "You sure it's a girl?" He practically had to yell to be heard over the blower.

"Unless you wore pink nail polish and had breasts when you were a pre-teen," I yelled back.

Just then his radio barked. He listened, then unlatched his door and a blast of cold air poured in. "I gotta go," he said, turning to get out. "Keep at those files. I'm betting you'll find something." The door slammed and blessed warmth once again filled the car.

～❦

When I got to my neighborhood, instead of pulling into my own driveway, I continued a little further down the street and pulled into a drive alongside the brick Georgian-style house where my best friend Paulette lived.

Paulette and I had been friends for nearly twenty years, and we'd shared our lives over coffee and some of Paulette's baked creations every other day or so. There was nothing we didn't share, but no matter what we talked about, it always stayed between us. Paulette was also Pequod's answer to Paula Dean, while I was Mr. Bean in the kitchen. Or at least had been. Under her tutelage, I was becoming a passable cook, which was depriving both Sam and Will of funny stories to tell at work.

Before I could knock on the back door, Paulette jerked it open and asked, "Okay, what's going on? Where have you been?" The previous fall, Paulette had impersonated a graduate student looking for easy money as an escort to help me in my investigation, and we barely survived a car chase. Ever since, her thirst for crime-solving had way outpaced mine. She'd overcome her aversion to blood and guts, at least on the written page, and had taken to reading crime scene investigation manuals and murder mysteries by the dozen.

"You planning on inviting me in, or do I have to beg?"

She stood aside and waved me into her kitchen, with its usual mouth-watering aromas, this time meaty and spicy with an overlay of something fishy with fresh baked bread.

"What's on the menu today?" I asked, giving her a hug. Paulette was tiny, her head barely coming up to my chest, so she hugged back around my waist.

"I've got a beef stew for tonight in the crockpot," she replied, stepping back. "But I also made clam chowder and some sour dough bread this morning. Want some lunch? Maybe then you can tell me what's going on."

"Bribe away."

While she set the table for lunch and I sipped from a mug of decaf coffee, I told her about the finger, which she already knew about, and then gave her the rundown on the morning's activities, but still omitted any gory details. She put her hand to her mouth and paled a bit, but all in all, I think she handled it well.

"A child, Rhe! How horribly sad. Will Marsh be able to identify her?"

"I think so. There're only four children missing in the state. One of them is …"

"Deirdre," Paulette finished, sighing. "I'd almost forgotten about her. This must be hard on you."

"I'm okay. Sam gave me the files on all four. He said he'd like another pair of eyes on them, but finding this body could be a break."

"Well, let me know if there's anything I can do..." She stared at me for a moment, then something clicked and she practically yelled, "Good God, Rhe, what were you thinking? Rappelling down a cliff? Are you nuts?"

"That's what Sam and Marsh said. But honestly, who else could do it? No one from the State ME's office could get there, Marsh is acrophobic, Midori couldn't rappel, and the fireman didn't have the medical training. That left me, and you know I've got way more experience climbing."

"So what's Will going to say?"

"I can just imagine. But I'm going to have to tell him. If I don't, he'll hear it from Sam and there'll be hell to pay."

"I think there'll be hell to pay anyway, Rhe. Not good, especially now. Just when you two seem to have gotten past the problems with the last case you worked on."

"I know that. Maybe if I make him a nice dinner and wait to tell him until Jack's in bed?"

Paulette just shook her head.

"What should I make to soothe the savage beast?" I asked the Empress of the Kitchen.

I'd just begun inhaling my soup when the backdoor opened and a young girl blew in, followed by a blast of cold air. It was Paulette's daughter, Sarah. She yanked her hat off, unwound her scarf, and pulled off her boots by the door.

"Hi, Aunt Rhe!" She paused to give me a hug before asking her mother, "What's for lunch?"

"How come you're home? I thought you were supposed to be at your school of exceptional learning," I joked.

Sarah made a face at me. "Teacher half-work day." She was heading for the stove when Paulette replied, "Clam chowder. Go wash your hands and I'll dish you up." As Sarah left the room, Paulette shook her head and called, "and take off your coat and hang it up!"

"Sure, Mom."

I had known Sarah since the day she was born. I'd babysat her, been there for her first steps, and felt like her second mother. Lately, she'd taken to calling me about social things – clothing styles and girlfriend squabbles and a little about boys, mostly negative. I was probably the last person she should ask, but if Paulette was a little jealous, she had hidden it well so far.

N. A. Granger

Sarah came back to the table in a rush. She had her Mom's blond hair, but long and straight, lovely blue eyes framed by luxurious lashes, and so far, no acne. I knew she watched what she ate, but Paulette watched even more closely, determined that her daughter would not develop an eating disorder and turn into the stick figures we saw around town.

While we ate lunch, Paulette ran over some possible dinner recipes with me, and Sarah listened and commented. She liked to cook and frequently helped her mother on weekends. Will, Jack and I were regular recipients of the cookies, brownies and bread that she made, much to the distress of my waistline.

I left Paulette's with another hug from Sarah and buoyed by the thought that maybe a good dinner would solve my problems with Will, at least temporarily.

4

I prepared one of Will's favorite meals, a beef, lamb and pork meat loaf from a recipe of Paulette's, with garlic mashed potatoes and green beans. I made a sugar-free, coconut chocolate pudding for dessert – comfort food for Will and Jack.

After dishes and the nightly tussle to get Jack focused enough to finish his homework, he went more than willingly to take a bath. Will and I sat down in our family room with after dinner coffee – a good Jamaican brew for him and the usual dishwater for me. The soft couch was so comfortable, with the smell and crackle of a fire in the stone fireplace, I was tempted not to say anything about my high flying adventure that morning. I gave a deep sigh, knowing what would result if I didn't, and pondered how to phrase my words.

"Why the sigh?" Will asked.

"Just feeling comfortable."

"Any problems today? How's the baby?" This in a monotone that implied anything but real interest.

"No problems, except for the continuing need to pee every half hour."

Will grimaced. He asked about me and the baby infrequently and never really wanted any details.

"There was a child's body found today in Dornish Cove." I backed up. "Well, actually a lobsterman spotted it yesterday but didn't report it until after dark, so this morning was the first time anyone could take a look."

"Was that the phone call last night?" Will had stopped asking me directly about calls that might be from Sam.

"Yup. Sam asked if I would be there when they retrieved the body, so I drove out after dropping Jack at school."

"Dornish Cove...isn't that the place with the overlook?"

"Yeah, that little patch of sand with the cliff behind it."

"So how did they get the body? Come in by boat?"

"Nope, the sea was too rough. They rappelled down."

"So Marsh went down? I can just see him swinging back and forth, looking like a white balloon in that parka of his." He smiled at the thought, but when I didn't respond, he asked, "Marsh did go down, didn't he?"

"Actually, he's severely acrophobic. Couldn't handle it."

The smile had faded from his face. "So who did it?" A log crumbled in the fireplace with a loud crackle and a puff of sparks. I could see Will mentally considering the options. "Oh my God, not you! I can't believe it! Three months pregnant and taking a chance like that. What kind of idiot are you?" His voice rose and his face contorted in anger.

"Quiet down, Jack's just down the hall!"

"I will not quiet down! I'm married to a lunatic with no regard for her own life or that of her unborn child." He jumped out of his chair, knocking his coffee cup to the floor.

Nice touch. Her unborn child. "But you know I did a lot of climbing in college."

"I don't know," he replied stubbornly.

"Of course you do," I insisted. "I spent two weeks climbing in the Rockies and we climbed Mt. Katahadin before Jack was born."

He remained standing, looking down at me, unconvinced.

"I was the most experienced climber there this morning, plus the only one with medical knowledge. Honestly, Will, if a pregnant Kerri Walsh can win a gold medal in volleyball at the Olympics, I can scale down a hill with big, muscular firemen manning the ropes."

Will shook his head, then turned and walked out of the room. *That went rather well.* I didn't think for one minute his reaction had anything to do with the baby, but everything to do with my working with the police department.

Same old, same old. I picked up his cup and went to get a rag and some carpet cleaner.

Will slept on the sofa in his office that night.

ও৵ী

The next morning he was gone before I got up. *Great.* It was his day to drop Jack off at school, but since I had to do it, I was late for my shift at the hospital. I was in a sour mood when I arrived, which did not improve when I was handed a memo slip with the message 'Meeting with Dr. Manning as soon as you come in.' Luckily, the ER was fairly quiet. I made a double apology to the charge nurse, promised to be back as soon as possible, and hot-footed it to the elevator.

When the door opened on the fourth floor, I was struck by the contrast between the noise and seething humanity of the ER and the quiet ambiance of Administration just a few levels above. Plush dark green carpeting deadened footsteps, tasteful but bland landscapes graced the walls, heavy drapes in a coordinating color framed the windows, and the furniture was made in a rich wood. Quite a contrast to the stainless steel or white enamel of the ER. It occurred to me that while the ER needed to be kept sterile, the real sterility was here.

I quietly approached Dolores Richmond's desk and cleared my throat. Dolores was done up in her usual Queen of Administration regalia: a two-piece, navy Donna Vinci knit suit with a pearl necklace. Her hair was swept up in gray waves, sprayed into an unmoving helmet. A little too much foundation, which had clotted into her facial wrinkles, and, dear heavens, bright blue eye shadow. She was fixated on her computer screen and raised her head abruptly with a look of annoyance.

"Yes? What can I do for you?"

Clearly she had no clue who I was. "I'm Rhe Brewster. I got a message Dr. Manning wanted to see me first thing this morning?"

"You're late, Ms. Brewster. Didn't your shift start fifteen minutes ago?"

"I had to drop my son off at school..." The disdain registering in her frozen, polite expression quickly made me realize I had to take the offensive. "Is Dr. Manning ready to see me?"

She actually snorted, and I had to work hard to keep a straight face. "Yes, he can see you now." Dolores picked up the phone, pushed a button and spoke quietly into the receiver, then gestured me to the heavy double doors to her left. The doors had large, stained glass inserts. *Nothing too good for this administration.* After a first, ineffective try at opening one, I planted my feet and yanked to gain entrance to the inner sanctum.

Manning's office was a repeat of the lush environment in the reception area, but with a burgundy color palette. He was sitting behind a desk as large as a boat with his hands folded on its empty surface, as if in prayer. He made a papal wave, gesturing me to take a seat in an upholstered chair in front of the desk. Dr. Manning was actually quite young for a CEO of a hospital. Tall, early fifties, bland face topped with wavy reddish hair with a touch of gray at the temples. And dark, beady eyes, behind which lurked a shrewd political mind.

He also had an annoying habit of bobbing his head, as if agreeing with someone on a continual basis. He'd been nicknamed Woody the Woodpecker by the hospital staff, a name that was occasionally shortened.

"Well, Ms. Brewster. I had expected to see you a little after eight." Head bobbing.

"As I explained to Dolores…."

"Never mind. I'm willing to overlook the delay."

Well, thank heavens for that.

Manning frowned, then rearranged his face to appear serious and businesslike. It didn't work. "As you know," he continued, "the economy is not what it once was. Because of the hospital's bottom line, we've hired an efficiency expert to find savings in our day to day operations. One of our most expensive departments, as I'm sure you know, is Emergency Medicine. The cost of trauma treatment, coupled with the number of uninsured using our emergency room, puts us in the red on a daily basis. It's been determined the ER is overstaffed for the amount of business it does…"

I finally saw where this was going, and my stomach dropped.

"…and I'm forced to reduce staff hours. I see that you are already part-time, working three shifts instead of the usual four."

I nodded silently.

"We, and by that I mean the Board and I, decided that it would be unfair to reduce the hours of our full time staff, because they would lose their benefits.

And this would strongly affect staff morale. You, on the other hand, by virtue of being part-time, don't receive benefits. So we have decided to reduce your time to two shifts a week." More head bobbing.

This was the biggest bunch of bullshit I'd ever heard. If they really wanted to save money, they'd cut a full time person and save both the salary and benefits. I could see a twinkle of malice in his eyes as he told me; we both knew this was retribution.

I couldn't help myself. I stood up and leaned onto the desk to confront him. "You're doing this to punish me, aren't you? For providing the evidence that dismantled your transplant unit. And you barely avoided prosecution yourself!" I wanted to reach across the desk and wring his neck.

"Nurse Brewster! You are not only misinformed, but you're being disrespectful. This has nothing to do with you personally. I have also had to cut back on hospital security, along with other things."

The wind went out of my sails and I sat back down.

"Do you have anything else you want to say? More civilly this time?" he asked, a hint of a smile touching the corners of his mouth.

"No, sir." *Slimy bastard.*

"Your reduced shifts begin next week. If there is anything you wish to communicate, I suggest you go to Human Resources. That's all." He waved his hand toward the door.

I found myself back in the ER without remembering how I got there, wondering what to do next. Nancy Ennis, one of the full time ER nurses and a good friend, was manning the desk and I pulled up a chair.

"Thank God you're back, Rhe. We're starting to pile up." She looked at my face. "What happened? You look like your best friend just died."

"Manning cut my hours to two shifts a week."

"You can't be serious! Why? We have barely enough staff here as it is!"

"Let's talk about this on break. I need to ask you some questions." I took a deep breath and looked around. The number of people waiting patiently on the hard plastic chairs finally registered. "Where am I needed first?"

৯৯ ৶৩

The rest of the morning raced by, with a number of serious flu cases, a few broken bones, and a couple of construction workers who were trying to work in the cold and had shot themselves with nail guns. By one o'clock, things were fairly quiet and Nancy gave me the high sign to head upstairs to the cafeteria.

We grabbed a booth in a corner, opened our lunches, and both said at the same time, "So what's up?" I smiled for the first time since my meeting with Manning, then got serious.

"I need to ask you about the reason for my reduced time. Is it true Manning hired an efficiency expert to tell him and the Board how to save money? He told me the ER was the biggest drain on the bottom line."

Nancy nodded, and through her mouthful of chicken salad I thought I heard, "Well, we all know it is, but not because of us!"

"Did you actually see this so-called efficiency expert?" I stabbed a tomato in my salad with force, splattering the table.

"If you mean the little mousey guy with the Coke bottle glasses and the comb over who spent all of ten minutes in the ER last week, then I guess I did."

"Is that the only time he was there?"

"I'm pretty sure, but I can ask around."

"I've been trying to make a mental list of the other nurses who work only part-time, and I've only been able to come up with three, including myself, Sullivan and Donahue. Is that right?"

Nancy tugged on one of her red curls for a minute and then replied, "Yup. That's all."

"Have any of them had their shifts reduced?"

"Don't know. Sullivan hasn't mentioned it. Donahue and I don't work the same days."

"Could you find out? Carefully? I don't want it to reach Manning I'm asking around. I know he has friends in the ER."

"Rhe, you can't honestly believe this was deliberate!"

"You bet your sweet ass I do. He's been trying to find a way to get back at me. He had to fire his fair-haired surgeon, Montez, but somehow he tap-danced his way out of being fired himself."

"But that's too obvious! It really *could* be a money-saving issue."

"Well, he did say he had cut hospital security…"

"Yeah, Charles, that nice guy assigned to the ER, is gone."

I hadn't even noticed. I was still convinced Manning was playing with me, and I shook my head in exasperation.

She paused to take a bite of her sandwich, then said, "Okay, I can see you have a beef. But at least begin an appeal with Human Resources – you can go there at the end of your shift."

"I'll get there when I can. I really need to see Marsh first. I'm hoping he's done the autopsy on the body we pulled up from Dornish Cove yesterday."

"Yeah, I read about it in the *P&S*. The usual lurid headlines. Does anyone have any idea who it is?"

"Not yet." *Not for certain.*

☙ ❧

When I finished at 4:30, I headed to Marsh's office in the basement. The autopsy suites were dark, and Midori's office door was shut, but Marsh's was open. I knocked on the doorframe as I entered and found him leaning back in his chair, staring at the ceiling. From the looks of the crumbs decorating his desk, and the empty package of Goldfish in the wastepaper basket, I'd interrupted him having an afternoon snack. "Hi, Marsh. Got the autopsy results?"

"Rhe! Have a seat." He removed some files from the chair next to his desk and added them to a teetering pile next to him. I dropped my bag and coat on the floor and sat, leaning my elbows on his desk, eager to hear what he'd found.

"I finished about two hours ago and just finished writing up my notes... Look, I'm so sorry about yesterday. It was my fault. You shouldn't have had to go down to the beach. I know this must have created problems with Will."

I could feel my face go hot with embarrassment and frowned at the thought of the confrontation with my husband. *Did everyone know?* "I made the decision to do it, and Will and I will just have to figure it out. So don't blame yourself. Maybe Midori can take some wilderness training?"

"Now that's a visual! I can just see her rappelling in that red coat, bobbing up and down...looking like a buoy on a fishing line!" We both smiled. "I really shouldn't joke," he then said. "She's a good kid and smart as a whip."

"So what did you find?" My smile evaporated with the question.

"Well, first of all, the finger from the lobster trap belongs to that body. The ends of the disarticulation are a match. I know you noted pink nail polish on her forefinger. I sent off a sample to the state lab to see if they can compare it to the sample on the other finger, but I'd bet dollars to doughnuts they'll be the same."

"How old is this girl?"

"I had Midori take a complete set of X-rays. They showed she is definitely prepubertal, based on the fact some bones in her skull hadn't fused. The growth plates in her long bones hadn't fused, either. I'd estimate her age at ten to twelve, because her first and second bicuspids have erupted, but not her second molars."

I leaned back, trying to relax against the chair, aware of the tension that had crept into my neck and spine. I bent my head from side to side to relieve it. "Did you find anything else on the X-rays?"

"There was an old break, at the distal end of her left radius. Looks like a typical FOOSH." I nodded at his terminology of 'fall on an outstretched hand,' knowing forearm fractures are nearly 50% of the children's bone breaks, and three fourths occur at the wrist end of the radius.

"Can you tell how long ago this happened?"

"Based on bone re-formation, probably four to five years ago. There's another more recent break in her right arm, a spiral fracture of the radius and ulna."

"How long ago?"

"Fairly recently, I would say within six months. But this child is extremely malnourished and the bones were not re-approximated. So it could have been a year or more ago. She must have been in constant, terrible pain for quite a while."

I sat quietly for a minute with a hand on my stomach. I hated to think of it, but spiral fractures had occasionally been considered an indication of abuse, especially in children. A spiral break could be caused by an adult grabbing and violently twisting a child's arm. "Abuse?" I finally asked.

"Can't say, but her parents would have to be ruled out because of the recent nature of the break."

"Anything else from the X-rays?"

"Just some wearing on the distal ends on her tibia and fibula, both legs, just above the ankle."

"Mmmm…so she was restrained?"

"That's what I was thinking."

"Dear heavens." We both pondered that for a moment. "You said malnourished?"

"Yeah, this kid had nothing at all in her digestive system, lots of bruises, very little subcutaneous fat. She's very underweight for a child her age."

"Poor girl!" I found myself getting light-headed.

Marsh looked at me, rose, and got something from his mini-fridge. I heard him crack a can open. "Here Rhe, drink this. It's ginger ale. I bought some to keep around just for you."

I gave him a grateful smile and drank deeply. When I refocused, there was an opened package of cookies on the desk. "Thanks, Marsh! You're a life saver. May I ?" I took a cookie.

"Be my guest." I noticed they were lemon cookies. Marsh liked lemon-flavored anything.

I sighed, and continued with my unhappy line of questioning. "Did you save her clothes? I noticed they seemed to be too small for her, at least in length. I read Savannah Engstrom's file, and the clothes described seem to be similar to what we had found on the body. If these were the clothes she was wearing when she was abducted, perhaps her parents can identify them."

"Midori bagged them. We can check that out. There's more. You up to hearing it?"

I shook my head but said, "Might as well know everything."

"Aside from the effects of malnutrition and the wear on the leg bones, there were a few more things about the body. Although the skin had started to slough, I noticed both the wrists and ankle areas were very discolored. Again indicates some sort of restraint, but the wrist restraints were either just recent or only used from time to time since the distal radius and ulna did not show any wear."

"Cause of death?"

"Nothing obvious. I sent off some blood samples for a tox screen, but if a fast-acting poison killed her, we might not find anything. So I also took samples of the vitreous humor in the one remaining eye. Do you know about this type of analysis?"

"I think so, but remind me?"

"Well, the vitreous humor, or the liquid found in the eye between the lens and the retina, is relatively isolated from the blood. So it's less affected by postmortem changes and can be ideal for chemical analysis."

"But would a poison persist in the vitreous?"

"It might. Changes in the concentrations of drugs in the vitreous lag behind those in the blood by several hours. So yes, there might still be something there. The other good thing is that we can get a fairly accurate determination of how long it's been since her death from a measurement of potassium and hypoxanthine."

"How long until you have results?"

"Knowing the state lab? Ten days to two weeks."

"Can you pressure them?"

"I can try, once Sam has read this report. Better if two people push."

"One more question, Marsh, and I really don't want to ask it. Any sign of sexual activity or abuse?"

"I won't lie, Rhe. There were signs of repeated rape." Marsh thumbed through the pages of the report in front of him, shaking his head in distaste.

"Did you do the standard rape kit?"

"I did, but with the time in the water, I don't think anything's going to show up from the vaginal or rectal swabs or under what's left of her fingernails. I'll know by tomorrow after Midori runs the samples. But I did note bruising of her breasts and on the inside of her thighs, and in her perineal area. There's no hymen, either." He shuffled the report's pages and then rubbed his forehead.

This is hard for him. "Why do you think there was long term activity?"

"Because she has genital warts. And because her rectum and her vagina are scarred and thickened. I took tissue samples in addition to photographs, because these changes need to be documented histologically. Do you want to look at the photos?" he asked, finishing his litany of horror.

"No! I'll take your word for it." By this time, I was holding my head in my hands. The mental images of what had been done to this child were almost more than I could handle. Child abuse had always been an emotional issue for me, from the first time I saw evidence of it when I was in nursing school. A sickening feeling had overwhelmed me then and had not eased up with more experience. There were no reasons I could ever accept for someone abusing a child.

Marsh and I again sat in silence for a few minutes. Then I asked, "When will you have an ID on the body?"

"Maybe tomorrow. Sam told me the FBI is sending an agent with the dental records of all three missing girls for comparison."

"I'd forgotten about the FBI. They must've run the investigations for all the kidnappings, and Sam got pulled in each time when they widened their search." I paused and took a sip of ginger ale, then munched on a cookie. "When will the report be finalized?"

"First thing tomorrow. I have some details to finish up before I can send it to Sam. You gonna meet with him?"

"I'm hoping I can wait until the fireworks with the FBI over jurisdictional issues are over. Sam is going to take this case personally. He's not going to want to hand it over. But first I have to go home and tell Will my shifts here have been cut."

"What? Why?" Marsh rolled his chair around his desk to face me and took my hand.

"Because Dr. Manning told me the hospital needs to make cuts to preserve the bottom line, and he prefers to cut the part-time people."

"That's just plain nonsense. It would be more cost effective to lay off a full-time person."

"Well, you know it and I know it, and everyone else in the trenches knows it. But that doesn't make it any less real."

"What are you going to do?"

"Haven't a clue. Probably gather some information, consult Human Resources and then maybe decide if it's worth the effort to fight it."

"This has been a hell of a day."

"Sure has," I replied, getting up and girding myself to face the ice cold wind outside and the white hot response I'd get from my husband when I talked to him about this.

5

When I arrived home at 5:30, much later than usual, Jack was fidgeting at the kitchen table, ignoring his homework. He looked up and smiled as I came in from the garage. "Whew!'" he said. "Am I glad you're home! Dad said he was *not* getting dinner, and I'm hungry."

"Did he give you a snack?" I asked, struggling to pull my boots off.

"No, he just sat me down, made sure I had my homework out, and went to his office. Is he mad at me or something? He didn't talk much on the way home."

"He's a little mad at me, hon, but he shouldn't take it out on you. Let's see if I can make him smile. I'll make cheeseburgers for dinner."

"Mmmmmm. I think that's a good idea," he said seriously, which was funny because Jack loved cheeseburgers. I tousled his hair and went to the fridge to get the hamburger, knowing full well the cheeseburgers wouldn't be nearly enough to counter the news about my new working hours.

I decided to get dinner on before I talked to Will. So I started with a salad, thinking it would balance the fat and cholesterol in the hamburgers. But then I gave in and whipped together a bread pudding with some stale sourdough I'd been saving for that purpose. If the carbs sank the meal, I didn't care. In between, I helped Jack with his homework. It was difficult for him to focus at the end of the day and frustrating for me, trying to get him to concentrate. As I watched him hunched over the table, I worried he was also responding to the tension in the house.

Once the aroma of sizzling beef permeated the house, Will wandered into the kitchen and told Jack to pick up his unfinished homework and go wash his hands for dinner. He then set the table without a word. I was still sitting in the doghouse, apparently. We ate dinner without addressing each other, avoiding eye contact. We did chat with Jack about his day, the next basketball game, his teacher, whom he adored, and mindless, trivial stuff just to keep the silence at bay. After dinner, Jack moved back to the table to finish his homework and Will retreated to his study again, leaving me with Jack and the cleanup. For once I didn't mind. The tension dropped to a manageable level when he left the room.

While Jack took his bath, I screwed my courage to the wall and went to Will's study. The door was usually open, but was now firmly shut. I knocked. He didn't reply, so I opened the door. "Want some coffee?" I asked.

"Sure. In here, though." He didn't look up from his work.

Just wonderful. "Look, there's something I need to talk to you about...not the case, but about work."

He finally looked at me, his forehead raised in a question. "Good news?"

"No," I gave him a frown, "bad news."

"What happened?"

"Manning cut me down to two shifts a week."

"What? Why? Because you've been distracted by this new case?"

At that point everything I'd been trying to handle came crashing down: the tension with Will, the determination to maintain a stiff upper lip with Manning and in the ER, and the horror of what I'd been told by Marsh. I sagged against the door and started to cry. Will paused, watching me, then finally came over, put his arm around me and led me to the small sofa opposite his desk. He swept off the papers and helped me sit down. I couldn't help it, I just bawled, leaning against his shoulder. At first awkwardly, then with more care, Will cuddled me and let me finish crying. When I had gotten to the shuddering and snuffling stage, he got me a Kleenex, shoved it into my hand and asked, "What's going on?"

"I knew Manning would try to get back at me, Will," I said in between blowing into the Kleenex. "Now he's got his chance."

"Just another reason why you should never have gotten involved in that case in the first place, Rhe. What reason did he give you?"

"He said he had hired an efficiency expert to figure out where the hospital could save money, and the ER was the biggest drain. He decided to cut my hours to save money."

"You're kidding, right? Why didn't he put some of the full-time people on part-time? That way he wouldn't have to pay their benefits. Everyone's doing that now."

"He said it would impact morale if he did that. That it was easier just to reduce my time."

"That's bullshit."

"I know that, but what are we going to do, Will?"

He sat quietly for several minutes, while I leaned into him, tired of the day and everything.

"I suppose I can pick up a summer course if I have to."

"But that's the time for your research. And you need the publications."

"I'll just find a way to cram it in," he said with some sarcasm.

"Maybe I can find some in-home nursing jobs. I'm going to HR tomorrow anyway. They might have some options."

"I don't think that's a good idea, Rhe. You've got the baby to think of."

"It wouldn't be a lot."

"Rhe."

"Just a day here or there. I'm still feeling great. Plus the private jobs pay more."

That got his attention. "You realize this is only a short term solution, don't you? You won't be able to work after the baby arrives." He paused, probably for effect, then dictated, "Okay, you can look into it. Let me know what you find before you go off making any huge decisions."

I sighed. "I promise." Then I thought, *What the hell, I'll be the first to apologize.* "Will, I want to tell you how sorry I am about yesterday. It was an impulsive thing to do and you were right. I never should have done it. If this last year has taught me anything, it's how I operate: full speed ahead, no thought of the consequences. I need to be more cautious and think before I leap." I smiled. "Literally, right?"

Will gave me a one-arm hug and said "That's my girl. Let's go get some coffee and check on Jack. He's probably puckered into a prune in his bath water."

How condescending he sounded. That's my girl? And no apology from him and he didn't even ask about the dead girl. I was so discouraged I bit my tongue in an effort not to rekindle the argument.

❧

The next morning, after dropping Jack off, I drove to the police station. I hoped to catch Sam early and needed some time to gird myself for dealing with HR. It didn't help that it was a gloomy day with spits of sleet, matching my feelings about my life in general.

Ruthie was at the front desk, although as usual, all I could see was the top of her head bobbing around behind it.

"Ruthie? You hiding out back there?" I called. She popped up on the desk seat, grasping the pen she'd obviously been chasing. Her face was red from the effort. Slips of hair had escaped from her reddish-gray bun and danced on her forehead; she blew at them with an irritated puff of air. When she saw me, she beamed.

"Hi, Rhe! What's up? How's the baby? How's Jack?"

I could see I wasn't going to get away without an update. The usual exchange of gossip this time stretched to a good fifteen minutes. I even pulled up a chair. Ruthie was the repository of all the family news for each departmental employee, something she'd assumed was part of her duties when she took the job at the front desk thirty-five years ago. In a way, she was the glue holding the department together, and she ruled Sam's non-emergent schedule with an iron fist. When we had exhausted pretty much all of the latest, I felt less gloomy.

Ruthie told me Sam was in his office. "He got the report from Marsh this morning. I made the mistake of popping in while he was reading it, you know, just to ask if he wanted coffee. He just waved me off without a word. I've never seen his face look like that."

"Trust me, that report would upset even the most thick-skinned person, Ruthie. I know you want to know what's in it," I said with a forced smile, "but it's not something anyone would want to read. I just pray Bob Morgan doesn't get his hands on it and then publish it in the *P and S*. Not even after the parents have had a chance to deal with it."

Ruthie nodded solemnly and patted me on the arm. "Sam will be gentle notifying them, don't you worry."

"I don't think Sam'll be doing that, since the girl's not from Pequod. Speaking of that, have you heard anything about the FBI dropping in for a visit?"

"Yeah. Sam got a call early this morning. Some hotshot agent's on the way. I think it's one of the guys who were here last year to interview you after your kidnapping."

Oh joy. I remembered them well. I just hoped it was not the hyperactive rookie, who'd spent the entire time tapping on the table or jiggling his legs. I gave Ruthie a kiss on the cheek and walked down the hall to Sam's office, knocking gently on the door. I could see Sam at his desk with his head in his hands. He looked up and beckoned me in.

"I'm sorry you had to read that first thing this morning. I was going to try to soften it for you." I took the hard metal seat next to his desk. "Not that much of anything could soften it."

"This poor girl," he said softly, shaking his head.

"Marsh said he could make a preliminary ID today, if he gets the dental records from the FBI. Ruthie said some agent was coming here this morning?" I was still hoping it wasn't true.

"Yeah, to claim jurisdictional precedent. But I'm going to fight him for at least a joint investigation. The body was found here and the autopsy done by our ME. I want to catch the bastard who did this so bad my teeth ache."

Just at that moment, Ruthie knocked on the door frame. Behind her stood Agent Bowers, just the man I didn't want to see. He was dancing up and down on his toes. *Does he ever stop fidgeting?*

"Special Agent Bowers has arrived," Ruthie announced, then stepped back and let him walk by her into the office.

Bowers walked over to Sam's desk and held out his hand. "Special Agent Michael Bowers, FBI. We met last fall over that case with the funeral home." He ignored me.

"Sure. You remember my sister-in-law, Rhe Brewster? It was her case," Sam reminded him. "She's now a consultant with the department."

Bowers finally looked over at me and gave me a nod. "I have the dental records here," he told Sam, removing a thumb drive from his pocket. "Where should this go?"

"To our medical examiner, Marsh Adams. He's at the local hospital. Rhe can take you over when we're done here."

Bowers gave me a look and I thought I saw a slight rolling of his eyes. *Yes indeedy, we're off to a good start.*

Sam rose to his considerable height, and I noticed Bowers back up. "How about we grab some coffee, go to the conference room, and get ourselves on the same page?" Sam asked and proceeded out the door, with Agent Bowers and me in his wake.

Bowers obviously didn't expect me to follow, because when we were all seated at the conference room table, he nodded his head towards me and asked Sam, "What's her involvement?" We were sitting at one end of the conference table with Sam at the head. Sam and Bowers had steaming mugs of coffee in front of them, while I had a bottle of cold water, the condensation from it pooling on the table.

"Ms. Brewster," replied Sam, emphasizing my name, "is the one who managed the crime scene yesterday. I've given her the old files on the other three missing girls, with the idea she may see something we've missed."

"Three?" asked Bowers. "I thought other than this one, there were only two."

"There's one from a long time ago, also was never found, from right here in Pequod," I told him. Bowers indeed fitted the image of a standard issue agent: neatly dressed in a dark suit with a striped tie, his thin, blonde-white hair neatly trimmed and combed to the side. Aside from his nervous ticcing – he was currently tapping the desk surface with the end of his pen – his most remarkable feature was his eyes, a luminous gray, peering out through dark-framed glasses.

"Do you think that case is related to the current one?" he asked Sam.

"Not sure. It's always possible," I answered, trying to get Bowers to look at me.

"Why don't you bring me up to date, Chief Brewster," he asked Sam pointedly, and Sam gave a brief summary of finding the finger and then the body, where it had been located and its recovery. Then he slid the ME's report over to him.

"I'll let you read that while I go top off my coffee. Rhe, do you need anything?"

"Yeah, I think I'll take advantage of the ladies room."

"What is wrong with that guy?" I hissed as soon as we had shut the door. "Do you think one of his FBI courses was Beginning Misogyny?"

Sam chuckled. "He does seem to have an issue with you, doesn't he? I think he's just young and new and feels he needs to prove himself. This could become a problem, so let me handle the discussion about where we go from here. Can you bite your tongue?"

"In half, if I need to."

When we returned to the conference room, I noticed that Bowers' face was nearly as pale as his hair. *Well, at least he's capable of feeling something.*

"You have any questions about the report?" Sam asked, taking his seat again.

"Not at this time."

"How do you think we should proceed?" Sam was polite, but I could see he was definitely not letting go of the case.

"I've been assigned to run the case," Bowers replied a little testily.

"Well, that's not going to happen without our involvement. I understand the investigations of the missing girls were handled by the FBI originally, but this body was found here in Pequod, and there needs to be local input. I planned to ask Rhe to run point for us, so she would be working with you and be the liaison to the department."

It was as though Bowers had sat on a wasp. He jumped up from his chair and sputtered, "That isn't possible...that is..." Seeing the startled looks from Sam and me, he caught himself, turned a fine shade of pink, and gradually lowered back into his chair.

He didn't speak again for a moment, and I knew he was figuring out how he could wiggle out of working with me. "I'll have to ask my superior," he finally said.

"And who is that?" I asked.

"Senior Special Agent Bongiovanni."

"I remember him. The tall guy who came with you last year."

Bowers nodded.

"When will you have an answer?" Sam asked.

Twenty minutes later I found myself riding to Sturdevant beside a very pissed off FBI agent. I had to give him credit; he had it under control except for clicking his ring against the steering wheel. I would have given a week's wages (before my hours were cut) to know what he and Bongiovanni had said to each other during the telephone call. Based on the gesticulations I'd observed and his walking in circles in the hallway, it must have been a barn burner. Now he was completely quiet.

We were in Bowers' standard issue government car, a black Ford Crown Victoria, a land barge with a threadbare interior, but I had to admit it was more comfortable than my old Jeep. We continued in silence for several minutes, except for my giving him directions. He'd initially snapped at me that his GPS unit would get us there, but I'd convinced him I knew a short cut that would save five minutes of driving time. I figured he was in a hurry.

Finally, when the silence was solid enough to chop with an ax, I asked, "So how long have you been with the FBI?"

"About two years."

"And before that?"

"Georgetown."

"Good school. Had you thought about law school?"

"In passing. But I was looking for something more challenging."

More challenging? "Do I have to call you Special Agent Bowers all the time?"

"Agent Bowers is fine. No difference."

"Have you had many interesting cases?"

"Well, the one you brought us last year."

He finally recognized me. Took him long enough. "Look, are we going to have any problems working together on this one? I'd like to know up front, so I can lay in an extra supply of Excedrin."

The corners of his lips turned up. I thought he might actually have a nice smile if they ever turned up all the way. "I'm not sure. You okay with my taking the lead?"

"No problem."

"Just don't get in the way."

Fantastic. I directed him into the parking lot at the rear of the hospital and noticed he backed into the parking space, with the rear of the car up against a bank at the edge of the lot. *Must be standard FBI operating procedure. Maybe he really does know his stuff.*

Once inside the hospital basement, we walked down the corridor to Marsh's office, but I saw through the glass that he wasn't at his desk. I turned and continued to the second autopsy suite on the left, where some light was leaking under the door.

"Ever been to an autopsy?" I asked Bowers.

"Uh, no..."

"You can stay outside if you want. Just give me the thumb drive."

"No, ma'am. It stays with me."

"Suit yourself." I opened the door to the suite and saw Marsh and Midori, one either side of a dissection table. Both of them were clad in white, fluid resistant, one-piece 'space' suits, plus shoe booties, surgical gloves and head coverings with face shields. Various containers were arrayed on a side platform table, and as we entered, Marsh was weighing a liver and talking into the microphone inside his suit. Midori had a range of instruments next to her, some of them already bloody. I grabbed a mask and booties from boxes on a shelf next to the door and turned to look at Bowers. He had stopped in his tracks.

"Here," I said, offering him the coverings. Taking pity on him, I grabbed a jar of Vaporub from the shelf. Vaporub was not generally used any more, since it had proved easier to get used to a noxious smell, and odors could tell you a lot about a crime scene. I had to admit, Bowers had cojones. He put a swipe of the Vaporub under his nose, donned the mask and booties and followed me toward the table. The autopsy was in full swing, with both the abdomen and thorax opened. I took a look at Bowers, who was looking everywhere but the table. He suddenly made an about face and raced over to a sink along the wall. Marsh turned at the sound of retching, saw me and raised an eyebrow in question.

"Rookie agent," I answered, indicating Bowers with my head. "We're here with the dental records of the missing girls."

"I need about thirty minutes to finish this up," he replied, voice muffled in the head gear. "Can you two find something to do until then?"

My stomach was rumbling. "We could have lunch. How are you with cafeteria food?" I asked Bowers with a sly smile.

☙ ❧

Forty five minutes later, my stomach was perfectly full of comfort food – macaroni and cheese, two hot dogs, and a slice of chocolate cake. Bowers, who'd selected soup and Jello because of his recent introduction to the autopsy sink, had looked at my plate with disgust. "How can you eat that stuff?" he'd asked. "It's loaded with carbs, preservatives, fat, and large helpings of other unhealthy things."

"Hey, I'm pregnant," I'd replied. "Happy to take advantage of the need to eat for two."

He gave me a hard look. I could tell he hadn't anticipated being partnered with a sack of hormones. I ignored the look and continued eating, guilt free.

We were now sitting in Marsh's office, introductions over. "So," said Marsh, "where're the dental records?"

Bowers found the thumb drive in his inside jacket pocket and handed it to Marsh, who plugged it into his laptop. "Before we start, do you still have the sail the body was wrapped in?"

"No, I don't. I sent it off to the state crime lab this morning. Why do you ask?"

"My superior wants me to find out where it came from, and for that I need to take a look at it."

"Well, I guess you're going to have to take a trip to Augusta, if you want to see it in person."

Bowers nodded.

"Which girl shall we start with?" Marsh asked him.

Before Bowers could answer, I said, "Savannah Engstrom. The clothes on the body resembled those described as hers when she was abducted." Bowers looked a little surprised.

Marsh pulled up the dental X-rays of the child we had found on the beach, then opened up the Engstrom file from the thumb drive. While we watched, he put his X-rays in the same file for comparison. I waited quietly and found myself holding my breath. Minutes passed while Marsh's gaze shifted from one image to the other. Finally he frowned, pushed back from his desk and sighed, "They match. We have Savannah Engstrom in the morgue."

6

Special Agent Bowers drove me back to the police station, where we once again sat with Sam in the conference room.

"So it's definitely Savannah Engstrom?" Sam asked.

"Yes." Both Bowers and I responded at the same time. Bowers continued, "I'll need to make the notification as soon as possible."

Boy, that sounded cold. I wondered if he'd ever had to confront the parents of a dead child before.

"I'd like to call the parents in here."

What was he thinking?

Sam started to say something, but I cut him off. "Look, it may be FBI protocol but you shouldn't tell them anything over the phone. And if you ask them to drive to Pequod to talk about their daughter's disappearance, you're going to torture them. They'll spend the whole time wondering whether you're calling them with some positive news or if you need them to view their daughter's body. Why not visit them at their home? Then they're in a comforting place when you tell them their daughter is dead."

"Just what I was going to say, Rhe, before you cut me off."

"Sorry."

Bowers was quiet during this exchange, seeming to wait for direction.

"That's what I want you to do." Sam directed this at Bowers. "And I want her," indicating me with his head, "to go with you. She's had to deal with death in her job, and she might be able to help you work through it gently." He emphasized the last word. "Especially if you haven't made a notification like this before."

Bowers didn't answer but he also didn't argue. "I'm thinking we should go this evening so we can find both parents at home. It's 2:30. How far is it to Camden?"

A good suggestion, but how to manage with Jack and Will? "It's an hour, hour and a half. Let me make a phone call first," I said. I went to Sam's office to phone Will and shut the door behind me, thinking the call was going to be contentious. When I told Will that he'd have to get Jack after basketball practice and why, he must have registered the angst in my voice. He whined for a minute or so but agreed to do it.

Then he added ungraciously, "I guess we'll have to get takeout. If there's any left over, you can have it if you're late getting home."

Still, he seemed to be in a better than average mood, and I couldn't help but wonder why.

❧ ❧

Bowers and I set out for Camden around 3 PM, once again in his Crown Vic. His heater actually emitted a continuous stream of warm air, so I was definitely not complaining. I decided to pump my new partner. With a series of questions, grudgingly answered, I found out he had a steady girlfriend who was also in the FBI, assigned to computer crimes. I asked him whether an FBI agent could marry another agent.

"We're not at that stage and I'm not sure we'll ever get there," he replied curtly. "And please stop asking me personal questions. I don't like being interrogated."

Interesting choice of words. But I shut up.

Camden was a coastal town, with a narrow main street crowded in summer with tourists and lined with flower boxes containing a profusion of white, pink and purple flowers. Today, though, there were just a few people scuttling from warm store to warm store, trying to avoid the bitter breeze blowing off the ocean. The Engstroms' house was on a steep, narrow street off of Bayview, which ran along the southern edge of the harbor. The car lumbered up the street, wheezed into a parking spot by the mailbox sporting a neatly painted #14, and shuddered to a stop. Bowers gave me an apologetic look when I frowned at the shaking car.

Painted decoratively in a light tan, house number fourteen had clearly undergone reconstruction: two stories with a peaked roof, each story with four tall windows and a gable above. Stone steps cut through a neatly trimmed hedge, ascending to the front door.

Bowers consulted his watch as we started up the steps. "Quarter to five, think they'll be home?"

"Lights are all on, so I'm thinking yes." *Duh.*

He rang the doorbell to the side of the storm door, and we both stood back on the stoop, stomping our feet in the cold while we waited for someone to open the inside door. After a minute, he rang again. Finally the door opened, and without opening the outer storm door, a woman asked us, "Yes? What can I do for you?" The woman who I assumed was Mrs. Engstrom was painfully thin, with bones that poked through the picked gray pullover she was wearing. Her dishwater brown hair was threaded with gray, and her round face was lined with both deep and fine wrinkles that belied her age, which I knew was mid-forties.

Bowers held up his shield. "Special Agent Michael Bowers, FBI. Are you Mrs. Anna Engstrom?"

She nodded vigorously. Then her hand went to her mouth and her eyes opened wide in recognition, filling with tears as she unlocked and opened the storm door. "It's about Savannah, isn't it?" she asked before we'd even entered the house.

"Yes, ma'am," answered Bowers. "Is your husband at home?"

"Yes," and turning from us, she yelled, "Tom, come quick! The FBI's here about Savannah."

We came in, closed both doors and followed Mrs. Engstrom into the living room. I heard the sound of quick footsteps approaching from the rear of the house. Mr. Engstrom towered over his wife, broad in the shoulders and muscular, with thinning blond hair and a trim beard. I knew from the files he was a lobsterman. Mrs. Engstrom ran to him and wrapped her arms around him.

"Can we sit down, Mrs. Engstrom?" I asked, since Bowers seemed to have lost his tongue.

"Certainly, certainly," she replied, her voice quavering with fear, and indicated a pair of comfortably stuffed blue chairs opposite a similarly overstuffed sofa. She and her husband sat down on the sofa, clasped hands, and leaned forward.

Bowers remained quiet but watched me intently.

"My name is Rhe Brewster, and I'm a consultant with the Pequod Police Department. This is Special Agent Michael Bowers of the FBI," I began again, for Mr. Engstrom's benefit. I looked at Bowers and nodded.

Finally he said something, but it came out as a croak. "We're here about your daughter." He swallowed several times and his Adam's apple bobbed up and down. "I'm afraid we have some bad news for you."

"She's dead, isn't she? I knew it, I knew it," Mrs. Engstrom cried, tears now streaming down her cheeks. "Where did you find her? Can we see her?"

Mr. Engstrom put his arm around her, struggling to keep his emotions in check but losing the battle.

Under her barrage of questions, Bowers wilted back into his chair and looked at me again, so I picked up the conversation. "Mr. and Mrs. Engstrom, I can't tell you how terribly sorry I am to have to bring you this news. I know you never lost hope. But at least Savannah's been found."

Her mother nodded, dropping her head. Her shoulders shook with her sobs. "How did she die?" her father asked.

"We're not sure. There are no indications of anything physical that might have killed her, so we're waiting on the toxicology report." It wasn't exactly a lie, and it was better they didn't know, at least for now, about everything else.

"Where was she found?"

"Her body washed up in a cove near Pequod two days ago, which is why we're here. We only identified her today."

"She didn't d-drown?" her mother asked.

"No, and she'd only been in the water for a couple of days at most." Silence weighed down on the room. I felt like I was being pushed into the floor under its mass.

After a while, when Mrs. Engstrom's sobs quieted, her husband asked, "When can we see her?"

"Tomorrow, if you wish, but I have to warn you her body's been partially destroyed by marine life."

"I've seen that before," he replied. "I can handle it."

I reached into my bag and pulled out a picture of the clothes we'd recovered from the body. I handed it to Mr. Engstrom. "Do you recognize these clothes?"

He stared at the picture and shook his head, but his wife grabbed it and took a sharp breath. "Those're what Savannah was wearing the day she disappeared. How could I forget?" she said, almost angrily. Her tears abated momentarily.

"I just wanted to make sure," I replied. More silence.

Finally, Mr. Engstrom turned to his wife and said, "These people have come a long way and we should at least offer them some coffee." Looking at me, he asked, "Would you like some?"

"Yes, thank you, I would."

Mrs. Engstrom rose to her feet, wobbled a little and headed towards the door leading to the back of the house. "May I help you?" I asked. I got up and followed her out of the room. Through all this, Bowers sat quietly, watching but not commenting. Maybe he would be able to talk to Mr. Engstrom, man to man.

Mrs. Engstrom bustled around in their retro 1950s kitchen, putting coffee in the incongruous espresso machine on their counter, getting out mugs, and finally leaning over the counter and sobbing once again. I put my arms on her shoulders, and she turned into me, shuddering against my chest. I felt tears forming in my own eyes, imagining how terrible this must be for her.

"I know how to operate this machine," I told her. "Why don't you sit down while I make the coffee?" She nodded and slid into a chair at the kitchen table. I handed her a piece of paper towel from the roll under the cabinets, so she could wipe her eyes and face. Ten minutes later, carrying a tray, I re-entered the living room with four coffees and cream, not caring whether Bowers wanted one or not.

There had clearly been a breakthrough, because the two men were leaning toward each other, talking in quiet voices.

"Anna," Mr. Engstrom asked immediately, "is there anything you've thought of since our last visit with the FBI?"

"Anything at all," Bowers added, as I placed the tray on the coffee table and sat down.

Mrs. Engstrom sat, and to my surprise said, "Yes, maybe. Savannah used to hang around at a local art gallery on weekends in the summer. She's very artistic and wanted to become a professional artist one day. She liked to spend time with the artists who showed their work at the gallery and the owner taught her how to mat and frame." She paused, seeming to gather her strength. "I told the FBI all about this when she disappeared. But I forgot to mention one of the artists had asked her to come to his studio to see his work. She told me she was so excited and really wanted to go, but the owner, Jill McMillan, had stepped in and said Savannah would be too busy at the gallery. Savannah told me she didn't know why Ms. McMillan had done that. She was a little angry. It was such a small incident, and it happened a year before she disappeared. I can't believe I forgot it until just now."

I sensed Bowers' ears pricking up like a Doberman at a chain link fence. "Can you give me the name of the gallery and where Jill MacMillan lives," he asked.

"Yes, but the gallery's only open in the summer. I don't know where she lives in the winter, somewhere in Florida, I think."

I took my coffee mug and took a small sip of its contents, knowing it wasn't good for me. Neither of the Engstroms was drinking theirs and Bowers hadn't touched his.

He had pulled out a small notebook and taken down the information about the gallery and its owner, then finally, maybe noting the aroma of the fresh coffee, helped himself to a mug. The room went silent yet again, and I had no words of comfort to fill it.

Finally I took one of my cards and a pen from my bag, wrote down Marsh's telephone number on the back and handed it to Mr. Engstrom. "That's the name and number of our medical examiner. If you call tomorrow, I'm sure he can make arrangements for you to see your daughter." I doubted Mrs. Engstrom was strong enough to handle it, but her husband was.

"When do you think..." Mr. Engstrom swallowed hard, "we can bring her home?"

"I can't say," I replied. "That'll be up to the medical examiner, probably once all of the evidence has been collected and analyzed. I'm so sorry..."

Mrs. Engstrom began sobbing again.

Bowers rose. "Thank you for being willing to talk to us." At that point, he turned to me expectantly, looking for help.

"Again, we're so sorry to have to deliver this news," I said. "If there is anything we can do, you have my card and I'm sure Agent Bowers will give you one of his." I glared at him, so he hastily fished in his wallet for a card.

I could still hear Mrs. Engstrom crying as her husband let us out the front door.

&⋯&

On our way back to Pequod, I said to Bowers, "Thank you for having the good sense to know when it was time to leave. Those people need to grieve alone, then call their family and friends to support them."

"I only did it because I was so uncomfortable I couldn't stand it anymore. And thanks for taking the lead in there. Chief Brewster was right; I've never had to notify anyone of a death in their family."

Well, how about that? Honest and a bit humble. He might be a good partner after all. "Remind me of the name of the gallery owner?"

Bowers pulled his pad from his coat pocket and handed it to me. I opened it to the first page. "Jill McMillan. I've heard of her. She's quite famous in her own right. Does primitive paintings of Maine islands and fishing boats and coastal sites. How will you find her?"

Finally, Bowers smiled. "The FBI is very good at finding people, living people at least. I should have an address for her by tomorrow morning."

7

The next day was the last of my Monday-Wednesday-Friday schedule in the ER. I not only needed to find out what days I would be working the following week but also had to visit Human Resources.

I took the elevator back to the 6 floor, where I'd met with Manning, but this time turned left. Same plush rugging in the hallway, but beyond the frosted glass door with 'Human Resources' etched on it, there was an alternate universe – a square room with rough commercial carpeting the color of vomit, four institutional metal desks arranged in walled cells, and none of the drapes and art work of the CEO's office. There was a front desk with a name plate 'Receptionist,' where I stopped and asked for Sylvia Hutty, the head of HR.

I'd known Sylvia since grade school. Even though she was a year older, we'd been neighborhood friends, Sylvia, Deirdre, and I, the three Musketeers, always looking for adventure. Of our three, she was the cautious, no-nonsense one. She reined in our more dangerous ideas for fun, such as climbing around in the collapsing and condemned hotel that sat on the property where I now lived. We'd shared our suffering when Deirdre disappeared with long sessions of crying and reminiscing, exacerbated by our early pubescent emotions.

We'd met again when I'd started working at Sturdevant, refueling the friendship with lunches together every few weeks and occasional dinner swaps. I'd called her right after the meeting with Manning and should have seen her then, but I had more interesting things on my plate. *I am getting good at playing the avoidance game.*

The receptionist, an overweight young woman with bad acne and long blonde hair dyed pink at the ends, made a call, then said, "You're expected," flicking her hair towards the office at the back of the room.

Sylvia opened the door before I got there, giving me a huge smile. "Rhe, it's about time for us to have lunch again. I'm glad to see you!"

"Wish I could say the same, Syl," I replied, giving her a quick hug.

"Yes, I know." She closed the door behind me, walked to one of two plumply upholstered chairs and sat. I sat in the other, enjoying its softness against my aching back. Sylvia was a feast for a fashionista's eyes. I knew she shopped at Target and TJ Maxx, but she always projected the image of a consummate professional, reed thin and dressed in with a timeless style. She was wearing an aubergine knit dress with a mosaic scarf in blending colors, artistically tied at her neck, and black, high-heeled boots. The outfit was a stunning contrast to her graying, close-cropped hair.

"You look fantastic," I said with envy, thinking how frumpy I felt being pregnant, with my crumpled blue scrubs and scuffed black Crocs. I took a deep breath. "So. What's the real reason Manning's reducing my hours? Have anyone else's hours been trimmed?"

"It's a mess, Rhe, and I've been warned not to talk to you about this."

"Not to talk to me? Why ever not? Manning was pretty clear when he told me the hospital needed to cut costs. And he told me to see you."

Sylvia shook her head, frowned, and then seemed to make a decision. "We've been friends for a long time, and what he's doing is just wrong. So I'm going to tell you as much as I know, but you can't use the information. He threatened my job if I told anyone…he doesn't know we know each other, so please, Rhe, keep this to yourself. I know you'll figure something out."

I was stunned at this and Manning's hubris. "Of course I promise. But how can he do that?"

Sylvia took a deep breath and let it out slowly. "Because he knows something that could damage me and he's using it as leverage. I can't lose my job, not in this economy. I've got kids to support and you know Mitch is chronically behind on child support payments."

I knew Mitch, her former husband, was mean, small-minded and vindictive. A real jewel of a man. "So what could he possibly have on you? You've always been the cautious one."

"Yeah, well, this is a biggie. I don't know…I'm afraid. Really."

"You don't have to tell me anything. I know you well enough to accept that Manning is being a piss ant with something he knows about you. It's okay."

Sylvia seemed to be having an argument with herself for a moment or two. Finally she said, "Oh, what the hell, Rhe. If I can't trust you, who can I trust? I'm having an affair with someone in Accounting. Manning saw us together one evening and put two and two together."

"You're allowed a private life, Syl. He can't tell you who to date."

"Yes, but he can use what he saw as leverage. I was having dinner with a woman. What he saw was clearly more than friendship."

I smiled at her. "Would you be upset if I tell you this is *not* a surprise?"

"That's my Rhe. When did you know?"

"I guess as far back as high school. But you were so uptight and closeted, I would never have asked. I was a little confused when you married Mitch, but figured you had your reasons. Just like I figured someday we'd have this conversation. Your sexual orientation shouldn't make any difference. There are laws to support you." I could just imagine what Manning threatened with that information.

"Who else knows?" I asked.

"Besides you? Only Manning and Theresa, of course. At least I think that's all."

"So Mitch has no idea?"

"He'd take the kids if he found out. You have to promise me you won't tell anyone." Sylvia had tears in her eyes. I'd certainly been seeing a lot of that lately.

"I promise." I reached over and took her hand, and we just sat that way for a few moments.

Then her professional persona made a reappearance, and she smiled at me. "Let me tell you about that so-called efficiency expert."

"There really was one?"

"Yup. A bird-necked, officious pencil pusher who roamed around the hospital with his pad for the grand total of one day."

"I take it you weren't the one who hired him?"

"No, Manning did," she replied. "I don't even know if he was for real. Manning might have just hired an actor."

"Who paid him?"

"I asked Manning, since the hiring wasn't from HR. He told me the money came out of discretionary funds, whatever they are."

"Did anyone ever get a report from that guy?"

"Not as far as I know. I did ask around, since any information from him might help me increase the efficiency of this department."

"You could get rid of the Christina Aguilera wannabe for starters," I joked, indicating the outer office with my head.

Sylvia shrugged her shoulders and gave me a sheepish smile. "She's Manning's niece."

"Nice that you have a mole. Actually, there is some information you *can* give me," I continued.

"Name it. I owe you."

"Do you have the name of anyone needing home nursing care?"

"That I do. Let me get you a list of names. The pay is pretty good, I'm sure you know that. I doubt Manning's figured out you can make more money in private nursing, for less time. So strike one for you. Maybe you should think about doing this all the time?"

"I'll definitely think about that, especially if I can work out a roster of regular clients."

࿐

I reported a little late for work again, but with the mood I was in, they could shove the job. Nancy Ennis saw me as I walked in and asked, "That bad, huh?"

"Yeah, but I guess it could be worse. Sorry I'm late. I was visiting HR."

"It's okay, I covered for you, but you need to know the Woodpecker's gunning for you. Emphasis on the Pecker part. He personally called down here, checking up on you, making sure you were here on time and working your shift. I laid it on thick about how punctual you are, how your expertise and care contribute so much to the ER, yada, yada, but nothing untrue."

"Thanks, Nancy. You're a good friend."

"Dollars to doughnuts, he's looking for an excuse to fire you."

"I believe it. How dandy."

"I know you, Rhe. You're gonna survive this. On another note, I've got you scheduled for Thursday and Friday next week. That okay?"

"No problem. So what's on the board for our walk-ins?"

∾∽

Before I left the hospital for the day, I called Agent Bowers to see if the FBI had found the owner of the gallery, Jill McMillan.

"We did," Bowers told me. "I have her address in Florida. Called her, but she refused to talk over the phone. She is one weird lady."

Or maybe it was your approach?

"Anyway, I have clearance to fly down to talk to her tomorrow. Imagine, I had to make an appointment with her. Do you want to join me?"

"Nope. Can't leave my child and the police department wouldn't spring for it, but call me when you get back, will you?" I wondered if he would be able to get anything out of Ms. McMillan. I hoped she liked FBI agents with nervous tics.

On my way out to the parking lot, I checked in with Marsh to see if there were any results on the samples he'd sent off for analysis. The autopsy suites were dark, but there were lights on in both his and Midori's offices. I knocked on his door, heard a hearty "Come in, Rhe!" and walked in to find him on the floor, gathering papers.

"How did you know it was me?"

"You're the only person who visits me this time of day. I figured your shift just ended."

"Right on both counts. What are you doing?" I asked, bending down to help him with the avalanche of papers on the floor.

"I had all the reports on Savannah in a pile on my desk, and clumsy me, I went to pitch something into the wastebasket and hit the pile."

"I never took you for a Roger Clemens, Marsh. What the heck were you throwing?"

"A cookie bag," he replied, looking a little guilty.

I noted the crumbs on his desk and figured he'd had more than one.

"There," he said, sitting down in his chair and shuffling the papers into some sort of order. I sat down next to him, squirming with eagerness at what he had to say. "Where do you want me to start?" He gestured at the papers.

"Anywhere."

"Well, the cause of death was an overdose of propofol," he said, lifting the top report from the pile.

"Propofol? That's the drug that killed Michael Jackson, right?"

"Yes, and you know it's only available by prescription, so maybe that's a place to start."

"Or maybe not. I've only ever seen it used in hospitals, mainly on ventilated patients, so it might be a long shot trying to find a prescriber. Anyone could lift it from a hospital. And vets use it, too, so that's going to make the search much wider. I'll bet you can even get it over the internet. I'll check. What else?"

"I found what looked like some flower petals in one of her pockets and sent them off with the sample I scraped from under her fingernails."

"Flower petals?"

"Yup, this little girl was into picking flowers. She must have been allowed some freedom."

Why didn't she run away? Maybe she was being watched? Or Stockholm syndrome?

"Anyway," Marsh interrupted my thoughts, "the results came back quickly and are really interesting."

"How so?"

"The botanists at the state lab identified remains from an English Sundew, Marsh Valerian, and a Ram's Head Lady Slipper, plus remarkably acidic soil under her fingernails."

I thought for a minute. "Bog plants, right? She was being kept somewhere near a bog! I wonder how many bogs there are in Maine?"

"I can think of four right off the top of my head. We need to find out if there is one bog that has all three of those flowers."

"You got a botanist who owes you a favor?"

"Well, I have a friend in the Bureau of Geology, Natural Areas and Coastal Resources who might be able to narrow it down. Oh, and that guy I talked with last year...what's his name?" he looked puzzled for a minute, "at the University of Maine. He's into bog plants. Never mind, I can find him."

"Hot damn. Now we're getting somewhere! Anything else we didn't already know?"

"No, that's about it. Oh, the fingernail polish was a match to what was on the isolated finger..." he paused, then asked, "What's going on with you and Inspector Clouseau?" Marsh attempted a French accent that sounded like Serbo-Croatian.

"We talked to the Engstroms yesterday, but you probably already know that."

"Yes, the father called here this morning. They'll be down tomorrow to see the body. I think with the information we're getting in, I can release the body to them fairly soon."

"I know they'll be grateful. One thing ... the mother is very fragile. If you can manage it so she doesn't see the body, it'd be for the best."

"I'll see what I can do."

"Think you might have some info on those flowers by tomorrow?"

"It's possible. Why don't I call you after the Engstroms leave?"

"What time are they coming?"

"Early, around ten."

"Talk to you then." I pushed myself out of the chair and shrugged into my coat. There was something else I'd meant to ask him...what was it? *Lightbulb.* "Marsh, one more thing. Savannah wasn't wearing her braces when we found her. They must have been removed. Is it possible to tell when, from looking at her teeth?"

"I'm not sure. I could ask a forensic dentist."

"I'd esteem it a favor from my favorite ME."

"Consider it done. Now get home and put your feet up!"

Ordinarily I would have happily complied with that order, but with the friction at home, I dragged my sore feet getting there. While I was dragging, I had a lot to think about: the flower petals, the braces, and possibly something from Bowers by that evening. We were starting to get somewhere, but where it would lead, I hadn't a clue.

8

Saturday morning was gray and overcast, with an ocean over-punctuated with white caps, and a light snow beginning to fall. The aroma of warm coffee in the kitchen almost convinced me to stay home by the fire and read more of the case files on the missing children, but Will had started grading papers early and insisted he was too busy to go grocery shopping with me. So I resolutely encased myself and Jack in our winter wear and left the house for my least favorite chore. There was a nor'easter brewing, so if we were going to be snowed in, we would need some food in the fridge. Jack came along because of my promise of a pancake breakfast at McDonald's. Yes, it would be a carb overload…but my son, the perpetual motion machine, had never met a pancake he didn't like. The baby wanted pancakes, too. As we drove out, I wondered if the Engstroms would still make the drive down to identify their daughter.

❧ ❧

By the time we emerged from Hannaford with our groceries, the promised winter storm had hit full force, with snow descending in fast flakes, my Jeep already covered by over an inch of white. The wind had picked up by the time we got home, and as we came in the door with the first of our bags, I called to Will, "Got the generator primed?"

"Yup," he called back. "Paulette called. She wants you to come over. I think you should go." I heard the sound of his office door closing.

Since he clearly wanted to be incommunicado for the next while, I said to Jack, "Let's put this stuff away and walk over to Aunt Paulette's. I'll bet Tyler needs some company."

Twenty minutes later, cheeks red from the cold, we were banging the snow off our boots by Paulette's back door. She flung it open with a "Come in, come in. And close the door! It's miserable out there!" Her kitchen was, as usual, bright and filled with the wonderful smell of baking bread. "Jack, after you get your coat and boots off – put your boots on the mat by the door, dear – you can go on back to Tyler's room. He's been hoping you'd come over. Rhe, can you guys stay for lunch?"

I was struggling out of my coat for the second time that morning. "What's on the menu?" As if it mattered. I took another whiff of the aromas in the room and tugged off my boots, dropping my hat and mittens on top of Tyler's.

"Chicken corn chowder and I made some sourdough bread," she replied.

The breakfast pancakes were history and my taste buds did a happy dance. "I got the impression from Will he wanted me out of the house, for what reason I don't know. Did he say anything to you?"

"Nothing. Just that he'd tell you I called."

"Well, lunch is a great idea. Can I bring some back to Will?"

"I've already got the containers out. I made a ton of soup, enough for everyone. The snow is keeping Sarah and Ted at home, too. No malls, no hardware store."

Just then my cell phone rang. After some fumbling, I retrieved it from the depths of my bag and noted the caller. Bowers. "Whatcha got, Agent Bowers?" I answered.

"I wanted to report that I called on that art dealer this morning. Mrs. McMillan. She lives in Palm Beach. Her house is a palace, and I surmise she must be doing very well for an art dealer. Marble floors and Greek columns and..."

"Bowers, I appreciate the decorating tips, but can you get to the point?"

"Yes, right. She met me beside her swimming pool. It was the size of Lake Erie, and she had a pitcher of mimosas and was wearing a bikini. Not a good look at her age."

"Did you enjoy the mimosas?" I asked, ignoring the bikini comment.

"FBI agents can't drink when they're working, and I don't drink anyway. I thought you knew that."

Note: no sense of humor. "So what did she say?"

"When I told her we needed the name of the artist who'd showed interest in Savannah, she first seemed confused about what I was referring to. After I'd repeated myself a couple of times, she said she didn't remember. I persisted. Then she said she remembered the incident but didn't remember his name. I think she'd been into the mimosas for a while."

"So did you get anything?"

"She said she would go through her gallery records and see if any name rang a bell."

"When will you talk to her again?"

"She invited me to dinner."

"You be careful there, Bowers. I think she has designs on you."

"FBI agents can't fraternize with subjects of an investigation."

Bowers had clearly memorized the manual. "If I were you, I'd call her late this afternoon, tell her something's come up at Quantico, pile on the FBI lingo, get that information and ride your horse out of town ASAP."

"I'd planned to do that. I'll call you tomorrow, when I'm back in Portland. Did you talk to the ME yesterday about the COD?"

Ah, the official lingo. "Yes. She died from an overdose of propofol. Not sure if there is any way to follow up on that because of the many places it's found. But there *was* one really interesting find."

"What was that?"

"Some flower petals in her pocket. They're from plants only found in peat bogs, and we're hoping they're indigenous to only one bog here in Maine. Marsh has a couple of friends he's going to consult, so maybe we'll know something tomorrow or Monday. Did you say you were coming back to Portland?"

"Yup. I was going to head to Washington to see my girlfriend, but the airport's closed because of a storm. How's Portland?"

"That storm is here too, so your escape may have to be delayed 'til tomorrow. Call me and let me know where you are."

"Sure thing." We disconnected without a good-bye.

"What say I give you some coffee, and you tell me what that was all about," said Paulette, her newly emerged forensic antennae twitching.

Over a couple of cups of decaf, I caught her up as much as I could without going into detail and was just about to bounce my future plans off her when my cell phone rang again. It was Marsh.

"Rhe, I think I've found something. All three of those plants are only found in one bog area in Maine – the Crystal Bog in Aroostook County."

"That's great! So Savannah was probably held, at least lately, near that bog." I paused, then said, "Or not so great. That bog covers a lot of territory." Aroostook County was Maine's largest and most northern, bordered on the east, west and north by Canada, and Crystal Bog was huge, if I remembered correctly.

"If that's so, then I'm not sure we can narrow it down, but I'll see if there is one area within the bog where all three plants grow."

"We have another problem, Marsh. What's the connection between Crystal Bog and Pequod?" That was the big question. Maybe the artist whom Jill McMillan couldn't remember was the link.

After we hung up, I told Paulette about Crystal Bog and that I'd use some of our snowbound time to go over the other files.

Paulette waved her hand. "Can I help?"

"Not yet, but in any event I'd have to get Sam's permission for you to view them. You'll be my sounding board if I find anything, bet on that."

Paulette paused where she stood, taking silverware for lunch out of a drawer. "Rhe, can I ask you something?"

"Sure, anything, what's up?"

"It's Sarah. She's become sort of private lately. We don't talk the way we used to. I know she calls you about stuff."

"Ah, sweetie, I figured you'd ask me about that sooner or later. There's nothing for you to worry about. Sarah's growing up, and your relationship with her is going to change no matter what. I know whereof I speak." I winked at her. "I did grow up in a family with three girls. Not counting my mother of course, although she liked to think of herself as one of the girls." I smiled, thinking of my mother, Autumn, the forever hippie, and my sisters Summer and Sage.

"Did you pull away from your mother, too?"

"More like a total rebellion. I was the ultimate tomboy, and she didn't get me. The things Sarah has called me about, well, I've not been a great help to her. They're things *you* know about – makeup, hair styles, fashion. Just hang on, she'll be back."

"You think so?"

"Just look at me! Do you see a fashion model?"

Paulette looked me over – baggy, pilled sweater, seat-sprung jeans, and a rubber banded pony tail – and chuckled. "At least Sarah's not into scrubs."

At that moment, Sarah burst into the kitchen, gave me a hug, and started pulling out bowls and spatulas, then flour, sugar and chocolate chips. "I promised Tyler some chocolate chip cookies," she announced by way of explanation.

"But we're just going to sit down for lunch!"

"This won't take any time at all, Mom. What? Are we going somewhere in a hurry today?"

ॐ∾

We ate lunch gathered around the kitchen table – Sarah, Ted, Jack, Tyler, Paulette and I. It was a real family gathering, with lots of banter and teasing. Jack and I certainly missed that at home. After lunch, I trudged home with a large container of chowder, Sarah's cookies and some fresh bread for Will, leaving Jack to play with Tyler for the afternoon. Will wasn't home when I got there, and, considering the weather conditions, I wondered where on earth he'd gone. At least he'd taken the Jeep, which had 4-wheel drive. I was still wondering when he returned around four, telling me that he'd had to go to his office at the college. When I asked him why, he said he'd left his notes for his next lecture on his computer there. But I knew he didn't have a lecture for another week.

ॐ∾

Sunday proved to be a stay-by-the-fire day. The snow had continued over-night, slowing to tiny dancing flakes by mid-morning. When the sun came out, we ventured outside and found the neighborhood covered in three feet of daz-zling whiteness. Will used the snow blower to clear the driveway, but it was a shame to sully the stunning silence with its noise. Jack and I shoveled the side--walk in front of the house. Well, I shoveled and he threw snowballs at me and Will. We didn't hear plows on our road until late afternoon.

Our electricity had miraculously survived the storm, so I put chili fixings in a crock pot after lunch, and Will had made a roaring fire in the stone fireplace in the family room. It was one of those rare, cozy afternoons at home, with each of us concentrating on something interesting – Will in his office and Jack and I in the family room. Tyler had dug his way over through the snow to play with Jack, and, after building a huge snowman on the front lawn, they were busy creating a small town with buildings and trucks on the floor. I sipped hot chocolate, indulged in two of Sarah's cookies, and slowly went through the files on the other three missing girls. Somehow, given my surroundings, I wasn't as chilled as I was when I first opened the file on Savannah.

The second missing girl was Rachel Vance, aged ten, from Ellsworth, Maine. She's vanished two years before Savannah had disappeared. I'd never been to Ellsworth, so I looked it up online. It was an old town, with a population of just over seven thousand year-round residents, located south and east of Bangor, on the route to Bar Harbor. It had just one main street in the downtown area, but there were many historic stately homes surrounding it. The Vances lived on Pine Street, in what looked like, from Google Earth, one of the older, larger homes. Her father was the manager of the local bank, her mother a school teacher. Rachel had disappeared on a January afternoon from in front of Ellsworth Elementary School, where she had been waiting for her father to pick her up following a science club meeting. As with Savannah, there were no clues, no ransom notes, nothing on the family computer, and nothing came of interviewing her friends and family. Another set of frantic parents, another seemingly normal ten-year-old, and the similarities didn't end there. Like Savannah, the abduction had been in January, and Rachel looked a little like Savannah: blonde, big smile, and braces. There the similarities stopped, because Rachel had brown eyes and wore fashionable glasses.

I sighed and reached for the third folder. Just then my cell phone rang. I went into the kitchen with my cocoa mug, picked up the phone and saw that it was Bowers. "Hey, Bowers, have you managed to talk to Jill McMillan?"

"You don't waste time on niceties, do you?"

Silence on my end. *He should talk.*

"Okay, yes, I have."

"And?"

"After a diatribe about being sued, losing her business, liabilities, yada, yada, she gave me a name: Robert Cornwell. He's an artist, works on a sheep farm in northern Maine but migrates down to the coast to paint in the summer. Does oil paintings, the kind that tourists buy to put over their sofas."

"Northern Maine? Anywhere near Crystal Bog?"

"I don't know where Crystal Bog is. Why do you ask?"

I told him about what Marsh had discovered and then asked again, "Where does he live?"

"Near Presque Isle. Is that near the bog?"

"Hang on a minute." I grabbed my computer and called up a map of Maine and the location of Crystal Bog. "I'm checking...no, it's north of the bog, but not by a lot. What did she say about him?"

"Just that he gave her the willies, and for that reason she didn't want Savannah to be alone with him. And she wouldn't volunteer to go with her."

"So what else do we know about him?"

"I've got the computer geeks working on that now."

I wondered if he meant Pam. "Call me when you have some answers, will you? Do you think it might warrant a trip to Presque Isle?"

"We'll see..." He was silent for a minute, and I wondered if he wanted to continue talking.

"Are you back in Portland?" I asked.

"Just got in."

"Where are you staying?"

"At a house the FBI maintains for agents."

"Got any company?"

"No, the Portland agents all have homes here."

I bet they weren't interested in hosting a nervous rookie agent from Washington, which was a pity. He wasn't a bad guy, just odd. "Most of the main roads should be plowed out by tomorrow," I told him, "but I'm not sure how soon stores, schools and offices will open up. I'm guessing Tuesday. So if you need to check out Cornwell, you should be able get on the road by then. Keep in touch."

I made myself a second, indulgent mug of hot chocolate and returned to the files. The third victim was Jane Alderson. Age ten, but her picture showed a girl younger than that, with light brown hair, brown eyes, a big smile. I wondered if she wore braces, would have to check on that. Could be a link. I made a mental note to follow up on how long it had been since Savannah's braces had been removed.

I tried to pore through the rest of Jane's file, but my eyes were getting heavy, the couch was feeling softer, the warmth from the fire was like a blanket, and the boys' voices had receded into the background. I drifted off, thinking about sailing, running before the wind with the Trinket's sail wide on a crisp summer day. Something about sails hovered around the edges of my consciousness, before I fell deeply asleep.

I was shaken awake. "Mom, Mom, are you awake?" Good old Jack.

I opened my eyes. It was dark outside and the fire had burned down to a pile of hot embers.

"What, honey?"

"We've played all the games and it's 5:30. When are we going to eat?"

"You boys hungry, huh? Well, the chili should be ready in about thirty minutes. Will that work?"

"Yeah, but can we have some crackers? Tyler's tummy is rumbling."

I looked at Tyler and raised an eyebrow. "You really hungry, Tyler?"

"Uh-huh."

After adding more logs to the fire and stoking the embers, I found some cheese crackers in the kitchen and filled a small bowl. The boys grabbed the bowl and headed to Jack's room, whispering plans to do something with the snow the next day. I wondered if it *would* be a snow day. Just as my hand reached the crock pot lid, I realized I hadn't seen or heard a peep from Will all afternoon. I figured I'd better let him know we'd be eating soon. The door was shut, but I could hear him on the phone with someone. I knocked, but opened the door at the same time.

He hung up the phone as I stepped into the office. "Can't you give me any privacy? I'd appreciate it if you'd wait until I tell you to come in."

Really? Since when? He'd only recently started closing his door, but I thought it was because he was disturbed by Jack's noise. The pile of papers he had said he had to grade still sat undisturbed on his desk.

"I just wanted to tell you the chili will be ready in about thirty minutes. The boys are hungry."

"Okay, I promise to put in an appearance. Any of that good Pinot Noir left?"

"I think so, but you'll have to do all the drinking." I forced a smile.

He got up and followed me into the kitchen for the wine.

కి∽కి

The following morning, although our road had been plowed, a lot of the secondary roads were still blocked. Will had been up early and checked his cell phone for a notice that the college was closed. It wasn't, apparently, which he told me along with the road report when he came back upstairs. I was still tucked under warm covers and watched him languidly as he dressed.

"I take it the schools are closed, too?" I asked him.

"That they are. The boys were up before me, watching a cartoon channel."

"Why can't they ever sleep in on a snow day? I suppose they want breakfast?"

"You got it."

I stayed in bed until he clumped back downstairs, then groaned, sat up, grabbed my bathrobe, and followed him. Tyler had stayed over the night before, since we were fairly sure there wouldn't be any school. Both boys were sitting at the kitchen table, looking expectant, when I got there. Will was already in the garage because I heard the garage door going up. He drove out without saying good-bye.

I made Belgian waffles at the boys' request, balanced by orange juice and some cut-up fruit, and was pigging out with my second waffle when I remembered that I needed to call Marsh. It was 8:30 so he would be at his office. The hospital never closed. It felt strange, this first Monday when I was not working an eight-hour shift.

Marsh was indeed in.

"Hey, Marsh, I'm living the life of luxury here at home. How bad was it getting in this morning?"

"Not too bad. Things will be up and running by tomorrow morning. How was your weekend?"

"Cozy. Listen, did you find out anything about when Savannah's braces came off?'

"Rhe, yesterday was Sunday and there was a snow storm. Hold your horses. I'll get to it this morning!"

"Sorry, I know I'm pushing. I spent yesterday looking at the files on the other victims, and I noticed something. The third victim, Jane Alderson, doesn't have braces in her photo, but it appears the picture was taken maybe a year or two before she disappeared. I'm wondering if she was also wearing braces when she was abducted."

"Are you thinking the braces are a link for the girls?"

"Enough that I'm going to ask Sam if he can find out. There was something else I was going to ask you, but it seems to have slipped my mind. It'll come to me. See you Wednesday if not before." Something was definitely flitting around in my gray cells, but for the life of me, I couldn't get a grip on it.

❧❦

Later that morning, Bowers called. "I got the information about Robert Cornwell," he replied to my immediate question. "His record is spotless, except for one speeding ticket about a year ago. He's in his late sixties, was an Army Ranger in his twenties, and left the service with an honorable discharge. Let's see," and he paused as if he were reading from notes, "he returned to his parents' farm outside of Presque Iles, married, but the wife died about fifteen years ago. No cause of death. Two grown daughters. He inherited the farm from his parents when they died, lives modestly and supplements his income from the sale of his sheep with his paintings. He began painting about ten years ago, bought the small condo in Camden about the same time. Someone runs the farm for him when he's not there."

"He doesn't exactly sound threatening, does he?"

"And he doesn't fit the profile of a pedophile, but I still need to check him out. Do you want to come along?" He'd been very good about including me in his investigation, but my home life would never let me be an FBI agent.

"I'd love to, but I have two hyperactive boys to keep an eye on today."

"You're not going to work? I thought hospitals never slept."

"No, but that's a story for another day. Have a safe trip."

I was pretty busy for the rest of the morning, outside with the boys doing boy things: making another snowman, then a fort, compacting a pile of snowballs to launch at their fathers when they came home. After lunch I remembered I needed to call Sam, but the forgotten question that was worrying at me like a pebble in my shoe, remained elusive. We made a date for lunch the next day to catch up.

After dinner that night, Will and I sat down with the list of private nursing jobs I'd gotten from Sylvia and picked a couple of prospects I could check out the next day. I didn't tell him about my conversation with Sylvia and what I'd learned about Manning. It wasn't the right time, and maybe never would be.

9

Tuesday morning I hadn't heard from Bowers, and I tried his cell number several times without getting an answer. It didn't even go to voice mail, which bothered me. By the time I met Sam at Ernie's, I'd gotten anxious.

Sam was already there, sitting in his favorite booth by the steamed-up window, perusing a menu. *As if I didn't already know what he would order.*

"Hey there! I take it Jack's back in school?" He beamed one of his huge smiles at me, stood up and gave me a bear hug. Without waiting for an answer, he gestured at the booth. "Have a seat. Gonna have your usual rabbit food today?" Then he noticed my face. "What's up? Did you get a hold of Bowers?"

"No, and I called him four times. Didn't even get voice mail. I'm worried something's happened to him. He's so by the book, he'd never not check in."

"Well, hon, let's have some lunch and then we'll go over to the station and I'll make some calls, okay? It's probably nothing. Maybe his car got stuck in the snow somewhere out of cell phone coverage."

"Exactly why I'm worrying."

"He's a big boy. I think he could handle it."

The smells of baking pizza crust had been assaulting me since I opened Ernie's door and just then my stomach let out an alert for food, so we sat down and I grabbed the menu from Sam. "You're just going to have a pizza with sausage, green peppers, mushrooms and, oh, let's not forget the onions, so I don't know why you're even looking at this!"

The waitress appeared and Sam ordered his usual, a large, then invited me to share it. How could I refuse? I was eating for two. But worry about Bowers crept in and I asked him if we might eat it back at the station.

"Rhe, another fifteen or twenty minutes is not going to matter, and you know I don't like cold pizza."

"Okay, but let's eat fast." When the pizza arrived, we dug in. Through a mouthful of delicious gooeyness I asked, "How can you be sure that Bowers is just out of phone range? I worry that with his nervous jiggling, he'd shoot himself in the foot if he ever drew his weapon."

"He had to get through Quantico, so I assume he did well enough in training not to shoot himself." Sam smiled at the thought. "If it'll make you feel better, I'll call his supervisor, too."

I thoroughly enjoyed not worrying about my waistline through nearly half the pizza, but just as we were finishing, I happened to look out at the street. There, staring at me through the fogged-up window, was James Barnes.

I must have started, because Sam asked, "What's wrong? You look like you've seen a spook!"

I turned back to face him. "James Barnes is staring at us through the window!"

"Where?" We both looked. There was no one there. "Are you sure?"

I thought a minute. "I could be mistaken. Why would he be looking at me? I only met him that once."

"Yeah, well I've had some run-ins with him. Nasty temper. Bet it was me he was checking out."

∾∿

Back in Sam's office, with both of us feeling just fine from the infusion of fat and carbs, Sam made a call to the Presque Isle police. After the cop greetings and usual garbage, Sam asked about Bowers, and, not getting any information, gave them a description of his car and Robert Cornwell's name as the person he had been planning to interview.

"They promise to check it out ASAP," he told me after he hung up. Then he called Agent Bongiovanni. I gathered from the noise coming from the phone that Agent Bongiovanni hadn't heard from him either.

Sam leaned back in his chair, put his feet on the desk, and explained in detail what he'd done so far, concluding with "What would you like me to do further, Agent Bongiovanni?" Silence, then nodding his head, Sam replied, "Will do," and hung up.

"So... what are we going to do?"

"*We* are not going to do anything," he said firmly, sitting up. "Bongiovanni was already irritated that Bowers hadn't checked in. My calling the Presque Isle police was embarrassing. He's not a happy camper. You, my dear, are going to sit tight and I'm going to wait for a call from Presque Isle. If the police are unable to locate him, Bongiovanni's going to send a team up there. Now what the heck is going on at the hospital?"

I'd completely forgotten he didn't know and filled him in on everything, avoiding any mention that Manning was blackmailing Sylvia. As a cop, Sam would charge in like a bull, and I needed to keep Sylvia safe. "There's no way to get at him, is there?" I asked.

Sam shook his head. "Not likely. You have to admit, Rhe, he's holding all the cards at this point. You and I both know he's a son of a bitch, but there just wasn't enough evidence to park his ass in a jail cell. So did Will take this okay?"

I nodded.

"What are you guys gonna do?"

"I'm actually going to interview for a home nursing job once I leave here. I've got two possibilities and I've already made the appointments."

"Can you manage that kind of a job?"

"Heck, yes. It's way less demanding than the ER and the pay is better."

"Let me know if a job doesn't materialize and maybe I can find some more money for you in the department budget."

"Thanks for the offer, brother-in-law, but I know you're strapped. I'm sure I'll find something." I suddenly remembered what I needed to ask him about the case. "Sam, the picture of Jane Alderson in the file seems to have been taken a couple of years before she disappeared. She's not wearing braces. I was wondering if she was wearing braces when she was taken. Just a thought, because both Savannah and Rachel had them."

"Don't know, sugar, but I'll find out for you. Who are you interviewing with today?"

"One family is the Carlsons. They have a truck farm north of Pequod. The mother has dementia and they need help caring for her. The other family is the Noonans. I think the husband knows you…Andy? His eighty-year-old mother is living with them and needs some nursing care – she's pre-diabetic and broke her hip last year. She lived next door to Deirdre and made great cookies, so I sort of know her."

"Andy Noonan? Pretty much lost track of him after high school, but I've seen him around town recently. He was on the basketball team with me and Deirdre's brother."

"This is serendipitous. I can ask them about Deirdre." I stood, belched a little garlic and fished for a breath mint in my bag. I didn't want to impress my potential clients with pizza breath. "Gotta go, thanks for lunch. I'll call you later this afternoon about Bowers. I hope they found him. He's growing on me, sort of like a fungus."

The interview with the Carlsons was cordial, but a brief physical examination of Mrs. Carlson's mother, Olive, revealed that her dementia was far advanced. With some directed questioning about potential problems, Mrs. Carlson admitted that Olive was occasionally violent. I wasn't willing to risk having to deal with that, especially since I noted some bruising on Mrs. Carlson's arms. So I advised the Carlsons that Olive had, in my opinion, reached a point at which she needed to be institutionalized. There was a local psychiatrist I knew who would be gentle in helping the family with this decision, and I gave them his number.

The meeting with the Noonans got me a job. Mary Noonan, Andy's mother, remembered me and was delighted I'd be taking care of her. She was chipper, bright, and energetic, capable of doing many things for herself. What she needed was a little medical supervision and help with some of her physical needs. I agreed that I would work with her one day a week, but since the job was mainly for an LPN or Certified Nursing Assistant, I gave her son and daughter-in-law the names of several people who could help her the rest of the time. I drove home on a high, because working just one day with Mrs. Noonan almost made up for my lost salary at the hospital.

My cell phone rang just as I was sitting down at the kitchen table with a cup of the usual slop. I grumbled, got to my feet and fetched my phone from the counter. The call ID said Sam Brewster. I sat back down at the table and put my feet up on another chair before answering.

"Hey, Sam, what's the news?"

"They found Bowers."

"Found him?" My feet went down on the floor. "Is he okay?"

"In a manner of speaking. The local PD found him unconscious and half-frozen in his car on a dirt road just south of Presque Isle. He might have died if a local hadn't chosen this morning to take a drive out to see his father, who lives alone nearby. The guy saw the Crown Vic on its side in a ditch and stopped to check if someone was in the car."

"Then Bowers was really lucky. Where is he now?"

"In the local hospital, getting warmed up and coming around."

"Any injuries?" I shivered, thinking of what might have happened. He might have been a fungus but he was *my* fungus.

"Nothing apparent, but they're doing blood work. Bongiovanni and another agent are headed up there to take his report. I guess they'll be interviewing Cornwell, too."

"So someone set Bowers up to make it look like an accident and figured he would freeze to death?"

"That's my Rhe. Always jumping to the wildest conclusion. Don't you think it's more likely he got drunk and ended up in the ditch?"

"I don't think he's got a drinking problem, Sam. I haven't spent much time with him, but he's just too uptight and by the book."

"Those types drink, hon."

"Nah, he told me emphatically he didn't drink and I believe him. When will you hear back from the Fibbies?"

"Bongiovanni said I could call him tomorrow. How did your interviews go this afternoon?"

I told him about Olive Carlson. He didn't seem surprised, and I figured he may have been called out to their house once or twice. "But I did get a one day a week job with Mary Noonan, which will just about make up for my lost salary."

"Did you get a chance to talk to them about Deirdre and her family? If the Noonans were close to the Dunns, maybe they know where you can find her brother."

"Crap. With all the talking about Mary, I forgot. Next time." I was definitely rattled by Bowers' accident, if it was an accident.

૰৵৶

Later that evening, when the house was quiet and I'd been able to get back to the files on the missing girls, my phone rang. Sam, again.

"Hi, Rhe, hope I'm not disturbing you."

"Nope, just going over those files again. It's what you said when you handed them to me; there has to be something in here that we're missing. Haven't found it yet. What's up?"

"Bongiovanni called a few minutes ago. Bowers is lucid and talking. Turns out he was given a high dose of propofol. Sound familiar?"

"Dang. So I was right?"

"Guess you were, madam sleuth. He remembers visiting Cornwell, then nothing. Bongiovanni is heading out to the sheep farm in the morning."

"So maybe we've poked a hornet's nest?"

"Seems like it, but there's no way to prove Cornwell gave him the drug. Bowers says he had nothing to eat or drink at his place, remembers driving away. Without some evidence, they can't get a search warrant."

"There's something there, I know it. Maybe I'll go up there myself."

"Not without me you won't."

"Okay, when do you want to go? I don't have a shift tomorrow, and Will can't object if I go with you."

"Let me see what my schedule is, but I think tomorrow's fine."

"Can you let Bongiovanni know we're coming up? Maybe they can hang around long enough so we can talk face to face?"

"I'll make it happen. I'm looking forward to another road trip with you — the last one was so much fun."

He was referring to the funeral we had attended the previous fall for a murdered Pequod College student, my first case for the Pequod PD. My car had been keyed while we were in the church, and he and Will had had a colorful discussion about who would pay for the damage. Will never knew Sam paid for it himself.

Will was already in bed reading when I came upstairs. He looked at me over his wire-rimmed glasses. "Was that Sam?"

"Yup."

"You seem to talk with my brother more than you do with me."

Maybe it's because we don't have anything to say to each other that doesn't lead to a disagreement.

When I didn't reply, he asked, "What did he want?"

"We need to go to Presque Isle tomorrow to see Agent Bowers. Someone tried to kill him." I brought Will up to date on what had happened to Bowers.

"This the guy you went with to Camden?"

"One and the same. He's still in the hospital and we need to talk to him, hopefully catch the other FBI agents before they leave. I can take Jack to school in the morning, can you pick him up?"

"You going to be home for dinner?"

"I doubt it. It's a four hour trip up there. I suspect I'll be home late."

Will grumped, but didn't put up an objection. Very strange.

"Oh, by the way, I got a one day a week job working with Mary Noonan. Do you know the family?"

"No. How much will it pay?"

"Almost enough to cover what I would earn in the ER for a day. I don't think you'll have to pick up a summer course."

Will pulled off his glasses, thought a minute, then replied, "Finally, some good news. But we're going to have to put something aside for when you're out of work with the baby. I was going to have to teach a summer course, anyway."

"Well, maybe I can squeeze another day in here or there to make up the difference. I'll go over the names Sylvia gave me again."

Will patted the covers beside him. "Come on to bed. You look tired. Another job would help, but you'd wear yourself out."

As I undressed, I tried to figure out where this more supportive Will had come from. I got into bed and slid over to cuddle with him, feeling grateful and hoping maybe we would weather our differences after all. Silly me. He said "Good night," turned out the light and rolled over, facing away from me.

10

Early the next morning my old Jeep, Miss Daisy, was pressed into service to take us to Presque Isle, with Sam at the wheel. Paulette, bless her, had packed us some still-warm oatmeal-cranberry muffins. Their odor was so tempting that between us, Sam and I polished them off in less than thirty minutes. I'd brought a pillow to bolster my lower back and leaned into my seat, watching the wintery landscape zip by on 95N. We had about three hours to go, making good time on the interstate, but slowing once we hit US 1 in Houlton. For some reason, the Jeep's unreliable heater seemed to be happily chugging out warm air, although I had brought a blanket and kept my coat on just in case.

"Whatcha thinking?" Sam asked after a prolonged period of silence.

"Lots of things. For one, I'm a little worried about Bowers and whether this attempt on his life will affect his career with the FBI."

"Are you getting soft on him, Rhe?"

"No, it's just…"

"I suspect he'll be fine. Bongiovanni seemed genuinely concerned about him and I didn't get the sense he blamed Bowers for what happened. Anything else got you thinking?"

I took a deep breath and blew it out slowly. "Will. Have you noticed any changes in him lately? For the last several months, he's avoided talking to me and has been spending a lot of time either at the college or holed up in his office at home."

"Have you talked to him about it?"

"Yes, and he just said he'd been busy lately. Am I making a mountain out of a molehill?" Another deep breath. "Maybe it's just my hormones."

"Are you far enough along to have raging hormones? If so, I'd better be careful where I leave my gun!" Sam said with a smile, and I had to smile back. "He hasn't mentioned anything to me, if that's what you're asking, Rhe. Did he tell you I ran into him yesterday morning?"

"No, but knowing Will, it's likely he forgot. Where did you see him?"

"In front of the Pie and Pickle around nine. He seemed really surprised to see me, almost nervous. Turned me down when I asked if he'd like to have coffee. Strange, because he always has time for his big brother. I'll make a point to ask him for lunch soon, maybe figure out what's going on, if anything."

The rest of the trip north passed comfortably, with chit chat and then a stop for lunch at the Café Terracotta in Littleton, where Sam knew the cheesecake intimately. We got to Presque Isle around 1:30 and went directly to Aroostook Medical Center. When we entered his room, Agent Bowers was lying on his bed, eyes closed, fully dressed except for his shoes.

"Hi, Bowers! How are you feeling?" I asked, sitting on the bed beside him.

He opened his eyes in alarm, then relaxed as he registered who was there. "Ready to be discharged, if the damn doctor will ever get here," he replied unsteadily.

I looked him over carefully. His face was definitely lighter than his usual shade of pale. He had dark circles under his eyes and looked like he'd lost weight. He looked from Sam to me and said quietly, "I guess you think I blew this assignment."

"How so? You couldn't help it if someone decided to put you to sleep permanently. We're all lucky you were found."

"I should have been more alert. Seen what was coming. Mostly I wish I could remember something, anything. It's just a big blank after I left the Cornwell Farm." He paused, then, as if finally recognizing Sam and I were in Presque Isle, asked, "Why are you here?"

"Rhe and I decided we needed a road trip," Sam answered.

"But why?"

"Sam and I wanted to talk to both you and your boss face to face, and I'm dying to see the Cornwell farm for myself. You're just the excuse I needed." I gave him a smile but he wasn't amused. "Where's Bongiovanni?"

"He left just a minute ago to re-interview Cornwell and look around the farm. If you hurry, you can catch him. I'd come with you, but I can't find my shoes and that damn doctor..." He frowned, started to sit up and then fell back.

I sensed some confusion and didn't think he was ready to be discharged yet. Maybe his physician not showing up was a good thing. I put my hand on his arm. "You rest. We'll catch up with you later. We're just happy you're alive."

Bowers' sense of time was definitely wobbly: Agent Bongiovanni was not in the hospital. So we hit the road again using my Garmin and the address for the farm that we'd got from Bowers. Poor guy was so muddled, he couldn't remember the directions. The place was about ten miles out of town and off the main road to the left, marked by a leaning mailbox on which the name 'Cornwell' had weathered to a faint script. We bounced and jiggled along a rutted gravel road with fields on either side, enclosed by weathered and crooked split rail fencing. What sheep I could see had thick coats and were huddled in three-sided wooden wind breaks. We came over a rise and saw a Crown Vic parked at an angle in front of a two-story farmhouse.

The wind insinuated itself into my sleeves and inside my collar as soon as I stepped out of the car. I leaned back and took in the house. It was built with an ell on the left side, with a porch and its sagging roof filling in the corner. Its original color was anyone's guess because the years had scoured the house of its paint, leaving a scabrous gray behind. Based on the arched windows, some gingerbread work along the eaves, and the general air of collapse, I figured the house was close to a hundred years old. We climbed three creaky wooden steps to the porch and were just about to knock when the door opened with a screech. Agent Bongiovanni stood glowering in the doorway.

"What are *you* doing here?" he asked, sotto voce, the annoyance in his voice reflected on his face. He folded his arms across his chest. "This is an FBI investigation."

"Not completely," replied Sam, drawing himself up to his considerable height, which was only an inch or two less than the agent's. "Rhe and I drove up to talk to you personally about what happened with Agent Bowers. Since it just so happened you were at Cornwell's farm, we decided to head out here and have a look for ourselves. Sorry if we interrupted anything."

"Well you have. Agent Bowers should not have involved you."

"You can't blame him," I replied. "He's still muddled from the propofol. It was our decision."

The agent seemed to consider that for a moment, then sighed and backed out of the doorway. "You might as well come in. It's pretty cold."

We closed the door behind us and followed him down a wide hallway, stepping around neat stacks of newspapers, passing by closed doors. I noticed parts of a small engine on a narrow table, just outside the kitchen at the back of the house. The kitchen itself was large and wallpapered in a flower print so old and faded that the blossoms looked like dingy turtles. Seated at the end of a long wooden table in the center of the room was a man I assumed to be Robert Cornwell, hunched over, hands wrapped around a coffee mug.

"Mr. Cornwell, let me introduce Chief Sam Brewster from the Pequod Police Department and Rhe Brewster, the Pequod police consultant who is the liaison to the FBI on this case."

Mr. Cornwell lurched to his feet and held out his hand to Sam and me in turn. "My farm seems to be a popular stop today. Pleased to meet you."

We all sat in unoccupied chairs and I took a closer look at Cornwell. He was not exactly what I expected: probably in his mid-sixties, on the short side, with a shock of white hair, piercing blue eyes, and the craggy, worn face of a man who'd spent his life outdoors. He was dressed in worn Carhartt overalls that hung off his thin frame.

"Sorry I can't offer you anything but coffee. Would you like some?" He gestured at the back wall, against which sat a cast iron stove. An old-fashioned metal coffeepot rested on one burner.

Although I was still cold from the brief arctic interlude between the car and the house, I shook my head no. The coffee would not be decaf and had probably been sitting there for some time.

"How about you, Chief Brewster?"

Sam answered in the affirmative, and while Cornwell pulled a mug from a shelf over the stove, I glanced around the room. There was a fireplace with a snapping fire on the left-hand wall, with two old but comfortable-looking chairs sitting in front of it. A sink with a hand water pump and an old green wooden cupboard with punched tin doors sat along the back wall next to the stove, and a neatly made bed covered by a quilt stood to the right. Mr. Cornwell clearly spent his winters in this sparest of rooms. *Probably has an outhouse*, I thought. *Please, God, don't let me have to go.*

When we were all settled, Agent Bongiovanni, with apologies to Cornwell for having to repeat some of his questions for our benefit, resumed the conversation. Sam and I sat silently.

"You said that Agent Bowers showed up here day before last, correct?"

"Yes, at about two in the afternoon. I was out feeding the sheep and didn't realize he was here until he blew his horn."

"Can you describe the gist of your conversation?"

"He asked me about a little girl I met a few years ago in Camden. Savannah...?"

"Engstrom."

"Yes, Engstrom. She used to hang around in the gallery in Camden where I show my paintings. He asked me if I'd ever seen her outside the gallery. I told him I couldn't be sure, maybe downtown somewhere. I knew she'd gone missing, but didn't understand why he'd be talking to me."

"Did he tell you?"

"He asked me if I remembered inviting her to see my studio in Camden, but I honestly didn't remember. Then it hit me, maybe the FBI thought I had something to do with her disappearance. When I asked him if that were the case, he said the girl's body had been found and he was following up on several leads."

"Was there any further conversation about this?"

"No, at that point I asked to call my lawyer. Guess he didn't have much evidence, 'cause he left right after that."

"Do you know why we're here today?"

"Same thing, I figure. I'm just going to repeat what I told that young fella two days ago. Not saying anything more without a lawyer."

"Do you know where Agent Bowers was going when he left here?"

"Didn't say."

"Did he eat or drink anything while he was interviewing you?"

"Just some coffee, same as you are."

Sam pushed his coffee mug away and cleared his throat.

"Did something happen to him?" Cornwell asked.

"Yes, he was drugged and left to freeze to death in his car on a road not too far from here."

"Is he alright?" Cornwell seemed genuinely surprised. Without waiting for an answer, he said, "This is the first I've heard. You can't think I was involved? I don't know anything about that!" He partially rose from his chair, looked at the three of us, then sat down again.

Bongiovanni paused for a moment, then said, "Mr. Cornwell, I have a search warrant for your premises here. I hope you'll be willing to come with us to the Presque Isle Police Department while we're executing it. I'd like to ask you some more questions. Of course you can have a lawyer present, if you wish, but we're not arresting you."

Cornwell looked dumbfounded. He sat there, shaking his head, muttering "I don't understand this," over and over. Finally he said, "I'll go with you, but first I'd like to make that call to my lawyer. And if you don't mind, another call to a neighbor who can check on my sheep later."

"No problem, go ahead."

While Cornwell made his calls on an old fashioned black landline phone, we stepped out into the hall.

"I can't see him doing this," I told Bongiovanni. "I work with people every day under the most awful circumstances, and I'm pretty good at telling when someone's lying. That guy's not lying. He's as baffled as we are."

Sam had been silent this whole time and finally spoke. "I'm not sure I agree with Rhe. He could be lying. Practiced liars are pretty convincing."

Bongiovanni didn't seem surprised that we'd disagreed. I got the feeling he wasn't set on Cornwall as a suspect either, but he had to cross his t's and dot his i's anyway.

"Can I ask Mr. Cornwell a couple of questions?" I didn't want to wait, not knowing if I'd have another chance.

"Sure, what about?"

"The bog."

At that moment, Cornwell emerged from the kitchen, pulling on a heavy gray woolen coat.

"I told the neighbor I'd be back by tonight. That okay?" he asked Bongiovanni.

"Fine. We should be easily done by then. Ms. Brewster here wants to ask you a question."

"Do I need to have my lawyer here?"

"I don't think so," I replied. "I'm just curious about the land around here."

"Then sure, the way this day is going, what's one more question?"

"Mr. Cornwell, can you tell me how close this farm is to Crystal Bog?"

"Not far, maybe a few miles as the crow flies."

"Do any of the flowers or shrubs found in the bog grow on your land?"

"Not as far as I know. I doubt the soil here is acid enough. Can't be, because we grow grass to feed the sheep. Why do you want to know?"

"Just following up on something. That's all I needed."

Cornwell locked his front door and we drove back to Presque Isle, where he was placed in an interrogation room at the police station. Bowers was waiting for us at the station, looking even paler, if that were possible, and for once not fidgeting. Sam asked Bongiovanni if we could all get on the same page before we headed back to Pequod. The Presque Isle Chief of Police thoughtfully provided us with a room and some coffee, along with the inevitable doughnuts. These, however, were fresh and still warm, thanks be to the doughnut gods. I took two to my seat, along with a requested bottle of water.

"Sooo...," began Agent Bongiovanni, "what do you have that we should know?"

"You first."

He shrugged. "I'm not sure there *is* anything on our side you don't already know. You sat in on the interview with Cornwell and saw his place."

I turned to Bowers. "But what about your interview? Cornwell basically told us nothing. Did you get anything at all from him?"

Bowers pinched the bridge of his nose with his right thumb and forefinger before answering. "He didn't tell me much. Hardly remembered Savannah, knew she'd gone missing but couldn't help. That's about it."

Agent Bongiovanni looked at Sam and me. "It's a shame you came all the way up here for nothing. If we get anything further out of Cornwell, we'll let you know. Now I have a question for you. Why did you ask him about Crystal Bog?"

Sam nodded at me, and I proceeded to go over what I had learned from the flowers found in Savannah's pants pocket.

"So you concluded she'd been held somewhere near Crystal Bog?" Bowers asked.

"We did," replied Sam, "and since Cornwell's farm is not too far from the bog, we thought coming up to take a look wouldn't hurt."

"I'll call the search team then and have them look around the farm for someplace a child could be hidden, maybe restrained."

The thought of a young girl chained in a dark place sprang to mind. I put my doughnut back on the plate, then asked, "Agent Bongiovanni, could you have your people take some soil samples to test for acidity?"

"Good thought, Ms. Brewster. Consider it done."

I turned to Sam. "I was so sure we were going to find something! I'm sorry it turned out to be just a long ride and a wild goose chase."

"Maybe not," Sam replied. "We got to see the farm, got an idea about its proximity to the bog."

"And maybe something will come from further interrogation of Cornwell," Bongiovanni added. "We'll call you if we find out anything." He turned to Bowers. "Have you thought of anything else?"

"No, sir, and I'm really trying."

"Well, maybe you should *not* try and just let the memories come back naturally."

Bowers looked down at his lap and mumbled, "Yessir."

I had an inkling he was in trouble with his superior and just had to say something. "Agent Bongiovanni, can I say something on Agent Bowers behalf?" Without waiting for a yes, I continued, "Agent Bowers has been nothing but professional. Now that we've gotten used to each other's, uh, investigative styles, I believe we make a good partnership. I hope you won't take him off this case." My face felt hot as a radiator. *Where did that come from?*

Bowers looked shocked, and Bongiovanni smiled at me for the first time. "I wouldn't think of it, Ms. Brewster. Have a safe trip back to Pequod."

Our trip back was uneventful, and I dozed part of the way, my head against the window and eyes half open to the passing scenery. We passed a boatyard, and all of a sudden, the thought that had been eluding me for the past several days made a front and center appearance. "Sails," I yelled sitting straight up.

"Good grief, Rhe, you scared the bejesus out of me. What about sails?"

"The sail Savannah was wrapped in. Bowers was supposed to look into the sailmaker."

"Has he said anything about it?"

"No, but I haven't asked. Maybe I can help. I wonder Marsh has any pictures from the state lab."

"Well, it's too late to call now. Relax. Whatever they found isn't going anywhere. Plenty of time to find out tomorrow."

Silence reigned again. Then I had a thought. "Sam, when Savannah disappeared, did the FBI question all the local PDs in the state about all unclaimed bodies?"

"I'm pretty sure the FBI would have already been notified if there were any. Where are you going with this?"

"I'm thinking there might be another body out there. Are you sure they talked to PDs in towns around Crystal Bog?"

"To tell you the truth, I don't know. I can check tomorrow. Along with that question about Jane Alderson and braces. Maybe we can contact her dentist."

"Good," I replied, snuggling back against the window with a hopeful feeling that we might actually get a lead. *Heaven knows, we need one.*

11

Tension was palpable in the ER when I arrived for work on Thursday, and I asked the charge nurse what was going on.

"Woody's coming down to spend some time observing," she replied. "Wouldn't you know, things have been quiet this morning. With our luck, he'll cut more personnel, as if you and the security guard aren't enough."

I was the one he would spend time observing, so after I stowed my coat and changed my boots for Crocs, I set about making sure all of the cubicles and suture kits were stocked and prayed an unkind prayer for some patients to show up. Five minutes later, just as Manning emerged from the elevator, the outer doors opened. Three gurneys came in, with the attendant EMTs reciting patient injuries and vitals to the nurses and MDs, who took over for them. More gurneys arrived within minutes. A big rig collision with several cars had occurred on US1 and for the rest of the morning, I didn't even think about Manning.

I finished my shift at four totally exhausted, but stopped to see Marsh on my way out. He was in one of the autopsy suites, finishing up on a body from the crash that morning. I stood inside the door while Midori zipped the body in its bag and stored it in a refrigerated locker and Marsh took off his paper suit and head gear. He rubbed his face with his hand, then smiled at me.

"Couldn't stay away?"

"Bad one this morning, huh?"

"Yeah, three dead, one a child."

Midori walked by, wishing us a good evening. "How's she working out?" I asked after she'd left.

"She's not Oliver, but you only have to show her once how to do anything. I frankly think she's too smart for the job, but she says she needs the money. I'm going to give her more training in forensics, so she can make extra money working with the techies, like Oliver did."

"You're a marshmallow," I commented, wincing at the pun. "I need to ask you something I totally forgot about from when we recovered Savannah's body."

"Come on in the office. You want some ginger ale?"

I followed him across the hall, piled my stuff in a corner and moved the neat piles of folders from the chair next to the desk. Marsh retrieved two ginger ales from his bar refrigerator and popped them open, handing one to me. I took a long drink, realizing how little fluid I'd had that day.

"So what did you forget?"

"The sail, Marsh. The sail Savannah was wrapped in. Remember I told you I thought it was a foresail or a jib?"

He looked at me, puzzled. "What about it?"

"We haven't gotten any information about the sail from the state lab, have we? You know, possible make, age, distinguishing characteristics."

"So if you can identify the source of the sail, you might be able to find out who bought it."

"Right. Bowers was supposed to look into it, but he's been busy following another lead and I I forgot about it. What if it was made by a local sailmaker?"

"Okay, I'll call the lab. What specifically do you need?" Marsh picked up a pen.

"Can I get a picture of it? I also need close-ups of the tack and the clew."

"The tack and the what?"

"The tack and the clew, the corners at the bottom of the sail. Sometimes sail makers have their own way of hand-binding the grommets at those corners, and occasionally they add a corner patch at the tack that's uniquely theirs. I also need to know the material it was made from. Hopefully it wasn't made by one of the conglomerates that send sail specifications to China for manufacture."

He scribbled notes on a piece of paper. "Let me see if I can get those photos for you and an analysis of the material. If not, you can always go to the state lab and look at it firsthand, like I told Bowers."

"That wouldn't be anytime soon. Tomorrow is my first day as a private duty nurse."

"I'd forgotten about that. Damn Woody." He hit his desk with his fist; he disliked Manning as much as I did. "I hope it's going to pay well."

"Enough so we can get by." *Hopefully.*

❧ ❧

The next morning I dropped Jack off at school, thinking I might have to pick him up in just a few hours because another snow storm was forecast. As usual, Will had left so early, I hadn't had a chance to talk to him about it. And he wasn't answering his phone…again. I really didn't want to know why.

I drove out to the Noonan farm, admiring the neat red house, barn and outbuildings as I drove down the plowed driveway. A couple of milk cows were sheltering in a lean-to in a near field, and the other fields surrounding the house were covered with snow that rippled from the plowed rows beneath. When I got out of the Jeep, I could hear chickens scrapping in a small hen house near the barn. *Fresh eggs.* I knocked on the weathered front door and shortly heard footsteps approaching. The door opened with a yank and there stood Mary Noonan, who greeted me with a big smile and a hug. From behind her came a whoosh of warm air smelling deliciously of baking bread.

"Come in, come in, Mrs. Brewster. It's a fine cold day out, isn't it?" I could hear the sweet Irish lilt in her voice.

"Yes, but there's more snow on the way. How are you doing, Mrs. Noonan?" I walked by her and took off my boots as she closed the door. "Baking something good by the smell of it."

"Some Irish soda bread, dear. It will be out of the oven in a few minutes. Would you like some? And please, call me Mary."

"Only if you call me Rhe. And I'd love some, Mary. Are your son and daughter-in-law here?"

"No, they left early to get some feed for the stock and some groceries. You can get isolated out here with heavy snow. Hang your coat on that hook, dear. Would you like coffee?" She bustled down the hall toward the back of the house, where the kitchen with its wonderful aroma was located. The house was old but lovingly maintained. The hallway was papered with a small flower print and a polished wood stair on the right, with carved bannister and spindles, led up to the second floor. The kitchen was bright and cheerful, painted yellow with dated, but sparkling, white metal cabinets, a modern six burner gas stove, and an enormous chest freezer dominating the wall by the back door.

"Please, sit, while I take care of this," Mary said as she opened the oven door. Two round loaves of golden bread appeared. She pulled out the pans, set them on top of the stove and turned to face me. "I see you're eyein' the one with raisins. Let me cut you a slice or two." After removing the loaves to a bread board, she cut two thick slices and placed them on a plate along with a slab of butter. *Yum.* When I asked if she had tea instead of coffee, her round face and rosy cheeks lit up with pleasure. "I'd love a cuppa myself," she said and got out two mugs and teabags, poured in hot water from a kettle on the stove, and let them steep while she brought milk to the table.

I took a big bite of bread and savored its warmth and flavor. When my mouth was no longer full of heaven, I told her, "Mary, this is wonderful, but we need to talk about you. Tell me how you've been feeling this past week? Are you sleeping well? How's your appetite?"

She returned with the mugs, and sat down across from me at the table. I noticed that she wasn't eating any of her own bread. "My appetite's not there," she replied, "and I'm not sure why. Everything else is fine, but when I cook, I don't want to eat."

"How about when your daughter cooks?"

"Oh, I eat what she makes. I don't want her to think I don't like her cookin'."

Mmmmm. After further discussion, we went to her bedroom and I did a physical exam and took her vital signs. Her blood pressure was a little high, but she assured me she was taking her medication. In the past, she'd had bouts of atrial fibrillation, the most common type of heart arrhythmia. But now that she was on medication for that, her heart was beating regularly. Her son had told me she'd had a fainting spell about two weeks ago, so I listened to her lungs and checked her respiratory rate, which was low. *Probably time for an EKG.* I had her get up, walk across the room and back for me, but saw no balance problems. Then I checked her ears and eyes, did a physical exam of her abdomen, mouth and neck, checked her lymph nodes, the pulses in her arms and legs and did a breast exam. Nothing abnormal.

When we returned to the kitchen, I asked for another cup of tea. I figured I could gently recommend a more thorough exam from a cardiologist and hopefully drift into a conversation about Deirdre Dunn and her family. All of which went well.

"I'd forgotten how close you were to Deirdre," Mary commented when I brought up the subject.

"Deirdre was my best friend. It was horrible when she disappeared."

"I seem to remember that." Her eyes took on an unfocussed look as if she were far away, reliving the past.

The silence went on for more than a minute, and finally I said, "Mary? Are you okay?"

She came back to the present with a start. "Oh, I'm fine. I tend to drift off from time to time, or at least that's what Andy says."

Note to me: schedule her to see a psychologist for a mental evaluation of her cognitive function.

"What were they like then, the Dunns? Did you know them well?"

Mary perked up. "Well? I would say so. Their house was about ten feet from ours, separated only by the driveway. Those houses! Built so cheap you could hear everything goin' on next door. And my, there was always a lot goin' on."

"Like what? Deirdre never talked about her family and, come to think of it, I didn't get invited to visit very often."

"Well, I shouldn't say this – it's bad to speak ill of the dead, you know..." and here Mary crossed herself, "but Sean, the father, was a drinker. I heard him ragin' on weekends, things breakin', and that poor mother. I never saw her but she wasn't hidin' a bruise. I used to bring food over to her after one of those fights."

"Did he beat his children? I never saw a bruise on Deirdre."

"No, he doted on her, talked sweet to her, but he beat on that boy. What was his name?" Her face crinkled in thought.

"Art... Artie."

"That's right. Artie. Sweet little child, but wasn't very talkative when he got older. He seemed unhappy most of the time."

"Do you know what happened to them after Deirdre disappeared?"

"Lots of yellin' every night. The mother blamed the father, the father blamed the mother, it never stopped. Artie spent a lot of time hidin' under the back porch when he wasn't at school. I used to sneak him food."

"How long did that go on?"

"Seems like forever, but about a year later, I saw a truck out front, lotta men carryin' boxes and furniture out, and the next day, the house was empty. I never saw them again."

"Did you see Artie or his mother on moving day?"

"I saw Artie but not his mother. In fact, I hadn't seen her for about a week before they moved."

"I didn't know any of this. Did you have any contact with Deirdre before she disappeared?"

"Sometimes she'd come over to sit with me on the porch when her folks were fightin'. We'd wait until things got quiet and then she'd sneak back in."

"Did she say anything about her parents? Anything about what was going on?"

"No. She was real quiet. I don't think I ever saw her laugh. Did she laugh with you?"

"Yes, she did, a lot. She was a little wild, to tell the truth."

"Well, good for her. I'm glad she had some joy in her life."

I shook my head in sorrow. "Why didn't you report the fighting to Social Services or the police, Mary?"

"I was always afraid that Sean would come after me or mine if I did. He had an awful temper, that Sean. I just did what I could, Rhe, but I've had times when I feel real bad, thinking I shoulda done somethin'. Maybe things would have turned out different."

I glanced out the window and saw snow coming down thickly. Just then the back door opened and the Noonans came in, arms full with bags, bringing in a stiff breeze of frigid air.

"Hi, Rhe!" greeted Andy. "You and Mom been having a good visit?" He set the bags on the counter, alongside his wife's.

"We have, and I've been enjoying some freshly baked soda bread. A real treat." I looked again out the window. "I see it's starting to come down, so I'd better go before the driving gets tough. Mary, I'll see you next week. Andy, got a minute?" I asked quietly. He nodded.

When I got up, Mary wrapped the rest of the raisin soda bread in parchment paper and gave it to me to take. I gave her a hug, said good-bye to the younger Mrs. Noonan and headed down the hall to where I'd hung my coat. While I rewrapped myself and thrust my feet into my boots, I told Andy,

"There're some things I'm concerned about. Mary's respiration rate is lower than normal, and her blood pressure is up, even though she said she was taking her meds. Do you give her the meds, or does she take them herself?"

"She takes them herself."

"She might be forgetting and thinking she took them. That happens with the elderly. I don't want her to develop congestive heart failure. Maybe you or your wife can make sure she takes them? She'll complain, I'm sure, but be tough."

Mary's son smiled. "She's stubborn as a mule. This'll be war."

"Make sure you win it! One more thing. While we were talking, she sort of spaced out on me, and she mentioned you'd noticed that, too. I think it might be good to have a psychologist check her cognitive functions. I'd recommend Dr. Ferguson. He's wonderful with older people. I'll email you his number."

"Will do, Rhe. And thank you."

"No problem. Your mother is a delight and I look forward to seeing her next week." I pulled open the door and almost fell back from the blast of air that hit me. "See you then," I said, as I stepped out onto the porch. Andy shut the door firmly behind me.

Miss Daisy started right up, and despite the soda bread, my stomach reminded me it was lunch time and the baby needed food. *Maybe I could corral Sam for lunch.* I gave him a call and we agreed to meet in thirty minutes at the Pie and Pickle, a much needed change from the Italian carbs at Ernie's.

☙ ❧

The Pie and Pickle was a great café for breakfast, but they also had wonderful soups and other lunch items. By the time I got there, my cell phone had informed me that Jack would be getting out at 2 PM, giving me just enough time for a nosh with my brother-in-law. The windows of the P&P were steamed up, and the snow on the sidewalk was more than an inch when I pulled open the door to the friendly bell ring. The P&P had a homespun, welcoming décor: blue and white checked tablecloths, red paper napkins, and an old, creaky wooden floor. I spotted Sam sitting at a two person table in the back, near the coffee counter, devouring a menu with his eyes. Guess he was hungry. I hung my coat and scarf on the back of my chair and swiped the menu from him.

"I know what you're going to have…. a Reuben, right?"

"You know me too well, honey." *Ah, his cowboy is on today.*

The waitress, a tired-looking older woman I didn't recognize, put water and napkin-wrapped silverware on the table and took our orders. Miss Daisy's heater had been less than efficient during the drive into town, so I opted for a bowl of clam chowder, with a side of fried onion rings, a craving I'd developed with the pregnancy.

"So how's Mary Noonan?" Sam asked when the waitress left.

"She doing pretty darned well for an eighty year old, although I suspect Andy and his wife have their hands full. I did get to talk to her about the Dunn family. Got some questions for you. Did you know that Deirdre's father beat her mother?"

Sam twirled the salt shaker between his thumb and forefinger for a moment or two before answering. "I knew something was going on. Artie never invited me to the house and during our junior and senior years, I saw some really bad bruises. When I asked him how he got them, he said sports or clumsiness. I guess I really never wanted to know so I didn't press."

"According to Mary, Sean Dunn beat both his wife and Artie, but treated Deirdre like a princess. I wonder if something else was going on, perhaps sexual abuse, because Deirdre was really wild with some of the older boys at school. I know you asked me to find Artie, so when I visit Mary next week, I'll ask her more. The younger Noonans came home in the middle of our conversation, and I didn't want it to appear I was pressing her. Can the computer geek of the Police Department give me a hand with an online search for him?"

"Phil?"

"Of course Phil. The man who rescued a phone that'd been in water for three days. The wizard of Windows."

"Right, I'll ask."

I thought of something else. "Did you manage to find out whether Jane Alderson had braces?"

"We found her dentist, and he told us she'd never had them. Of course he was curious as to why we were asking."

"I hope you obfuscated."

"Obfuscated?"

"Make obscure or unclear." I sighed. Sam was not a reader.

"Oh. Yeah, I told him we were bringing our files up to date."

"Darn it. I'd hoped the braces would be a link."

"Keep at it, darlin', you'll find something."

'I wish I could be so sure."

Our food arrived and Sam tackled his Reuben with less than his usual gusto. When I'd finished eating, there was still a half sandwich on his plate. In fact, he didn't even try to snitch one of my onion rings. Sam was definitely not being Sam.

"Okay, Hopalong, what's wrong?" I tried to get him to smile. "You are definitely out on the range today."

"I tried to talk to Will again, gave him a call to ask him to have lunch with me. He accused me of nosing into his business and told me to butt out. I don't know what's wrong, Rhe. I know you've been worried about him, but I don't think he's going to talk to me."

My stomach sank, and suddenly lunch wasn't sitting so well. If Will was being hostile with Sam, something definitely was going on, and I didn't want any bad blood between them. I reached across the table and squeezed his hand. "I'm sorry I asked, Sam. This is my business and I'm sorry I dragged you into it. I'll try a little harder to see if I can get him to open up."

Sam picked up the check for lunch, and we didn't speak again until we were outside the café. I gave him a hug. "I'll call you tomorrow to see what Phil might have found. Would you call Bongiovanni to get an update on Cornwell?"

"Sure thing. Talk to you tomorrow."

Before I pulled out of the parking space, I turned Miss Daisy's radio on and looked for some soothing music. I was anxious, thinking about having to confront Will. I found Whitney Houston on an oldies station, singing *Didn't We Almost Have It All*, and thought how appropriate it was for the moment. As I headed for Jack's school, I thought about everything I'd tried in order to get Will to open up, respond to me, even notice I was there: making gourmet meals, buying him small gifts, sending him a card at work for no reason, surprising him with tickets to a hockey game. What had I gotten in return? Little or no response, and the last time I'd asked him what was wrong, he'd yelled, "Nothing, I don't know why you're always on me about this."

If anything, he'd become even more remote since then. So much for wishing and hoping there was nothing wrong. There clearly was, and I couldn't deny it or make it go away. There was nothing left to do now but make a full court press. It was way past time.

12

After I picked Jack up from school, we drove home, where I had him change into warmer clothes before he walked over to Paulette's to play with Tyler. Since it was only 2:30, I was left with two things on my mind: what to have for dinner and the full court press. What should I do? I decided on turkey burgers and carrots for dinner and got the ground turkey out of the freezer. With that settled, I made myself a mug of hot chocolate and went into the family room for a comfortable chair in which to think about my other problem. Will's remoteness had begun after I'd helped solve the murder of the Pequod College student, along with the related closing of a local brothel using college students as escorts. Right after, he admitted he'd visited the brothel – once, by mistake. Or so he said.

The announcement of my pregnancy hadn't improved our relationship one whit, and I rubbed my stomach thinking about that. How could I ask him what was going on without having him explode or lock himself in his office? We'd had a loud argument last fall, and he had shoved me in anger. Would he become physical if I really made him mad? The thought was unnerving.

I looked out our French doors at the gray ocean, roiling with whitecaps, framed and blurred by the heavy snow coming down, and let my mind wander to other things. I needed an update from either Bongiovanni or Bowers, I needed the information about that sail, I needed to find the bodies of the other two girls, I needed...

The sound of my phone ringing woke me up, and I groggily got up and found it on the kitchen counter. It was Sam.

"Sorry to bother you, Rhe. I hope you had your feet up."

"I did. What's up?"

"You're probably getting dinner right now…"

Dinner! I looked at the clock; it was 5:30. I really needed to get going. "Yeah, I'm kinda in the middle of things." *So I fib sometimes.*

"So let's powwow tomorrow after work. Phil has some information for you, Bongiovanni called, and I need your input on where the case is heading."

"You bet, Sam. Gotta run, bye." Will would probably be coming in the door any minute and nothing was underway. Jack was still at Tyler's, so I called Paulette and told her to send him home. I got out the hamburger buns, chopped and fried out an onion, and mixed that into the turkey meat, along with bread crumbs, an egg and some seasoning. After scraping the carrots and chopping them into chunks, I set the table. By then, Jack was home and it was well after six.

Where was Will? I tried calling him but he didn't pick up.

Jack had done his homework at Tyler's, for which I blessed Paulette, since I knew how hard it was to get him settled down and focused. By 6:45, he was definitely hungry. "Where's Dad?" he yelled from the family room where he was busy on the floor with some toys.

"Not sure, kiddo. Let's give him another fifteen minutes."

"But I'm hungry now."

"Why don't I start the veggies and if we haven't heard from Dad in another ten minutes, I'll put your hamburger on."

"Okay," he replied in a grumbling tone.

Jack and I ate at seven, and I left food in the oven for Will. I had just gotten Jack into his bath when I heard the garage door open. *Will. Don't be angry, Rhe. You've done the same thing to him several times, forgotten to call.* I went to meet him, calling, "Will? Your dinner's in the oven."

He had his coat off and was pulling his plate out with a hot mitt when I got there. "Why didn't you wait for me?" he asked in a tone that was half accusatorial.

"Jack got really hungry and I couldn't reach you on your cell."

"Battery's dead."

"Why don't you give it to me and I'll charge it for you. The charger's right here on the counter."

"You don't need to do that. I'll take care of it later."

"Sure. I've gotta find some clean PJs for Jack. Be right back." When I returned, I found him picking at his dinner. "Not up for turkey burgers tonight?"

"Not really hungry. I had a big lunch."

He wasn't hungry, hadn't called and now was pissed we hadn't waited for him? Two can play that game!

"Oh, where'd you go?" I asked innocently.

"Moe's, with some of the grad students."

"Anyone I know?"

"No."

"Did you have the lobster roll?" He knew I was a sucker for the lobster rolls.

"Fried clams," he answered without enthusiasm or returning my smile. "What is this? An interrogation?"

"No, I just like hearing about your day." *Right.* "How 'bout some coffee? I'll make you the real stuff." I shook my head while making the coffee. Our dinner conversations had always been so easy, filled with details of the day, local gossip and of course, Jack tales. Now it felt like pulling rocks out of the yard.

Just then, Jack came into the kitchen, fresh from a bath and wearing his dinosaur PJs, and asked Will to read him a story. A few minutes later I could hear them laughing together in Jack's room while Will read him a story using funny voices. *We sure don't laugh together anymore.*

When Will returned, the coffee was done and he poured himself a mug. Although I was sitting expectantly at the table, he headed across the family room to his office. "Hey, got time for some conversation?" I called after him.

"Not tonight, Rhe, I'm busy."

I followed him into his office and perched on the arm of the old sofa. He swiveled his desk chair toward me with a prominent crease between his eyes, a sign that he was irritated.

"What?"

"Will, what is going on with us? Maybe it's me, maybe it's the pregnancy, but you have to admit you've become increasingly remote. We don't talk, you're hardly ever here, you barely have any time for Jack. Whatever it is, I miss you and I want to work to make things better." *This came out the wrong way, I was groveling. I wanted to be strong, forceful.*

"How many times do I have to tell you nothing is going on? Why don't you get that?"

"When was the last time we had breakfast together? You're gone every morning I'm not working. We haven't gone out for a meal, gone snow camping or antiquing in such a long time."

"If this is about my coming home late tonight..."

"It's not. I know I've done the same thing to you a number of times. You're allowed."

"You bet I am!" he exploded, turning back to his desk. "Now get out... please. I have work to do. Sorry I didn't do justice to your dinner." This was said with more than a hint of sarcasm.

I couldn't let it go. Not this time. "Can't we just talk the way we used to? Let's have a fire and sit in the family room. You haven't asked about the baby in a while."

"Not now! How many times do I have to tell you I'm busy?" He said this with his back to me, but then turned around again. "Are you thick? Leave me alone!"

I sat there, stunned, then stood up and walked over to his desk, anger rising. "What in hell is going on with you?" Louder than I liked. "What have I done to merit your back?"

He gripped the arms of his desk chair as if trying to control his anger. Then he took a deep breath and looked up at me. "There's nothing the matter, nothing. I'm just under a lot of pressure right now – midterm exams, my annual review coming up. I'm really sorry if I've been inattentive. I don't mean to, really. I just...forgive me for yelling at you...I shouldn't have said that." He rubbed his forehead with his hands for a few seconds, then grabbed my hand and kissed my palm, a move he used to make when he was apologizing.

At this point in our usual argument, I would soften. Not this time. I might have wanted to believe him, but couldn't, and this conversation wasn't going anywhere.

"We'll talk soon," he promised.

Right, and the bear's Catholic. I left his office without saying anything more and retreated to the kitchen, where I poured myself a cup of coffee in spite of it being the full caf. I didn't see Will's phone and figured he had left it in his coat pocket, so I went over to where the coat was hanging and dug it out. *Well, well. It was fully charged.* I put it back in his coat pocket. *Oh, Will, who are you involved with? What have you done?* I started to cry.

For some reason, I slept like a log that night. Maybe because I had finally accepted that nothing Will said was the truth and that there really was a huge problem, one I was going to solve, one way or another.

༒

By the next afternoon, feeling lighter than I had in a long time, I stopped by Marsh's office. It was becoming a ritual. The door was open and Marsh was sitting at his desk. When I knocked on the doorframe, he motioned me to come in. "I have that information about the sail for you," he began.

"Oh yeah? Got pictures?" I sat down in my customary place on the chair next to his desk. We could probably put my name on it at this rate.

"Yup." He slid a manila folder across the desk. As I opened it, he added, "The sail is Dacron, and they think it's a foresail, just as you thought. Can you tell the maker from those pictures?"

I laid the four prints side by side on his desk and closely examined the stitching as well as the tack and clew. "I think I can. This looks like one of Tom O'Neil's sails. It's been a while since I've seen him, but I think his loft is still in operation. He made sails for the Glass Trinket when I was a kid."

"That your boat?"

I looked at Marsh and realized how little we knew about each other outside of work. "It sure is. It's moored down at the marina. Wanna go sailing some time?"

"I've never been out on a sailboat, so definitely yes. But not now!"

We'd gotten five inches of snow the previous day. "Oh come on, Marsh. Winter sailing is fun!"

He knew I was pulling his leg and gave me a thumbs down.

"Can I take these?" I asked.

"No problem. They sent two copies of everything."

"Off to see Sam," I said as I bundled up. I was getting so tired of the coat, scarf, hat and gloves routine. "I'll check with you Friday."

❧❦

Sam was in the process of putting on his coat when I got to his office. "Thought I wasn't going to see you today," he said as he removed his coat and hung it on the slightly bent coat tree in the corner of his office.

"I'm sorry. Were you going someplace?"

"Doughnuts." He looked abashed. "But it can wait. What've you got to tell me?"

"I stopped to see Marsh. He had some pictures of the sail Savannah was wrapped in. It looks like it's one of Tom O'Neil's and I plan to see if he might be able to tell me who he made it for."

"Good idea. You need me to go along?"

"I think I can handle it. We're old friends and I don't want him to think he's a suspect."

"Okay, it's yours. Why don't you take off your coat and stay a while? Want some coffee? Oh, I forgot, you're on the decaf diet. How about some water?"

I threw my coat on the tree, on the opposite side from his, along with my scarf. The rack wobbled but held. "No, I'm fine, thanks. So tell me what you learned from Bongiovanni." I sat down next to his desk, in another chair that should have had my name on it.

"So he called me yesterday afternoon to tell me his agents had found propofol on Cornwell's farm, so they're holding him."

"But that doesn't prove anything. I did a little online research and it's a common veterinary medication. Available by prescription. He might be using it on the sheep, during lambing or something like that."

"That's exactly what he said. But for now they don't have any other suspects."

"Thin evidence. He'll be out once he gets a lawyer."

"He already has. But there was one thing he told Bongiovanni during questioning. Apparently there's a guy who works the farm for him in the summer, when he's in Camden painting. The guy's name is Charles something..." he fumbled around in the piles of papers arranged haphazardly on his desk, "...here it is. Harkin. Charles Harkin." Sam had an unerring ability to find whatever he needed in those piles, a remarkable talent.

"So he'd have access to the propofol as well. Do they know where this guy lives when he isn't working for Cornwell?"

"That's the thing. He seems to be an itinerant laborer. No permanent address. No driver's license in that name. Cornwell says he just shows up at the beginning of every June."

"I take it the FBI has put their considerable powers into looking for him."

"They have, but nothing so far."

"They got a picture of him?"

"Nope. Cornwell gave them a description, but it was pretty generic. He's an artist, so they asked him to do a drawing. I'm hoping they'll share that with us. But there was one thing...he has a cola-something in one of his eyes."

"Coloboma?"

"Yeah, that. What is it?"

"It's a gap in part of the structures of the eye, like the iris – the colored part of your eye – or the lens. It's caused when the baby's eye doesn't develop properly during pregnancy." My hand went inadvertently to my stomach and I saw Sam's eyes notice it.

"What does it look like?"

"The gap can be large or small but usually occurs in the bottom part of the eye. It's very noticeable if it's in the iris. Then the pupil, the black area in the center, has a keyhole shape."

"Oh." Sam didn't see it; he'd need a picture. He changed the subject. "Speaking of babies, how are you feeling? Baby okay? Aren't you due for a checkup soon?"

Just like him to be concerned about me. "Not for a while yet, but I'm feeling pretty good. Thanks for asking."

My mind shifted gears. "Have you asked Bongiovanni to look into the possibility of unclaimed bodies? Maybe query the smaller police stations in the area around Crystal Bog that maybe the FBI skipped when the girls went missing?'

"Dang it, Rhe, I forgot. I'll get to it this afternoon, I promise." Sam smiled at me. "You come up with some strange ideas," he shook his head, "but your track record is pretty good. Mmm...how did things go with Will last night? Did you two have a chance to talk?"

I must have flushed because he almost immediately added, "No, forget that, it's none of my business."

"It's okay. I did talk with him last night, but nothing came of it. He said he's been under pressure with exams and his promotion review. That's all he told me, but it would explain why he was so short with you." *Can I lie or what?*

"Yeah, alright." He squinted one eye and regarded me for several seconds. I figured he knew there was more to it and wasn't convinced by what I'd said, so I gave him a reassuring smile and nodded.

Then he said, "You look sort of different today, Rhe. I don't know, less worried?"

"That's nice to know." *What else could I say?* "Talk to you tomorrow." I rose and once again went through the ritual wrapping up. It reminded me how much I just hated, abhorred, loathed winter.

13

Will actually stayed home for breakfast the next morning and took Jack to school. He joked and laughed with Jack, a little too forced to my ear, and even kissed me on the cheek as he left. *Why had he put on this act?* After I had cleaned up the breakfast dishes, I called Tom O'Neil to see if he'd mind a visit. No problem.

Tom's loft was a way up the coast in Little Monmouth Harbor, a tiny place with maybe twenty houses. His barn was next to the 150-year-old house where he'd lived all his life, and he was walking across the lawn when I pulled in. At one time, Tom had been blond and tall; now he was still tall and lanky but with a shock of white hair. I remembered having a crush on him when I was teenager, spending a lot of time in his loft while my sails were being made. I picked up the envelope with the photos as I got out of the car and greeted him.

"Hiya, Tom. Good to see you."

"Rhe! You look great." He gave me a bear hug.

"That's good to hear, considering baby number two is on the way."

"Congratulations. Pregnancy agrees with you. Up to climbing up to the loft?"

I nodded vigorously. In fact, I couldn't wait. The loft was on the second floor of the barn, and when Tom opened the ground floor door for me, it was like stepping back in time. The same pictures of sailing ships were on the wall, along with a bunch of newer ones, rooms with old sails and cordage, and the same massive carved wooden head of a woman, which Tom had told me was the figurehead from an old whaling vessel.

"Head on up, Rhe," Tom said, indicating the stairs at the left. I climbed up to the second floor and into a huge room, filled with the light from large windows all around, with a wide expanse of polished wooden floor. There were sail maker's benches on three sides of the room, two of them occupied. The assistants looked up momentarily and gave me a smile, then bent back to their work. These benches were almost works of art: low, wooden, elongated, worn smooth, scored with years of use. On the benches, there were hand tools that probably hadn't changed in shape or use in two hundred years, and around the loft, several industrial sewing machines, a large drafting table to one side, and charts on the walls. Here Tom and his three assistants engaged in the real craft of sail making. I remembered my sails being cut on the floor and shaped by eye and experience. I inhaled my surroundings, appreciating the fine art I was witnessing.

"So what can I do for you?" Tom asked. "You sounded mysterious on the phone."

"I'm hoping you can give me some information. You know I'm a consultant for the Pequod Police Department now?"

"Doesn't surprise me one bit," he replied with a smile. "You were always nosing around here, asking questions."

"Well, I'm an official noser now, badge and all. That's why I'm here. You heard about the young girl's body found on the beach in Dornish Cove?"

"I did. Terrible thing."

"She was wrapped in what I think is one of your sails."

"One of mine? Are you sure?" He backed up to the drafting table and collapsed on a stool. A change came over his face as he realized the implication. "You don't think I did it, do you?"

"Not for a minute, Tom. I'm here to find out who bought that sail." I knew he could be a suspect, but based on our long years of friendship, both Sam and I had him way down on any list, for now. I opened the envelope and took out the photos from the state lab, spreading them on the table.

Tom looked at them very carefully. "Yes, that's definitely one of mine. I recognize that stitching. Corner patch at the tack. Guess you did, too. Headsail, Dacron, old."

"Head sail?"

"It's the smaller sail on a fractional rig sloop, bet you haven't seen one. Forestay doesn't run to the top of the mast and the main sail does most of the work. It was made for one of two people I can think of, but I can't tell you which right, off the bat. Didn't keep records on a computer back then."

"Would you check for me?"

"Sure, you want to wait?"

I recognized I'd asked him for time, and as with any artist, time was money. "Tell you what, Tom. Why don't you check as soon as you're free, then call me?"

"I'll do it tonight. You'll be at home?"

"You betcha." I gave him a hug. "Thanks, Tom. I appreciate this." I looked around the loft one more time and headed back down the stairs, stopping to admire the photographs of the sailing ships and their sails decorating the wall. I knew Tom had crafted all of them, and I hoped he wouldn't move up on the suspect list.

∾∾

It was not yet lunchtime, although my stomach was rumbling, so I decided to visit Sam to see if the FBI had located Charles Harkin and if Phil had found any unclaimed bodies in the Crystal Bog area. When I entered the police station, Ruthie was sitting at her desk, working on what appeared to be a Word Jumble in the *P & S*. *Must be a slow morning.* She looked up at the sound of the front door opening, smiled, and gave me a come here signal with her index finger. Although I was anxious to check in with Sam, I obeyed. You didn't irritate Ruthie. "Guess what?" she asked when I reached her desk.

"You solved the Word Jumble?"

"Nope. Phil found another child's body, or at least they think it's a child." Ruthie knew absolutely everything that went on in the police station, so I guess I shouldn't have been surprised.

"They *think* it's a child?"

"The preservation's a little wonky."

"What do you mean, a little wonky?"

"Sam'll have to explain, you need to see him." She gestured with her head towards the hallway to his office. "But first tell me how Will and Jack are doing."

"Jack is great, playing basketball in the town league. Will is, well, fine I guess. Working hard with teaching and writing. The usual."

Ruthie gave me a quizzical look as I walked past her to see Sam. *She'll know all about our troubles in a cold minute,* I thought. Sam looked up just as I reached his door and motioned me in.

"What did Phil find?" I asked.

"And good morning to you too," Sam said sarcastically.

"Okay, okay, good morning, Sam. How are you? Now tell me what he found!"

"I'm fine thank you." He handed me a report Phil had typed up. He had contacted the Crystal Crossing police and discovered they'd had a body stored in a local meat house freezer for the last two years.

"Meat house freezer?" My mouth fell open.

"When there's only twenty people in the town and an elected but unpaid police chief, there aren't too many options."

I read on. Some hikers in the bog had discovered an arm poking out of the ground while walking off trail and had high-tailed it back to the gas station that *was* the town, looking for help. It just so happened that the garage's mechanic was the police chief, Milton Saunders. They were so horrified by what they'd seen, they refused to return to the site, but they did describe pretty accurately what they'd discovered and where. Chief Saunders and the owner of the garage found the site and dug out the body attached to the arm. It was so desiccated they figured it was probably that of a MicMac buried long ago.

"MicMacs, Sam?"

"I had to have Phil look that up. They've lived for centuries in northern Maine and southern Canada. Discoveries of bodies like this happen once in a while and they're usually identified as MicMac and given a tribal re-burial."

"So how did it get to the freezer?"

"Saunders didn't know what else to do with it, so he had a local beef farmer store it, thinking he'd eventually figure it out. I think the idea of the state police or the FBI never crossed his mind because he thought the body was ancient."

"So was it identified as MicMac?"

"That's the interesting thing. Our message about unidentified bodies lit a fire under Saunders and he finally got around to contacting the tribal center. An elder was sent to Crystal Crossing, and he told Saunders the body wasn't MicMac. There wasn't anything with the body to suggest it was a native burial, and the body wasn't buried sitting up, which is normal for a burial in the ground."

"Wow, some story. When can we get the body?"

"*We're* not getting anything. The State Examiner's office is having it transported and will do the autopsy. I called them and the FBI as soon as Phil handed me this." Disappointment must have shown in my face because he added, "That's just proper protocol, Rhe. Marsh is only an assistant ME. Any finding like this has to be sent to the state lab."

Undaunted, I pressed on. "When will the results of the autopsy be available?"

"Probably in a few days. I told them the body might be that of a kidnapped girl, the FBI's involved in the case, and they agreed to rush it. I talked to Bongiovanni, and he's all over it."

I shook my head. All the interagency protocols were making my head swim. "Did Phil have any luck anywhere else?"

"Nope, that was it." I watched as he carefully replaced the notes from Phil in the middle one of the piles on his desk. My face must have brightened, because when Sam looked up, he asked, "What?"

"I was visiting Tom O'Neil before I came here. He positively identified the sail as one of his and is going to look through his files to see who ordered it."

"Good news, pardner. Maybe this will lead us in the right direction. You heading home?"

"Yup. Time for lunch. The baby is complaining and my stomach is, too."

"Wanna grab something in town?"

"Not today, Sam. I really need to give the house a lick and a promise and figure out what to do for dinner, just in case Will shows up." This last was only slightly bitter, and Sam ignored it.

I didn't get home for lunch until after one, because one of Miss Daisy's tires decided to go flat. I had to call Triple A and wait around for them, stomping my feet in the cold. Turned out something had punctured the tire.

The repairman who sealed the hole for me asked if I'd been playing with knives. I was sure it was just a piece of glass on the road, but his sarcasm doused my previously upbeat mood. What I really needed was food, so I drove straight home.

When I pulled into the garage, I noticed there was a paper bag with the Munch Box logo on it sitting on the stairs going into the kitchen. The Munch Box was a local sandwich shop which was not one of my favorite places, but which Sam swore by. I picked up the bag and brought it inside, figuring it must be a present from Will. *Who else could get into our garage? Plus he had done the things-are-back-to-normal play act this morning.* When I saw what was inside, I knew it was from him: a fancy tuna salad on ciabatta with lettuce, tomato and a pickle on the side. He knew I could never resist tuna fish salad. I took off my coat and put the sandwich on a plate. After grabbing a bottle of water, I went into the family room to eat and watch some news. I had to admit, the sandwich was really, really good, and I ate every crumb of it.

About thirty minutes later, I started to feel nauseated, which increased when I stood up to take my plate back into the kitchen. I threw up in the sink and wondered if my early pregnancy queasiness had returned with a vengeance. I felt better after throwing up again but decided to lie down on the couch, where I blanked out until I heard my phone ring. When I went to get my phone, my head suddenly felt like it would explode. It was Paulette calling.

"Rhe, are you okay? I was late picking up Tyler and Jack was still there. I tried calling you but since you didn't pick up, I brought him home."

I looked at the clock. *Five! What had happened to me?* "I'm okay, just a massive headache. Will left me a tuna fish sandwich from the Munch Box on the doorstep in the garage. It must have been off or something because I threw up shortly after eating it. Then I was out like a light on the couch."

"Sounds like food poisoning. Could it affect the baby?"

"Most of the time not. But I'll push fluids tonight."

"You should call the Munch Box and let them know."

"I will. Can you send Jack home? He needs to start his homework. Thanks so much for picking him up. What would I do without you?"

My headache was not helped by Will that night. At 7:15, I was rinsing off dishes for a run in the dishwasher, glancing out at the blackness of our back yard through the window over the sink, and drinking a third glass of water. Jack was sitting at the table, grumbling and jittering through his homework. I didn't hear a car, Will just blew in through the back door, took off his boots and coat and asked, "Dinner in the oven? Faculty meeting ran late."

'What faculty meeting?"

"I told you last night, didn't I?"

"Not that I remember."

"Oh well, it just got out. Sorry. I must have forgotten to tell you."

"Dinner's in the oven."

"Good, I'm starved." He grabbed a hot mitt, then removed the platter of aluminum-covered fried chicken from the oven, chicken which I'd made at Jack's request. Unfortunately, Will also loved it; he probably thought I made it for him. He swore when he burned his other hand removing the bowl of mashed potatoes and plate of asparagus. I smiled to myself, amazed at my cruelty. I finished the dishes and sat down at the table, after pouring myself a mug of decaf. While demolishing everything, Will chatted with Jack, helped with a couple of math problems, then brought the plate to the sink and rinsed it. He didn't even notice me rubbing my forehead.

"Thanks for the fried chicken, babe."

I looked up. "Have a good day?" I was totally uninterested but keeping up a front.

"Yeah, more or less. Office hours and student complaints, then the usual blah, blah at the faculty meeting. How about you?"

"I visited Tom O'Neil this morning. You remember him? The sailmaker." Will nodded.

"He hasn't changed one whit in twenty years...well, except for the white hair. His sail loft was exactly as I remembered it from when I was a kid. Oh, there are some baked apples in the pan on the counter, if you want one."

Will took out a bowl and helped himself to an apple. "How did you get to know him that well?"

"He made the sails for the Trinket."

"Oh? So why did you visit him today?" He got ice cream from the freezer to put on top.

Jack, who had taken his finished homework to his room, came into the kitchen just then. "Those are really good apples, Dad. Mom let me put some whip cream on top of mine. Which do you think is better – ice cream or whip cream?"

Will made an effort to look like he was thinking seriously about Jack's question, then said, "It's a toss-up, scout. I just felt like ice cream tonight."

"You don't feel like ice cream to me!" Jack laughed.

Will made a face and asked, "Where does he get this stuff?" He paused, sat down at the table, then asked again, "So why were you visiting the sail loft?"

I gave a tiny nod towards Jack. "Oh, just found a sail we needed to identify." Turning to Jack I asked, "Hey kiddo, how would you like to go see where sails are made?"

"Yeah! Do they have big machines there?"

"No, the sails are small and made by hand." His face fell. "But they have lots of pictures of big sailing ships and the head of a woman carved from wood, as big as you are."

Jack's face lit up. "When can we go?"

"How about the next teacher work day?"

"Great! Can Tyler come, too?"

"Sure!"

Will finished his apple and took his dish to the sink.

"Will, did you leave me a sandwich for lunch on the step in the garage today? From the Munch Box?"

"No, not me. I had lunch at my desk, working on a paper."

"Then how did it get in the garage?"

"No clue. Maybe it was Paulette. She has a key to the house. What's the problem? Wasn't the sandwich any good?"

"No, I got sick after I ate it. I called the Munch Box, but it seems no one else got sick on the tuna fish." Just then my cell phone rang. I picked it up, walked into the family room and promptly forgot about our conversation. It was Tom.

"Hi, Tom, what did you find?"

"How did you know it was me? Oh, you've got one of those new-fangled phones that tells you who's calling!"

"Yes I do, and I'm sorry if I startled you."

"You'd think I'd remember that by now. My sons do that to me all the time. Anyway, I found the name of the person who ordered that sail. It was twenty years ago, so I'm not sure how helpful this is going to be. It was for the sloop owned by Robert Morgan."

"Twenty years ago? Then he must be the father of the guy who's now editor of the *Post and Sentinel*."

"Yup, that's the one, Morgan Senior."

This case couldn't be more convoluted if I made it up. "Thanks so much, Tom. I really, really appreciate it. By the way, if we get a teacher work day anytime soon, can I bring Jack and a friend over to see your loft?"

"Jack your boy?"

"He's a ...very energetic seven-year-old."

"Any time, Rhe. Just give me a day's notice."

"Thanks again, Tom."

By the time I returned to the kitchen, Will had left, leaving all his dishes piled in the sink. *Really concerned about my apparent food poisoning.* I went to his office door, called through it to ask if he wanted a cup of real coffee, but he didn't answer. No way was I going in there, not after the previous night. Later Will came out, got a cup of the decaf, tasted it and made a face.

"Why didn't you make me some real coffee?"

I looked up from reading the *P&S*, opened on the table in front of me, and shrugged. "You didn't answer me when I asked you."

He turned and left, calling over his shoulder, "I'll be working late tonight." As soon as his office door was shut, I opened my lap top and logged in, going online to check the Psychology Department's website and calendar. All of the departmental events for the week were listed, and there was a faculty meeting listed, but it had been the day before.

Honestly, how stupid did he think I was? And how long was he going to continue this charade? Maybe it was time I did a little nosing around on him.

14

The next morning's shift at the hospital ER began simply enough with sprains, pink eye, broken noses, and migraines. Luckily, my own headache had disappeared with a good night's sleep. Just before noon, an EMS bus pulled up to our loading dock and three techs struggled in the door with a gurney. On the gurney was an enormous man, who hung over the edges. To make things worse, he was barking instructions at the EMTs, telling them not to jiggle him, cursing when they went over the door frame, and then yelling for a doctor. One of the EMTs, a wiry old-timer named Joe, grabbed me while his partner recited the patient's vitals to the charge nurse.

"Watch this guy. He's mean," he warned. "Name's Donnelly. He was in a fender bender and swears his neck is broken. There's no indication of that, but we put him in a collar anyway. I think the worst he'll have is whiplash, but in my opinion, this is a case of 'whipcash'." Joe smiled, showing a broken tooth. We saw cases of 'whipcash' from time to time, people who came to the ER with facetious injuries, looking to launch a lawsuit for big money. "And stand back when he talks to you. He's loaded. Blew a point two-five on the breathalyzer."

"Thanks for the info, I'll wear a mask." I smiled at him, grateful for the warning.

"He's going to need a C-spine if he thinks his neck is broken," I told an orderly. "You can take Mr. Donnelly to radiology for a cervical spine X ray as soon as I'm sure he's stabilized."

With the help of the orderly and another nurse, I managed to push Mr. Donnelly into a treatment room. It took four of us to get him off the gurney and onto the bed, working to a litany of groans, moans and curses. The smell of sweat and alcohol wafting off his body was nauseating, but I had to re-check his vitals and get him on an IV before the neurosurgeon came in.

After the others had left the room, I took a pressure cuff from the stand next to the table, then explained what I would be doing, using as soothing a voice as I could manage. "Mr. Donnelly, I have to take your vital signs. I'm just going to place this bracelet around your wrist. I want you to hold your hand up to your heart and I'll tell you when you can relax." I carefully strapped the blood pressure cuff around his wrist, lifted his arm across his chest, and pushed the button.

He lay there calmly for a minute with his eyes closed, then suddenly opened his eyes, saw the pressure cuff and flung the arm with the cuff to the side. "What is this thing?" he bellowed, trying to lift himself to a sitting position. I immediately knew he'd blacked out. I gently placed my hand on his shoulder and tried to coax him back to a supine position.

"You're alright, Mr. Donnelly. I'm Nurse Brewster and I'm taking care of you."

"What are you doing to me?" he yelled and, using his arm, pushed me back so violently that I hit the floor, banging my head on the IV stand. The stand started to wobble, but I caught it before it fell. Using a chair, I pulled myself up to a standing position.

While I was saving the IV stand, Donnelly managed to sit up, swing around and push himself off the table. When I turned to face him, he hit me in the jaw with his fist. I fell again, this time taking the IV stand with me. The crash brought the charge nurse, Nancy Ennis, into the cubicle. Before she could grab him, he started kicking me, his work boots smashing into my legs. I curled into a ball to protect my stomach and wrapped my arms over my head, which did nothing to soften the repeated kicks to my arms, back and legs. I tried to take my mind out of it, smelling the wax and disinfectant on the tiled floor as I breathed deeply, hoping each kick would be the last.

Dazed by the attack, I dimly heard Nancy screaming for Security and saw her feet between me and Donnelly. He must have pushed her aside because the kicking continued. At some point, someone else or maybe two other people came into the cubicle, and I heard a prolonged scuffle. The kicking stopped and the mayhem moved out into the main room. Finally there was a thud, and when I opened my eyes, I could see three people holding Mr. Donnelly on the floor and Nancy kneeling beside him, plunging the needle of a large syringe into his butt. *Where was Security?*

I must have blacked out momentarily, because the next thing I felt was someone gently removing my arms from my head and doing a quick examination of my arms and legs to determine if anything was broken.

"Rhe, where does it hurt?" I recognized the voice of Dr. Moran, one of the ER physicians.

"Mmm, sort of everywhere, don't think anything's broken."

"I concur, but you are lucky, my dear." He slid a cervical collar around my neck. Two sets of hands slid me onto a gurney, lifted it and carried me into another cubicle, sliding me onto the table. I had my arm across my eyes, a little dizzy, still dazed, and now shaking from an adrenalin rush.

Nancy came in and took my vital signs and checked my eyes. "How are you feeling?" she asked with concern.

"I've felt better." I kept my eyes closed to quell the dizziness.

"Can you move your legs?" she asked. I did, but grunted with the pain. "Can you put your index finger on your nose?" I did, but again groaned. "Can you tell me what day it is?"

"Thursday, and I'm fine, Nancy. You can quit with the Glasgow scale." I had used the Glasgow Coma Scale myself many times to assess the consciousness of a patient.

"Dr. Boudreau's coming down to check on the baby; then we are going to take X-rays to ensure nothing's broken. As soon as we're sure the baby is okay, I'll give you something for pain."

"No, I'm fine, really. I don't need X-rays and as soon as Boudreau checks on the baby, I need to finish my shift. I can't give Manning any excuse to fire me."

"Are you nuts? Some booze-crazed idiot tried to beat you half to death and you want to go back to work? I don't know who's more crazy!"

With that, I opened my eyes and smiled.

"Do you want to call Will?" Nancy asked.

"No, he's impossible to reach these days. This would just set him off. I'll let him know when I get home."

"I called the police as soon as Donnelly was down."

"You're my hero, Nancy. How much did you give him?"

"Enough to keep him sleeping for a little while."

I frowned. "Where was Security? Didn't anyone call?"

"We did but no one came. I can't figure out why."

At that moment, I heard Sam's voice loudly calling my name. "In here, Sam." The curtain to the cubicle was flung aside and Sam barged in, hat in hand, out of breath. He came and stood over me, looking from me to Nancy and back.

"Is she okay?" he said, gently taking my hand,

"We'll know as soon as she's checked out, Chief Brewster. Would you wait outside while she's examined? And while you're at it, you might want to put some restraints on Sleeping Beauty there. We decided not to try lifting him." Nancy very efficiently guided him out and Dr. Boudreau took their place.

I let everyone do their thing. A thorough obstetrical examination, total physical, blood work, and X-rays. Sam stood up when they wheeled me to radiology, but I gave him a thumbs up and he sat down again. Much to my relief, the baby was fine, and except for bruises seemingly everywhere, I was too. After Dr. Boudreau authorized some Percocet and insisted I rest, Sam came in, twisting his hat in his hands, and sat down next to me.

"Where's Will?" he asked.

"I didn't call him. I haven't been able to reach him on his phone for a while now."

"Do you want me to send a patrol car over to the campus and get him?"

"Heavens, no. There'd just be a scene when he got here. I'd rather let him find out about this at home."

He shook his head and bit his lower lip, not pleased. "Well, when you're ready, I'm taking you there. No arguments." His eyes never left my face and seemed to get a little watery; when he saw me staring back, he looked away. After a moment, he resumed a professional demeanor and asked me to give my version of what had happened, placing his ever-present recorder on the stand next to the bed and turning it on.

When I had finished, I asked, "Where's Donnelly?"

"They took him up to the psych ward a while ago and have him locked down. This is not the first time he's attacked someone while under the influence. Did he threaten you at all before he attacked?"

"No, the first clue was when he socked me in the jaw."

"Do you happen to know why there wasn't any security?"

"Manning told me he had to let go the guard here in the ER, for budget reasons apparently. What happens now, Sam?"

Sam took my hand, holding it between his two. "Donnelly will be charged with battery, Rhe, but since you're pregnant, it'll be pushed up to aggravated battery. He'll do some time. Which may be good for him."

At this point, there was a commotion outside the cubicle and I could hear Nancy say, "The police chief is with her now, Dr. Manning. You might want to wait." *Fat chance.*

The curtain was flung aside yet again, and Manning walked in. "I should have suspected you'd be the one involved," he said, without a preface.

"What do you mean?" Sam rose to his full height and looked down at Manning.

Manning took a step back before answering. "Mrs. Brewster's unprofessionalism and disrespect has been noted before. I wouldn't be surprised if she said or did something to cause Mr. Donnelly to fend her off."

"Fend her off?" Sam yelled. "From what I have learned, that inebriated loon attacked her and might have killed her, if the ER staff hadn't dragged him off! And where was Security? What kind of hospital are you running here, where your personnel can be half-beaten to death before anything is done?"

"For one thing, no one was present when the altercation began, so you have no evidence Mr. Donnelly initiated it," Dr. Manning replied officiously. "Security was cut for budgetary reasons, which I am sure Mrs. Brewster can confirm." He turned to me. "Mrs. Brewster, you are suspended until this situation has been resolved. We cannot continue to pay you during this time. I plan to visit Mr. Donnelly shortly and I only hope he won't decide to sue you and the hospital. So you should understand why I cannot let you continue to work here."

My mouth started to form the word 'What?' but before I could say it, he turned and walked out. I sagged back on the bed and finally began to cry. I couldn't get a break.

❧ ❦

Nancy collected my belongings from my locker, and as per hospital protocol, made me sit in a wheelchair to leave. Sam wheeled me out to his Jeep and lifted me into the front seat. I was still overwhelmed with what had happened and just stared out the window on the way home. Sam, however, was positively garrulous, cursing Manning and insisting he was getting me a lawyer. He would personally take Mr. Donnelly to the police station as soon as he'd sobered up and assured me he would be held for arraignment. He knew all about the bad blood between Manning and me.

"That pile of crap Manning got away with it last time, Rhe. This time there'll be consequences for the bastard, I promise you."

With a wince, I placed my hand on his arm. "I don't think that's what a Police Chief should be saying, cowboy. Be careful where you express your pig-headed opinions!"

He gave me a big grin.

"I appreciate your being there for me this afternoon. You have no idea how much."

We pulled into the driveway, and Sam helped me out of the car and up the steps to the front door, where I pulled out my house keys. I unlocked the door and turned to Sam. "I've got it from here. Go on and get back to work. I'm going to call Paulette to pick up Jack, then take a long bath. I'm sore but I'll be fine."

"I'm here for you, Rhe. Know that." He put his hands gently on my shoulders.

"I do. Believe me, I do."

He gave me a quick kiss on the cheek and walked slowly back to the car, not driving off until I closed the door behind me. When I got inside, I called Paulette. Of course I had to tell her *why* I needed her to get Jack for me. She gasped when I explained what had happened.

"Does Will know? Did he come to the hospital?"

"No, Sam brought me home. I haven't been able to reach Will on his cell for the last week or so and decided it wouldn't help things if Sam sent a patrol car to get him. I'll tell him when he comes home."

"Well, girlfriend, I'm bringing over dinner, so you won't have to cook tonight. No arguments. Now get yourself in a warm bath. I'll see you when I bring Jack home. What are you going to tell him?"

"Probably that I fell down at work. Something simple he can understand. Thanks, Paulette. I'll have some coffee for you when you get here."

"Don't bother, you know I don't like your stuff."

☙ ☙

True to her word, Paulette arrived around five, with Sarah, Jack and Tyler, carrying two casserole dishes, fresh bread and a container in which I could see a chocolate cake. The first casserole was a chicken fricassee in a creamy sauce, giving off the rich aroma of chicken and vegetables. The other was for the next night, a lamb cassoulet, made with lamb chops, pork sausage, white beans and other vegetables, seasoned with rosemary, thyme and orange, according to Paulette. *How does she do this?* I wondered for the umpteenth time. The chocolate mousse cake, Sarah announced proudly, was her creation.

The soak in the bath tub and another Percocet had done me a world of good, although I still moved gingerly as I headed over to the coffee pot. "I made regular coffee just for you," I announced as I poured two mugs. Jack and Tyler had disappeared into the family room, and Sarah and Paulette sat at the kitchen table. Sarah looked darling, her hair in a ponytail and wearing a hot pink terry jacket and a pink and white striped turtleneck. I figured she was talking to her mother again.

"You're having regular?" asked Paulette, surprise registering in her voice.

"Yup. After what happened today, damn the caffeine for once. Plus I took another Percocet and I need something to keep me awake."

"Is it safe for the baby?"

"I grilled Dr. Boudreau about it — she gave me a thumbs up. The baby's still fine and healthy."

"Aunt Rhe?" Sarah looked pointedly at my mug. "Can I have some coffee, too?"

"Sure! You can have what I used to have when I was your age. My mother called it coffee milk." Taking another mug from the rack, I poured in about a half cup of coffee, then filled it with milk from the fridge.

Paulette added some cream and sugar to her mug from the containers on the table and handed the sugar to Sarah. "Go easy," she warned. Mother and daughter settled in their chairs for a good chat, Sarah looking proud to be included.

After I answered a few more of Paulette's questions about the attack, carefully because of Sarah's presence, she asked, "So what is the hospital going to do for you? Don't answer that! They'll give you a commendation and expect you back at work tomorrow."

"Not likely. Sarah, would you mind checking on the boys?" I asked. What I had to say was not for her ears. She nodded and went to look for them.

As soon as she left, I said, "Dr. Manning has suspended me without pay for provoking the altercation. He also indicated that Mr. Donnelly is likely to sue both me and the hospital for unspecified damages."

"What?" Her eyebrows reached her hairline. "Are you serious? You can't be serious!"

"Oh, but I am. Apparently the time has come to get a lawyer. I'm thinking of calling Sawyer Smith, Ruthie's nephew. She'll be all over this by tomorrow morning and Sawyer will probably call me before I call him. I can't wait until Will hears about this. No money coming in and now we'll have lawyer's bills."

"Sweetie, don't worry about the money. It sounds like you're the one with a case against the hospital and Donnelly. What you need to worry about is getting healed up. And figuring out a way to sweet talk Will into taking the whole thing calmly."

"I wish I knew how to do that. Speaking of Will," I said, looking at the clock over the fridge, "I need to shove the three of you out the door. He'll be home soon, and I need to put your good food in some of my containers, so he'll think I made it. Is that too devious?"

"Here, let me help you."

Sarah reappeared with the boys, and I put her "coffee" in a travel mug.

৵৽

By seven, Jack and I decided to go ahead and eat and were gifted with the delicious chicken stew, to which I added a salad, and the chocolate mousse cake for dessert. Jack didn't seem to notice my jaw, but I'd put some makeup over the red area. When Will didn't show by eight, I got Jack into bed and read him three stories, the last one with his eyes closed. I took a warm shower at ten and fell into bed, totally exhausted but having a hard time finding a position where something didn't hurt.

At some point I was aware of Will coming into the bedroom, opening the closet door and then using the bathroom, but when I awoke the next morning to the annoying buzzing of the alarm clock, he was not in bed with me. I almost screamed with the pain as I got out of bed and had to lean against the wall for a minute before walking down the hall to rouse Jack. After he went into his bathroom, I went back down the hall to our bedroom, stood in front of the floor length mirror, and dropped my nightgown to see where the pain was coming from. The sight was discouraging. I had large black and purple bruises on my arms and back. When I turned, I saw my multicolored buttocks and some dark bruises on my legs. My ribs hurt with every breath, but worst of all, I now had a large purple swelling on my jaw where Donnelly had first hit me. Jack had been too sleepy to notice it. I took my last Percocet and put on a long-sleeved loose sweater and sweat pants.

I had cereal in bowls for both me and Jack when he finally arrived for breakfast. He sat down, started to slurp the cereal and then looked at me. His spoon clanged into his bowl. "Mom, what happened? Who hit you? It wasn't Dad, was it? Does it hurt?"

"No, of course it wasn't Dad!" *Why would he think that?* "What happened is that I got slugged by a drunk in the ER. A real KO! Do I look like I've been in a boxing match?" I tried to give him a reassuring smile.

"Yeah, and you lost! Where's Dad?" He didn't smile back.

"He came home late and left for work early. He said he'd see you tonight." *I'm such a liar.* "Maybe we can do something together this weekend. How about a movie?"

He nodded but still didn't smile. What was that song? *I must be a cock-eyed optimist.*

15

Right after I got home from taking Jack to the bus stop, I poured myself another mug of coffee and lowered myself gingerly into a kitchen chair. My feet went up on another chair. My cell phone rang; I groaned because I'd left it on the counter. I got up, cursing the phone gods, and retrieved it. I didn't recognize the number. "Rhe Brewster."

"Rhe? This is Sawyer Smith. Ruth Hersh's nephew. The lawyer?"

"Hi, Sawyer!" Sawyer and I had become acquainted the previous fall, when I was looking for a lawyer to represent a Pequod student, Zoey Harris, caught up in the raid of the local brothel. "So Ruthie told you what's going on, right?"

"You know my Aunt Ruthie. There's not much about the police family she doesn't know, and in this case, I think the chief asked her to call me. I'd like to come over this morning to discuss the possible suit against you and maybe find a way to take the offensive with this. Do you mind if I bring a photographer? We need to document your injuries as soon as possible."

"Sure. I'm not going anywhere. What time?"

"How about right now?"

"You're on. One thing – how much is this going to cost?"

"Don't worry about that now. We can discuss it later, and I promise you won't go bankrupt."

I had to smile at his eagerness. Not five minutes later, the phone rang again. This time it was the lovely and painted Dolores Richmond, Manning's secretary. I knew what was coming. "Good morning, Dolores. What can I do for you?"

"Dr. Manning wanted me to call and tell you that Mr. Donnelly is indeed suing you and the hospital for what occurred yesterday. So you will remain on unpaid leave." With that, she hung up. *So much for courtesy and respect.*

After I hung up, I called Will, figuring more bad news would be better over the phone. No answer, for which I was grateful this time. He would explode at the message I left.

❧ ❦

True to his word, Sawyer was at my house with a female photographer in tow within fifteen minutes. "This is Heidi Warren," he said, making the introductions. Heidi was in her thirties, petite with short dark hair, and radiated confidence. "I've worked with Sawyer before. He figured you'd prefer a woman to be taking the pictures."

"I actually hadn't even thought about that, but I appreciate it. What do you want to do first?" I asked Sawyer.

"Let's get the pictures out of the way."

I took Heidi upstairs to my bedroom, where I took off everything but my underpants and bra. She gasped. "Sorry, but you're pretty hard to look at. Are you sure you're feeling okay?"

"I'm so wicked pissed, I can handle anything this morning."

"I'm going to need everything off. I know this is embarrassing, but I'll blur out the sensitive areas in the final pictures," she told me. So everything came off.

What the hell, as a nurse, I see nakedness all the time.

She photographed my face and all the areas with bruising, close up and at a distance, and from several different angles. When she was done, I dressed and we both went downstairs.

"Sawyer, you're going to have one easy defense here," Heidi said as she put her coat on. "This is one tough lady. I'm surprised she's not in the hospital. These photos will be delivered to you as soon as I've finished. No email this time." I walked her to the front door, where I gave her an air hug because of the pain.

She laughed. "Take care, Rhe. I hope everything works out for you,"

Sawyer had helped himself to coffee by the time I got back to the kitchen and made a face when he tasted it. "Decaf, right?"

I nodded. Should have made the real stuff.

"Okay, let's get down to business." He sat down at the table, took out a recorder and a pad and pen, and took another sip of coffee.

"I can sweeten that for you, add some creamer, maybe make it taste better?"

"No, this is fine. I drink too much of the caffeinated stuff as it is."

Over the next hour, I told him what had happened in the ER, repeated several things that needed clarification, and answered what seemed like an unending stream of questions, including naming witnesses. He took copious notes. When I mentioned that Security had been called when Donnelly first attacked me, but had never shown, his ears perked up. Then he asked for a detailed description of my past interactions with Manning; I told him plainly why Manning didn't like me and about our confrontation when he reduced my work hours. He was shaking his writing hand by the time we'd finished.

"Did you go to HR for an explanation when he reduced your hours?"

"I did, but there's a situation between Sylvia Hutty, the head of HR, and Manning I can't talk about without Sylvia's permission."

One of his eyebrows went up. "Do you think you can get me permission?"

"I doubt it. It's very personal and going public would cause irreparable harm to Sylvia. I'll call her tonight anyway. I don't think it would be a good idea to show myself at the hospital right now."

"I agree, let's avoid any possibility of confrontation." He turned off the recorder, took my hand and looked me straight in the eyes. "There's no question I can get any lawsuits against you dismissed, based on what you've told me. The photos should clinch it, but the fact hospital security didn't show up is a big issue. I plan to interview the ER personnel, Mr. Donnelly, and Manning. Donnelly's arraignment on charges of aggravated battery will also play into this."

"Do you know when he'll be arraigned?

"A week from Monday, I think."

"Good, I want to be there."

"I'm sure there'll be some dancing around with Donnelly's and the hospital's lawyers, but I'm hoping Donnelly will see the wisdom of dropping his suit against you, particularly if there's the threat of a countersuit. How much do you want to countersue for?"

"Countersue? I haven't even thought about that. To be fair, I want to know more about Mr. Donnelly before deciding."

"Then there's the fact you can sue the hospital for lack of security. You should seriously consider that move, Rhe."

"If I countersue, I'll never work there again."

"But what if you win, Rhe?"

Mmm, I hadn't even thought of that. More unpleasant things to talk about with Will. Whenever I see him again.

"Can I think about that? I'd like to talk this over with Will and maybe Sam." Actually Sam was the first person I wanted to talk to. How easily I'd slipped into thinking of him first.

"No problem. I need to do those interviews first. We'll talk at the arraignment."

❮❯

That evening, Will showed up at 5:30. Jack was doing his homework with a lot of my help, and I was heating up the lamb cassoulet from Paulette and preparing some carrots as a side dish. When I turned to greet him and he saw my face, he lurched back. "What happened to you?"

"Shh, Jack's doing his homework. I was punched by a patient in the ER yesterday." I nodded toward Jack.

Will shook his head but didn't pursue any details. "Are you okay?" He didn't ask about the baby.

"Fine. When I didn't see you last night, I called you and left a message. Why didn't you answer? Where were you?" I waited for the lame excuse, and I wasn't disappointed.

"I was doing some research in the library; I turned my phone off."

"Why didn't you call?"

"I forgot the time. You know how it is when you're really focusing. When I realized what time it was, it was after Jack's bedtime and I didn't want to wake him with the phone ringing."

Couldn't he come up with a more believable excuse? I willed myself not to say something sarcastic. "Well, go get cleaned up, help Jack with his homework, and we'll eat in about an hour. Paulette made us dinner."

Jack looked up from the table. "Yeah, Dad, I found a really cool video game that Mom approved. Wanna play?"

"Finish your homework first, slugger, then we'll play."

The two of them spent an hour after dinner laughing and having a good time with the game, and the sight was a sad echo of the fun Will and I had once had. For just a brief moment, I wished... *fat chance.*

After Will had tucked Jack into bed, he came back out to the kitchen. "Want to tell me what really happened?" he asked without any preface, sitting down at the table.

I turned and leaned against the sink, not wanting to be close to him when the eruption occurred. I told him everything, including what had happened with Manning, assured him the baby was fine, and then watched while he did a slow burn. *Time to take the offensive.* "I met with a lawyer this morning."

"Yeah, and how much is that going to cost us?"

"I don't know, but here's the thing. Sawyer – Sawyer Smith, my lawyer – assured me he can get Donnelly to drop the suit if I countersue."

"What does that mean?" He looked interested for the first time.

"I sue him back for some amount of money he can't afford to pay, for pain and suffering. Sawyer also recommended I ask the hospital for a chunk of money to offset the fact I might have lost the baby or been killed. The pictures of the bruising alone might do it. Since hospital security didn't show up, my case is even stronger. Then it wouldn't matter if I couldn't work at the hospital any more. We'd have some money for when I'm on maternity leave and later."

There was no explosion. Instead, Will's face brightened. "Really? How sure was he about this?"

"Pretty sure. We're going to talk again next Monday after Donnelly is arraigned." I kept my voice neutral, while thinking Will was a little too interested in the money angle.

"The lawyer'd be paid out of any settlement money?"

"That's what I figured."

Will didn't ask me any more questions, but retreated to his office as usual. I finished cleaning up the dishes, too tired and sore to have any more conversation with him that evening. If he had cared at all, he would have at least offered to help. So I was surprised when Will went upstairs with me at our usual bedtime. I quickly figured out why when he asked to see my bruises. He was definitely thinking about the money. He retreated back to his office, saying he still had work to do, and I realized I didn't care anymore.

☙ ❧

Early the next morning, Will was gone again. It was Saturday, and I was still sore and now I was cranky because Will was nowhere around to keep an eye on Jack. Sam had called me around nine to let me know he'd take me to retrieve my Jeep from the hospital parking lot. Once again Paulette stepped into the breach, without asking about Will, and took Jack for the day. *What a good friend.*

On the way to the hospital, it occurred to me yet again how incredibly thoughtful Sam was. I told him about the visit from Sawyer and the photographer and the idea that I might countersue.

"How did Will take everything?"

"Not bad. He was interested in the possibility of my suing the hospital. He also inspected my bruises, I think to see for himself how good a case we might have."

Sam said nothing, but I knew he was thinking about Will. He was frowning, so his thoughts were probably not kind. I needed to get his mind on something else, something I had let slip.

"Hey, Sam, with all the excitement at the hospital, I completely forgot to tell you about the sail! Tom some digging in his records, and it was made for Robert Morgan Senior.

"Bob's father?"

"One and the same. What do you want to do with this lead?

"Well, Morgan, Sr. is dead, and since you're such good friends with Morgan, Jr..."

"I know, you want me to follow up with Bob. He does owe me a favor."

"Yeah, you saved his life. I'd call that a really big favor."

"I'll take care of it early next week. I see Mary Noonan again on Monday. I plan to talk to her more about Deirdre. Has Phil made any progress on finding Artie Dunn?"

"You know, with everything going on, I forgot to ask him. You want to swing by the station when you're finished seeing Mary? Maybe I can buy you some lunch, Annie Oakley."

I smiled at the sobriquet. "You're *always* buying me lunch, Buffalo Bill. First, I'm going to sneak into the hospital and talk to Marsh to see if he's heard anything about the body from Crystal Crossing. If it's not past lunchtime when I finish, I'll stop by. Otherwise, I'll call, okay?"

"You sure you're going to be up for all that by Monday?'

"I'm just going to walk slowly and take a handful of Tylenol."

"Hmmmph."

He parked next to my Jeep. "Now sit tight, I'm coming around to get you out." He walked around his Wrangler, opened my door and gently helped me down. Even with support, I couldn't hold back a grimace. He helped me into Miss Daisy with a warning, "Go straight home and soak in a hot bath."

"So you're the nurse now?" I almost laughed at the thought of him packed into scrubs.

Mary Noonan was her usual apple-cheeked grandmotherly self when we met Monday morning. I was wearing a long sleeved sweater and walked carefully down the hall to the kitchen, where I managed to sit down at the table with nary a wince.

"And just how did you get that great bruise on your face, Rhe?" she asked.

Dang, I was hoping she wouldn't ask. I decide to prevaricate, otherwise the conversation could be endless. "I fell in the ER, Mary. Nothing serious, just hit an IV stand."

"You need to be more careful, a chara." Mary had a cup of hot tea in front of me in a minute, and this time she had baked oatmeal cookies. I chewed on one enthusiastically before asking her how she'd been for the past week.

"I'm not away with the fairies, as it turns out." I raised an eyebrow, not having a clue what she meant. "Ach, that's Irish for crazy, my dear. Andy took me to see a psychologist last week and he ran a bunch of tests. I'm not an idiot. I knew what they were for. Turns out my mind is just fine."

"So did you also see your cardiologist?"

"Yes, and he thinks he knows why I'm dreamin' durin' the day. At first he thought it was some sort of little seizure. Travelin' schemes or somethin' like that."

I thought for a minute. "Transient ischemic attacks?"

"That's it. Scared the whey out of me when he told me what they were. But then he looked at the results of my blood tests. Turns out I have an electric imbalance."

"Electrolyte imbalance. That can sometimes mimic a transient ischemic attack. I'll bet it's because you haven't been eating properly and may not be drinking enough water."

"That's what he said, and gave me a rousin' lecture. Let me tell you, he sounded like my dear departed..." and here she said something that sounded like 'far Kayla', which I took to mean a term of endearment for her husband. "Told me I needed a good slap of stew. Now how would he know any Irish?"

"I don't know, but he sounds like a wise physician. So are you eating and drinking regularly?"

"Oh, yes, and I'm doin' much better! How about another cuppa?"

"Let me take a look at you, then we can come back here for tea."

Mary's heart did sound better, and her vitals were right where they needed to be, so we were back in the kitchen very quickly. Over more tea, I gently probed Mary for any information about Deirdre.

"Mary, you know Deirdre Dunn was one of my best friends. I'd give anything to find out where she went. Have you thought at all about our conversation last week? Deirdre's been missing all these years. Do you have any idea where she might be?"

"Have another cookie, dear. I did think on this, and I can't remember hearin' or seein' anything before she left, as to where she might have been goin'. It was so long ago, you understand."

"That's okay, I was just hoping for some little clue."

"I can tell you where Artie went."

I tried not to choke on the cookie in my mouth, swallowed with a gulp, and sat back in surprise. "You can?"

"Well, I'd forgotten, but it came to me one night when I was lyin' in bed, tryin' to fall asleep. Plain as day. I was standin' by the fence, talkin' to Artie. The movin' van was out front, and his athair – that's his father, dear – called over and told him to stop yappin', they would be late for the ferry."

"Ferry to where?"

"That's what I asked. 'Ferry to where, Artie?'" I said. And he said Swans Island. I'd never heard of it, but I remembered the name. There are these wonderful wild swans in Ireland, you know."

I reached over and grabbed her hand. "Thank you *so* much. This is great information."

She beamed. "Will you let me know if you find him? I'd like to know he's all right. I was wonderin' what he looks like now he's all grown up."

❧❧

I left the Noonans feeling elated and couldn't wait to tell Sam what I'd found out. But first I needed to see Marsh. I parked my Jeep at the far edge of the employees' parking lot behind the hospital, hoping Miss Daisy wouldn't be noticed, and walked toward the back doors on the loading deck. I took it slow but convincingly, like I still worked at the hospital. They hadn't taken my employee ID badge. I needn't have worried because Lyle Pendergrass, the old hospital guard whom I'd known since I started working there, was at the check-in desk. He broke into a huge, yellow-toothed smile when he saw me and just waved me in. I'd expected some problems, but he gave me a wink.

I walked quickly down the hall, knocked on Marsh's door and sidled in before he could answer. Marsh shook his head when he saw me. "I heard what happened last week. Are you okay? You face is a little swollen on one side."

"Darn, I'd hoped the makeup had taken care of that."

"It's all over the hospital Manning's gunning for you."

"Yeah, I know, but I got myself a lawyer." The Tylenol must have worn off because it hurt when I lowered myself into the chair next to his desk.

Marsh noticed, because he pulled a bottle of the stuff from his desk drawer and reached around to get me a water from his mini-fridge.

"I know that guy gave you quite a beating. What are you doing here? You should be home, healing up." He opened the bottle for me.

"Hey, I'm still alive and kicking, so you can't look at the evidence," I joked. "Thanks for this, just what I need." I indicated the pills and water.

"Is it true security never showed up and Nancy had to stick the guy with a full load of chlorpromazine?"

"No, no one showed up, and I don't know what she gave him, but he went out like a light. Have you heard any scuttlebutt on why no security from another part of the hospital?" I took a sip of water with two pills; I was already sloshing from all the tea.

"Not a word, but you might ask Lyle. He was here when you were attacked."

"Lyle? They would hardly call him. He couldn't wrestle a butterfly."

I got a big smile from Marsh with that. "I know you've snuck in here to find out about that body from Crystal Crossing, Rhe. I do have some information for you and Sam. Maybe Sam got a report, too."

"Do tell…"

"Well, the body, as you know, is not that of a Native American. It's a young girl, age between ten and twelve."

"So this could definitely be one of our missing girls?"

"It's entirely possible. She was buried in the bog, although the preservation was not as good as some of the Iron Age bog people they've found in Northern Europe. But good enough, between the acidity of the bog, the lack of oxygen, and the fact that Maine bogs are pretty cold most of the year. We were lucky it hadn't been a long time since her burial because her bones were still intact."

"What do you mean, bones still intact?"

"In the Iron Age bodies, the bones have been dissolved by the peat over the centuries."

Ugh. A body with no bones inside, essentially a sack of skin. "So what else did they find? Anything useful?"

"The body still had hair and her teeth were intact. With the dental records and DNA analysis, they should be able to identify her. Results should be available soon."

"I think Bowers is going to have to make another notification, poor guy."

"Will you be going with him?"

"I don't know. I haven't heard anything from him lately. I think he's lying low, still embarrassed by what happened in Presque Isle. Even though it wasn't his fault. Sam's been keeping him informed of anything we find on this end, since he's still the lead investigator." I rose and put on my coat. "Mustn't overstay my welcome at here."

"Don't forget to check with Lyle on the way out," Marsh reminded me.

After a much needed bathroom break, I did stop at the security desk. Lyle was a little surprised because I'd never stopped to talk to him and our entire relationship consisted of greetings and waves.

"How're you doing, Lyle?"

"Fine, Miz Brewster." His face lit up at my greeting, breaking into a thousand wrinkles. Lyle was probably in his late seventies and way past retirement, but I suspected this job was his life. He'd been here since Sturdevant was first built, maybe even before. At his age, this assignment was perfect because it involved no demanding physical activity and was not something any other security guard would want. But Lyle was sharp: he knew every employee and was very protective of our privacy, as he had proven the previous fall when I'd been followed by a bunch of reporters.

"Lyle, could I ask you something?"

"Sure thing." His voice sounded like a cackle. "How are you feeling? I heard about the fracas in the ER last week, it's all over the hospital. I see where you got hit in the face. Must hurt."

So he did know. "Did you happen to get a call when it happened?"

Lyle's face lit up. "You betcha! And I woulda gone up there to help you, Miz Brewster, but I was told to stand down."

"Really? Why?"

"I don't know. Some woman called. I know Manning dismissed you, and I want you to know I don't like that guy. Bastard, if you ask me. As if you could do something wrong."

"Thanks, Lyle. You've been a huge help. Take care of yourself." *Wow! I have a real friend. I need to bring him some cookies when I'm reinstated — or even before.*

16

Lyle Pendergrass's compliment really had made me feel better; even my bruises weren't feeling so sore. While driving to the police station, I marveled that someone with whom I'd only exchanged a few words over the years was truly concerned about my well-being. What a sad contrast to my husband, who didn't seem to care much about me at all any more.

Also running around in my head was all the information we had found – the involvement of Crystal Bog with the flower petals and the body of a second girl found there; the relationship of Cornwell to Savannah; his farm being near the bog; the attempt on Bowers' life.

Suddenly I felt a need for revenge. I wanted revenge for the girls, revenge for Bowers and revenge for me. *Did it take my getting beaten up to feel this for the first time?* I stepped on the gas and roared into the police station parking lot, coming to a stop with a satisfying squeal of tires.

I stopped and said hello to the massive reception desk, then walked around it to find Ruthie on the floor, picking up paper clips. "Hey, Ruthie! Thanks for getting Sawyer to see me on such short notice."

"Are you kidding? After I heard what happened to you at the hospital, I was all over it. No one gets away with hurting one of my family. I take it he's going fix this for you?"

"More like make it go away. I'm going to see him again at the arraignment next Monday."

Ruthie scooted up onto the desk chair, so she was more at eye-level with me. "Honey, are you feeling better? I can see where he got you in the face, you poor thing."

"Yeah, nothing like a good whuppin' to improve the complexion. Plus lots of makeup." I winked at her and walked down the corridor to Sam's office.

He looked up as I got to the door. "Why don't we get some coffee and go to the conference room to talk. I've been sitting at this desk all morning and need to stretch." To prove it, he rose to his full height, raised his arms almost to the ceiling, then lumbered to the door.

After he'd gotten a mug of the boiled acid from the departmental coffee pot and I'd found a bottle of water, we settled as comfortably as possible in the hard plastic chairs at the conference room table. "Who goes first?" I asked.

"How about you? I sense a tsunami of information about to hit." He took a sip of coffee, made an awful face and pushed the mug away.

Could have told ya. "Let's see, where to start? I saw Mary Noonan this morning. She's a hot potato for her age, and now she's seen some specialists, I may have lost a job. Anyway," I said, reaching into my bag, "she sent you these." I pulled out a waxed paper-wrapped packet containing half a dozen oatmeal cookies.

Sam ripped open the packet and devoured the first cookie in two bites. "Mmm...good. That lady can bake! And?"

"She told me where we might find Artie Dunn. She remembered hearing the father tell Artie to hurry on the day they left. That they'd miss the ferry to Swans Island. He might still be there. Any chance you can check on that?"

Sam took out his notebook and wrote down Swans Island and the word 'police' with a question mark next to it. "I'll do it today. Good work, Rhe. What's next?"

"I snuck into Sturdevant to see Marsh after leaving the Noonans. Have you got the state ME's report on the body from Crystal Crossing?"

"Not yet. Later today."

"Guess Marsh has an inside track. The body's a ten to twelve year old girl. No time of death yet, but that might be hard because of the bog preservation." I explained what Marsh had told me. "The state lab is doing a dental comparison and DNA analysis, so we should know soon if it's one of the other two girls, Jane Alderson or Rachel Vance. Can Bowers do the notification?"

"I'll ask Bongiovanni as soon as the ID's made." He squinted at me and said, "I sense there's more."

"Very perceptive, Holmes. I talked to Lyle Pendergrass on the way out of the hospital."

"The old geezer who mans the desk off the loading dock?"

"That's him, and he may be a bit creaky, but he's not a geezer. His mind is sharp! He knows everyone in the hospital and everything that's going on. Sawyer told me the ER had called for security when Donnelly hit me, but the word came to stand down. Lyle confirmed that."

"Who gave the order? Does he know?" Sam asked.

"A woman. I'm betting Dolores Richmond, Manning's secretary. I'll tell Sawyer and he can subpoena her. But she might lie; she's Manning's toady."

"Well, I'd like to be the one to serve her."

I stared at him. "Really? You couldn't scare a fly."

"You've never seen me at my best," he said, drawing himself up in his chair and giving me a grin. Then he hesitated, frowned, hesitated again and finally said, "Rhe, I'd have to be deaf, dumb and blind not to know something's wrong between you and Will. I don't want to interfere and I've tried to stay out of it. Really I have. But after last week, I'm concerned. He's not there for you. What's going on?"

I frowned and looked down, trying to think of how I could handle this. "Yes, something's going on, but I – we – need to work it out ourselves. I really appreciate you wanting to help, Sam. But Will and I have to work through this as a couple. Do you mind if I just don't share at this point?" I smiled to take the sting out of my rebuff.

Sam sat back in his chair, took a deep breath and relented. "I'm sorry. I shouldn't have asked. But if you need anything…any time…" Then he colored right up to his receding hairline.

"I know, Sam, and I'm very grateful. I'm not sure what I would have done lately, without you there to back me up." The conversation was already way down the road to uncomfortable, and I had to change the subject. "You know the lead on the sail?"

Sam nodded and straightened up. I had his professional interest back.

"I'm following up on that this afternoon. As you suggested, a meeting with Bob Morgan."

"When?"

"Right after lunch, if you're still willing to pay."

Sam smiled. "Of course, Watson. Where shall we dine?"

With that, we resumed our comfortable routine and ended up going to Moe's, probably because Sam knew their lobster salad po' boy was one of my favorite things in the world. He didn't seem to suffer, plowing through a plate of fried clams and French fries in record time.

I completely forgot to tell him about the tuna fish sandwich.

❧❧

I was standing at the door to the managing editor's office of the *Post & Sentinel* by 2 PM. Bob Morgan and I went back a long way: during his swash-buckling run through most of the girls in our high school, he had paused with me for an inordinate amount of time, several months, building to an intimacy I wasn't ready to give. I'd sent him on his way but sensed his interest in me had not waned in the intervening years, marriages for both of us, divorce for him. The previous fall, I had saved him from a crazy woman who had sworn she loved him but had tried to kill him anyway.

The office door flew open at my first knock. "Rhe! Right on time. Come on in. Want some tea?" His warm reception almost made me forget how much I loathed reporters.

"No thanks, Bob. But I could use some information."

"Let's trade." He'd called me several times during the previous week, seeking new material for an article on Savannah Engstrom. I wondered if he'd heard about the other body, or worse, about the incident at the hospital.

He walked back to sit at his desk, a massive piece placed in front of huge, multi-paned windows that characterized the old building now housing the newspaper. He gestured for me to take a seat in a chair directly in front of this desk. The glare from the windows made me squint.

"You run into a door?" he asked, looking at me in the harsh sunlight.

"Something like that." I wasn't about to elaborate and sat there quietly, waiting for his next question.

"I heard what happened at the hospital, you know."

"Figured you would. You're a reporter. Do you have to do a story on it?"

"Hadn't planned to until he goes to court."

"Keep me out of it as much as you can, will you? I don't need any more notoriety. It's bad for my family."

"I can understand that," he replied gently. "So what exactly do you need? You know what *I* want," he said with a sly smile, the double entendre dripping. *He never gives up, does he?* "Yeah, a story."

"That's Rhe. Never one to waste time with social stuff." He nodded, agreeing with himself. "What *I* want, in case you're interested, is something new on the Savannah Engstrom case."

"We're working on it, and you can quote me."

"That's it?"

"Look, Bob, this case is several years old. The trail is cold and we have very little to go on."

"Okay, but I heard you visited Tom O'Neil. Must have been about the sail the body was wrapped in."

I laughed out loud. "Your spy network never fails to surprise me."

"My spies had nothing to do with it – he called me."

I leaned forward and put my elbows on his desk. "Then you know why I'm here. Your Dad bought that sail for one of his boats and I'm hoping you know what happened to it."

"Tit for tat, Rhe. I need something in return."

"Not in this case, my friend. This is a police investigation, and if you hold anything back, then you're guilty of obstruction of justice. This is a federal case, so it would be a felony." I tried to sound knowledgeable. It worked.

"You've been reading up on the law?" He didn't wait for an answer. "Okay, okay, you can't blame me for trying. That sail was made for some unusual boat my Dad bought me, I think it was a sloop, when he had visions of me becoming a transatlantic sailor."

"Tom said it was a fractional rig sloop, forestay didn't go to the top of the mast."

"Yup, that's it. I was never like you, you know. I didn't like sailing all that much, more of a tennis and golf kid, so after a few summers, Dad sold the boat. I knew I'd be seeing you so just to be nice, I went through some of Dad's papers, hoping I would find the buyer."

"And?"

"The person who bought the boat was a seasonal, lived in Camden part of the year."

My antennae went into high twitch mode. "Robert Cornwell?"

"How did you know?"

"Astute guess."

"C'mon, Rhe. You have some information. Share."

"I can't, Bob, I really can't. It's part of a federal investigation and I can't divulge anything."

"That's okay; I'll put a reporter on it. Thanks for the heads up."

Just then, I realized I'd blown it by mentioning Cornwell's name before Bob told me. I could be in deep trouble if he used this. "Damn me all to hell!" came out of my mouth.

From the curse and the look on my face, Bob must have figured it out, too. "Look, Rhe, I know I owe you from last fall. You probably saved my life, no, you *did* save my life, and the last thing I want to do is cause problems for you. I won't publish anything until you say I can, and I won't mention where the information came from. Is that okay?"

I knew he was going to start snooping the minute my back was out the door, but was *pretty* sure he wouldn't betray me. "Deal."

He relaxed back in his overstuffed editor's chair. "So how's family life? How's the baby?"

"Well, it's nice not to be nauseated any more, otherwise you might have some new decoration on your lovely rug," I replied, nodding my head toward the plush Oriental on his floor.

"How's Will? Excited about the baby?"

Does he know anything about what's happening with Will and me? Nah, I'm just paranoid. "He worries about the bills." *At least that's honest.*

"You've got a lot on your plate right now, kiddo. If there's ever a time when you need help or a shoulder to lean on, I'm here. Just know that."

Lord, he sounds like Sam. Every man in my life but Will...wait! Did he know something? I felt my cheeks flame. *Two conversations about my marriage in one day! And this one brought back some strong memories from high school.* "Thank you," I mumbled. "I'm really okay. I've got to get going."

I got up and scooted out of his office as fast as I could. When I got to the street, I took a deep breath of cold air and tried to relax. *He didn't mean anything by it, just his usual line. For heaven's sake, Rhe, what could he possibly know? Stop acting like a teenager.*

As I walked to my Jeep, I pulled out my phone and called Sam. Without even saying hi, I blurted, "Sam, you're not going to believe this, guess who bought the sail from Tom?" Then I realized I was talking to his pre-recorded message and waited for the beep to repeat the same thing. I started to drive home, but couldn't subdue the excitement of this new information and decided to visit Paulette. Maybe she could calm me down or give me something good to eat. *Same thing.*

Twenty minutes later I found myself sitting across the table from Paulette in her kitchen, drinking tea for a change and eating a cinnamon roll. Paulette had figured out some new lead had turned up the minute she saw my face. "I know that look – sort of like a cat with a bowl of cream. Something's happened on the case, I know it."

"Well, I found out where Deirdre Dunn's family moved."

"Where? How?"

I took a long sip of tea, just to build the excitement. "My new patient, Mary Noonan, she remembered. It's Swans Island. Do you know that place?"

Her head bobbed vigorously. "I went there once with my parents; we visited different islands during our vacations every summer."

"What's it like?"

"Not many people, mostly lobstermen. There's a store, a couple of villages, some cottage industries. We took the ferry over, drove around a bit and came back."

"Mmm, wanna take a road trip?"

Paulette almost jumped out of her chair. "When?"

"Calm down, sweetie. I have to wait until Sam finds out if Artie Dunn still lives there."

"Okay, anything else?"

"Well, I found out where the sail wrapping Savannah was made. Tom O'Neil's. And you'll never guess who he sold it to."

"Surprise me."

"Robert Morgan, Sr."

"No way! Bob's father?"

"None other, and I went to see Bob today to find out what had happened to it."

"Did he make his usual pass at you?" Paulette actually started eating a bun, tearing it into shreds in her excitement.

"Well, he did, sort of. I just ignored it."

I must have stopped at the thought, because Paulette prompted me, "So what did you find out?"

"Turns out his father sold the sail, along with the boat it was made for, to that sheep farmer I went up to see in Presque Isle."

"So that's another piece of evidence against him, right? He knew Savannah and had asked her to his studio. Have you told Sam yet?"

"Left him a message. You know you can't tell anyone what I just told you, right?"

"You know me, Rhe. I never talk about what you tell me. But this is getting exciting! You might be close to finding the guy!"

Just then my phone rang. I dug it out of my bag and saw it was my brother-in-law, who seemed to have ESP.

"Hi, Sam, did you get my message?"

"Yup, and I passed it along to Bongiovanni who passed it to Bowers, since he's still the lead investigator. Cornwell was released after a few hours, so they're going to re-interview him. Good work, Rhe! I don't know what I'd do without you…I mean, without your help."

I found myself beaming at the phone.

"And Rhe, Artie Dunn does live on Swans Island."

"Alright! I've already talked to Paulette about taking a road trip out there."

"Fine with me, but let's not have a repeat of your last road trip with her." The previous fall we had gone to Boston, been followed on the way home and nearly run off the road. "How're you feeling after being out and about all day?"

"Pretty good, thanks for asking. I should be an abstract in yellow and green by tomorrow."

"Keep in touch with me, Rhe, and let me know when you head to Swans Island."

"Sure thing."

After confirming with Paulette we indeed had a road trip, I told her the latest about the hospital law suit. When I told her that Donnelly's arraignment was the next Monday, she said was going with me and not to argue. I didn't.

17

Jack had been uncharacteristically hyperactive the past few weekends, even more than his usual ADHD restlessness. I knew this was happening because Will had been working on Saturdays and Sundays, not wearing him out with physical activities as he usually did. On the spur of the moment on Saturday morning, I decided to take Jack to a Portland Pirates ice hockey game that afternoon. I got two tickets on line, but thought if I could find Will maybe I could persuade him to come with us. He'd left early that morning, telling me he had some exams to grade and promised to be back by mid-afternoon. He usually graded at home, so I checked his class schedule, and as I suspected, he'd given no exams that week. *Lies on top of lies. Dumb-ass.*

I just knew he wouldn't be back that afternoon, and I banged on the kitchen counter in frustration. *I can't take this anymore. I know he's seeing someone and I'm going to find out what's going on, come hell or high water. I'm going to find my son of a bitch husband and have it out.*

Since *of course* he was not answering his office or cell phone, I told Jack we'd stop by his Dad's office to see if he might want to come with us. We bundled up around eleven, got Miss Daisy warmed up, and headed over to the Pequod campus. My anxiety at what I might find had me holding the steering wheel in a death grip. Jack didn't help

by bouncing up and down in his booster seat the whole way.

"Mom, is something wrong?" Jack asked as we entered the campus. "You look sort of mad."

"Sorry, kiddo, I was just thinking about something I'm working on."

"Well, cheer up! We're going to a hockey game!" He punched the air with his fist.

I had to smile, but suddenly I realized I hadn't even thought about the ramifications of Jack being there if I did find Will. *Stupid.* As I pulled into a parking spot in front of Will's building, I decided to have Jack stay in the car. Unfortunately, he bolted from his child seat and was out of the Jeep before I'd even turned it off. He was halfway up the walk to the psychology building by the time I got out and yelled at him. He kept on going, so I followed, hoping there would be nothing to find.

I'd always thought there must not have been any famous psychologists from Maine, because the building was named after the college founder's wife, Evangeline and looked like her, an unadorned square block of stone.

Jack was struggling with the heavy entrance door when I caught up and helped him open it, then he ran to the elevator. The building was deserted and the sound of his boots echoed in the large entrance hall. When the elevator opened, he ran in and punched three.

"That's Dad's floor, right Mom?" I nodded and he jiggled up and down until the doors opened on the third floor. He skipped down the hall to Will's office and turned the knob on the door, but the door was locked. "Dad's here, isn't he?" he asked.

"That's what he said this morning. Maybe we should knock?" Jack knocked on the door and yelled, "Dad, are you in there?" There was no answer.

"Maybe he went out for an early lunch and we missed him." *Trying to find Will had been a bad idea.*

Jack hung his head and his shoulders slumped. "Maybe he doesn't want to spend time with me anymore."

His words hurt me to the core, and I bent down and hugged him. "That is simply not so, Jack. He's been working really hard lately. He loves you and would be out running sprints with you on the basketball court, if he had time. You know that. He's out of shape and you'd leave him in the dust! He'd fall on the court gasping!"

Jack smiled at that, straightened up and took my hand. "Okay, let's just us go to the Pirates game. He'll be sorry he missed it. Can I have a hot dog? Maybe two hot dogs?"

"Sure thing, and maybe a pretzel, too."

As we walked back to the elevator, a young man with rosy cheeks, dressed in a green anorak, came out of the elevator. He stopped and turned, putting a hand on the elevator door to keep it from closing. "You're Dr. Brewster's wife, right?"

"I am, and you are...?"

"Seth Gordan, one of his second year students. You just missed him! I passed him coming out of the back entrance of the building."

"Thanks, Seth. You're a life saver." Turning to Jack, I said, "Let's take the stairs. Maybe we can catch him."

Jack and I ran down the stairway to the left of the elevators and exited in the basement, where I knew the corridor let out onto the back of the building. As we crashed through the door, which locked behind us, I saw Will's Camry turning onto the road that ran along the back of the building. Jack saw him, too, and waved and jumped up and down.

"Let's see if we can catch him, Jack. We'll have to plow through the snow to the front of the building. Are you up for it?" *What am I doing? Let it go, Rhe.*

But Jack was off again, wading through what for him was knee high snow, while I scuffled in his wake. We managed to get to the car, get buckled in and race through the campus in a matter of a few minutes, but we'd lost the Camry.

"Guess we missed him, huh?" Jack was again disappointed.

"We did, but let's take a swing through town. Maybe he went for lunch somewhere and we can spot the car. You take the right side and I'll take the left." I drove slowly down Pequod's main street and we both checked out cars parked near Ernie's Pizza and the Pie and Pickle Café. No white Camry.

"Let's just go to Portland. Okay, Mom?" Jack said with a sigh.

"We'll get him another time," I replied as I hung a U-turn and drove back to Jackson, the main road to US 1 and I 95. Jack had me turn on the radio to find a station with music he liked, and I relaxed for the first time that morning.

About five miles from Pequod, I noticed a white Camry in a parking lot in front of a restaurant called The Mariner, an upscale place Will had frequently mentioned we should try.

"Hey, that's Dad's car. Stop, Mom!"

I stepped on the brakes, flipped on the turn signal and just made it into the exit at the far end of the restaurant's parking lot. I swung the Jeep into a spot near where we'd come in and turned to Jack. "You stay here," I told him sternly, stopping him just as he was unlatching his seat belt. "I mean it, buddy. You are to stay here. I'm just going to pop in and see if he's here and if he's free. If he isn't, then we'll just head on to the game. Okay?" I left the Jeep running and got out of the car, heart rate going through the roof, telling myself this could be it, this could be where I found out what the hell was going on. I turned back and looked at Jack, who hadn't moved. Maybe this wasn't the time? *Coward! Do it, Rhe.*

I turned again and walked to the restaurant's front door. Pulling it open, I was greeted by soft music and the view of a nicely lit, comfortably decorated room. The enticing aromas of the lunch menu permeated the entranceway. A tall, well-dressed black woman approached and asked, "How many in your party?"

Up until her question, I wasn't sure what I was going to do, but just then I spied Will, sitting at a table toward the rear of the room. With him was a Pequod student I knew well, Zoey Harris. They were holding hands and looking into each other's eyes with undisguised lust. My face heated up and my heart dropped into my stomach. *You son of a bitch.* I waved the hostess off and walked slowly to their table.

Zoey was one of the undergraduates who had been arrested for prostitution at a high class brothel called East Almorel the previous fall. For some reason she'd asked for my help following her arrest, probably because I knew her from my investigation into the death of another student and she sensed I could be an ally. She'd had valuable information about Almorel, so Sam and I had found her a lawyer. I'd lost track of her after that and frankly hadn't thought much about her. Clearly, since she was still in Pequod, she'd been given probation or the charges had been dropped. Young, thin and gorgeous, she was everything I was not. *Fuck you, Will.*

Before I could figure out what the hell I was going to do, Will spotted me and yanked his hands away from Zoey.

"Rhe! What are you doing here?" he asked in a rather loud voice and with a big, fake smile I immediately wanted to scratch off his face. Like I was the one who had done something wrong.

"I might ask you the same." My voice didn't even sound like me, coming from deep within my chest.

"I was just having lunch with Zoey Harris, one of my students. You remember my wife, don't you, Zoey?" he asked smoothly. *He didn't lose a beat.*

Zoey had the decency to turn beet red. "Yeah, sure. You were a big help to me last year, Ms. Brewster. My charges got dismissed." Presumably Will already knew all about this, since he didn't bat an eyelash or ask what the charges were.

"So what *are* you doing here, Rhe?" Will repeated.

"I decided to take Jack to a Pirate's game this afternoon. You weren't answering your phones, so we went to the college to see if you might want to come along with us. I ran into Seth Gordan just after we knocked on your door. He said he'd seen you leaving. When we didn't see your car in town, we left for Portland. Jack spotted your car and he's outside, waiting." I blathered through the long-winded explanation. *Why? Get a grip.*

"Gee, I'm sorry, Rhe. I was trying to finish up a paper this morning and turned the phones off. When I left to get a quick bite for lunch, I ran into Zoey and she suggested we try The Mariner for lunch." Will sounded so rational, so believable.

Right, and pigs fly. Then I noticed a pink smear near his right ear. I checked Zoey's lipstick, and sure enough, it was the same color. I'd had enough. "Liar," I said quietly. Then louder, "LIAR! LIAR!" I turned to Zoey. "And you…you're a whore!"

I'm not sure if I said anything after that. Maybe I remembered my manners: "Well, I'll leave you to your lunch." Or "Well, I'd better get going if we're going to catch the game." In any event, I found myself back in the car and turning out of the parking lot before I even recognized where I was.

"Mom. Mom. What took you so long? Did you see Dad? Why aren't you answering me?" Jack's piping seven-year-old voice finally penetrated my fog. I pulled to the side of the road and turned to look back at him, using every bit of strength I could muster to generate a smile.

"No, I didn't see him, Jack. But I ran into someone else I knew. That's what took me so long, okay? You ready for the game?"

Jack looked at me uncertainly, the crease between his eyes so reminiscent of Will I had to turn back to face the road. "Sure. We're going to have a great time, right?"

"Right!" It took tremendous effort to chat with Jack in the car and then focus on the game, but I had to box away what I'd seen until I had a chance to think about what I was going to do. Jack's habit of noticing the most minute, interesting things helped distract me, but it was still the longest and most agonizing afternoon of my life.

❧ ❧

Will came home just as I was settling Jack into bed that night. He went directly to his office and closed the door. I stood in the hallway outside, wondering what to do. *Should I confront him? He won't talk, you know it. Should I ignore it? No, I can't ignore it. Think, what do you want to do?* I gave up thinking, put on my boots and coat and walked down the street to see my best friend. Maybe she could help me work this through.

Paulette answered her back door with her usual smile, which faded when she saw my face. "Rhe, what's wrong?" I pushed past her into her kitchen, took off my coat, sat down at the table and started to sob.

"What's going on? What's wrong?"

I couldn't seem to stop crying. I was sobbing so hard I couldn't talk. I think I howled at one point, and her husband Ted poked his head around the door from the family room. Paulette shook her head violently, got up and closed the door. She came back to the chair she'd pulled up beside me and sat down, putting her arms around me. I leaned into her shoulder, hiccupping and gasping for air. She handed me a napkin from the table and finally my breathing calmed and the tears stopped. I wiped my face and turned to look at her.

At that minute, she knew. "It's Will."

I nodded wordlessly.

"Who is it, Rhe?"

"He, he, he's having an affair with a student." I told her about my day, the search for Will and the scene at The Mariner.

"Does Jack know?"

"No, but he suspects something's not right."

"Where is Will now?"

"At home, locked in his office. He came in just as I was putting Jack to bed."

Paulette thought for a minute. "Zoey Harris. Isn't she the student who was working as an escort at Almorel last year?" I nodded. "And you and Sam helped her out with a lawyer?" I nodded again. "That little bitch. How could she? How could Will?"

"I don't know, Paulette, but maybe Will's night at Almorel, the one he asked you to cover for, wasn't so innocent. Maybe that's why he tried to hide it. Maybe he was seeing her there all along. I just don't know what to think at this point."

"Well, you've got to do something. You can't just ignore it."

"You know he'll deny everything. He never said a word to me about knowing what Almorel was until I confronted him. This is so much worse. I know we were having communication problems, but we'd agreed to work on them. Maybe my becoming involved in this investigation tipped the scales. I drove him to this," I wailed.

"Honey, you did no such thing. His actions are inexcusable. I just can't believe he'd do something like this. You're pregnant with his child for God's sake."

"I know what he sees in her, but what in hell does she see in him? He's fifteen years older, losing his hair and getting a pot belly. What's the attraction?"

"I don't know... father figure?"

"What should I do? What *can* I do?"

"Maybe you should confront Zoey first. Get her to admit what's going on. Then he can't deny it, and maybe you two can work things out, see a counselor, get back on track. You had a good marriage, at least until that bastard started cheating on you. *You* will have to decide if you want to try again. You're a strong woman. You can get through this, trust me! Ted and I are here, whenever you need us."

That makes four friends, counting Sam and Bob.

Over the next hour and several cups of tea, I gradually saw a path forward, determined to confront Zoey the next day to confirm what I already knew, but what Will would deny.

ॐ❦

Sunday morning I didn't even check to see if Will was in his office. I didn't care. Jack was very quiet, for him. He'd asked his father around ten if they could do something together, but Will had said no, rather rudely. So Jack played in his room. My heart broke for him.

I figured Zoey wouldn't meet me if I called first. So I left Jack with Paulette for the afternoon, thinking maybe Tyler and their dogs could cheer Jack up. I knew the location of Zoey's sorority house and parked slightly down the street, waiting for her to come out. She finally emerged around 3:30, talking on her phone. I got out of my Jeep and headed to intercept her. She was so engrossed in her call – *maybe with Will?* – she didn't see me until I stepped in front of her. Her eyes opened wide and she dropped her phone.

"You'd better pick it up. Your friend – or is it Will? – could get worried."

"It's not Will," she replied defensively.

"We need to talk."

"I don't want to."

"Well, you can talk to me or talk to a divorce lawyer when I name you in the suit."

"You can't do that!"

"Wise up. Zoey. Of course I can. Then it will be public knowledge. Wonder what the college would do about that?"

Zoey sagged and looked at her feet. "What do you want?"

"To talk. I want to know how this thing you have with Will got started, how long it's been going on."

"Can we talk somewhere else? It's a little public here."

"You should have thought about that before you went out to lunch with my husband. How about in my car?" I pointed to the Jeep and gave her a gentle push in its direction.

She looked at me with alarm. "What are you planning to do?"

"You know me, Zoey. I'm a police consultant. I won't do anything to you, I just want to talk." Somewhat to my surprise, she nodded and slowly plodded across the street, looking like she were going to a hanging, which is what I wanted to do with her. When we got there, I opened the passenger side door for her, waited until she got in, then ran around to my side thinking she might try to make a break for it. She didn't, but just sat there slumped in the seat, not looking at me.

"What do you want?" she asked again. Angry, resentful, sullen.

"Some answers. How long have you and Will been..." my voice trailed off because I just couldn't say the words.

"Lovers? About a year."

"A year?" My mouth dropped open. "Then you were seeing him before the raid at Almorel." An ugly thought popped into my head. "He was seeing *you* there?"

"Yeah, he was a regular customer. What did you think?"

"He told me...I don't know what I think." Will had in fact told me he'd been to Almorel once, that it had been a mistake because a colleague took him and he hadn't realized the place was a brothel. I'd been a fool and believed him. "So he's been seeing you all this time?"

"Yeah. After you got me that lawyer, I came back to school and he found me, wanted to continue seeing me. There must be something really wrong with your marriage, Mrs. Brewster."

That comment hit me like a ton of bricks and hurt to the core. I took a deep breath. "Does he still pay you?" My tone was seven-layered sarcasm.

"At first he did, but then he told me he loved me. I guess I love him too, so I stopped taking his money."

"Well, aren't you the ethical one! Knowing he was married with a child. I'm pregnant. Did he happen to mention that?"

Zoey shook her head. "No, he didn't tell me," she replied in a small voice. She processed the information for a moment and her face hardened. "That bastard. He told me he was leaving you. Guess that won't happen now."

"I wouldn't bet on that, little girl. Up to now we haven't discussed anything about his leaving, but I think you might get lucky," I replied bitterly.

"Is that all you wanted to know?" Zoey grabbed the door handle.

"Yeah, sure, leave. Wait. One thing. Have you ever felt guilty at all about this? Did you ever wonder what this would do to our marriage, to his family?"

"No, not really. People are who they are. I still think Will's a nice guy. Like I said, he wasn't all that into you, or his family."

After Zoey fled the Jeep, I sat in the car for a long time crying, with my head on the steering wheel. I didn't notice how cold it was getting or the start of another snowfall. I was just trying to get my head around everything Zoey had said. *My marriage wasn't at all what I thought it was. Will had shoved me when I confronted him about Almorel. That should have registered. How naïve could I be, trying to rekindle his interest when he had a prostitute for a girlfriend? How could he hurt Jack like that? Even if he didn't love me, I really thought he loved Jack.* I banged on the steering wheel in frustration until my hands hurt. Finally, mentally drained and tired to the core, I wiped my face, turned the key in the ignition, and drove to Paulette's on automatic to get Jack. Paulette's rude comments when I told her about Zoey were actually comforting.

Will didn't come home at all that night, not that I wanted to see him. I felt guilty at the relief. After six hours of tossing and turning in bed, rubbing my baby bump, thinking about what I should do, I decided I had to talk to Will before I made any decision. How and when that would happen, I hadn't a clue.

18

Monday morning I took Jack to school and swung by Paulette's on the way to Donnelly's arraignment.

She came out with her hands full – two travel mugs of coffee in one hand and a paper bag in the other, her bag over her shoulder. I leaned across the passenger seat and opened the door. "Have you thought more about what you're going to tell Jack?" she asked, getting into the car. The smell from the bag was delicious but made my stomach turn. I hadn't been able to eat any dinner the night before, much to Jack's consternation, and had passed on breakfast. Although I was hungry, I couldn't get my mind around actually eating.

She held out one coffee and the bag. "Here, decaf coffee and an apple muffin. You look very pale, Rhe. You didn't eat last night did you? What about the baby? You *have* to eat."

"Maybe later. Something bland, like eggs and toast."

"Okay, but I'm holding you to that."

We parked at the police station, and walked next door to the courthouse, a three story, neoclassic stone monster on the National Register of Historic Buildings. I couldn't figure out why, given its ugly countenance. We walked up the wide flight of short steps and into the atrium. "Where's your lawyer?" Paulette asked, and immediately put her hand to her mouth since her words reverberated loudly in the huge entranceway.

"Right here," came another much more moderated voice, and we turned to see Sawyer Smith coming in right behind us. He was dressed in a dark navy suit, ivory shirt, and gold and blue striped tie, looking altogether worthy of a Supreme Court appearance, except for his unruly red hair. "Come on, we're up in Courtroom One, top of the stairs." He nodded towards the imposing stairs facing the entrance. They went straight up, then wound away to the right and left. *Marble, with carved oak bannisters. Maybe this place did deserve the Registry.* I took my time climbing the stairs, feeling drained of energy.

Paulette and I were settled in for the arraignment by 8:45. I sat behind the Assistant District Attorney with Sawyer on one side and Paulette on the other. Donnelly came in from a side door with his lawyer promptly at 9 AM and sat at the defendant's table. His lawyer was a young black woman, attractive with sleek straight hair to her shoulders, clad in a 'See Me' bright red suit. Donnelly had been partially transformed. Although he was wearing an orange jump suit courtesy of the county jail, he was cleanly shaven and his hair was neatly trimmed. He looked everywhere but at me, but I shuddered when I looked at him. Sawyer felt me twitch and whispered, "Don't worry, you'll be fine. I know his lawyer. She was assigned from the Public Defender's Office and she's as green as I am."

The arraignment went smoothly. His lawyer argued I had baited him into attacking me and, since he was drunk, he didn't know what he was doing. She asked for a dismissal. Sawyer had sent my photos to the Assistant DA who was representing the people, namely me, and after seeing them, the judge ordered Donnelly remanded but set his bail at $10,000, an amount he could probably raise. As everyone rose when the judge left the courtroom, I grabbed Sawyer's arm. "So he can come after me?"

"Take it easy, Rhe. Donnelly and his lawyer want to meet with you to talk this over."

"I don't know if I can handle that right now."

"I think this might be to your advantage, and I'll be right there. He's not the same man who attacked you."

"No. he's sober. But he only needs a couple of drinks to get back there!" Sawyer waited patiently, looking at me but not saying anything. I calmed down and thought about it. "Okay, when?" I asked with a resigned sigh.

"As soon as he's released on bail. An hour or so. Can you wait around?"

"I need to take Rhe to get some breakfast, Mr. Smith," said Paulette. "Where should we meet you when we come back?"

"I'll meet you downstairs in the atrium. Rhe, you're looking a little pale today. Are you okay?" Sawyer touched my arm with concern.

"Didn't sleep too well last night. I'll be fine once I have some food in me."

"Okay, ladies, see you in, let's say, an hour fifteen."

❧ ❧

Paulette and I wandered over to the Pie and Pickle, where I ordered scrambled eggs, an English muffin and decaf coffee. "What? So my decaf isn't good enough for you?" Paulette asked with a smile, after she had ordered a stack of pancakes, with bacon on the side, juice and coffee. Despite her small size, Paulette could eat like a trencherman, and I wish I knew the secret to her hummingbird metabolism.

The waitress came and poured our respective coffees, and we sat there in silence for a moment. The café bustled and I saw quite a few people I knew, chatting animatedly, laughing and smiling, something I wondered if I would ever do again.

Paulette caught and held my eyes. "How're you holding up? What did you think about the arraignment?"

"I'm freaking out! Donnelly's going to be out on bail. What if he comes after me again?"

"Did you forget everything we learned in that self-defense class two years ago? I realize he caught you by surprise in the hospital, but next time you'll be ready for him. Remember? Elbow to the stomach, step on his foot, turn your head into his elbow and push up on his arm. Then a mighty kick to the naughty bits." Paulette seemed to be reliving our lessons with enjoyment: she was smiling and mimicking the moves, almost falling off her chair. I had to smile. "That's my girl. A smile, finally."

"Only you could do it, girlfriend." I gave a deep sigh.

"What's the sigh for?"

"I'm going to have to tell Sam what's going on. I don't think I can hide it from him any longer."

"Why don't you wait until after you've talked to Will?"

I thought for a moment. "Yeah, you're probably right. I'll tell him what I've decided once I've pinned Will down. If I can."

"He'll have to come home at some point. He'll need clean clothes. And if he insists on staying in the house, you and Jack are welcome to stay with us. Jack will love it."

Paulette's support was fierce and heartfelt, and I felt somewhat reassured knowing I wouldn't have to stay in the house with Will, if it came to that. Our breakfasts arrived, and we chatted about Sarah's latest pronouncements and everyone-else-has-one requests over our food. I felt a lot better having eaten. I even ordered a second English muffin.

⌘

Sawyer met us in the atrium and took us to a small conference room down the corridor from Courtroom 1. I stopped suddenly just inside the door. Donnelly and his lawyer were already sitting at the large table filling the room. Donnelly had changed into a suit, which was stretched tightly around his girth, and they both looked up when we entered. Sawyer was behind me and gave me a gentle push to keep me going. I screwed my courage to the wall and took a seat directly opposite Donnelly, forcing myself to look at him, while Sawyer sat across from the lawyer. Paulette sat on the other side of me and held my hand under the table. I found when I looked directly in Donnelly's eyes, my fear went away. *His* eyes darted everywhere, looking at everything but at me.

Sawyer introduced us to Donnelly's lawyer, Joan Alston, and then asked, "Will you please tell Mrs. Brewster what you proposed to me yesterday when you called?"

"Mrs. Brewster, my client is extremely sorry for what happened at the hospital last Friday. He was under the influence of alcohol, and he admits he has a problem."

I continued looking at Donnelly. "You knew you had a problem before you showed up in the Emergency Room. Why didn't you seek help earlier?" I asked.

"I thought I could control it." He hung his head and looked at his lap.

"Well, obviously you can't. I'm pregnant. You could have killed my child."

"I know that now, and I can't tell you how sorry I am." He looked up. Tears were forming in his eyes, and I wanted to believe they were real.

Ms. Alston said, "Please, let me continue. Mr. Donnelly has five children and is the sole provider for his family. If he goes to jail, the family will probably end up in a shelter."

And what kind of home life do his children have? Maybe they'd be better off.

"We were hoping you would be willing not to sue Mr. Donnelly and put in a word for him with the District Attorney..."

"What?" I rose out of my chair, barely able to contain myself. Sawyer grabbed my arm and pulled me back into my seat.

"In return..." continued Ms. Alston, "for his getting help for his alcoholism."

At this point, I was sputtering.

Sawyer gripped my arm a little tighter. "Let me handle this," he whispered. He turned back to Ms. Alston. "Let me see. My client was badly injured, could have lost her child, and was put on administrative leave with no pay by the hospital administrator. And now you're asking her not to sue your client and put in a good word for him with the DA. All that for the promise of his seeking help, with no supervision or guarantee he will do so. Does that about sum it up?"

0I found myself caught between a rock and a hard place. I didn't want this to affect his children, but I was angry and desperately wanted to lash out at him. What to do? "Let me talk with my lawyer for a minute," I replied, then got up and stalked out of the room. Both Sawyer and Paulette followed.

"What are you thinking?" Sawyer asked.

"That I need to know more. I want to talk to his wife and if there is a way, observe how he interacts with his family. How do I know he doesn't beat her and the kids when he's drunk? I'd just be letting him go back to hurting them."

"Sounds reasonable, I can probably arrange that. I'll check with Family Services to see if there have been any previous complaints. What else?"

"He tells Manning he won't sue the hospital, but only if I get my job back with pay for time lost. Otherwise, he threatens a huge suit. Manning will take the offer, trust me."

"Also good. I was going to suggest that myself."

At that point, Paulette asked, "What about your hospital bills? You know, whatever your insurance doesn't cover?"

Sawyer replied, "Way ahead of you. I already told Ms. Alston those bills would have to be paid. It won't be a lot, so they'll agree."

"One more question, Sawyer. The DA can't drop the charges, can he?" I was a little confused at this point.

"No, but if you agree to what they're asking, he could put Donnelly on probation with the supervised treatment for his addiction."

I sighed. "Okay, let's go tell them what we've decided."

A half hour later, with the lawyers chatting about billable hours, Paulette and I begged off. I needed to see Sam, and Paulette had some shopping to do. Donnelly shook my hand before we left the room. I still didn't trust him, but decided not to make final judgment until I'd seen the family.

Paulette and I walked back to the police station parking lot. I gave her the keys to the Jeep, told her to have fun and I'd call her when I was through talking to Sam. I had to laugh, watching her try to adjust the driver's seat to fit her short legs. *Definitely feeling better.*

Taking a deep breath and putting an almost real smile on my face, I pulled open the glass door to the police station, determined not to let Ruthie suspect a thing. Luckily for me, she was away from the reception desk and I hurried down the hall to Sam's office feeling relieved. Sam looked up with a smile when I knocked on the door frame, walked in and took a seat. "How're you feeling, darlin'?"

"Better every day. Bruises are fading, aches are fewer."

"How did the arraignment go?"

I gave him the twenty-five cent version and told him about the meeting with Donnelly and his lawyer.

"You sure you want to do that? Let him off so easy?"

"Not yet, but I need to know how he is with his family. The children need to be protected if he's abusive."

"Always the nurturer, right?." He paused, then said "I have some news for you, too. The results of the dental comparisons from the bog body came in, and it's definitely Rachel Vance. Bowers called and said he would like you to come along when he notifies the family."

"Oh joy," I sighed. "When is he planning this expedition?"

"Late tomorrow afternoon. He wants to get both parents at home."

"There's no way I can go on such short notice." *With everything else that's going on?* "Bowers needs to learn to fly. I'll call him when we're done. What else came out of the autopsy?"

"This girl's hyoid bone was crushed, so they're calling the COD strangulation."

"Could they tell if she'd been bound?"

"They could and they did. Same as Savannah."

"Could they determine how old Rachel was at the time of her death?" I asked, recalling that Savannah had been held for over a year.

"Possibly twelve to thirteen. Report says..." and here Sam dug into a pile of papers immediately in front of him, came up with three stapled sheets about one third down in the pile and read through the first page before continuing, "her second molars had erupted, consistent with an age of twelve to thirteen years. These molars had not erupted on her last dental examination."

"She was ten and a half or so, when she was taken," I commented, remembering the FBI report. "Anything else on that report?"

"Well," Sam continued, wincing, "she had the same changes to her nether parts." Apparently the word vagina was not in his vocabulary. "Here, you read the report," he said, thrusting it at me as if it were covered with killer bees.

I skimmed through the report, but nothing else jumped out at me. I needed to have time to read it through carefully. "Am I allowed to have a copy of this?"

"Sure thing, honey. Have Ruthie Xerox it for you on the way out."

Ruthie. Oh dear. "Anything yet on what happened to the sail boat? Has Bongiovanni interviewed Cornwell again?"

"Haven't heard anything, but you can ask Bowers when he calls you, which I know he will," Sam replied.

"I'm outa here. Gotta go pick up Jack."

Sam's raised an eyebrow. "I thought Will picked him up on Mondays."

Lord love a duck, I'd forgotten how much Sam knew about our schedules. "He called, got a meeting he can't get out of." *Damn.* Sam was long over accepting my excuses, but although his eyebrow stayed up, he didn't push.

He did ask, "You okay? You seem a little on edge."

"It's just the thing with Donnelly. Talk to you tomorrow!" I scooted out of his office, holding the report and carrying my coat over my arm, as fast as I could without running. My luck held and Ruthie was still not at her desk. I flagged down Phil, who was just coming out of his office, and he ran the copy for me. Once back in the parking lot, I spotted my Jeep parked in the front corner, engine running and Paulette in the passenger seat. We were primed for a getaway. I didn't even bother to put my coat on, but just tossed it on the back seat with the report and my bag, before getting in on the driver's side and peeling out of the lot.

"Trying to avoid someone?" Paulette asked with a frown.

"Yeah, Ruthie. You know if she started asking questions about the family, I'd be like butter in her hands. She'd know everything in a matter of minutes."

"She wasn't there?"

"Oh she was there, but just not at her desk. I had to get away before she knew I'd seen Sam. I'm going to pick up Jack, if that's okay with you, and we can get Tyler while we're at it."

"And miss the fun of two stir crazy seven-year-olds getting out of school? Never!" We both smiled. *Three smiles for me today, must be a record.*

৵৶

While I was preparing dinner, I called Bowers. He answered on the first ring. "Rhe, how are you? I heard from Bongiovanni about the beating you took in the hospital last week. Are you okay? Is the baby okay?"

Good grief! Another person more caring than my husband. I teared up at the thought. "I'm getting better, just a bunch of impressionistic bruises right now, and the baby's fine. Thanks for asking. What's this about wanting me to go with you to notify Rachel Vance's parents?"

"Yeah, I could definitely use some company. I'm just not as good at handling this stuff as you, and I could use a little more mentoring, if you know what I mean."

"I wish I could take the time right now, but I'm in the middle of some crap going on at the hospital with the man who attacked me." I opened the oven door to check on the Shepherd's pie, then closed it, and pulled two plates from the cupboard. "I need the next few days to work things out. You're going to do just fine without me." I heard a low groan on the other end of the line. "Just remember how we approached Savannah's parents. Be gentle, let them talk. They might know something important, just like the Engstrom's. It's your job to get them to open up." Putting my phone on speaker, I set plates on the table and opened the silverware drawer. "Have you heard anything about the sailboat? Did Bongiovanni interview Cornwell?"

"He did, and Cornwell sold the boat with the sails to the guy who works for him in the summer."

"The one with the funny eye?"

"Yeah, that one. The one with the coloboma. But we still haven't been able to locate him. He's totally off the grid. A hard thing to do in this day and age. You sure you can't go with me tomorrow?"

"I'm sure." I peeked in on the pie and turned off the oven.

He gave a deep sigh. "Okay, but I'm calling you before and after."

"I'll be waiting for your call." Dinner was ready.

☙ ❧

Will waltzed in for dinner that night. His hubris was astounding: he greeted Jack, set himself a place at the table and then sat down to eat as if nothing was wrong. I hardly spoke a word all the way through the Shepherd's pie, other than reminding Jack to eat his salad—which he did with way too much Ranch dressing. I decided to let him have his veggies his way for once.

Will talked with Jack enough for both of us but studiously avoided looking at me, except for the occasional sideways glance. After dessert and some play time with Jack before tucking him in, Will came into the kitchen where I was sitting with my feet up on a chair, reading the *P&S*. My feet dropped to the floor when he said, "We've got to talk."

You bet your sweet ass we do. I nodded, got up, and poured myself a cup of the decaf coffee I'd made while he was in with Jack. Out of habit, I poured him one too. *I could've made the real stuff, but what do I care what he likes?* We both sat down at the kitchen table. *We've spent so much time at this table as a family.*

I decided to make the opening move. "I've talked to Zoey, so I know pretty much everything."

"You what?" Will's face contorted in anger. "You had no right to do that!"

"No right? No right?" My voice was rising, so I took a deep breath, willing myself to calm down, placing my folded hands quietly on the table. "By what right did you break your marriage vows, screw her while married to me, get me pregnant, and tell her you were leaving me and Jack to be with her? What gives you that right?"

"I never wanted another child. The pregnancy was your fault, not mine."

I looked at him in stunned disbelief. *Who was this man?* I forced a laugh. "It takes two to tango, Will." If anything, that made him madder. I decided to go ahead and ask the hard question. "When are you moving out?"

"As soon as possible. I rented an apartment near the College several months ago. It's where I spent last night. Zoey will be moving in with me at the end of the school year."

"Before we're even divorced?"

"I consider that we've been separated for some time now and filed for divorce earlier today. You want to know the reason I gave? Alienation of affection." He said this with a smirk, proud of himself.

I thought of a quote I'd once read: the look of a toad breakfasting on fat marsh flies. *He's a toad alright.* "Maine's a no fault divorce state, do you know that?"

"It doesn't matter. You haven't been here for me since last fall, when you started working for the police department."

"But you agreed to that!"

"Only because you would have made my life hell if I hadn't."

I almost laughed out loud again. "You were *already* seeing Zoey at Almorel, in case you don't remember. And I was here every night that you weren't. What had I done to deserve *that?*"

"Can't fault a husband for looking for something on the side when he's not getting it at home."

I couldn't believe my ears, but one thing was now clear to me: Will was living in another world, one ruled by his libido and a desire to be young and free of responsibility. There was no point continuing this conversation. "Then go ahead and get the hell out of the house. Just don't move your things when Jack's around." *If he doesn't do it soon, I'm gonna love throwing his things in the front yard.* "Are you planning to talk to Jack?"

"No, I'm leaving that to you. It's your fault, you take care of it."

"Are you so into your new life that you don't even care about your own son?"

"Of course I care about him. If I get my way, I'll have sole custody. With all the danger you put yourself in, you're an unfit mother."

I was mightily tempted to throw my coffee at him, but stopped, thinking of Jack in the room down the hall and hoping he wasn't listening. If I hadn't been so frigging angry, I might have felt sorry for the pathetic caricature he'd become. "You're a joke, Will, you know that? A joke!"

Will stood up and went to get his coat off the hook by the door. Before he left, he hit me with a parting shot. "Oh, and Rhe, I'm putting the house on the market. The mortgage is in my name only, so there's nothing you can do."

Really? And in February? Then I did the one thing I knew would annoy him the most: I laughed. And continued laughing for several minutes after he closed the door behind him. Then I had a good long cry and two more mugs of coffee. A stiff drink would have really hit the spot at that point. I picked up the phone to call Sawyer. I'd already asked him if he could handle a divorce. Just in case.

19

Tuesday morning found me in Paulette's kitchen, after taking Jack to school. We sat at her table, drinking coffee, as I rehashed the conversation I had had with Will the night before. I did my best not to let it get overblown or to let myself get too emotional. I'd had enough angst in the past several days to last a lifetime.

"Will's turned into a monster. What's happened to him?" Paulette asked when I'd finished.

"I wish I knew. Mixed marital arguments with extreme cheating?"

"What're you going to do?"

"Well, I've already talked to Sawyer. Called him early this morning and told him to go ahead and file the papers on the grounds of adultery with Zoey, even though this is a no fault state. I couldn't help it, tit for tat. I suspect Will will move his things out today or tomorrow. What next? A 'For Sale' sign on the front lawn? It's laughable, Paulette. No one will be looking to buy a house in Pequod in February! What an idiot!"

"You'll get half of the proceeds, Rhe, plus child support, so don't worry. I looked up the divorce laws for Maine last night on the computer. But this might move forward quickly, the separation can be as short as sixty days."

Only my best friend would start working for me right away. "So what you're saying is I have roughly two months."

"That's about it... and you look like you haven't been eating again. Did you have breakfast?"

"Couldn't. Stomach is roiling."

"I'll make you some oatmeal. That should sit well."

"Please don't bother, Paulette. I promise I'll eat something later. Really."

"Do you want more coffee?" Without waiting for an answer, Paulette refilled my mug, which had a picture of Eeyore on it with the words "Good morning. If it is a good morning, which I doubt." *Perfect.*

"Okay, but I'm going to make sure you eat," she insisted. "Let's talk about the trip to Swans Island. I've already found someone to pick the kids up after school."

At that point, my cell phone rang. "Who's this?" I wondered out loud, as I grabbed my bag from the floor, rummaged around and pulled it out. "What a surprise! It's Sturdevant... Rhe Brewster," I answered.

"Mrs. Brewster, this is Dolores Richmond, Dr. Manning's secretary." *As if I didn't know.* "You have an appointment with HR this afternoon to straighten out your employment status."

"My employment status? I thought I was on unpaid leave indefinitely."

"There have been some recent developments with regard to the situation with Mr. Donnelly, which means that you are back on staff as soon as you wish."

Her voice was as imperious and unctuous as ever. I decided it would be nice to see her squirm, since she probably didn't know I had made the arrangement with Mr. Donnelly. "And what recent developments might those be, Ms. Richmond?"

"I am not at liberty to discuss that, only to tell you that you may resume your duties in the ER as soon as you are able."

"I'll do that. Please tell Dr. Manning to expect a call from my lawyer. I'm planning to sue the hospital."

"But, but you can't do that. You didn't require hospitalization! You went home under your own power!"

"No hospital security, Ms. Richmond. The hospital has to take responsibility. I'll visit HR this afternoon. Thank you for the call." I hung up before she could utter another sputter.

Paulette and I smiled at each other. "Are you really thinking of suing the hospital?"

"You can bet your sweet ass I am. I know Manning probably directed Dolores to make the stand down call when he heard what was going on, and I'm going to flush both of them out. I'd give anything to see Dolores' head explode when she discovers she's named in the suit. Bright blue eye shadow all over the walls of that fancy office."

That elicited another smile from Paulette, who took a sip of her coffee and toyed with her spoon. "Hmmm, maybe if you did sue, the money would be enough to let you buy another house or buy out Will's half."

"Sweetie, it's a nice thought, but it's so far ahead I don't even want to think about it. Let's get back to Swans Island." I really, really needed to get away, if only for a day.

"Well, your friend here did some research on that, too." She gave me a two finger salute. "If we can get to Bass Harbor by eleven, we can catch the ferry and be on the island a little before noon. What do you think?"

"Sounds like a plan. How about tomorrow? No storms in the forecast, and you said you had someone who could pick up the kids and take care of them after school?"

"Yeah, Beth Smith said she could take them, and she'll pick up Sarah, too. I can have Ted stop at Beth's on his way home, and I'll leave supper all made in case we're late."

"The boys will enjoy playing with Michael, but poor Beth. She'll need ear plugs!"

"So we're set for tomorrow?"

"Yeah, I'll come here right after I take Jack to school."

Paulette made me eat some oatmeal, which led to toast and bacon, which led to lemon cake. I left on a sugar high to visit HR and Sylvia. Apparently all the HR personnel knew what was going on because they looked up from their cubicles in unison when I came in, and the receptionist just waved her hand in the direction of Sylvia's office. The door was open so I knocked on the jamb.

"Come in, come in," Sylvia said with a big smile, getting up from her desk to join me in her comfortable chairs. "You look better than I expected, Rhe."

"Yeah, when you're not working you tend to get more rest." I noted her outfit today: a deep green pantsuit with a blue-green paisley silk blouse and a string of silver beads. Smashing, as usual. "And you're looking just gorgeous as always. I don't know how you do it."

"I'm going to show you sometime, when you find the time to climb out of your scrubs. You got the call from the Queen of Mean?"

"I did. She said I've been reinstated."

"Not only reinstated, but back to three days a week with pay for the time you've been out. All of your hospital expenses have been taken care of. What's going on, Rhe? Manning had you right where he wanted you!"

"Let's just say I have a good lawyer, and the guy who beat me up was in a receptive mood after court yesterday. He's not suing the hospital and is going into rehab for his alcoholism. But I don't know how the rest going to play out, because I'm suing the hospital for lack of security."

"Good for you!"

"That leaves me pretty much holding all the cards right now. Manning can't fire me, even when he's notified of the suit. It would be too obvious. I'm not naming him, just the hospital and whoever made that call. It was a woman."

"Dolores!"

"That's what I'm thinking, and Manning will throw her under the bus in a heartbeat to weasel out of any responsibility. I'm hoping she'll bite back."

"Rhe, you sneaky devil! This is the best news I've had in years." She leaned across the space between us and clasped both my hands in hers.

"So, what do I have to sign to return to work on this leaky bucket?"

∂∞⌒

Thirty minutes later I was in the employee parking lot, having signed some papers attesting to my reinstatement with no fault and back pay, gotten my schedule for the following week from ER, and given both Marsh and the ever faithful Lyle Pendergrass the good news. When I got to my Jeep, there was a note tucked under the windshield wiper. I wondered what it was, since I didn't see any similar notes on the other cars. I waited until I was inside the Jeep with the motor running before I unfolded it.

"Ms Bruster keep yur fuckin nose out of my life. Back of. If you don't, someone neer you will be next."

My stomach took a nose dive. *Is this from the girls' killer? If not, who else could it be? Not Donnelly, he was in rehab. Or was he?* My hands were shaking so hard I could barely steer myself out of the parking lot and to the police station. I had handled the note with my gloves on and got out of the car holding it between two gloved fingers, carrying it at an arm's length as if it were poisoned.

"Whatcha got there, Rhe?" Ruthie asked as soon as she saw me.

"No time, Ruthie, gotta see Sam." As I headed down the hallway to the left, I heard her call, "He's in the conference room. He's with..." I didn't hear the rest.

I opened the door to the conference room without knocking and came face to face with not only Sam, but also Agents Bowers and Bongiovanni, all of whom looked up in surprise. I frowned. *I thought I was part of this team, and here they are, having a meeting without me.* "How come I wasn't invited to this party?"

"We tried to call you last night and again right after lunch," replied Sam, "but your phone's off."

Crap, I had turned the phone off after Will had left the night before and never turned it back on.

"What are you holding? Some priceless artwork of Jack's?" Sam smiled at me.

"Maybe a letter from the girls' killer or maybe just a prank. If so, it's not a nice prank."

For a moment, the silence in the room was deafening. Then both Bowers and Bongiovanni jumped up and everyone started asking questions.

"I doubt it's a prank, Rhe," Sam said, looking at the note while I held it open for them all to read.

"Where did you find this?" asked Bongiovanni.

"On my windshield in the parking lot at the hospital."

"Has anyone else touched it?" Bowers this time.

"No."

"How would he know about you?" asked Bongiovanni.

"The *Post & Sentinel* would be my best bet. Have you been reading it? Bob published a story about finding Rachel Vance's body in Crystal Bog, probably based on a leak from the state lab, then linked it to me. I wasn't even involved in that. Well, not much."

"When do you think the note was left?" Another question from Bongiovanni.

"Well, I went in to visit HR around 1:30 and came out about 2:30, then came right here, so I guess during that window."

While I was getting the third degree, Bowers pulled a pair of nitrile gloves out of his pocket and put them on, taking the note from me and spreading it out on the table on a piece of newspaper. All three men looked at it again while I divested myself of coat and gloves.

"Not too well educated," said Bowers. "Or he's faking the bad grammar. Used pencil, cheap paper, we'll never trace it. But maybe we'll get fingerprints."

"This certainly ramps things up," said Bongiovanni. "Funny that the killer, if it is the killer, has focused on you and doesn't seem put off by the FBI. Is there a surveillance system for the parking lot?"

"I honestly don't know. I've never looked for one."

Bongiovanni turned to Bowers. "Can you get over to the hospital and see if they have any eyes on the parking lot? I'll get a warrant in the meantime, in case they do." Then he turned to me. "Ms. Brewster, I think you and your family need to be in protective custody until this is over, just to be on the safe side."

"No way. I have a child to care for, a house, a job, which by the way starts back next week, and I need the money. No. Way."

"How about I take care of the family's protection?" said Sam. "I'm local, she's part of the department family. We'll handle it here."

Bongiovanni thought for a moment. "Okay, if you think you can manage it with just your department. If necessary, I can assign Bowers to her detail as well, as soon as he's checked the hospital and notified Rachel Vance's parents." Bowers actually looked pleased.

"One more thing." I looked at Bowers. "Can you check on the where-abouts of Mr. Donnelly, the guy who beat me up in the ER? He's supposed to be in rehab, but there's an outside chance he left the note."

"Will do."

Bowers left for the hospital and Bongiovanni made a phone call, presumably to get the warrant, before we all sat down again. I was still jittery, taking deep breaths, trying to calm myself.

"So what did I miss?" I asked, taking another breath and blowing it out.

Bongiovanni filled me in, although I already knew most of it. "We haven't got a

track on this fellow with the odd eye, but I've got agents combing the area around Crystal Bog, talking to residents to see if he's holed up there. We'll find him, but it's going to take time."

"What if he doesn't live in that area?" I asked.

"We've issued a BOLO with fliers and the sketch provided by Robert Cornwell to all the local PDs. Someone must have seen him somewhere."

"Can you show me the sketch?" I asked.

"Sure thing." Bongiovanni opened the briefcase at his side, flipped through some files and pulled out the sketch, putting it in front of me.

It was clearly artistic, not like a police sketch, but it was more generic than specific. Large head, chiseled features, very dark eyes. The drawing niggled a memory. I'd seen someone who looked like this, but I just couldn't place him.

The meeting ended shortly after that, with Sam and me remaining behind to talk about my security detail. *There was no hope for it. I was going to have to tell him about Will.*

"Sam, before we even start I have to tell you something. Will and I have separated."

He didn't even flinch at my words. Not an eyebrow or muscle twitch. "I suspected something like that."

"Why?"

"The idiot put me down as a reference when he rented the condo on College Way. I called him and he told me he was divorcing you."

"When was that? He didn't even tell me until last night."

"Maybe a couple of months ago? I really thought he wouldn't go through with it, so I didn't say anything. When you told me to stay out of it, I figured you two were working it out. I'm so sorry, Rhe." He reached over and put a hand on my shoulder.

"So you knew all along? I'm such an idiot!" I stared at Sam for a minute. His face registered such sadness and regret, I just couldn't be angry with him. This mess wasn't his doing, just his brother's. "It's okay, Sam. It's not *your* fault." I put my hand over his. "Did he tell you he wants a divorce on the grounds of alienation of affection? Imagine that!"

"What did he do, Rhe? I know that's not the whole story. You'd fight for your marriage."

"Damn straight. But I can't fight *this*. He'd been seeing Zoey Harris at Almorel for several months before the raid. Did you know that? After I helped her avoid prosecution, he sought her out and they started back up again. Not for money this time. She's moving in with him at the end of this year." I stopped and looked at my hands, folded in my lap. Suddenly, a tsunami of all the feelings I'd held behind a mental breakwall crashed through, and I started to cry. "I don't know what I could have done differently, Sam. Maybe I *am* at fault for working with the police, I just don't know any more. Will isn't the person I married. What happened to him?"

Sam pulled his chair close to mine and enveloped me in a huge bear hug. I sobbed into his shoulder, relieved to finally have told him. "Don't you worry about a thing, darlin'. You're going to get through this just fine. I'll see to it. I know you've got a good lawyer – have you talked to him yet?"

"This morning. I told him to go ahead and file. Sam, Will wants to sell the house right away. What am I going to tell Jack?"

Sam just let me cry it out, which was probably the best thing to do. Finally, I stopped, sat up straight and wiped my cheeks with the back of my hand. Sam handed me his handkerchief. He was probably the only man I knew who still carried one. While I snuffled into it, he said, "I figure Will's moving out, right?"

"Right."

"So I or another member of this department will be outside your house every night until this is over. You don't have to worry about that, okay?" He held up his hand when I looked at him in surprise. "I can spend some time with Jack, too. And no, I won't stay *with* you – too many ways that could be misinterpreted."

I could see the sense in his reasoning, and I *did* feel safer knowing he would be at least outside the house. "If that note is real, do you think this guy would go after Jack?"

"I doubt it. He's into preteen girls. But we shouldn't take any risks."

We talked on for a few minutes after that, going over my plans to go to Swans Island the next day with Paulette, which he still thought was a good idea. He told me Phil or a patrolman would guard Beth Smith and the children after school. He'd also decided that since this man posed a threat to the community, he was going to notify all of the schools in the area personally. The schools could then notify the parents, handing out the rough sketch at the same time. Knowing the parents at Jack's school, this community would be buttoned up as tight as a drum. When we finished, he asked, "Where are you going now?"

I looked at my watch and discovered I had fifteen minutes to pick up Jack. "To the school to get Jack and right home."

Just then Sam's phone rang. It was Bongiovanni. They talked for a few minutes, Sam scowling the whole time. After he hung up, he said, "Rhe, it's not good. They actually had some footage from the parking lot this afternoon, and a small, dark-colored car pulled up next to yours. What appears to be a fairly large guy got out and put something white under your windshield wiper."

"Did they ID the type of car? How about a license plate?"

"The car was boxy and looked old. They're working on a make and model. No luck with the license plate, the resolution wasn't good enough."

"What about the guy? Could they see his face?"

"No deal. He was wearing a hoodie and had it pulled over his head."

"Did they rule out Donnelly? He's a big guy."

"That was the first thing they did. He was in rehab at the time. Counselor vouched for him."

"I'd figured as much."

"I'm sending Phil over to your house to meet you when you get there. I want him to go in with you when you get home and check everything out. I'll be over around seven. Keep the doors locked. Do you still have your Taser?"

"I do, and you know I can use it."

❧ ❦

That night, I sat down with Jack in the family room after an early supper, one of his favorites – hot dogs and macaroni and cheese, with ice cream and chocolate sauce for dessert. To hell with the calories. He clearly sensed something was wrong, because he'd been asking when his Dad would be home and now was scuttling around on the family room floor, throwing his cars around on the rug. I had to tell him but I felt like I was walking on thin, cracking ice and my head pounded from tension.

"Jack, can you please come over here? I have something important to tell you." He reluctantly got up and flopped down beside me on the couch. "I want you to know what I'm going to tell you has nothing, nothing to do with you. Can you keep that in mind?"

He squirmed, thought about it, then said, "Sure, Mom. Does it have something to do with Dad not being here?"

"Yup, it does, honey."

"You and Dad are getting a divorce, aren't you?" More squirming.

I fell back into the sofa. *How did he know?*

He answered my question before I even asked it. "I heard you last night. Actually I've heard you lots of times at night. Daddy doesn't like you working with Uncle Sam, does he? He seems mad at you all the time. Is that the reason he's not here?"

"You're right. He doesn't like me working with the police. But I'm pretty good at what I do for them, tracking down the bad guys. There are more reasons he's not here, Jack, but they're not something you need to know about now. Maybe later. I'm so sorry; I never wanted you to hear us arguing." I leaned over and put my arms around him, and after wiggling for a minute, he finally let me cuddle him. "Your Dad and I just can't live together anymore. It's gotten really hard for us to be around each other. It doesn't mean that we don't love you, and your Dad will still be here to take you to games and movies and play ball with you. All the regular stuff. He just won't be living here."

"That's okay, Mom, he showed me where he's living now."

What?

"And I met this friend of his; I think her name is Zoey."

"When did this happen?"

"About a month ago. The last time we went out for some fun on a Saturday. I think you were working."

My head now felt like there was an iron band tightening around it. *Migraine definitely on its way.* "Where were you when you met Zoey?"

"We had lunch with her at McDonald's. I think she's a student. She likes Big Macs. Dad told me not to tell you, but I guess it's okay now."

Holy shit! Even Jack knew about Zoey. I leaned back and took a deep breath, trying to release the anger I felt at Will for dragging his seven-year-old son into a sordid situation. After a long minute, the tension released a little. I had to know more of what Jack thought about all this, but I didn't want him thinking I blamed him, for doing what Will had asked.

"So what do you think, Jack? Can you handle all this? I know it's going to be hard, but I'm pretty sure you and I will get through it."

Jack nodded solemnly.

"Tell me the truth, kiddo. We've taught you always to be truthful."

He seemed to be thinking about it, for just a moment. Then he said, "It's okay, Mom. Dad's never here anyway, and when he is, you're sad and the fights make me feel bad. You're happier when Dad isn't here, so I think that's better."

I hugged my wiser-than-I-could-ever-believe son for a long while. Finally he squirmed out of my arms and went back to his cars. "I have something else to tell you. Your Uncle Sam is going to be staying here for a few days. There's a bad guy out there who is threatening children in this town," *better to make it generic*, "and he doesn't want us here by ourselves."

"Great! That'll be great! Will he play some games with me, maybe toss the ball around?"

My poor kid, starved for male attention. "Of course, but remember he has an important job, so he probably won't be here until late." Just then there was a pounding on the front door. "That's probably him now!"

Jack raced to the front door and started to undo the lock. "Wait, Jack!" I yelled. "Don't open the door!" Jack stopped short and looked at me curiously. "We have to know who's outside first, don't we? No strangers." I peered through the side glass and saw Sam standing on the stoop, stamping his feet. "It's okay, it's Sam." I unlocked the door.

"Yeah, Uncle Sam's here!" Jack yelled and jumped on him.

Welcome, Sam.

20

The next day was sunny as predicted, and for the end of February, rather warm, in the low 20s. The ocean outside my windows that morning was smooth and gray-blue, making it a perfect day for a boat trip. I arrived at Paulette's promptly at 8:30, looking forward to time away from the tensions that had overtaken my life recently. Just the thought of forty minutes on the water, even on a ferry, lowered my blood pressure.

Paulette appeared in the driveway with a large food basket, flung open one of the rear passenger doors to my Jeep and put the basket on the seat. "We're not going hungry on this trip!" she announced, shut the door and went back inside, coming out with the usual two travel mugs gripped in one hand, the paper bag in the other, and a large tote over her shoulder. Paulette was always prepared.

We drove north out of Pequod, sipping warm coffee, and munching on apple pecan muffins.

"When do you find time to do all this cooking?" I asked Paulette, before finishing off my muffin.

"Sometimes late at night when I can't sleep. Sarah was up working on a project last night, so I stayed up with her and kept busy in the kitchen."

I could just see her bustling around, throwing ingredients together. Sarah was a miniature of her mother with her love of cooking and fashion; the drama queen genes had definitely been passed down.

"She's gotten so tall," I said. "What happened to that boyfriend...Todd?"

"Todd is so last week," replied Paulette, mimicking her daughter with a wave of the hand and an eye roll. "This week it's someone named Jock. He's polite and sweet, a little shy. I like him, but guaranteed it'll be someone else next month."

"How's Ted handling the hairdos? He looked pretty fierce the week she went to school with feathers in her hair. I kinda liked it." I winked at Paulette.

"He's watching her like a hawk but so far has swallowed most of his criticism. I think he wants to keep the lines of communication open. We're well aware we've got some rough years coming up, and I ought to know. She's just like me!"

The thought of Paulette at that age was more than amusing. "Your mother must have had the patience of a saint."

"She did, but I took years off her life. Say, I saw Sam's Jeep outside your house last night... does he know about Will?"

"Yup, he does. In fact, he apparently figured out what was going on quite a while ago. I just confirmed the details. So far he's staying pretty much out of it, which is good. He's in a terrible position, caught between me and his own brother."

"Was it Sam who had the flyer about the kidnapper sent out? Ted is up in arms, literally. Got out his shotgun last night. Sarah's going nowhere without an escort. Is that why Sam was at your house?"

"He said he doesn't want Jack and me to be alone and is alternating with one of his deputies until we find the guy. I think the FBI is getting close." I deliberately chose to leave out the detail about the note I'd found on my car, but was glad to hear that Ted was on guard. Sam had mentioned he would talk with Ted today, to be on the safe side.

"Hmm, I wonder what Will would think if he knew Sam was keeping such a close eye on you?" Paulette asked with a sly smile.

"Probably absolutely nothing, since he was so eager to get out of my life. You know, at this point, I could care less. Really." I banged on the steering wheel to make my point.

Bass Harbor is a quaint little fishing village on the side of Mount Desert Island opposite to Bar Harbor. We circled the island, driving around a large portion of Acadia National Park. After parking in the line for the ferry, I ran inside the ferry office to purchase a ticket plus a reservation for the trip back. The *Captain Henry Lee* was making the run to Swans Island, and just before 11, we drove the car onto the ferry. After a lumbering start, the ferry's engine thrummed powerfully and the boat made solid headway in the waves. Paulette and I sat in the car, which rocked gently with the ferry. Occasionally a wave splashed over the rail on the right side, hit our windows, and froze into slush. No way was I getting out.

"Where should we start looking?" asked Paulette, after wrapping herself in an extra scarf. The car was turned off and getting cold.

"Well, the island has a town office and a year-round store, so I'm thinking someone at either place would know where Artie lives. I read online there are only three hundred people on the island in the winter."

"Can't imagine living in such an isolated spot," she replied.

"I know that. Whatever would you do without a Macy's or Crate and Barrel?"

"You interested in a sandwich?" She reached into the back seat and retrieved the wicker basket.

"Sure, whatcha got?"

"Contain your disdain – egg salad or, in consideration of your fixed lunch menu, tuna fish salad."

"I'm going to live dangerously. Give me an egg salad."

Paulette's eyebrows registered her surprise. "You're going to make me eat tuna fish?"

❧ ❦

After the ferry tied up at its dock at the north end of Swans Island, we drove onto the pier, parked, and asked for general directions at the ferry office. Following a map we were given, we headed south on Atlantic Road and continued right onto Harbor Road. The houses we passed on the way were tidy, a mix of old and new and painted mainly white. Large neat stacks of lobster traps could be seen in virtually every front yard, an indication of the primary industry on the island. Just after passing a three-story, weathered brown building with a sign that said Odd Fellows Hall, we bore to the right and found the Carrying Place Market, a small one-story building built of vertical planks.

"A good place to start, I guess," Paulette remarked wryly, looking at the four cars in the parking lot. "What do people do here all year, other than lobstering?"

"I saw an advertisement for a Swan Island Blanket Company," I replied as we got out of the car.

There was an old truck and an older SUV parked directly in front of the store, and two men were having a laugh together at the rear bumper of the rusted Range Rover. They were both dressed in jeans, old duck boots, and dirt-stained Carhartt jackets. One had on a plaid hat with ear flaps and turned to look at me as I approached.

"Excuse me, sir, can I ask you a question?" I asked.

"How can we help you ladies?" he replied with a smile revealing a gold tooth.

"We're looking for an old friend we were told lived here on Swans Island. Artie Dunn? We grew up with him in Pequod and thought since we were visiting Bass Harbor, we'd take the ferry out and see if we could find him."

The second fellow, wearing a black wool watch cap pulled down to his eyebrows, looked at his companion and said, "I know Artie. Doesn't live too far from hee-ah."

He stopped, and I waited for directions. When none were forthcoming, I asked, "Could you give me directions?"

"Ayup."

I waited a few moments, looking from one man to the other. "Well?" I finally asked.

"We kin give you directions," said the flap-hatted man, winking at his friend. Apparently there was a joke going on I was missing.

I raised an eyebrow at Paulette, but she stood there transfixed by the interaction. *No help there.* After a bit I said, "I would esteem it a great personal favor if you could give me the directions to Artie Dunn's home."

"Well now, since you asked so nicely," said flap-ear, "I'll do just that. Turn 'round and head back up Atlantic towahds the ferry. House is on Hahbah, on the right about a half mile from the dock."

"Can you tell me what the house looks like?"

"I can tell you something bettah. Look for the name on the mailbox." And with that, the two men burst out laughing.

Trying to preserve some shred of dignity, I gave each one a nod and said, "Thank you very much for the help. You've been most kind." *Do these guys have nothing better to do than tease visitors?*

We retreated to the Jeep, and as I started the car I remarked to Paulette, who still hadn't said a word, "You were a great help back there, partner."

"Those men were downright rude! What was that all about?'

"Local humor. Some fun with the tourists."

"Why didn't you use your Maine accent? We-ah not from he-ah, came from Bangah this mohnin." Paulette did a pitch perfect imitation of their Down East accent. "It might have been fun to see how they reacted."

I had to laugh. "Maybe, but we got what we needed."

We turned back onto Harbor and both focused on reading the mailboxes. Finally, when I figured we'd missed it, Paulette yelled, "There it is!"

The mailbox read 'Dunn' in faded white paint. It sat erect at the end of a gravel driveway that led to a trim white mobile home on a solid foundation, with a large bump-out addition on the right side. Lobster traps were piled in huge stacks to the right of the drive, and there was a well-worn path to a wooden front porch. We pulled up beside a battered Tahoe.

"Do you think he's home?" Paulette asked, excitement in her voice.

"If that's his car, he is. C'mon, time's awasting." Actually, I was feeling a little nervous about seeing Artie. I hadn't thought much about how I'd ask him what happened to Deidre and was worried how he'd respond to my questions.

The front door opened as we reached the front steps, and a small, wiry man with short salt and pepper hair and a few days' worth of beard appeared. "What can I do for you? Are you lost?"

"Artie Dunn? It's Rhe. Rhe Hadley. Now I'm Rhe Brewster. Do you remember me?"

He peered at me and a look of recognition came over his face. "Rhe Hadley! For God's sake! What are you doing here? Come in, come in." He held the door open and backed in to let us pass. Once inside, I introduced Paulette and had a chance to look him over. His features were much the same as I remembered, but his face had weathered with a lot of fine lines.

He invited us into his tiny kitchen, where we sat on plastic chairs at a small, scarred wooden table while he bustled around making coffee. I looked around. The trailer was comfortable enough, but the furniture was old and the rugging showed wear. I doubted he made much money.

As he waited for the water to heat, he told us his wife, whom he'd met when he first came to Swans Island, was on the mainland visiting friends for a week. He'd been nursing a cold and stayed home. They had no children, but a passel of relatives in the area. I gave him a synopsis of my life since I'd last seen him, and how we'd found him via Mary Noonan.

"Mary Noonan? She's still alive? She must be in her eighties now. How's she doing?"

"She's living with her son and daughter-in-law and is pretty spry for an eighty-year-old," I told him, "and she wanted to know how you were. She's been worried about you all these years."

"That woman is a saint. Did she tell you about my father?"

I nodded. "It sounded like a horrible situation. I never knew."

"She was the one person I could turn to when things got rough with him," Artie said as he poured coffee into the mugs he'd set out for us.

"Is your Dad still alive, Artie?" I lifted the mug and inhaled the aroma, then warmed my hands around it. Paulette, who was being noticeably quiet, did the same. Guess we were both chilled.

'No, he died about five years ago. There hasn't been a day gone by I haven't rejoiced at his passing."

"Is he why your mother left?"

"Yes, and thank God for it. He was a mean and nasty drunk, but no one would have done anything if she'd complained. The police force was made up of his friends. Who could she have gone to? I found Mom after Dad died, and we're close. Say, your husband wouldn't be related to Sam Brewster, would he?"

"Sam's his older brother, and actually Sam is why we came here today."

"How's Sam doing? There was a time in high school when we were thick as thieves."

"Sam's now the Police Chief in Pequod, and other than some weight and missing hair, he's not changed much."

Artie smiled and looked out the window, as if remembering when he and Sam were young.

"I'm actually working as a police consultant. A girl missing two years turned up dead on a beach near Pequod, and it seems she's one of four who've disappeared over the years."

There was a pause after I said that. "Deirdre...you're here because of Deirdre," Artie finally replied. He looked at his coffee mug and took a deep breath.

"Yes, I am. Deirdre disappeared long before any of the other three girls, but it's still an unsolved case and Sam asked me to put new eyes on it. Is there anything you can tell me?"

At that, Artie got up and started to pace back and forth in the small room, running a hand over his hair and rubbing the back of his head. "I always knew this day would come. When I'd have to face what happened to her."

"Sam told me you didn't seem surprised when she disappeared. That you seemed to accept she wasn't going to be found."

Paulette, who had been watching Artie carefully, suddenly stood and led him by the arm back to his chair. "Put your head between your knees, Mr. Dunn. I can see you're getting a little light-headed." I had been so intent on what Artie was saying that I hadn't even noticed how pale he had gotten, and my non-medical friend had.

I mouthed the words "Thank you" as she sat down again. I leaned over and took Artie's pulse. His heart was racing. "Artie, are you on any heart medication? Do you have atrial fibrillation or high blood pressure," I asked him.

"No, I'm healthy as a hog. I, this, I ...I'm just not prepared for this."

"For what, Artie?"

"For telling someone what happened to Deirdre. I couldn't, not as long as Pop was alive. He would have killed me. Then he went mental and had to be institutionalized, and there didn't seem to be any point."

"Are you able to tell me now?"

Artie slowly raised his head, and, hand shaking, took a sip of his coffee. "Yeah, it's about time Deirdre was laid to rest."

Paulette grabbed my hand under the table.

"When Pop got drunk, he beat my mother, but he reserved something worse for Deirdre."

My mouth went dry and I swallowed hard. "He abused her?"

"Yes. From the time she was four or five."

"Oh dear God!" said Paulette. "That poor girl! Why didn't you do anything? Why didn't she say anything?"

"What could I do? I was just a kid. Who would believe me? I socked him once after he'd... touched her. He beat me to a pulp. Deirdre stood there screaming, telling him she'd do anything if he'd just stop. So he did. Deirdre, you know, she just accepted it, at least until the year she disappeared. I think hanging around with you and Sylvia...Sylvia, right?...I don't know, made her see that what was going on was wrong, that she deserved better. She started refusing him." Artie swallowed hard, paused, then found the words to continue. "At first, he just threatened to hurt her but didn't do anything. But she kept it up and threatened to tell one of her teachers and all her friends if he came near her again. I've never seen him so, so...crazy."

Artie swallowed again, and took another deep breath. "Then she disappeared," he finally managed to say.

"How do you know he was involved?"

"Because I hounded him during those first days when everyone was out looking and the police were around. Kept asking him where she could be." Artie was now shaking his head, as if trying to deny the memory. "Finally, about a week later, he got roaring drunk and told me if I ever asked him again what happened to her, I'd end up the same way....he killed her, Rhe. I couldn't prove it, but I knew he killed her."

"Oh, Artie, what a burden to bear and not to be able to do anything about it! I'm so sorry." I reached over and grabbed his hands.

Artie just continued, clearly wanting to get it all out. "Then he just packed us up and took me here, said it was for a fresh start. It wasn't. He kept on drinking, only now I was old enough to know how to stay out of his reaches. When I wasn't in school, I worked as a stern man on a lobster boat. Learned the trade, got my own boat and eventually when things with Pop got so bad, got some help to have him committed."

"Do you think he just said that about Deirdre to frighten you?" I asked. "Just created it out of whole cloth?"

"No, definitely not. Once when I was visiting him at the hospital, he was having one of his more lucid periods. We got talking about old times, and Deirdre came up. He started to cry, saying he hadn't meant to do it, that he was drunk and didn't know what he was doing."

"What did he tell you he did?' Paulette asked breathlessly, totally caught up in Artie's story.

"That they got into an argument when she came home from school, and he slugged her – God, he had powerful fists. She fell and hit her head on the corner of the kitchen table. He figured she was dead."

"Figured? He didn't know for sure? How could he not know?" What had happened to Deirdre turned my stomach.

"He said he didn't feel a pulse. Who knows if he even knew what a pulse was? He said he panicked and got rid of the body."

"Where, Artie? Where did he bury her?"

"I don't know, Rhe. He lost it at that point, and I never had another opportunity to bring it up. He may have had other days when he was lucid, but never when I came to visit. Maybe it was an act? Anyway, he died about three months later."

"Was he gone for a long time the day she disappeared?"

"No, he was there when I came home for dinner. I guess he didn't have much time to hide the body."

"Did the police search your house when you reported her missing?"

"They nosed around, looking in rooms and the basement, but as I recall, it wasn't a very thorough search. Pop was friends with so many guys on the force, they never considered him a suspect." Artie slumped down into his chair, looking for all the world like a deflated balloon, shaking and still pale.

"Artie, have you got anything stronger than coffee in the house?'

'I do, but I don't indulge much. Too many memories of what it did to Pop."

"Where is it?"

"In the cupboard over the sink."

Paulette jumped up, retrieved a bottle of Maker's Mark bourbon, found a jelly glass and poured Artie a healthy tot. He looked at it for a second, then downed it in one gulp. Within a minute, the color had returned to his cheeks.

"Do I need to see Sam? Do you think I'm in some kind of trouble?" he asked.

I put a hand on Artie's shoulder. "No, I doubt it, but I'm pretty sure that Sam will want to take a statement at some point. Could you manage to do that?"

"Sure, I can do that. Do you want me to go with you now?"

At his question, Paulette looked at her watch. "We've got to go, Rhe, or we'll miss the last ferry!"

I stood, grabbed my coat, bent down and hugged Artie. "Wait 'til you hear from us. Are you going to be okay here alone?"

"I think I might call my wife."

"You do that, Artie. I don't know her, but after all your years of marriage, I bet she's a good listener."

"Yeah, she is. Let me give you our phone number here." He got up, pulled a pad and pencil from a kitchen drawer and wrote the number down for me. Just doing that seemed to exhaust him and he sat down heavily again. "Can you see yourselves out?"

I hugged him again and Paulette and I left. We didn't speak until we'd passed the long line of cars waiting for the ferry and had slid into one of the spaces marked reserved.

Paulette turned to face me. "Lord, Rhe, did you ever expect to hear that?" She took a good look at me. "Are you okay?"

By that time my mind was roiling with horrible images of Deirdre and I felt sick. I rolled down the window for some cold air. I couldn't reply and just sat there, looking at the water. Finally I said, "I'd hoped for a clue, something to follow up on, but not to find out what actually happened to her. Poor Deirdre." I started to cry. "And Artie, having to keep it to himself all these years. I hope once he talks to Sam, he'll find a little peace. He clearly blames himself for not having done something to save her."

After giving me a Kleenex and some quiet time, Paulette asked, "Where do you think the body is?"

"I have an idea."

21

We drove into Paulette's driveway a little after 8 PM and I was gifted with a tired seven-year-old who had been fed and had finished his homework. Oh, and a huge container of beef stew with fresh biscuits made by Sarah. When I drove into my garage, I noticed Sam just pulling into the plowed spot in front of the house. After sending Jack off to get a shower, which he now preferred to baths, and reminding him to brush his teeth, I unlocked the front door and waved at Sam to come in. He went around through the garage, put the garage door down and came into the kitchen. By the time he tugged off his boots, I had the beef stew in the microwave and the biscuits on a plate on the kitchen table. I took out some butter and Maine blueberry jam, just in case.

"Something smells good. Haven't you eaten, Rhe?" Sam took off his parka and hat and put them on the hooks next to the garage door.

"No, and I'm betting you haven't either. It's beef stew. You up for some? No, never mind, I know you're up for anything edible." In answer, he went to the silverware drawer and brought out two settings, which I countered with bowls and napkins. "Sit, this should be ready in a minute."

Sam lowered himself into a chair with a grateful sigh.

"Tough day?" I asked him.

"No, just long. I had to go down to the harbor and separate a couple of guys who got into a fight over trap locations."

"Anyone I know?"

"Yeah, James Barnes, the guy you thought you saw in the window at Ernie's that day. He's one very intense guy, doesn't say much, but when he does, look out."

The microwave dinged and I used a mitt to transfer the container with its steaming contents to the table. I grabbed a ladle and dished a healthy portion of the stew into Sam's bowl. The aroma sent my salivary glands into overtime. I gave myself only slightly less than Sam and slid into a chair. Without another word, I took a spoonful, blew on it, and slurped it up. *Perfection. Sarah's definitely competition for her mother.*

Sam had two spoonfuls to my one before he spoke. "This Paulette's?"

"No, Sarah's. Can you believe that? Chip off the old block." I ate some more. "So what happened with James?"

"He got into an argument with Rollie Holmes, who's been lobstering for probably forty years. James only helps his brother out during the winter, but it didn't stop him from complaining Rollie'd put some traps just south of Little Squirrel Island. He claimed it was his brother's area."

"Did it come to blows? Where were they?"

Sam took a biscuit, slathered it with butter and popped the whole thing in his mouth before continuing. In Sam's defense, it was a small biscuit and he swallowed before he tried to speak. "On the main pier by the lobster co-op, where most of the boats are tied up. They'd just started getting physical when Phil and I arrived. It still took a few minutes before we could get them separated." He paused and selected another biscuit from the plate. "You know how territorial these guys can be, but in this case, I was inclined to believe Rollie. He's been around a long time and this is the first time I've had to deal with him in any official capacity. He's got a reputation for absolute honesty. James is a hot head."

"So how did you leave it?"

Sam buttered the biscuit. "They agreed to back off. It was either that, or I was going to take them down to the station to cool off. James finally said maybe he was mistaken, but I could tell he didn't mean it."

"Why does James only help Peter during the winter? Lobstering is slow this time of year."

"I asked him, and he said he had other things to do that paid more in the summer months. Normally I would disagree, but the glut of soft-shell lobsters this past year meant the Pequod fleet was getting less than two dollars a pound at the co-op. Hardly worth lobstering, and the price of menhaden's going up." I knew menhaden were the small, oily fish used to bait the traps.

"So what does he do that pays more than working for his brother?" I grabbed a biscuit before they were all gone and spread on some blueberry jam. I also helped myself to a little more beef stew and gave the remainder to Sam, whose bowl was empty.

"He didn't elaborate and I was so relieved the guys backed off, I didn't ask. Phil and I both got thrown around a bit trying to separate them." He paused for a large spoonful of stew. "How did your day go today? I heard you found Artie."

I told him about our trip to Swans Island and getting directions, which gave him a chuckle. "Typical Mainer's idea of humor. You should be used to it by now, Rhe."

"Any news about that note yet?" I'd wanted to ask him as soon as he'd gotten in the door, but food had to come first with Sam.

"Not yet."

Dang. By this time, we had finished eating and I was putting on a pot of coffee. Sam pushed his chair away from the table and leaned back. Now that dinner was over, I could tell him about our conversation with Artie, including what had happened to Deirdre.

At that, he leaned forward, elbows on the table, all ears. "Son of a gun! I never suspected. Poor Artie, thinking it was somehow his fault all these years. And that SOB father of his got away with it." Sam frowned, pensive for a moment. "He must have been really scared of his father, never to have said anything. I can confirm that Artie's father was tight with the Police Department. They used to drink together on Friday nights, down at the Salty Dog. So he hardly could have gone to them."

"The Salty Dog…that bar closed a while back, right? I seem to remember it had a really bad reputation. Where do you all hang out now?" I grabbed the coffee carafe and poured two mugs.

"We don't. The job's a bit more consumptive now. No time."

I put the mugs on the table with cream and sugar and sat down. "Sam, I have an idea where Deirdre might be buried. Artie said there was not a lot of time between when she came home and he himself got there. What do you think his father could have done, in that short a time?"

"Backyard or the basement. But I know the police searched the house and yard, it's in the report."

"Yes, but how well? Remember, the police wouldn't have considered Mr. Dunn as a suspect. How about you talk to the house's current owners and get a cadaver dog over there tomorrow? I have a bad feeling we're going to solve Deirdre's disappearance."

"Okay, I'll make some calls." He added cream and sugar to his coffee, took a sip and made a sour face. "What the heck is this crap?"

"Oh lord, I'm so sorry. I just went ahead and made decaf out of habit." I got up. "I'll make another pot of the real stuff."

Just then Jack came into the kitchen in his X Men pajamas, hair wet but combed. "Who's Deirdre?"

"Nobody you know, big ears. You ready for bed? Shall I tuck you in?"

"I think I can tuck myself in, Mom." *Shocker.*

"Well, give Uncle Sam a hug and kiss, and me, too, then off with you. I'll check on you in a few minutes. Pick a book to read."

After he'd left the room, Sam asked, "So how's he doing, Rhe? Is he okay with Will not being around?"

I leaned back against the counter by the coffee maker and crossed my arms. "For him, he's been quiet, really quiet. Jack's already seen Will's apartment and has met Zoey, but was afraid to tell me. We, or rather I, talked yesterday, and I've tried to reassure him that we both love him and will still be his parents. He hasn't asked any questions about why we've separated. Maybe Will said something. If so, I can't imagine *what* he told him."

"So why don't you give him your side of it?"

"Because I think he already knows my side. He wasn't exactly absent when Will and I were fighting the last few months. I don't want to load him up with more than he can handle."

"So you're willing to let Will's side of things stand?"

"For the time being. Jack is a bright kid, and the fact he's been comfortable with me suggests he understands some of it."

Sam got up and came around the table to give me a hug. "Let me know if there's anything I can do to help Jack. Right now I'm going to head out to the Jeep, turn the heat on high, and make those few phone calls. You lock the door after me and make sure everything is buttoned down, okay?"

"Sure thing, but let me give you a mug of the real stuff to take with you."

❧ ❧

Sam called me while Jack and I were having oatmeal the next morning and told me he'd arranged for the owners to be out of the Dunn's old house by noon. A cadaver dog would be there with its handler. I promised I'd be there, too. Then Sawyer called. The social worker assigned to the Donnelly case had assured him there no abuse in the home, but agreed I could meet Mrs. Donnelly and the children to see for myself. It had been arranged for that morning. *How did I get so popular?*

❧ ❧

The Donnelly's house was a neat Craftsman-style bungalow fairly close to the Pequod College campus. I had a fleeting thought of Will but banished it by the time I parked. There was a snowman on the lawn that reminded me of the Wicked Witch of the East – *I'm melting, I'm melting* – and sleds on the front porch. Mrs. Donnelly answered the doorbell on the first ring. "Come in, come in," she urged. She was hardly what I'd expected: roly-poly, pink cheeks, hair pulled into a disheveled pony tail with strands hanging on her face, an apron wrapped around her substantial middle, and chapped, reddened hands.

She emanated energy, and after taking my coat and telling me not to worry about my boots, she led me into the living room on the right of the foyer. I could see why she wouldn't worry about the boots. The hard wood floor was largely covered by a worn, stained rug I thought might have been blue at one time. Toys were piled neatly in every corner of the room, but I could hear a cacophony from the back of the house. Sensing what I was about to ask, Mrs. Donnelly said, "I kept the kids home from school today because I wanted you to meet them. I can't tell you how sorry I am for what happened. I know you expect me to say my husband is a good man, and he is, really. He just has a problem when he drinks. But he's getting help now, and we're all going to help him."

"Yes, he does have a problem, Mrs. Donnelly…"

"Please call me, Josey, Mrs. Brewster."

I nodded but didn't return the favor. "Can I look around, talk to the children?"

"Of course, of course, come on back to the kitchen." She started down the center hallway and I followed her into a big kitchen that extended from one side of the house to the other. "Excuse the mess, the children are busy making cookies, or something that'll resemble cookies."

There was a large, scarred kitchen table and chairs on the right side, and the children were kneeling or standing on stools around an island on the left, reading and yelling directions at each other from a cook book. Flour and sugar covered everything, including the children, like a layer of snow; there were broken eggs on the counter. It was clear they were having a good time. I glanced at each child in turn and noted that, like their mother, there were no visible bruises and they were well-fed.

Josey had to raise her voice to be heard over the noise level. "Children, this is Mrs. Brewster. She wanted to meet you, which is why you're getting a day off from school today." The children turned to look at me as one, and big smiles lit up their faces.

"Hey, thanks Mrs. Brewster!" the oldest one said.

"That's Jason, our oldest, he's nine," Josie said by way of introduction. "Say hello to Mrs. Brewster the rest of you, and introduce yourself."

"I'm Jill and I'm seven," said a little elf with egg smudged on her cheek.

An identical elf chimed in, "I'm Jane and I'm seven, too. We're twins!"

A moppet with a head of curly dark hair gave me a huge smile and said, "I'm Brian and I'm one-two-three-four-five! And he's Jeremy, and he's three," pointing to a smaller version of himself. *I saw a pattern.*

"Well, I'm delighted to meet you all. Can I make cookies with you?" They looked at their mother, who nodded, and then they all nodded too. I rolled up my sleeves and joined in. Two hours and three batches of sugar cookies later, ears ringing from the children's voices, I left the house exhausted, with a box of cookies for Jack. Mr. Donnelly's drinking had not impacted his family…yet.

Before I pulled into traffic, I called Sawyer's office and left a message that I concurred with the social worker about the family. I asked him to drop the more serious charge against Mr. Donnelly, but to go full speed ahead with the law suit against the hospital. I also told him I'd called Sylvia; she refused to talk about her situation with Manning, as I'd thought.

Then I headed to McDonald's to treat myself to a Big Mac and fries for lunch, feeling a little lighter of the intangible weight burdening me for the past week. *Even better with a Big Mac.* I inhaled it sitting in the parking lot before heading out to Cedar Street, where the Dunn's house had been built sixty years before.

It hadn't changed much: a two-story white farmhouse, front porch and a dormered roof, surrounded by a chain-link fence. But it was well-maintained, like most of the other houses on the street. As for the run-down ones, I felt sorry for what home owners were dealing with in the current economy. Sam's Jeep was parked in front. He was on the sidewalk, talking to a tall woman with what looked like a Doberman-Rottweiler mix, wearing a service dog vest and sitting patiently by her side. The woman was laughing and poked Sam with her elbow. I parked in a slot I found two doors down, got out and walked back to meet them.

"Hey, Rhe, glad you made it. Meet Debbie Maynard, the owner and trainer of Sampson here."

"Pleased to meet you, Rhe. Sam's told me a lot of good things about you."

I laughed. "Nice to meet you, too. I've paid him well for that. I know I'm not supposed to, but may I pat Sampson?"

"Of course. He looks fierce, but he's a marshmallow," Susan replied. "Samp, say hello to Rhe." Sampson gave me his full attention and offered a paw, which I shook with a smile. After letting him smell the back of my hand, I gave his head a riffle. He leaned into my hand and gave me an 'I adore you' look. I gave him another pet.

"Are we ready to go?" I asked Sam. "Are the home owners out?"

"They are. We're just waiting on a couple of my patrolmen." He looked up. "And here they are." He opened the front gate and held it back for Debbie, Sampson, and me. The patrolmen followed.

"I need you to stay on the front porch," Sam said to me and the patrolmen. "I promised the owners as few people as possible in the house. Rhe, I'll call you if Sampson finds anything." He and Debbie put on paper booties, and Debbie wiped Sampson's feet clean with a small towel she pulled from her pocket. Then Sam followed Debbie and the dog inside.

Left to my own devices, I gave a half-smile to the patrolmen and proceeded to pace up and down the front porch. The porch was as far as I'd ever gotten when Deirdre lived there; she'd always rebuffed any requests to come in. As I paced, I looked at other houses – normal, ordinary homes, just like this one, but hopefully not containing the evil this one had.

After a few minutes, Sam poked his head out the door and said, "Rhe, you can come in. Here are some paper booties and leave your coat in the hall-way. The door to the basement is on your left at the end of the hall." I swooped in while the two patrolmen got their marching orders, which was to wait for Sampson and Debbie and watch them grid the back yard when everything was finished in the basement. Booties on, I dropped my coat and hat on a chair and made a beeline for the basement stairs.

Sam stayed in the kitchen but called after me, "Watch your step, Rhe. The stairs are narrow. Hold onto the railing."

At the bottom of the stairs, a dimly-lit, partially cement-floored room emerged. There were two or three bare light bulbs overhead that barely dispelled the gloom. Some light came in from the high-set basement windows, filtered by the filth that covered them. I stopped on the last step and yelled up to Sam, "Does the family do anything down here? Sure doesn't look like it." The basement was essentially empty except for an old iron wash sink and a ton of cobwebs. I shivered involuntarily.

"Not according to the homeowners," he called back down after a moment. "Their washer and dryer are upstairs; rehabbing this space is on their list of things to do, but they haven't gotten around to it yet. Their kids think it's creepy."

"They're observant." Just then I noticed Debbie standing still on the part of the floor that was still dirt, furthest from the basement steps and the light. Sampson sat rigidly beside her. "Debbie, Sampson something?"

"Yup, within about a minute of being down here, he signaled."

"Signal?"

"He sits down and whines."

"So there's some human material where you are standing?"

"I'm 100% sure. He didn't hesitate."

At this point, Sampson started wagging his tail and looked up at Debbie expectantly. She pulled a dog treat out of her pocket and gave it to him. "Good dog, Sampie, good dog."

"Sam, have you called Marsh and the forensic techs?" I yelled up again.

"Just finished doing that." He clumped back down the stairs and stopped at the bottom. "Debbie, I think you and Sampson can walk a grid in the back yard now. I want to make sure we only have the one site."

"Sure thing. Come, Sampson." She slapped her thigh and moved to the stairs. Before going back up, she bent down and gave her dog a hard rub along his side and repeated, "Good dog."

☙ ❧

I spent the rest of the afternoon, until it was time to pick up Jack, sitting on the basement stairs, watching the technicians and Marsh dig and sieve dirt, while Midori catalogued and bagged anything they found. Sampson had not found anything in the back yard, for which we all were grateful.

A skeleton emerged after about thirty minutes of careful soil removal, and Marsh was nearly finished brushing it clean when I left. "Call me when you have anything?" I asked Marsh as I stood up from my spot on the steps.

"Will do, Rhe. I already have her dental records, so this should be a quick ID if it's Deirdre."

Sadness welled up and washed over me as I drove to Jack's school. Somewhere in my heart of hearts, I had always hoped she was safe and happy somewhere and I would see her again. Even Artie's confession hadn't completely dimmed that hope. Now my friend was really and truly gone, and I had to accept it. I thought about the homeowners, too. What would they think when they found out they'd been living over a burial site all this time, one of a young girl?

22

As we were driving home, Jack said, "Mom, you smell funny. Like wet dirt." *What a nose!* "Well, that's because I've been sitting in a cellar for the last few hours."

"How come?"

"I was with some people who were digging up bones. Sort of like what you've seen on TV where they dig up dinosaur bones."

"Not dinosaurs?"

I shook my head no.

"So what's for dinner?"

Thank heavens for his ADHD mind.

When we got home, I discovered I'd left my phone on the counter that morning. When I checked it, I saw that Agent Bowers had called me several times. Darn! With everything going on, I'd forgotten Bowers had gone to tell Rachel Vance's parents we'd found her body. Once Jack was settled with his homework, wiggling on a chair at the kitchen table and drinking chocolate milk, I returned his calls.

"Hi, Bowers, sorry I didn't get back to you earlier. How did it go?"

"Just what you might think. Not sure I was any comfort."

"No one bringing news like that could be of any comfort. Any more news on the case?"

"The name of the guy Cornwell sold the boat to is an alias. We haven't been able to locate anyone by the name of Charles Harkin. And since it was a cash transaction, we've got no other way to trace him. I guess this is the way they do business in northern Maine. Even though we didn't find any boat or sails or anything nautical on the farm, Cornwell's still our main suspect."

"What about that note I gave you?"

"There were no fingerprints on it, sorry."

"Ah, well, I figured we weren't going to get a break. But good news that we still have a suspect. We're still missing the third girl on the list of four I started with, and I need to concentrate on her now."

"Four girls? I thought there were only three."

"The fourth was a case from right here in Pequod, about twenty years ago. We found her body today; at least I'm pretty sure. Should have confirmation by tomorrow."

"Congratulations. I think you have a real talent for this, Rhe."

"Well, it's not talent I'm celebrating right now. Anything else going on?"

"Bongiovanni wants a meeting sometime tomorrow, but we haven't been able to get a hold of Chief Brewster to set it up. Do you know where he is?"

"Yeah, he was with us, locating that body." *More like he was avoiding answering his phone.* "I'll see him tonight. Should he call you or Bongiovanni? What's the meeting for?"

"I think he wants to spread out what we've got and brainstorm for some ideas."

More likely they've run out of their own ideas and want to pick our brains for where they should go next. "I'll get Chief Brewster to call Bongiovanni tonight."

∾∾

Sam showed up just as we sat down for dinner, early for once. I'd already calculated he'd be there and had made extra lamb patties and ratatouille. I was experimenting with new recipes now I had time in the afternoon and a kid willing to try them. And Sam, the gourmand. I looked pointedly at Jack, then Sam. "We need to talk *later* about what I'm going to be doing next."

Sam got the hint. "You bet...Jack, what's happening at school?" Dinner became a relaxing smorgasbord of small talk, laughs, and food. It seemed like ages since I'd enjoyed a meal like this one. Jack finished his homework with Sam's help, and when he disappeared to take his shower, Sam helped me clear the table and put the dishes in the dishwasher. *Just like an old married couple*, I thought.

"I'm glad you left when you did," Sam said as we were slotting the plates. "It took Marsh forever to finish uncovering the bones." I closed the dishwasher door, pushed the wash button, and we sat down again at the table, water sloshing in the background.

"What happened after the bones were freed?" I asked quietly.

"Marsh took the remains back to his autopsy suite and was kind enough to compare the skull's teeth with Deirdre Dunn's dental records right away. It's her, just as you thought."

Despite the fact I had accepted it, tears tickled my eyes.

"She had a broken jaw and a depressed fracture of the back of the skull. Fits Artie's story."

"Is there any way to know if she was dead when Mr. Dunn buried her?" I asked, swallowing hard.

"According to Marsh, no, not absolutely. But he thinks the depressed fracture would have knocked her out, not killed her. The resulting internal bleed would have been slow and she eventually would have suffocated."

I shook my head at the horror of that picture. *May Dunn rot in hell.*

"I'll call Artie tomorrow, let him know what we found, get him back here for a statement. He'll need to claim Deirdre's remains for burial." From the look on Sam's face, I could tell he didn't want to talk about it anymore.

"Oh, Sam," I whispered, "this has been horrible." I reached across and wrapped one of his huge hands in mine. "I'm just glad we finally know what happened to her, after all these years." We just sat there for a long while, letting our memories fill the silence. Finally, I spoke. "Now if we could only find Jane Alderson and give her parents some peace of mind."

He nodded. Silence resumed. I got up and made a pot of real coffee to have something to do. When he'd drunk some, Sam asked, "Speaking of peace of mind, what's happening with the situation at the hospital?"

"Other than starting back to work on Monday, I'm pushing forward with the law suit. Security *was* called off the day I was beaten, and with any luck, I'm going to be able to show the order came from Manning." I leaned back in my chair. "By the way, I had a good visit with Mr. Donnelly's family today, and he doesn't seem to be an abusive husband…yet. I told Sawyer to let his lawyer know we won't press charges if he gets help for his alcoholism."

"Rhe, you are way too forgiving. I hope this decision of yours doesn't come back to bite you on the ass."

"That's a swear word, Uncle Sam." Jack bounced into the kitchen. "You gotta put a quarter in the jar."

"Will do, kiddo." Sam stood up. "Where's the jar?" Jack brought it over from the counter and Sam duly deposited a quarter on top of the pile already in the jar. Mostly mine.

"Can you stay and play a game with me?"

Just then I remembered my promise to Bowers. "What Uncle Sam needs to do is call Agent Bongiovanni, right Sam?"

He frowned. "Sorry, Jack, but your Mom's right. I do have some phone calls to make.

"How about tomorrow night?"

We all turned to the sound of my cell ringing in the family room. It was Paulette, and her voice told me she was bordering on hysteria. "Rhe, have you seen Sarah? She wasn't outside of school when I went by to pick her up after basketball practice this afternoon. We've been looking for her everywhere. Is Sam there? What are we going to do?"

Dear God, not Sarah.

23

Ten minutes later, Sam and I were both in Paulette's kitchen. Sam had called another deputy to watch our house, and Jack had gone to bed without complaint when I told him Sam and I had to visit Paulette. He's normally a nosy kid, but he didn't ask why. He hadn't been asking a lot of whys lately and I wondered if it had to do with his parents' separation ...or maybe a sense of insecurity?

This kitchen had long been a place of security and calm for me, but now you could cut the tension with a knife. Ted was on the phone, still making calls from a list of Sarah's friends. Tyler was supposedly in bed, but I caught a glimpse of a small worried face peeking in from the adjacent family room. Paulette started out sitting at the kitchen table with me and Sam, her face drawn and pale with worry. But soon she got up and paced back and forth across the kitchen floor, then started making coffee and frantically pulling food from the refrigerator.

Sam watched her for a bit, then said, "Paulette, come and sit down. I need you to give me a precise timeline of what happened this afternoon. Don't leave anything out. Ted, could you join us? I need your information, too."

Paulette and Ted both sat, and I moved my chair next to Paulette's to put my hands over her ice cold ones, clenched in her lap.

"First of all," Sam told them, "we have an Amber Alert out already. I phoned it in before Rhe and I left her house. The entire police department has been put on alert and is looking for Sarah. FBI Special Agent Bowers has been called in as well. We're going to do everything in our power to find her. What I need you to do is to stay as calm as possible and let us do our work."

I wanted to tell Paulette we'd find Sarah, swear to her we would find Sarah, but I couldn't do that. I was sick with guilt; the threat against me had not involved Jack, but Sarah. How could I not have foreseen this mad man would carry out his threat against my best friend and take a little girl who meant the world to me? *Do I tell her? How do I tell her?*

I vaguely heard Sam directing Paulette to begin with when she first realized Sarah could be missing.

"I was supposed to pick her up after basketball practice today. Oh God, this is all my fault." She was wringing her hands now. "I picked Tyler up when he got out, came home, got distracted, and didn't realize until it was too late that I'd forgotten to get Sarah. Why did I do that? If I hadn't, Sarah would be safe!" she wailed.

I rubbed her hands. "If this person was determined to take Sarah, he would find a way," Sam said quietly. "This isn't your fault, Paulette. She was targeted. If he hadn't snatched her today, he'd just look for another opportunity."

"Targeted? Why? Why would he target Sarah?"

Sam immediately realized where this was heading. "Each of the other girls who were taken was also targeted, and we don't know why."

Paulette thought for a minute, and then asked the question I was dreading. "Is it because I'm friends with Rhe, and Rhe has been working with the FBI and you to find those missing girls?" Her eyes grew wide with realization. "He threatened *you*, didn't he?" she practically spit at me. "That's why Sam's been sitting outside your house at night! And since he couldn't get to you, he chose Sarah. She fits the bill, doesn't she? How could you let this happen, Rhe?" She pulled her hands away from mine and glared at me with a hatred I'd never seen. I shrank back into my seat.

"This is not Rhe's fault, Paulette," said Sam. "I know how distraught you are but blaming her for the actions of this lunatic is not going to help the situation."

Tears came unbidden as I looked at my best friend. "I never wanted this to happen," I pleaded with her. "Yes, someone did threaten me, but never in a million years did I think he would target anyone but me! We did warn the schools, and you all got a notice, didn't you?"

Paulette turned away from me. Sam asked her to continue, which she did with a wavering voice. "By the time I got to Sarah's school, there was no one outside. I went inside, looked around for Sarah, and finally found her basketball coach. She told me Sarah had gone out front to wait with some of her teammates. She didn't know what happened after that, but the assistant coach was supposed to be out there with them."

"Did any of her teammates see her leave? Ted?"

"Some of them talked to her while they were waiting. But so far, all of them left before she did. I still have two calls to make."

"Why don't you go ahead and make those calls now? If you find anything, I'll head over to talk to the girl in person."

Ted stood up, gave me a long look, and walked into the family room to make his calls.

"Paulette, do you know the name of the assistant coach?" Sam asked. "I need to talk to her."

"It's Lydia, Lydia Waters. But I already called her. She didn't see anything because she went back into the school for a couple of minutes to use the bathroom."

"Give me her number anyway. Maybe she's remembered something by now."

Paulette got up, fished a roster out of the drawer under the toaster and thrust it at Sam. He stepped away to make the call. Paulette went into the family room to stand beside Ted.

Sam snapped his phone shut and shook his head. "She's so defensive, I'm going to need to see her in person."

Overwhelmed, I leaned my head down on the kitchen table. *I can't even cry. It's just too much to bear.*

I felt Sam's hand on my shoulder. "I'm so sorry, Rhe, I opened a can of worms, didn't I? Me and my big mouth."

I raised my head and saw the concerned look on his face. I took a deep breath. "It's not your fault either. I would have had to tell Paulette sooner or later. There's no way I could have kept this from her. Plus she would have figured this out on her own without any hint. She's smart."

"At least it's out in the open. She's going to need you more than ever now. You two have been so close for so long, I know you'll work this out."

At that point, Ted came back into the kitchen holding his phone out. "It's the Pattersons. Their daughter Casey may have seen something."

Sam stood and grabbed the phone. "Hello?" Pause. "Yes, this is Chief Brewster. Yes, I need to talk to Casey." Pause. "Yes, I can understand she'd be upset, but I still need to talk to her. Can I come over?" Pause. "Yes, I know where you are. I'll be there in a few minutes. See if you can calm her down in the meantime. Thanks."

To Ted and Paulette, he said, "I'm going to see the assistant coach after the Pattersons. Stay here, just in case there's a phone call. I'll let you know whatever I find out, and I'm sending a Community Outreach officer over here to be with you.

I stood as well and went to follow Sam. "I don't want her working on this case," said Paulette just as we reached the door.

"And why not?" asked Sam. "She's done what no one else could do with the other cases. Why would you cut off your nose to spite your face?"

There was no answer and when I looked back, Paulette had turned away. Once again Sam had come to my defense.

It was such a relief to be outside that kitchen. I took deep breaths, burning my lungs with the cold air, and got into Sam's Jeep.

߭ࠍ

We were at the Patterson's in less than five minutes since they lived in the same neighborhood, just in a newer, add-on development which had been built about five years later than mine. The homes looked more cookie-cutter: square two-story boxes in various shades of brown or gray or blue with white trim. The front door of the Patterson's gray house opened before we'd even climbed the front porch stairs.

"Mr. Patterson?" asked Sam as he reached the porch. "I'm Sam Brewster, Chief of Police." He pulled off a glove and extended a hand.

"Nate Patterson," replied the man who filled the doorway. They shook hands, then Sam turned and introduced me, telling him I'd been working on cases of other girls who'd disappeared under similar circumstances. We followed him into a wide, hardwood-floored foyer and then into a square room on the left, plainly furnished with a soft gray rug, comfortable chairs and a long blue couch along the far wall. A short, rather stocky woman was perched on its edge. She was holding the hands of a thin, anxious-looking girl, who regarded Sam with wide eyes. Mrs. Patterson was introduced as Sharon and her broad, rather plain face lit up with a polite but nervous smile as she greeted us.

Casey, their daughter, was an interesting amalgam of mother and father. She was tall, like her father, but thin, and had her mother's plain face and light hair. She turned her head into her mother's shoulder when Sam, who sat in a chair opposite the sofa, asked her softly, "Casey, I need to know what you saw this afternoon, who picked up Sarah, what the person looked like, what the car looked like. Can you do that?"

Casey nodded with her face still buried in her mother's sweater. At a prompt from her mother, she turned and faced Sam. He took out his ever present notebook and pen, while I sat, transfixed by the scene, in a chair adjacent to Sam's.

I hadn't been introduced, and when Casey got a good look at me for the first time, she asked, "Who's she? Is she a policewoman?"

I smiled at Casey and her mother, told them who I was, and then added earnestly, "I'm hoping I can help find Sarah. I know whatever you tell us, Casey, will be very, very useful and may lead us to Sarah."

Casey nodded, and looking at me, began. "Okay. After practice, Sarah and I were standing with the other girls from the basketball team, you know, in the area where students wait to get picked up. My mom always comes rolling up late," here she gave her mother an accusatory look, "so Sarah and I were the last ones there. I wasn't worried, but Sarah said it was odd her mom was late because her parents had been hovering lately. You know, watching everything she did. My parents have been doing that, too, but Sarah was ticked off 'cause she thought they weren't trusting her. I think she just got tired of waiting, so she told me she was going to walk home."

"Walk home?" Mrs. Patterson asked. "That's such a long way!"

"She was pretty mad, Mom."

"Where was Ms. Waters? Wasn't she supposed to be out there with you?" Sam asked.

"She had to use the ladies' room and left when there were still several of us there," replied Sarah. "I don't know why she didn't come back."

That fit with what Sam had heard from Ms. Waters herself. "Then what happened?" I asked, anxious to hear what she had to say. "Did you see something, Casey?"

"Well, there was this car, parked just as you turn into the pick-up lane. I noticed it because it was just sitting there. I figured maybe it was a parent, waiting for their kid to come out of the school. But when Sarah walked off...I begged her not to, Mom, really..." Casey looked at her mother and started to tear up.

"Shhh, dear, it's okay, it's not your fault." Mrs. Patterson tightened her hold around her daughter's shoulders. "Tell them what happened then."

Casey looked back at me and seemed to calm down. "Well, when Sarah got to the other side of the street and was heading down Warren Avenue, the car sitting there pulled out and tried to turn around. But there was a car just pulling into the pick-up line behind him, and he couldn't. So he drove through the pick-up lane and around the parking lot to get out."

"You said he," said Sam. "Was the person driving this car a man?"

"Yeah, it was definitely a man."

"Can you describe the car?" Sam moved to the edge of his seat, leaning forward, hanging on her every word.

"Well, it was blue and old, you know, dented and a little rusty. It was small, too."

"By small, do you mean it had only two doors?" I asked.

"No, it had four doors, but it was low to the ground and small. It was very squared off," Casey replied.

"Good girl, Casey. You're very observant." I figured a little encouragement wouldn't hurt.   "Then what?"

"Then the car just drove by me and headed down Warren, you know, the way Sarah was walking."

"Can you tell me more about what the driver looked like?" Sam asked.

"I couldn't see him very well. He had on a wool hat and it was pulled way down. I'm sorry." Casey's face crumpled and she started to cry. "I wish I could have seen him better. That would help, wouldn't it?"

Mrs. Patterson put her arm around her daughter's shoulder and pulled her close. "Is that all?" she asked Sam.

"Think, Casey, just a little more," he replied. "Is there anything else you can tell me about the car or the driver?"

"No," she said in a tiny voice, crying harder.

"Casey, why don't you go out to the kitchen with your mother and maybe get us all something to drink," I suggested. "What about cocoa? Would that make you feel better?"

Casey nodded her head, and Mrs. Patterson got up, taking her by the hand and mouthed a 'thank you' to me, grateful she had something she could do with her daughter. They left the room and I sat back in my chair. Sam raised an eyebrow in a question.

"She needed a break. She'll calm down. When they come back, would you let me question her?"

"What do you have in mind?" asked Mr. Patterson.

"A little visualization. Once she's calm, I bet she'll remember more."

❧ ❧

Casey returned with cocoa for all of us, and I smiled my thanks to Mrs. Patterson. The warm, comforting chocolate taste made me feel a little more relaxed myself as I sipped it. Taking my mug, I moved over to the sofa to sit alongside Casey. After putting the mug on the coffee table, I turned to face her. "How would you like to play a game?" She nodded slowly. "Okay, here's what we're going to do. Give your mug to your mom, then we're going lean back on the sofa and relax."

Once we had settled back, I told her, "Now I'd like you to close your eyes. I will, too." She nodded again and closed her eyes. "Casey, I'd like you to think about being at school, see yourself standing outside the school today, waiting for your mom, who's always late." She giggled. "Can you see Sarah standing near you?" I opened one eye to check that she was nodding. "What's she wearing?"

"A red parka, striped scarf, blue hat pulled down over her ears. It looks dorky but I didn't tell her. And those Uggs she loves. Blue ones."

"Sounds pretty colorful."

"Uh huh. Sarah likes to be colorful."

I hesitated a minute. "You told me the blue dented car drove by you, right?"

"Uh huh."

"Take a good look at that car, in your mind. Just let your eyes wander over it. Is there anything else about it that you remember? Take your time. Just focus on the car. Tell me again what color it was."

"Dark blue."

"Great, you're doing fine. What else can you see?"

"I can see the license plate."

Maine requires front and back license plates, so she'd had two chances to get a look. "Think about the car. Can you tell me what the license plate looked like?"

"Well, it was dented. Mmmm, I remember it was sort of different. There was a lobster on it." *A vanity plate. Great, that reduces the number of possibilities from maybe a million to several thousands.*

"Can you see any numbers or letters, Casey? Just relax and focus on the license plate."

It was quiet for a few moments, then she answered hesitantly, "Well…it says Maine at the top." Another pause. "There's an A. And a nine, I see a nine."

"Anything else about the license plate?"

"Nooooo….."

"Okay, Casey. Keep your eyes closed. You're doing great!"

"Am I really?"

"Yes, you are. Now I want you to think about the driver. Concentrate on the man. Can you remember anything else about him?"

Silence. Then, "He was really big."

"What do you mean really big?"

"Well, the car was small, and he seemed to fill the whole front of it. And he was wearing a parka. Dark, maybe green?"

"Anything else, dear?"

More silence. Time ticked by, and I thought maybe Casey had fallen asleep, so I opened my eyes. I saw Sam had been taking notes in his little notebook and when I looked at Casey, her forehead was wrinkled. She was still thinking. Finally she said, "There was a sticker on the back window. It looked like a tennis ball with a bird on top. You know, with its wings spread?"

That particular detail didn't mean anything to me, but it did to Sam. He scribbled something in the notebook. Casey opened her eyes and looked at me. "That's about all I can remember. Will it help?"

I gave her a big hug. "You were wonderful, Casey. You remembered a lot and what you told us will be a big help. Thank you so much!"

Casey beamed, then yawned, so I stood and indicated with my head to Sam that we should go. We shook hands with both Patterson parents, and thanked them and Casey again. Sam handed Mr. Patterson his card, then told him to call if Casey remembered anything else.

"So what now, Sam?" I asked as we walked back to his Jeep. Just then his cell phone buzzed, and he stopped to answer it.

"Yeah, we just finished talking to the little girl who was outside the school with Sarah. Got some leads...Now? ...Sure, see you at the station."

"Who was..?"

"Bongiovanni. He wants to meet with us. Now." He looked at me. "You okay with that?"

"Yeah, but I'll need someone to be in the house with Jack, in case he wakes up. I could call Will, but that will open a real can of worms."

"Anyone else you can think of? Other than Paulette?"

Sigh. "No. I'll call him." *Could things possibly get any worse?*

24

Thirty minutes after calling Will, I sat at the scarred wooden table in the Police Department's conference room, yawning and drinking freshly made coffee. I really didn't care about the caffeine at that point.

It turned out Will had been surprisingly accommodating when he heard Sarah had gone missing. He said he'd do anything to help, arrived in fifteen minutes, and took the sleepy Jack to his place, with a promise to get him to school on time the next morning.

"So what are we looking at here, folks?" asked Agent Bongiovanni. He was seated across the table next to Bowers, who looked energized and ready to roll. Both of them looked expectantly at me.

I suddenly felt like I'd been flattened with a spatula and just couldn't muster the strength to tell them about Sarah. Sam stepped into the breach. Clearing his throat, he opened his little notebook. "Sarah McGillivray left Cardinal Middle School today at approximately 4:30 PM to walk home. She never made it. Her mother called me a little after seven, after she and her husband had done a preliminary search. Casey Patterson, a friend of hers, had been waiting with her for their rides to show up. According to both Casey and Sarah's parents, Sarah was wearing a red parka, striped scarf, and blue hat and blue Uggs."

"What are Uggs?" asked Bowers.

"You know, those soft suede boots with a furry lining the kids like to wear," replied Sam. He looked at Bongiovanni, who nodded in agreement. Sam then relayed what Casey had told us. He finished by saying, "An assistant coach was supposed to be outside, waiting with them, but according to Casey, she went inside to use the ladies room and didn't come back. I called her, but she's defensive and I didn't get much. I'll interview her tomorrow, unless you folks want to."

"I'll do that personally," said Bongiovanni, taking out his notebook. "What's her name?"

"Lydia Waters."

Bongiovanni wrote it down. "Maybe the FBI shield can shake out some information."

"Anything more on the car?" Bowers asked, taking notes.

"Yeah. Old, square and dark blue, with a Maine vanity license plate with a lobster on it. Casey remembers an A and a nine. And on the back window of the car there was a sticker that looked like a tennis ball with a bird sitting on it."

"Interesting," said Bongiovanni. "The surveillance video of the hospital parking lot around the time Rhe got that note showed a similar car pulled up next to hers. Too grainy to make out anything more than that and we couldn't enhance it. But the guy who got out of the car was big." He paused. "Anyone got any further ideas?"

No one responded. I sat there in a fog of my own emotions.

"If not," Bongiovanni continued, "I'm going to amend the BOLO and the Amber Alert. Bowers, I need you to get moving on that license plate." Bowers jumped up and left the room.

Bongiovanni turned to Sam. "Chief, you got any ideas on what kind of car it might be?"

"I gave the description to Phil, and he's going to compile a lineup of possibilities we can show to Casey tomorrow."

"What about the sticker?"

"Well, it sounded to me like maybe a military sticker. Both the Navy and the Marines have an insignia with a bird, but only the Marines have something resembling a tennis ball, you know, the globe with an eagle sitting on it. We'll show it to Casey as well and see what she says."

Bongiovanni turned to me. "Any thoughts?"

I shook my head. The knowledge that Sarah was missing and all of the associated horrible thoughts that went with it, plus the confrontation with Paulette, had sapped whatever energy I had. I tried to get to my feet, swayed, and slid back into the chair. Sam jumped up, asking if I was okay, and took my arm as I tried to stand again. "Rhe, you need to get some rest." Turning to Bongiovanni, he added, "If it's okay with you, I'm going to take her home and will meet you back here in about thirty minutes."

⧉

When my alarm went off at seven, I groaned, rolled over and shut it off. I'd had a restless night, only falling deeply asleep sometime after four. For a minute I just lay there, enjoying the comfort and warmth of my bed and the colors of the quilt my sister had made me, eye-dazzling in the early morning sun. Then the events of the day before crowded in, and I turned my face into the pillow, trying to hide from the truth, much like Casey had turned into her mother's shoulder the night before. The pillow didn't offer any comfort. I went over mentally what I needed to do that day: call Sam, find out what had turned up overnight; pick Jack up after school; talk to Paulette. There was no way to avoid that one.

I rolled out of bed, took a hot shower and by 730 was in the kitchen, dressed and sitting at the table with my cell phone, again drinking real coffee. I also had a stack of cinnamon toast. My phone rang. *Bob Morgan. Just what I need. And at this ungodly hour.* I knew what he wanted and it ticked me off.

"Hi, Bob. What's it this time?"

"Is that anyway to greet a friend?"

"I'm never sure if you're a friend, a reporter or a Lothario." Silence. "I'm sorry, Bob, that was uncalled for. I'm out of sorts today." *And the last thing I want to do is talk to you.*

"It's okay. I'll just chalk it up to your hormones."

"Look, just color me bitchy. What can I do for you?"

"I was going to ask you how the old kidnapping cases were coming along, but I got word this morning that Paulette McGillivray's daughter is missing. What can you tell me?"

I didn't answer. Whatever I told him, there'd be reporters hounding Paulette and Ted and even Tyler every time they stepped outside their house. If I didn't say anything, he'd find out anyway.

"Rhe? Are you still there?"

"Yeah, I'm still with the program. I know you've seen the Amber Alert, and it has as much information as we have." *Lie.* "We don't have much to work on right now." *Another lie.* "But please, please, you've got to promise me that you will not bother the family. *Do not* send out reporters and photographers to their house. They're suffering enough. I'll talk to them today about naming a spokesperson who can interact with the news media. With regard to the *Post and Sentinel*," this last was dripping with sarcasm, "the spokesperson will deal directly with you. What about it? Deal?"

Now it was Bob's turn to be silent. Finally he replied, "Okay, I'll do it your way. But I can't keep the rest of the press away."

"You can if you wait a day or so before putting it out there."

I could hear him hissing between his teeth on the other end of the line. "I've got to think about the paper, Rhe. It's going to look bad if everyone in town knows what's going on and the paper doesn't print anything."

"Just one day. Let the FBI get a handle on this."

"Okay, one day. But I expect a statement from the FBI and that spokesperson tomorrow bright and early."

"You'll get it, and thanks, Bob. I owe you for this one."

"Consider us even."

As soon as Bob hung up, I dialed Sam. He picked up after the first ring. "Rhe, how're you feeling?"

"Good...okay, not so good. I didn't sleep well. What's happened since last night?" I couldn't keep the nerves out of my voice and got up and poured myself another cup of coffee. When I sat down again, I realized my toast was cold but started eating it anyway.

"Well, Phil came up with several cars similar to what Casey described. And I've printed out some images that might fit her description of a bird on a tennis ball. I'm heading over to the Patterson's house now. Wanna come along?"

"I think I'll pass. I need to go talk to Paulette and Ted." I sighed and pushed the rest of the toast away.

"I was going to go there after I meet with the Pattersons. Why don't I swing by and pick you up? Maybe you could use a little backup."

"Thanks, Sam, you're a dear. I'll be ready when you get here. And Sam? You should know Bob Morgan is hot after this story. He called this morning, and I managed to talk him into waiting a day to publish anything. I also told him that Paulette and Ted would have a spokesperson so they're not hounded by the media. Can you think of anyone to do that for them?"

I heard a low chuckle. "Well sugar, I think the best spokesperson would be you."

"Paulette will never agree to that! I think she'd rather have the devil himself in that role before me."

"Let's wait and see before we reach that conclusion, okay?"

"Sure, but I'm not hopeful. And Sam, could you make sure the heater is working in your Jeep?"

☙ ❧

When Sam arrived about an hour later, I was waiting in the kitchen with some fresh coffee for him. He looked tired, the bags under his eyes pronounced and his whole body sagging in on itself. He gave me a brief hug before slumping into one of the kitchen chairs without taking off his coat.

I put a steaming mug in front of him and sat. "I figured you might need this. Did you get any sleep last night?"

"A couple of hours." He wrapped his hands around the mug before pouring in some cream and adding four spoonsful of sugar.

"So what happened at the Pattersons?"

"Casey picked out what she thought was the car. I showed her pictures of common cars from the 1990s, since the shape of cars became more rounded after 2000."

I snorted. "Yeah, Jack and I call those jelly bean cars. What did she choose?"

"A Ford Escort."

"Was she sure? The Escort looks a lot like a 1990's Festiva or even Tempo."

"How do you know that? Don't tell me you ran a garage in your youth?"

"Don't you remember my Uncle Charlie? The guy with the gas station out near US1?"

Sam thought for a minute and then nodded. "Vaguely."

"When I was in high school, I liked to hang out there. He showed me how to repair cars that came in for service. If I hadn't become a nurse, I coulda been a righteous car mechanic."

"No doubt," he replied with a wink.

"So was Casey positive about the Escort?"

"Not completely but almost. She identified the eagle and orb Marine insignia, though, so that's a big help. We're going to identify anyone locally who served in the Marines and see what they have for a car and license plate. Bowers is on that."

We sat there without speaking for a while, not really having much else to say, and Sam needed time to get energized with coffee. Finally he pushed away from the table, rising with an effort. "Okay, let's go talk to Paulette and Ted." I put on my coat and followed him out the door.

We ended up walking to their house. Sam needed time to clear out what mental cobwebs the coffee hadn't, and I needed to work on what I could possibly say to mend fences with Paulette. We were both bracing for what waited for us there. I automatically headed down the drive and around to the kitchen door, so deep in thought that I left Sam heading up the walkway to the front door without even realizing it. He stopped when he realized I wasn't with him and caught up to me at the stairs to the back door.

As soon as I opened the storm door, Paulette had the kitchen door open. She looked awful: puffy, bloodshot eyes, hair in a rat's nest, still wearing the same clothes from the previous night. She gave us an anxious look, but stood back and let us both in without a word. Typical Paulette: she wanted to know but she didn't want to know. Ted was standing at the kitchen counter, coffee mug in hand. "Sam, is there any news? Officer Danforth," and here he indicated a uniformed policeman standing in the door to the family room, "hasn't had anything to tell us we didn't already know."

"I think we may have a place to start. Let's sit down so I can bring you up to date." Sam took off his coat, slung it over a kitchen chair and sat down, then motioned for Danforth to join us. Paulette was in her usual seat before I even got my coat off. She and Ted listened quietly as Sam summarized what he'd learned from Casey that morning and where the search would now head. He reiterated that a BOLO and an Amber Alert were in effect with the latest information. When he finished, Paulette's eyes filled with tears.

"It's been almost twenty-four hours, Sam. What are the odds we're going to find her alive?" Ted asked, his voice wavering.

Sam rubbed his face with his hand. "I'm not going to paint a rosy picture, Ted. The odds aren't great, but this time we have some leads. Plus we know this guy doesn't kill the girls he kidnaps, at least not immediately."

"So what! He rapes and abuses them. What am I going to do? My daughter is out there with that monster and I can't help her!" Paulette put her head in her hands and shook with silent sobs.

Ted moved his chair over and pulled her to him. "Paulette…honey… I feel the same way. But you've got to hold it together, if only for Tyler. We can't let him feed on our emotion. He's not old enough to handle it." Gradually Paulette's sobbing quieted and finally she sat up and wiped her face with a napkin. I wanted so much to throw my arms around her and tell her everything was going to be okay, but I knew she'd shove me away if I even got near her.

"We've just got to let the FBI do their work and stay calm," said Sam in a quiet voice. "I know that's going to be pretty much impossible, but you've got to try. Especially since the press now has word of Sarah's abduction and could be here soon."

"What next!" Ted threw his hands up in frustration. "Those people are insatiable. They'll never leave us alone. Look what they did to Rhe last year!"

With those words, Paulette made eye contact with me for the first time. I was surprised not to see anger, but a little recognition, a little understanding. Then she looked away. I realized Sam was talking. "….think you need a spokesperson, to act as an interface with the press, until and unless you are willing to speak with them."

"So this person would talk to them for us?" Ted was a little calmer.

"Yup. They would provide any information you and the authorities are able to share plus any messages from you to Sarah," answered Sam.

"I think a spokesperson would be a good thing to have," Paulette said. "But who are you thinking of? You? One of your deputies or an FBI agent?"

"No, it can't be the police or the FBI. It's usually a family friend. I want to tell you that Rhe's already managed to get Bob Morgan to wait a day before trying to interview you."

Both Paulette and Ted looked at me. Talk about being on the hot seat. I hadn't said a word since I'd entered the kitchen, and now when I opened my mouth, my words came out in a semi-squawk. "Look, I know you blame me for this, and believe me, I've been blaming myself ever since you called yesterday evening. I should have realized that when I'm threatened, everyone around me is in danger. I'm so sorry." Now, I did cry. I couldn't bear what had happened to my closest friends because of me. "I never dreamed in a million years he'd go after Sarah..." I felt a pair of arms wrap around me, and looked up to find Paulette hugging me, tears streaming down her face, too.

"Oh Rhe, I was so mad at you last night, so frightened by what was happening. I had to lash out at someone, anyone. There's no way you could have known this would happen. Ted and I talked and realized you're a victim here, too. We know you would never want anything bad to happen to Sarah. I can't imagine trying to get through this without you." We were both blubbering by the time she finished saying the words I had hoped to hear, but hadn't dared imagine I would.

After a few moments, the ever practical Ted, who by then had tears in his eyes as well, said, "Ladies, if Rhe is going to be our spokesperson, we need to get going on what she's going to say." Over the next half hour, with Sam's help, we outlined a series of releases to the press, both from the PD and from the family. It was decided there would be a press conference in the reception area of the police station at 7 PM that evening, and I would say something then.

When I got home, I called Bob so he could be the first to know. After that, I made myself a tuna fish and pickle sandwich and sat quietly on the couch in the family room, munching and mentally going over all of our clues so far, which were pitifully few. I looked at my sandwich and realized yet again, I'd forgotten to tell Sam about the one from the Munch Box that had made me sick. The only other thing I'd not followed up on were the marks on the sail wrapping Savannah's body. I found my phone and called Marsh.

"Hey, Rhe, long time no see," Marsh said when he picked up.

"I know you're not serious, but I've been a wee bit preoccupied with family stuff, and now there's another girl missing."

"Anyone we know?"

"Unfortunately, yes. Paulette's daughter Sarah."

The silence on the phone was deafening. Finally Marsh cleared his throat and asked, "Anything I can do?"

"I don't think so, but thanks for the offer…listen, I forgot to ask if you or the state lab had figured out what made the marks on the sail Savannah was wrapped in."

"You're right and I never looked at the report for that. Let me check now. Can you hold on a minute?"

"Sure." I sat down in our recliner and realized as I sank into it, how tense and tired I was. I could hear a drawer open and close and some papers rustling on Marsh's end.

"You still there, Rhe?"

"Yup."

"It says the marks lined up with a type of anchor chain, the kind used on a fairly heavy boat, not a recreational sailboat or anything like that. Probably something commercial. They had no idea of anything specific. It's not much help, sorry. So how're you doing? I heard via the grapevine you're coming back to work on Monday."

"I am, the eight to four shift. I'll stop by on my way in or out to say hi."

"You make sure you do that."

"Thanks, Marsh." The chair was so comforting, I dropped off to sleep, waking with a start some two hours later when Tux, our cat, jumped in my lap and began to kneed and purr. He was hungry. One look at the clock and I realized I needed to hurry to pick up Jack from school on time. Even though the schools were now on alert and a patrolman was watching Jack, I still worried he could be a target.

25

That evening, the press conference took place as scheduled at the police station. There were fifteen or twenty reporters crammed into the reception area, all waving their microphones at anyone they thought might have even a tidbit of information. Ruthie sat at her desk, glowering at the reporters, daring anyone to ask her a question.

When I stepped to the makeshift podium, cameras started to roll and the lights for TV made the room so bright, I had to turn away. Sam asked in a stentorian voice for someone to turn off a few lights, and the room immediately went from blazing to just bright. I turned back to face the reporters, all of whom began yelling questions.

Once again, Sam stepped in. "If you don't stop yelling, there will be no information provided." The room became nearly quiet. "Rhe Brewster, the spokesman for the McGillivrays, will read a statement from the family." Bob Morgan was right at the front, nodding encouragement to me as I began to speak.

I took a deep breath and tried to keep my voice moderated and steady. "As most of you know by now, there was a kidnapping yesterday here in Pequod. Sarah McGillivray, aged eleven, was taken on her way home from school. We will circulate a picture of Sarah to you, if you don't already have one." I went on to describe what Sarah was wearing and asked that the family not be harassed at this time (*as if that would do any good*). "The family does not want to make any personal statements to the press right now, but there will be regular announcements here at the police station as we learn more. And that's all I have at this time."

Then I turned the podium over to Sam, who basically told them what I had already said, but added, "There will be a law enforcement presence at both the family home and at Sarah's school. Any attempt on the part of the press to get to the family or Sarah's teachers or classmates will be met with a trespass arrest."

As if that will do any good.

He did not reveal the information we had on the car, because we were still unsure if it was accurate. Sam also felt it might engender vigilantism. He then introduced Agent Bongiovanni, who basically told them what Sam and I had said. Bongiovanni announced they would take a few questions, at which point I tried to slip out of the room and out of the building without being followed. This proved easy because every reporter but one was trying to shout over the others in their eagerness for new information. Bob caught up with me as I reached the station's parking lot.

"Wait, Rhe, can I ask you a few questions?"

"Not really. You heard what Sam said." I'd known this was going to happen but was irritated nonetheless. "We can't offer anything more, but we'll give you an exclusive, just as we did last fall, when this case is resolved."

"That's great to hear, but I need something for tomorrow's paper. I've got nada, ziltch, goose eggs here."

"Okay, how about this? I'm the spokesperson for the family and I can tell you they're devastated. Although everyone's been taking precautions since the flyer went out three days ago, it wasn't enough. We're working with a very clever man."

"Are you certain it's a man?"

I chuckled. "Did you see the flyer? And when was the last time you heard of a female serial kidnapper of young girls?"

"I'll give you that one. Anything else?"

"How about you do a little investigation of your own?"

"What do you mean?" Bob looked interested.

"Well, you're supposed to be, or were, an investigative reporter. How about finding the guy your father sold the sails to? The FBI and the police haven't made any headway and the sail was a good lead."

Bob frowned and nodded. "You're right. I should have followed up on that."

"Well, make some magic. Sorry, but I need to get home now to …" I hesitated, "…to get Jack to bed."

"Let me walk you to your car."

Miss Daisy was parked a way down the street because of all the reporters' cars in the parking lot. The street, thanks to a couple of lights being out, wasn't particularly well-lit.

"This also gives me a chance to chat with you, more than our usual confrontations," he said, slipping his arm around my free one.

Uh oh. "Chat about what?"

Bob cleared his throat and hesitated a bit before answering. "I don't know why you've been so short with me the last few times we've talked, but you need to know I'm still your friend."

"Short with you? I'm pregnant, in case you haven't noticed, and the hormones take me up and down a lot. And I'm getting clumsy, which *is* irritating." Right on cue, I stumbled on an uneven brick in the sidewalk. Bob put his arm around me to steady me.

"No, it's not that," he said smiling. "You look just as gorgeous with this pregnancy as you did with the last, by the way."

"Ah, that's my Bob – ever the silver-tongued wordsmith," I replied with a barely suppressed smile.

He hesitated again. "Rhe, something's off with you lately. You're usually so upbeat, but you're, well, you seem down. Is there anything I can do?'

"Didn't I just explain I'm pregnant? Trust me, if there were something you could help me with, I'd tell you. But there's not, really." *I'm such a liar.* "And that's all I'm going to say."

We had arrived at my Jeep, and I fished in my bag for the key. Bob looked at me for a long moment. "You're an amazing woman, do you know that?"

I felt myself flush. He was still the handsome man I had known for so many years, casually tousled, tawny hair and warm hazel eyes that had once melted my heart. *Where the heck is he going?* I tried to deflect him. "Go on with you. I know you're trying to make me feel better, and if compliments alone would do it, you're succeeding."

"I mean it, Rhe. You're incredible." Suddenly, he leaned over and kissed me on the lips, lingering just long enough to let me know that this was a more than friendly gesture. Surprisingly, I didn't jerk back, but found myself enjoying it. When he pulled away, my feelings were jumbled. I liked that kiss. *Get a grip, Rhe. This is Bob, the womanizer.* I must have been staring at him and lost my concentration because I fell back against the car door.

"You must know I still have feelings for you," he said softly.

I finally came to my senses and shook my head in amazement. "What are you doing? Hitting on a married woman! We're not teenagers anymore!"

Bob had the decency to flush. "Yeah, I was a real shithead back then, wasn't I? But I'm serious now. I never lost track of you over the years and I'd hoped we would link up again one day. Then I got ambitious and you got married."

"That's just it, Bob, I'm married...m-a-r-r-i-e-d. And pregnant! You just *think* I'm having problems, so you make a move on me? Even for you, that's low." *How could he make me so angry?*

Bob just smiled his usual lop-sided, aren't-I-cute grin I knew so well. "Tell me you didn't enjoy that kiss, just a little. I know you did."

He was right, of course, and that just made me angrier. I lost it and slapped him, not hard, but it surprised both of us. "You're never going to change!" I yelled. I turned around, unlocked the door, got in the car and slammed the door behind me. I laid rubber getting out of the parking space. When I looked in my rearview mirror, he was still standing there, rubbing his cheek.

⚫

Saturday morning, Sam called with a possible break. "We tracked down three former Marines here in Pequod. Two of the three have cars match Casey's description. One of them is Peter Barnes'."

"Peter Barnes! That's a surprise. What's the plan?"

"I'm going to start by visiting Scott Gunnerson, then Peter. Want to come along?"

"I can't, got Jack this weekend. Call me as soon as you know anything?"

"Will do."

I hung up and stood for a minute in the middle of the family room, where Jack was watching his Saturday morning Nickelodeon shows. *I can't help it, I have to know. There's no police outside to follow me right now...* "Come on, Jack, we're going to buy some lobsters for dinner." Jack, who loved to watch the lobsters in the tanks, got into his coat and boots in record time and five minutes later we were on our way to the lobster co-op, where I hoped we might find Peter's car in the parking lot.

After we parked in the co-op lot, I got out, telling Jack to stay in the car for a minute.

"Why, Mom? Aren't we going to buy lobsters?"

"Yes we are, but I need to look at my tires first. I think one of them is soft."

I started walking carefully around the car, taking in every car in the lot while pretending to look at my tires. There was a red Ford Festiva I'd noticed coming in, parked behind where I'd stopped, and since Jack was for once sitting still and facing front, I backed away and walked over to it. I circled the car and sure enough, there was a globe, anchor and eagle insignia stuck on the back window. Unfortunately, the car was red. However, it was really shiny for winter driving on the roads in Pequod, no rust, no salt ring. I took out my key and made a tiny scratch in the paint low on the rear bumper, where I thought it wouldn't be seen. There was dark blue underneath.

I heard the Jeep door open and Jack yelled, "Where are you, Mom? When are we going to buy the lobsters?"

I looked up and noticed two figures come out the side door on the second floor of the co-op building and start down the stairs. I crouched to keep hidden from their line of sight and scurried back to the Jeep, emerging from its rear just as Jack climbed out of the car and the two figures hit the bottom of the stairs. It was Pete and James.

I closed the door and grabbed Jack's hand. "Let's go!"

As we came up to the two brothers, Pete said, "Hi, Rhe, what brings you here today?" He smiled and although his greeting was friendly, I nearly froze in my tracks. *What if he knew?*

I forced a smile. "Hi, Pete. James, right?" James nodded. "I decided to treat us to some lobsters tonight. Haven't had any in quite a while. How's the co-op's supply?"

"Stocked, especially for the bigger ones, but they're really hard shell. You'll need some nutcrackers and shears to get at the meat."

"Thanks for the advice. See ya." I hurried Jack into the ground floor store. Once we'd gotten inside, I turned to watch the brothers. James was walking around their car. I hoped he didn't see the scratch, or if he did, he wouldn't think I'd made it.

As soon as we were back in the car, lobsters in tow, I called Sam to tell him what I'd found out. As usual, he was apoplectic I'd gone off on my own. "Go home and lock your doors. There will be a deputy there when you get home. For God's sake, Rhe, when are you going to get some common sense? No, don't answer that. I already know the answer."

❧

Sam knocked on my front door around 7 PM, took off his coat and boots in the hallway and carried them into the kitchen. I could tell from his face he was still grumpy with me because of my trip to the lobster co-op.

Two, one and a half pound lobsters were steaming on a platter in the center of the newspaper-covered kitchen table. Nut crackers and shears were at the ready, along with three cups of melted butter, a roll of paper toweling and a large bowl to throw the shells in. Jack was already sitting at the table wearing a plastic bib, provided by the co-op, tied around his neck and covering his front. I was wearing mine as well. There were three dinner plates on the table, and a bag of potato chips and a salad ready to complement the lobster.

"Sit. You're just in time." I smiled at him to counteract his scowl.

"Rhe, you only got two."

"Don't worry, Uncle Sam," explained Jack. "Two is plenty. I can't eat a whole one. Mom just gives me a claw and I like to pick for body meat."

Sam relaxed and sat down, tucked a napkin into his shirt, and taking one lobster, easily disconnected both claws and the tail and handed one claw to Jack. The other claw and the tail remained on his plate and he returned the body to the platter. I handed him the salad and gave one of my claws to Jack, which he manfully struggled to crack. Sam took it from him, easily splitting it open.

"So have you picked up anyone today?" I asked, deliberately making my question neutral.

"We tried, but it seems they've disappeared."

"Got a line on where they might have gone?"

"None, but I've got Phil working on it."

"Is that Deputy Pierce, the guy that likes computers?" asked Jack.

"Yup. He's a whizz. He can find anything," I said.

"I should have him help me on my science project, Mom." Jack gave me a sly grin.

❧❧

The following day, Sunday, Will had Jack. I was at sixes and sevens after I'd cleaned the house, done all the laundry, including my scrubs for work the next day, and sorted and folded Jack's clothes. My refrigerator was pretty empty, so I reluctantly decided to do some grocery shopping. Grocery shopping was the worst chore in the whole world, and on top of that, I needed to stop to see Paulette and Ted. A depressing thought. I called Sam, got his voice mail, and left him a message to say where I was going. I emphasized I didn't need police protection to buy food.

❧❧

I'd finished shopping at Hannaford, packed my groceries in the trunk, got into the driver's seat and turned the key in the ignition. Nothing. *Oh crap, and it's starting to snow.* I tried again. Nothing. I got out and went to the hood, releasing the latch and pushing the hood up. The battery was disconnected. *How in heck...?* I leaned in to reconnect the cables. At that moment, I felt a sharp push into the middle of my back. A nasty combination of sweat, grime and something else, sweet and metallic, hit my nose. *Blood?* A harsh voice whispered in my ear, "Don't turn around Miz Brewster. Just close the hood, slowly."

Where had I heard that voice before? I straightened up and slowly closed the hood, leaving it unlatched, then took my chances and turned around. It was James Barnes. He was dressed in a parka covered with dark stains and so much grime I couldn't tell the original color. With a gray knit cap pulled low on his head and two days growth of beard, he was menacing, but when I looked closely at his eyes, they were normal. No coloboma. *Does he know the police are looking for him? Of course, you idiot! But his eye...*

241

He jabbed me again, this time in the abdomen. I looked down and saw the gun. "Turn back around." Louder, more insistent.

I complied.

"Now you're going to get in my truck, nice and quiet. That's a real gun I have stuck in your back, so do it!"

I noticed a truck pulled up on the other side of my Jeep with the driver's side door open. He must have just gotten out. As he pushed me toward the truck, I scanned the parking lot frantically, trying to find someone, anyone, who might notice me. Not many people, but there were some. If I got in his car, I'd give up any chance to get away. *This man is a killer. But he wouldn't be dumb enough to fire a gun in front of Hannaford's.* I started screaming at the top of my lungs, "Help me! This man has ..." and that's all I got out, because his arm came around my neck in a choke hold, cutting off the rest of the words. The gun dug more deeply into my back.

He started dragging me by the neck, but I kicked and thrashed, and I could feel him losing his grip. Suddenly, I couldn't feel the gun. What I did feel was a horrible pain on the side of my head, and then nothing.

෧෧෧

I had a vague recollection of being dumped on the ground while a door was unlocked or just opened, then being dragged over a threshold and thrown onto a hard surface. Some mewling sounds came from somewhere, and then things faded again. I don't know how much time passed before I became fully aware of my surroundings, but I came to with the nasty taste of gasoline in my mouth, which was stuffed with a gasoline-flavored something. It was completely dark and body-piercingly cold. I discovered I was bound hand and foot, with my hands behind my back. *Damn it was cold.*

I rolled on my back and wiggled myself to a sitting position, head pounding. My eyes began to make out some darker blobs in the dimness, and from one of them came the mewling sound I'd heard before. I inched my way over. It was Sarah! She was alive, but similarly bound and gagged. *Now what do I do? How do I get us out of here?*

26

I rubbed my mouth up against Sarah's coat but couldn't dislodge the gag. "Ara, el ee." I tried to ask her to help me, but the rag got in the way. I flopped over and scrunched so my face was near her hands, then butted her hands with my head until she got the idea. After a few tries, she managed to pull out my gag. Sucking in huge gulps of fresh air, I tried to clear my head. The side of my head where James had hit me hurt like a sucker, and I had a throbbing headache. I probably had been bleeding because the side of my face felt stiff with something dried. A *concussion? Good thought. At least he hadn't tried to kick me in the stomach.*

"Sarah, honey, are you okay? I'm going try to sit up with my back to you. Then you lie next to me and put your face near my hands." She complied, and I managed to get the gag out of her mouth.

As soon as it was out, she started to sob. In between gasps of air, she told me, "Oh, Aunt Rhe, it's been horrible. I'm so cold. Can you get us out of here?" She sat up and continued gasping and crying, leaning into me until she was spent.

"Aunt Rhe, your coat's all sticky. What is it? It's so dark, I can't see it."

"Don't get scared, it's probably blood, but I've stopped bleeding."

"Did he hit you?"

"Yes, he hit me, but it's not serious. I'll be okay." I needed to reassure her, even if I wasn't too sure myself.

"Where are we? Why is this happening? Can you get me out of here?"

"I don't know, sweetie."

Sarah started to cry again. I couldn't blame her. I felt like crying myself because I had no idea how to answer her questions.

I snuggled up against Sarah, hoping maybe our combined body warmth would help, and tried to soothe her. After a few minutes, I told her, "You sit still a minute. Let me figure out where we are, okay?" I butt-scrunched backwards until I came up against a wall, using that to push myself to my feet. I hopped toward the faint light illuminating the outline of a door, turned and worked at the latch with my hands, but couldn't get it to open. I peered through a crack in the door and saw the hall of the ground floor of Tom O'Neil's barn, with its shelves of marine rope and pictures of boats whose sails Tom had made. *Not Tom! Tom couldn't be involved in this. Now what do I do?*

I hopped back to Sarah and we both sat huddled together for warmth. Sarah leaned into me again and said, "We're not going to get out of this, are we?"

"Never say never, Sarah, I'll find a way." *Yeah, Rhe, if you were Wonder Woman.* "Has he touched you, hurt you in any way?"

"No, but I don't like the way he looks at me."

"I don't like the way he looks at me either. I feel like a piece of cheese being eyed by a rat."

I think Sarah tried to giggle but it came out as a squawk. *Maybe she isn't as badly off mentally as I thought.*

We chatted quietly for what seemed like a long time, then Sarah fell asleep with her head in my lap. I continued to think what I could do. Once, in a similar situation, I had been able to force my bound arms around my rear end and my legs, but this time I was impeded by all my winter layers. I wondered if there was anything in the room I could use to saw through the restraints. I had no time to think further because just then, I heard the creak of the outer barn door opening. I woke Sarah and whispered to her, "He's back. Don't let him see your gag is out. Yell when I tell you to."

The latch to the door jangled and screeched, raised, and the door opened. A man stood in the doorway, letting his eyes adjust to the dimness of the room, a dark menacing shadow in the light from the hall behind him. "Time to go, girlies," he growled. It was James. He strode across the room, picked up Sarah and slung her over his shoulder. He left the room, locking the latch behind him.

He didn't notice my gag was missing but as soon as the door shut, I bent down to the rag and drew it into my mouth, retching on the smell and taste.

Then I pushed myself up on the wall. A few minutes later, James returned. "Are you going to give me any trouble, or do I have to hit you again?" I shook my head several times in an enthusiastic no and waited for him to approach. I bent from the waist and tried to head butt him, but he was too fast, swinging around and catching me by the waist. Cursing and grunting, he dragged me out the door, down the hall and out into the driveway, where his truck sat. *Maybe he was just too tired to hit me again?*

Spitting the rag out of my mouth, I screamed at the top of my lungs, "Help! Help us! Help!"

He laid me on the ground, where I balled up, waiting for the strike.

"Forget it, bitch. No one is going to hear you. Look around. Do you see any lights?" Lifting my head and looking around, I had to concur: it was pitch black. He stuffed the rag back in my mouth, causing me to gag again. Then he stood me up and forced me into the truck bed, where he tied me by the waist with marine rope and knotted it through to a ring embedded in the floor, then shut the truck gate.

Sarah must be in the front seat. Good, at least she'll be warm.

The truck backed up, circled the drive and headed out, north I surmised, based on the constellations in the sky overhead.

&⋅&

The next two hours were excruciating. It was incredibly cold in the truck bed and bumps in the road threw me around. I sat up to look for other cars, figuring maybe I could signal them, get someone to see me, but the road was dark and empty. Finally, I wiggled as close as I could to the truck cab, given the length of the rope, in an effort to block the wind driving itself through my coat and freezing my hands. With my back to the cab, I did the best I could to burrow my hands into my coat. I had managed to rub the gag out of my mouth on the floor while I was wiggling forward, and my breathing got easier. Eventually, despite the cold and probably due to the hit on the head, I drifted off, waking only when the truck came to a jarring halt. I sat up, shivering violently, and noticed the sun was just over the horizon. I heard the truck doors open and close and the sound of a door being grated along the ground. Turning my head I could just see an old barn with rough-hewn sides, tinted here and there with moss.

Eventually James peered over the side of the truck bed. Seeing I was conscious, he said, "Good. Now I won't have to carry you." He climbed into the bed, cut the rope to the ring, dragged me to the truck gate, then cut the restraints at my ankles. After yanking me out, he propped me against the bumper. "You can walk yourself inside. Don't try anything; I've still got the gun." I didn't doubt him because he was holding it to my head.

The outside of the barn smelled of years gone by – must, decay, farm animals. Looking up just before I entered, I saw the open door of a hay loft with a chain suspending a sling, hanging from a strut above the opening. I knew it had been used for carrying hay bales up to the loft. Just below it was an old, painted metal sign, declaring 'Webster for Senate,' rusty with age. Incongruously, I wondered if he'd won. Inside I smelled old hay, corn meal, human feces and heard the scurrying of mice or rats. *I hate rats!*

James pushed me toward the back of the barn, where a curtain had been pulled aside to reveal walls lined with wood paneling. An electric heater sat in the middle, putting out enough warmth to raise the temperature to a habitable level. Two cots were arranged on either side of it. Sarah was now chained to a ring on the back wall, with enough chain running from her wrist cuffs to allow her to sit in an old chair near the heater or lie on one of the cots. A bucket sat on the outer edge of the three-sided room, with a roll of toilet paper next to it.

Just then I noticed one other person: a thin, almost translucent young girl with light brown, matted hair and dead eyes, sitting with her back to the right wall. She was wrapped in a tattered wool plaid bathrobe with nothing on her feet, which looked white and bloodless. When she looked up at me, her face showed no emotion or interest. But she was familiar to me. *Jane Alderson. The third missing girl. I've found her.* I stopped dead in my tracks and James ran into me, swearing and then shoving me ahead.

I saw a new, shiny ring protruding from the left wall. James cut my wrist restraints and grabbed one arm forcefully to turn me around. Facing him, I saw shackles in one hand. He must have thought I was half-frozen or half-dead, so I took advantage of that, lashing out at him with a leg toward his crotch. I swung my other arm, numb and unfeeling as a wooden club, to hit him in the face. He backed up and caught my arm as he fell, dragging me down with him. He was strong, wrestling me over until I lay beneath him, my face showered with his panting spit.

"Thought you had me, didn't you?" He smiled, and the last thing I saw was his coloboma. I passed out without him even hitting me again. When I woke, I was chained to the wall like Sarah and still lying on the dirt floor. Sarah was sitting beside me and was stroking my face.

"Wake up, Aunt Rhe! Wake up!"

I looked at her blearily – everything came rushing back: what had happened, where we were, what was going to happen, Jane Alderson. The headache returned with a vengeance. I rolled to one side and vomited, hoping beyond hope that I didn't have a subdural hematoma, slowly bleeding out into my brain. *Got to move fast, Rhe. Who knows how much longer you'll have any cognitive functions?*

"Are you okay?" she asked me in a quavering voice.

"Don't worry, Sarah, it was just the reaction to a headache. I'll be fine in a little while." I sat up, looked at Jane, who was watching with no expression. "Jane!" I called. She started a bit at the sound of her name but said nothing. "Jane!" I called again. "We've been looking for you. Can you talk to me?" Again, no answer. My stomach sank with the realization of how far gone this child's mind was.

"She wouldn't talk to me either, Aunt Rhe. I asked her what her name was, how long she's been here, but she just stared at me. Look! He brought us warm food and some blankets! You wanna eat?" Sarah had pulled a blanket that smelled of horse over me, but food was the last thing on my mind.

"No, you go ahead, while I rest up."

Sarah got up and walked over to a metal container and lifted the lid. The aroma of hamburgers and French fries wafted out, and my stomach turned again. I rolled on my side, away from Sarah, to get away from the odor and also to think. I had to find some way to loosen my shackles, hopefully before he returned. I *had* to get away, bring help, and there wasn't time to sit around feeling sorry for myself. "Sarah, did you hear the truck drive away?"

"Yes, just a little while ago."

I threw the blanket off and, leaning on the wall, gradually got to my feet. The room rocked for a moment, then settled down. I walked over to the ring in the wall and examined its attachment. There were two screws running through the faceplate of the D ring and into the wall. I worked on the D ring, yanking it up and down, this way and that, hoping James had not drilled both screws into a stud. If one were just through wood paneling, or only partially into a stud, maybe I could work it loose. After a long time, during which my arms became as heavy as lead, one of the screws appeared to loosen. *What to turn the screw with?* I glanced at Sarah and had a thought. "Sarah, can you give me one of your barrettes?"

She took one out of her hair and handed it to me. It was metal, not plastic. *This just might work.* After more yanking and pulling to loosen the screw even more, I put the edge of the barrette back into the screw and tried to turn it. No dice. More yanking, more pulling. After repeating this process several times, I finally got the screw to turn. *Hallelujah!* With a little more work, the screw came out of the wall. Just at that moment our luck turned. We both heard the truck in the driveway and looked at each other in a panic.

"Here, put your barrette back on." I tossed it to Sarah, then jammed the screw through the faceplate and back in the hole, pushing on it hard, to get it in as far as possible. Then I raced over to one of the cots, grabbing a blanket and covering myself as I lay down, turning towards the wall. The barn door swung open with a screech. After a moment, I heard footsteps and partially rolled over. James had changed his clothes for a new-looking dark blue parka, black watch cap pulled down over his ears, and leather gloves. His face remained frozen in a sneer, his black eyes boring into us.

"You ladies find supper to your taste?"

"It was good," replied Sarah, "but I'm still eating. Aunt Rhe isn't feeling good. She's been sleeping. Can I keep some food for her?"

"Sure." Then more quietly, "Although she won't be here much longer." He slung a couple of plastic jugs on the floor. "Here's some drinking water." He took the bucket out of the corner and returned in a few minutes with the bucket and more toilet paper. "Here, it's clean. The smell was getting to me. I'm sure you know what to do with it," he said with a chuckle, then left the barn, closing the door behind him.

I jumped up and raced to the far wall, pulling the screw out and sliding the D ring out from under the faceplate. I still had the shackles around my wrists with the clanking chain, and I looked at them carefully. They were cheap, not real hand cuffs; James had probably gotten them at a store that sold sex toys. Still, pulling on them, I realized I couldn't pull them apart without doing some serious damage to my wrists. I'd already made the big decision: I couldn't free both Sarah and Jane in any reasonable amount of time, and Jane would be a dead weight if we tried to run. I had to try on my own.

Sarah looked at me and, smart kid that she was, knew instinctively what the problem was. "You go, Aunt Rhe. Try to get away from here. I'll be okay and I'll try to protect Jane. It's me he wants anyway. Just don't take too long." This last ended on a quavering note.

Nevertheless, I took a quick look at the ring attaching her chain to the wall. I knew immediately it had been there a long time and was not budging. I went to the cot, rolled up some blankets and pulled another over them. *Not bad, but he'll know it's not me if he gets within ten feet.* I took off my scarf and wrapped it around and around the chain, to stop it from clanking and banging against me. Just then, I thought I heard James walking outside the barn. I'd seen a ladder to the hay loft on the right as I'd come in, so I kissed Sarah on the forehead and told her to be brave, took a look at Jane, who had fallen asleep, then ran for the ladder to the hayloft. I had just reached the loft when the barn door opened again.

"I'm here to get you, Miz Brewster. We're going for ride. You can ride in front this time." The menace was unmistakable.

Walking as quietly as possible to the chain hanging from above the hayloft door, I heard Sarah try to deflect him. "She's been vomiting. Maybe you should wait so she doesn't throw up in your truck." *Smart girl.* At that point I grabbed the chain, put one of my feet on the sling and pushed down, praying the chain was not locked and the contraption would hold my weight. It did, so I pushed myself out of the loft and jumped on the sling, which began to descend rather precipitously, to the accompaniment of a grinding sound from the chain. I just hoped the sound wouldn't register with James for a moment or two.

Just as I hit the ground, I heard him explode. "What's that noise? Goddamn it, where did she go? Where did she go, you little cunt?" There was an audible slap.

Time to move it, but which way? I couldn't stay on the road. Wait, that's east, the sun's not too far over the horizon. So I veered east from the barn, running by a one-story ramshackle house I hadn't seen, and headed across a meadow keeping the house between me and the barn. My goal was a thin stand of pine trees. I'd just plunged into the trees when I heard James yelling. "Where are you, bitch? You can't run far with that chain. I'm coming for you!" Then a guttural laugh. *Yup,*

I thought as I ran clumsily with my hands holding the chain, *I'm just a big piece of cheese. Sorry, little baby, you're in for a rough ride.* And I was leaving a track in the snow like a bright red neon arrow saying, 'She went thataway.'

As I ran, I noticed some tamarack and white pine trees, which I knew from a high school field trip were found in the outer ring of a bog. Based on those flower petals found in Savannah's pocket, I made a bet this was Crystal Bog. If I were right, it was about fourteen hundred acres in size. I vaguely recalled it was a domed bog because it rose several meters towards its center. In the center, there would be a pond or several ponds of water. *Oh goody, now I can be both cold and wet.* I would be passing through zones of vegetation, with lots of hollows and hummocks. *If I'm really lucky, I can break an ankle!* I could still hear James yelling after me, so I picked up my pace.

Although the snow had melted considerably, there was still a good six inches on the ground in the bog, and I couldn't see what was under it. I stepped in a hollow and fell flat on my face. *Shit, that hurt!*

I was slow picking myself up. I stopped to listen for any sound of James following me, then continued east, watching my steps, chain clinking. Where my feet kicked up the snow, I saw what looked like a bog moss lawn, with a dense and very wet layer of peat mosses. The duck boots I was wearing didn't help a bit. In some areas where the snow was deeper, it found its way down inside the boots and soaked my socks; my feet soon felt like blocks of ice. The rest of me, by contrast, was warm and sweating from the exertion. I wanted to take off my ski hat because my hair was damp, but I knew once my head got cold, I'd be unable to keep the rest of me warm.

In some areas, the surface of the bog was frozen, and I broke through repeatedly as I walked. Running was not an option. There were some stunted shrubs, but basically I was now in the open, hoping beyond hope James had decided not to follow me through the bog. Every few feet I stopped and looked back, but so far there was no sign of him. When I came to one of the bog's ponds, which I discovered by stepping into eight inches of water under the ice, I figured I was at least half way across. If I calculated correctly, another mile or so might find me out of it, with the possibility of finding a road or a hiking trail. Certainly there had to be hiking trails.

I had stopped hearing James a long time before, and it occurred to me that rather than track me through the bog, he had taken the easier and warmer way and would meet me on the other side with his truck. *Should I keep going or should I turn back?* He might have left the girls alone, but there was no help in that direction. Maybe I could find some if I kept on.

My progress slowed as I tired. I became colder, feet freezing, chain dragging on the ground, breath coming in deep pants. A thin, watery sun was overhead, giving no warmth, no heat.

I ran into what appeared to be a logging road about ninety minutes later and stopped in shock. *I made it out of the bog.* I took a guess and followed the road to the left, praying it was the right direction. Somebody had heard my prayers because I found the sign for a trailhead about twenty minutes later. A few minutes after that, an expanse of snow looking a lot like a parking lot came into view. A road angled off to one side. When I got there and kicked the snow aside, I saw gravel. *A double hallelujah!* I was so tired I had to force myself down the gravel road, feet dragging, head down. All I wanted to do was sit down and rest, but by now the winter sun was going down. In this densely wooded area, it was already growing dark. Then, suddenly, there was a main road, plowed and free of snow.

Which way to go? I decided to take a left and continue heading east. There were no cars on the road, but I remembered James would be driving around the bog, looking for me, his massive liability. Just at that moment I heard a car coming, so without thinking beyond the need to hide, I climbed the mound of snow by the side of the road and rolled down the other side. The car passed, and I peeked over the snow mound. It wasn't James' truck. If I could have felt my feet, I would have kicked myself. I really had to do something about my feet, so I stepped over the ice-filled ditch between mound and the berm, climbed the berm and pulled back into the trees. There I sank to the ground, leaned back against a pine tree, and almost gave in to my overwhelming need to close my eyes, just for a minute, and rest. It felt so wonderful to be off my legs.

However, I was more afraid of lying there permanently, and my abdomen was cramping. I rubbed it, thinking, *Calm down, baby, things will be better, soon we can both rest.* I knew I was seriously dehydrated from all the sweat, but had been afraid to take more than a mouthful of snow for fear of hypothermia. I sat up and took off my boots, socks and leather mittens. I shook the water out of my boots, wrung out my socks until they were as dry as possible, and massaged my feet as hard as I could, chain and shackles getting in the way of each movement. I

251

had an idea and dug down through the snow until I found a layer of pine needles and leaves. A little further down, they were pretty dry, so I dug them up and used them to line the bottom of my boots. I struggled to pull my socks on, then blew several warm breaths into my boots before sliding them back on and lacing them up. I took the scarf off the chain, double-wrapped it around my neck and pulled my parka hood up, lacing it tight. The sweat from my hike across the bog had soaked my turtle neck. Now that I wasn't moving, I was getting chilled and starting to shiver.

I wouldn't last long in this cold, especially after the sun went down. The longer I was gone, the greater the chance James would try to move Sarah and Jane.

James or no James, I had to try the road.

27

I heard another car off in the distance, coming my way. Pulling myself painfully to my feet, I emerged from the trees and started to walk down the berm. Halfway down, I slipped on wet leaves, then slid down the small hill and into the gulley between the berm and the snow pile. It was partially filled with ice, leaves and nearly a foot of dirty runoff water, which I could feel soaking through my parka and gloves. I dragged myself out of the water and crawled to the top of the snow pile to see where the car was. It wasn't a car, it was a truck, and it looked like James'. I dropped down to the bottom of the pile, back into the leaves and water. I was sure it was James; the truck moved by at a snail's pace, then stopped. I could hear a window being opened and after a few moments, smelled cigarette smoke. I put my hand over my mouth to deaden the sound of my breathing, sure he would hear me panting in fear. I only hoped he wouldn't see any marks where I'd crawled over the snow.

When the truck started moving again, I couldn't believe my luck. Maybe it was the diminishing light, maybe his position on the other side of the road. Or maybe it was just karma, to offset the fact I was sitting in icy cold water. I inhaled deeply several times as the truck moved on, but still waited several minutes before rising from my hiding place. I decided then and there to throw myself in front of the next car heading in the same direction, but I worried James would circle back.

I crawled over the snow mound and stood by the side of the road for a minute or two, shivering violently and dripping ice water, the chain attached to me clanking rhythmically. I couldn't hear or see a car coming east along the road. So I decided to start walking. At least it would warm me up, because by now my teeth were chattering uncontrollably.

Finally, headlights. I jumped into the middle of the road, waving my shackled hands and jumping up and down. The car slowed as it approached me, then suddenly veered around me and sped off. I saw an elderly woman at the wheel, eyes wide with fright, with someone in the passenger seat beside her. *Why didn't they stop?* I bent over, then knelt on the roadway in frustration, tears flowing freely for the first time.

Then it came to me. They'd seen a grubby, wild-looking person, clad in a muddy, bedraggled parka, waving at them with shackles and chains to get them to stop. They probably thought I was one of the undead. I wouldn't have stopped for me either, and I found myself laughing hysterically at the thought. *Okay, Rhe. Get up. Get going. Move that large butt. Sarah needs you.*

By now it was pitch black, and I could only walk straight by using the plowed snow as a guide. I picked up my pace, but despite the effort, my shivering was becoming more violent. *Oh goody, stage two of hypothermia.* I decided to try walking faster, to get my heart rate up, maybe raise my body temperature. *If I could only take off this damned sodden coat!* But the shackles and chain made this impossible. I did remove the wet gloves and rather than wringing icy water out of them, tossed them to the side of the road. After pulling on the chain, my frozen hands, still shackled, went into my pockets, which were only slightly less wet.

After another few minutes, I gave up; I had nothing left. I couldn't go one step further and sank to the roadway again, totally spent, hoping some time on the ground would give my batteries a little boost. I'd probably have to crawl back over the snow to avoid being hit by the next car. Which probably wouldn't stop.

Just then I heard the roar of a motor coming from the west. The sound propelled me to my feet, shaking, and I tried to climb the snow pile, digging in with my toes. *Can I roll over the top?* The vehicle came to a rubber-laying stop. I couldn't look, knowing it was James and there was nothing more I could do. It was over.

"Rhe! Is that you?"

I knew that voice! "Bowers?" I croaked, rolling back down to the road. What had stopped beside me was a four-wheel drive black SUV. Another door opened and suddenly two people were dragging me to my feet. Bowers and Bongiovanni. They'd never looked better.

"Gotta get her in the car and get this wet coat off of her," I heard Bongiovanni say.

"Can't," I rasped.

They stood me up, leaned me against the SUV, and examined the shackles. "Got any bolt cutters in the trunk?" asked Bowers.

"Not likely," replied Bongiovanni, shaking his head. "But I have an idea." He went to the back of the SUV, pulled out some sort of box from the trunk area and rummaged through it by the light of the rear tail lights. He returned with a flat head screw driver, then withdrew his Glock from his shoulder holster. After removing the magazine, he pulled the slide back and checked for any round in the gun, then locked the slide in the open position.

"Kneel down and put the chain on the ground, Rhe," he ordered. "This is a cheap chain. I think I can break it."

How did he know that?

Taking the screwdriver and holding the gun by the barrel, he bent down and placed the blade of the screw driver on the chain. He gave the handle of the screw driver several sharp whacks with the gun butt. A few more and the chain parted. Bowers helped me wiggle out of my coat, although my shivering didn't help. By that time, Bongiovanni had returned with some hand warming gel packs from the trunk and threw a thick blanket around my shoulders before helping me into the backseat of the car.

He pulled off my boots and socks, bent two more of the gel packs and placed them under my feet, then two in my armpits. The warmth from those packs was like heaven. "What are you doing here? How did you find me?" I could barely talk because my jaws were chattering.

Bowers was quick to answer. "We located some property owned by Barnes near the bog, and were on our way there when we heard a report from the local Sheriff that two of his senior citizens had seen an apparition in the road. A zombie with chains, staggering toward them. Since we were pretty sure Barnes had taken you, and knowing your …um…abilities, we figured it might be you." Bowers smiled, an honest to God smile.

Bongiovanni grunted. "We need to get you to a hospital."

"No, you can't! Sarah's in that barn. Jane Alderson's there, too. Sarah's okay, but Jane's in bad shape. You've got to go *now*! James drove by in his truck looking for me a little while ago. Since he didn't find me, he'll move the girls."

Bowers squealed the SUV around in a U-turn, throwing me into the door, and headed west on the road I had just spent so much energy traversing. I noticed he had a GPS locator in the dash, and our next turn was coming up. The SUV rounded the corner smoothly on two wheels and sped west. I needed to ask Bowers where he learned to drive. After what I calculated was four to five miles, he took a right onto a bumpy road. *I know this road!*

"It's not so far now, maybe a half mile," I told them. "There's a barn at the end of the road, with a derelict farmhouse to the right."

Bowers slowed the engine and cut the lights, but couldn't eliminate the crunching of the tires on the gravel and dirt. I could just see the outline of the barn ahead when he stopped the car.

"James has a gun, so be careful," I warned them.

"What kind of gun?" Bongiovanni asked, turning to face me.

"A handgun, big, bulky, looked old."

"His grandfather's Smith and Wesson M58," replied Bowers.

"How do you know?" I asked.

"Long story, tell you later."

"What's he driving?" asked Bongiovanni.

"A truck, Ram 150, parked somewhere near the barn if he's here," I replied.

With that, Bongiovanni and Bowers got out of the car quietly, and in synchrony whispered, "Stay put. Don't move from the car!"

I was still shaking and relished the warmth of the blanket and the gel packs, but I couldn't just sit there. I just couldn't. I had to do *something*. When the agents had moved out of sight into the darkness, I opened my door quietly and crept out in my bare feet, keeping the blanket around me. It was pitch black, the stars obscured by a thick layer of low clouds. There was no light from the direction of the old farm house, but I could just see the barn, its large door outlined in yellow by the light within. I stopped and listened, barely hearing the very soft crunching of shoes on gravel ahead.

Suddenly there was a screech on the gravel, and the door became a large, light-filled square. Two shadows entered the barn and I heard, "FBI.

Put your hands up!" Then nothing. The faint grind of a motor starting up came from behind the house, then a shadow, a large bulky shadow, slowly edged into the faint light spilling onto the driveway from the barn door. James' truck. *Why did both agents enter the barn? I'd told them he parked near the barn, hadn't I? Damn.*

I heard the truck coming toward me and raced back to the SUV with a mental *ow, ow, ow!* from the gravel biting my feet, opened the driver's side door and slid in. I felt for keys. None. *Push button, Rhe! This is a new SUV!* I found something round and flat and pushed, nothing. I pushed on the brake, then hit the button again; the engine started. I could just make out the truck coming toward me, so I shifted into drive, stepped on the accelerator, and swung the SUV left, blocking the road. In the darkness and without headlights, I knew James wouldn't see the car until it was too late. No time to jump, no time for the seatbelt. All I could do was brace for the collision and hope he didn't have the girls with him.

He hit the right side of the car with a shocking jolt. The air bag exploded and I was thrown into the driver's side door. A few minutes later, Bowers opened my door and shined a flashlight in my eyes.

"Hey, quit it! I'm okay. Get that out of my face," I yelled, while pushing the airbag out of the way and moving each of my extremities to make sure I hadn't lied. My left side felt like it had been hit by a train, but all my parts moved smoothly. As I swiveled to get out of the car, I noticed my neck was stiff and wondered if a cervical collar was in my future.

"I'm going to stay in the car," I told Bowers, turning back into the seat. "My neck is stiff and I want an EMT to check me out."

"They've been called and should be here shortly, whatever shortly means in this neck of the woods."

I leaned back in the seat, keeping my neck aligned and rigid. "How are the girls?"

"Bongiovanni is with them in the barn. He's busy trying to break their chains."

"And Barnes?"

"He hit his head on the window, no seat belt. He wasn't going that fast, and he was halfway out of the truck when I got to him. I have him handcuffed to his steering wheel."

"You could have fooled me," I replied. "It certainly felt like he was speeding."

"You okay staying here? I need to report to Bongiovanni."

"Sure. Leave me in my hour of need."

ත⬥ᖆ

Thirty minutes later, the gravel drive and the area outside the barn were flooded with police cars and EMS trucks, flashing red and blue lights, more illumination from car doors left open, and a lot of general noise and confusion. The local police and the FBI were conferring, well, arguing, over jurisdiction. I was sitting at the back end of one of the two EMS trucks, cervical collar around my neck as a precaution, Sarah cuddled beside me.

I'd watched while James was placed on a gurney, cuffed to either side, and loaded into an ambulance for the ride to the local hospital. A police car followed the ambulance. Jane had been brought out of the barn on another gurney, covered in blankets, an IV in her arm and an oxygen mask in place. She hadn't moved, staring blankly up at the sky, and hadn't reacted when she was loaded into the EMS truck.

All in all, Sarah was in much better physical shape than I was, but her psychological injuries were probably going to time to heal. Bongiovanni had called her parents and she'd talked to them briefly before they left to meet her at the hospital. Since Bowers was now an expert at delivering bad news, he'd been told to call Jane Alderson's parents. He'd told me they didn't believe him at first and thought it was some cruel joke, so he gave them an FBI number in Washington to call. They did and were routed back to him. After the initial shock, they promised to be at the hospital as soon as possible; he said he'd warned them to drive at the speed limit. *Only Bowers.*

In my heart, I knew that poor girl would never be normal again. *What a difficult time her parents faced. Would they be able to handle it?*

ත⬥ᖆ

Both girls had been found on the floor in the barn, trussed up like Thanksgiving turkeys, ready to be loaded into James' truck. Apparently he had abandoned them when he'd heard the SUV in the driveway, figuring they would be a liability.

Sam, who by now was on the scene, had relayed all this information. He sat on the other side of me, regarding my face (air bag burn), head (large knot on the side, now covered with a compress and gauze wrap), bloody hair, bandaged wrists and feet. Oh, and the cervical collar and several layers of blankets. He shook his head and said with all seriousness, "Rhe, you're in no shape to go back to work tomorrow."

I started to laugh. The tension of the last two days finally spilled over. I laughed until the laughs became sobs, and I leaned into his chest crying the tension into relief. He put an arm around me and stroked the part of my head that wasn't bandaged with his other hand. It felt so good I cried some more, for the girls, for my lost relationship with Will, and for everything that had gone wrong in my life during the past few weeks.

The next thing I knew, he was shaking me gently. "Rhe, honey, wake up. They're going to take you to the hospital now. They need to stitch your head and do another check of the baby. Can you stand up?" Groggily I stood and Sam and an EMT helped me onto a gurney, which was lifted into the back of the EMS truck. They covered me with more blankets, assessed my peripheral pulses and alertness, then put in an IV. Sam climbed in and sat beside me. Sarah started screaming. "No, don't take Aunt Rhe. I have to be with her!" In a moment or so, she was beside me in the truck. We held hands, all three of us. I was safe, she was safe. I drifted off again.

❦ ❧

I awoke to a hospital room filled with flowers and a roommate who turned out to be Sarah. She was sitting up and enjoying a McDonald's breakfast; clearly not hospital fare. Then I noticed some other happy faces: Paulette, Ted, and Tyler.

Someone patted my arm and I turned my head to find Jack standing on the other side of my bed. "Did you have a good sleep, Mom? Uncle Sam told us not to wake you up. They brought you breakfast, but it looks yucky!"

Suddenly I remembered what had happened, and looking around, found Sam, who had been sitting quietly near the door. I put my hands on my stomach but felt nothing. Panic took over. "How's the baby? I can't feel her moving!"

"The baby's fine, Rhe. Apparently she's as tough as her mother," he replied.

As quickly as it had come, the tension drained out of me.

"Yeah, Mom, she's fine. How come you didn't tell me? Am I really going to have a little sister?"

"I was waiting for a special time to tell you, Jack. I don't know if it's a little sister."

"Well, if you can order it, I want a sister."

I laughed and tried to lift my head and move to hug him. But the headache was still there and I felt like I'd been run over by a semi. I fell back on my pillow.

Jack smiled knowingly and pressed a button on the side of the bed. "Look, Mom, I can make your bed come up!"

"Thanks, kiddo." I opened my arms. He moved in for a huge hug and finally crawled onto the bed to snuggle with me. "When did you get here?" I asked him, when he'd finished squirming.

"I don't know but it was still dark. Uncle Ted drove like a madman."

Ted winced. "I was never over the speed limit by more than ten miles an hour, Jack, but it was a special circumstance." He came to the side of my bed, took my hand and pressed it. "Rhe, how can we ever thank you enough? You saved our Sarah. We owe you so much." There were tears in his eyes.

Paulette nodded, came over, and took both our hands. "He's right. Sarah told us what you did. You could have been killed." She looked over her shoulder at Sarah and turned back, tears running down her cheeks.

"But I wasn't, and I'm going to be fine. Stop crying, Paulette, you'll run your mascara." That got a smile.

All of sudden, I felt like I was easing down into a nice, fuzzy, soft place. My eyes closed. "The docs say she can sleep," said Sam. "But I need to wake her every hour or so to make sure nothing comes from that whack on the head. Jack, you want to stay with me? Then you can say hi when your Mom wakes up. Here's your Nintendo." The last thing I heard was the sound of a curtain being pulled.

By that evening, I was definitely on the mend. I was alert, sitting up, and eating what I thought was dinner: mystery meat, lumpy and bland mashed potatoes, canned green beans. At least the lime Jello looked tasty. Sam sat beside me, reading a magazine. I'd vaguely heard the discussion about Jack going home with the McGillivrays, so he wouldn't miss another day of school.

The overhead TV was on. "In today's news, the FBI, acting on a tip from the Pequod Police Department, raided a barn near Crystal Crossing and found Jane Alderson, who vanished more than two years ago. With her was Sarah McGillivray, the eleven-year-old kidnapped from Pequod last Tuesday. Before raiding the barn, the FBI found Rhe Brewster, a neighbor of the McGillivrays, walking on a road not far from the barn, seeking help. Ms. Brewster disappeared under mysterious circumstances on Sunday. It is not known at this time how or why Ms. Brewster disappeared or how she ended up on that road. The alleged kidnapper of the girls has been identified as James Barnes, a resident of Crystal Crossing, aged thirty-one. A conference was held earlier today with FBI and local police representatives..." I turned it off and looked at Sam. "Okay, you wanna give me the facts? What did I miss?"

He winked. "Quite a lot, actually. What do you want to hear first?"

"How I was found."

"Eat your dinner and I'll tell you."

I took another bite of the mystery meat and chewed. *Yuck.* "Okay, spill."

"Well, it was a pretty busy Sunday," he began, clearly relishing the telling. "First of all, we got a call from a neighbor of Pete Barnes, reporting what she thought were gun shots coming from inside his house. Phil and I went over to investigate and found Pete in his kitchen, shot in the chest. We think he's going to live, but right now it's touch and go."

"I'm really sorry to hear that. I just can't believe Pete had anything to do with this. I bet James shot him. James was clearly decompensating, with all the pressure on him."

"Whatever it was, we need to talk with him when he's able."

"Then what happened?" I leaned back and rolled on my side to face him, but not without wincing at the various aches and pains.

"When I got your voicemail and you didn't answer your phone, I drove over to Hannaford. Figured you'd gone there. I found your Jeep in the parking lot, bag, keys and phone inside." He glared at me.

"Heck, Sam, it was the middle of the day, I was going to a busy shopping center, and I couldn't imagine anything happening to me. I was totally wrong, I admit it."

Sam continued glaring but gave a low growl in agreement. "About the same time, the station got a call from a couple who'd been at the Hannaford store and thought they'd seen a kidnapping. They couldn't describe either you or James very well, but they were pretty clear on the make and license plate of the truck."

"I made a real mess of things, didn't I?"

"I couldn't agree more…"

"So how did you find me?"

"You can thank Phil for that. He'd been trying to locate where Barnes might have holed up, and found a farm their father had left both kids, up near Crystal Bog. The farm produced vegetables in season. Pete wasn't interested since he had his own lobstering business, so James took it over. Turns out he wasn't cut out for it. He took the summer job at Cornwell's sheep ranch because it was something he *could* do, and worked with Peter in the winter."

"I wonder what got him started kidnapping young girls? Is he insane?"

"Probably won't know until he's evaluated by a psychiatrist, which I'm sure his lawyer will want. What the FBI discovered is his part time jobs weren't enough to pay the bills and the farm is now in foreclosure. I don't think the bank was really interested in it, because nothing moved on the foreclosure. That's why James could keep the girls there. Maybe he had some arrangement with the bank. We're looking into it."

"And Pete couldn't help him out, not with the price of lobsters these last two years. So the pressure on James must have been growing."

"I agree. You finished with that gourmet meal? Can I move the tray?" He got up and walked to the side of the bed.

"It's all yours. Anything there that you fancy? Have you had dinner?"

"No, I'm going out to eat. This grub's not palatable, even for a starving cowboy."

I had to smile. "That's saying something if *you* won't eat it. Bring me something back? I could use a Big Mac and a frappe, chocolate please."

"Maybe tomorrow, after you're discharged, we can stop at a Friendly's on our way back to Pequod." I watched him move the tray to a desk and pull his chair closer to my bed.

"Pretty please. I'm so hungry!"

"No," he replied firmly.

"When did you get so mean?" He smiled. I gave up pleading. "So then what happened?"

"After we located the farm, we contacted the FBI. Turns out Bongiovanni and Bowers were already in the area based on some information they'd dug up. Before they went to the farm, they decided to contact the local constabulary. Guess they decided to follow protocol. That's when they heard about the old couple seeing you on the road."

My hand lifted to the side of my head, where I could feel the bandage and a wad of matted hair. *I'm a god-awful mess. Good thing I can't see myself.*

Sam saw my expression. "Don't worry, you look lovely and I'm sure they'll let you wash your hair in a day or so."

"Liar. Continue with your story."

"You know the rest. Except for the normal push and shove between the FBI and the Police Chief. I think they've straightened it out. You're going to be all over the news for the next week or so."

I groaned.

"By the way, Tom O'Neil's in the clear. He'd loaned the keys to his barn to Peter, so he could store stuff during the winter. James lifted them."

"I'm so glad. I just couldn't see Tom being involved in anything like that."

"Oh, and Bob Morgan has been calling your cell phone non-stop. I turned it off, figure you can talk to him when you get home."

I groaned again. "That man is like a plague of locusts. But I did promise him an exclusive."

I pulled the blanket up over my head. "Can I just stay here for the next month?"

28

Two weeks later, I met Sam at Ernie's for lunch. I was back working in the ER, feeling like myself again with no residual bruises and clean hair. Best of all, the baby had come through unscathed and was growing at a healthy rate.

I found Sam at his favorite booth by the front window, which was, as usual, clouded over with condensation from the warmth and baking. I shivered, thinking of my last time here and seeing James in the window. It wasn't Sam he'd been looking at, it was me. Sam stood up to give me a hug.

"So what are you going to have?" I asked him as I gave him a quick hug back and slid into my seat, not very gracefully. I drank in the warm, yeasty smell, and Sam handed me the menu. "Don't tell me, sausage with green peppers and mushrooms."

He nodded. "How are you feeling today?"

"Peachy. What about you?"

"Really good, now that the FBI is out of my hair."

"Aw, come on. I know Bowers was growing on you."

Sam grunted. "Great news about the hospital. Now you won't have to worry so much about your job."

The hospital's board decided, after a session or two with Sawyer, to pay me a large sum of money as compensation for pain and suffering, if I would drop the lawsuit and agree not to talk about the settlement. Manning had been asked to submit his resignation. He was fighting it, but clearly he was a lame duck, especially with his right hand, Dolores Richmond, gone. That was enough to convince me to sign on the dotted line. More enemies, but I didn't regret it one bit.

"Hey, I heard from Sawyer," I told Sam. "Donnelly's doing well in his rehab program."

"Don't get your hopes up, honey. You know the recidivism rate is thirty to fifty per cent."

"I do, but I'm still hoping this time he'll be able to stay sober. If only for his kids' sake."

"Optimist."

At that point our waitress arrived. I rubbed a hole in the condensation on the window and looked out while Sam ordered; the usual for him and two slices of plain cheese pizza for me. I was worried about baby weight.

"How are things at home?" Sam asked, reaching across the table and taking my hand.

"Not too bad. I thought Will would use what happened to me as further evidence of my dangerous life, but so far there's been nothing from his lawyer; other than the fact our separation is official as of this weekend."

"I'm surprised he was willing to let Jack stay with you during the week and every other weekend. What's going on?"

I smiled. "He discovered trying to care for Jack during the week was difficult with his class schedule and office hours. Also, Zoey apparently told him taking care of a seven-year-old with ADHD was not part of their relationship. She finally settled for having Will to herself every other weekend, but not without a knock-down, drag-out fight."

Sam smiled back. "I wonder how long that will last?" he said, more as a statement than a question. "So how's this arrangement working for you?"

"Me? Great! I get to be Jack's mother most of the time, and the huge load of guilt about our marriage is gone."

"You know it wasn't your fault."

"I'm not blameless, Sam. Marriage is a two way street. But his affair with Zoey was the main problem. I think he just used my work with you and the police as a way to offset his own guilt."

The pizza arrived and we dove in, munching with enthusiasm. Sam was clearly enjoying it, but I noticed how tightly his uniform shirt stretched across his stomach. *I need to get Sam to work on his weight.*

"How's Sarah doing?" he asked, in between bites. "I haven't seen Paulette or Ted recently."

"Well, I think, all things considered. She's seeing a child psychiatrist once a week, and Paulette told me the nightmares aren't as frequent. Being a school celebrity hasn't seemed to hurt either."

Sam smiled. More chomping. "Have you heard anything about Jane Alderson?" he asked, a little garbled because Sam often asked questions with his mouth full.

I swallowed carefully. "The Aldersons came to see me yesterday to thank me for finding their daughter. I'm not sure I did them any favors. That little girl is scarred for life. But they are so joyful to have her home, I don't think it matters at this point. They told me she knew them when they first saw her at the hospital and she cried. If so, that's the first emotion she's had in a long time."

We continued rehashing events: James' arraignment and his plea of not guilty by reason of insanity, that we might never know how Bowers was drugged unless James confessed. Suddenly, a sharp pain in my abdomen caused me to buckle over in my chair and an "Oof" came from between my gritted teeth. Another pain had me gripping the table.

"What's wrong, Rhe?"

"Pain, really bad pain." Just then I felt something warm and wet in my lap. I looked down and put my hand on the growing stain on my scrub pants. When I lifted my hand, it was bloody. Another cramp and I toppled sideways onto the floor. *No, no! Not now.*

I became wrapped in my pain, only dimly aware of Sam yelling into his radio for EMS, for everyone to get back. Then, in a minute or an hour, I was in an ambulance, the pinch of a needle in a vein on my hand, Sam there beside me. I remember laughing ridiculously, saying, "Three ambulance rides in one year, Sam. This can't be good." Then another cramp hit, and it really wasn't good. I tightened my grip on his hand and time warped.

❧❦

An hour later I once again lay in a hospital bed, Sam still there, still holding my hand, stroking my hair. When we'd reached the hospital, they'd rushed me to the operating room, where I delivered the fetus. I'd been given a sedative,

267

but it was wearing off and the horrible sense of loss pushed me down into the mattress and clouded my mind. "I lost the baby! I lost the baby, Sam!" I whispered, groggily, and gave into self-pity. "Why me? I wanted that baby so much! Am I being punished?"

"No, you've done nothing wrong. You're okay, Rhe. You're going to be okay," Sam repeated over and over. He had a look of misery on his face I'd never seen before.

"Where's Will? Why isn't he here? Didn't you find him?"

"I did, but he didn't want to come. Maybe later."

"He's happy about this, isn't he? He didn't want our baby!" I was becoming wild in my anguish, and Sam reached for the call button to summon a nurse. He pressed it, and Nancy Ennis came in within seconds.

"How are you, sweetie? Not doing so good, huh?" She stroked my face and withdrew a syringe from her pocket, the contents of which she injected into my IV line. "You need to rest, Rhe, and sleep. This will help."

"Do they know if it was a boy or a girl?" I asked her.

I thought Sam was going to cry.

"A girl," Nancy replied. "A beautiful little girl."

Just before I drifted off, I heard Sam say, "You're not alone, Rhe. We'll get through this together. You'll have another baby, I know it."

Acknowledgements

I mentioned in the Acknowledgement for *Death in a Red Canvas Chair* that there was a village to thank. My village has now expanded to a small town, and I owe each of its occupants a heartfelt thank you.

First, to my husband Gene, who, despite some physical problems, has continued to take on household management to give me time to write. He didn't flag at taking a trip to Maine in February and has enthusiastically joined me on several outings, including a long walk around the Orono Bog. My daughter Cameron has once again posed for the cover, and once again it was about the coldest day of the winter when we did the photo shoot – this time down on the beach, where she was wrapped in a sail.

The members of two critique groups have been invaluable in helping shape this book, especially the Early Birds: Bob Byrd, Elizabeth Hein, Elizabeth Calwell, Denis Dubay, Becky Abbott and Grace Wetzel. From my evening group, I want to recognize the contributions of Mark Craven, Diana Fritz, and Jennifer Riley. To my beta readers: You're the best. Thank you to Bob Byrd, Brian Lang, Laura Stone, Judy Kinnally, Stephenie Kennerley, Patricia Condon, and Christina Grimes. This group really made me aware of issues with my writing overall and I learned a lot from their comments.

I would also like to thank my editor, Alison Williams and my line editor, Mary Boutin, a high school classmate. Together, they ensured that *Death in a Dacron Sail* isn't riddled with the errors, large and small, that I didn't see.

I am deeply grateful to three people whom I interviewed for this book: Nathanial Wilson, possibly the premier sail maker in the United States, who patiently took time out of his day to give me a tour of his loft and talk about his craft; Capt. Clive Farrin, who, along with his stern man, Cage Zipperer, gave me a morning on his lobster boat in Boothbay Harbor, Maine, and schooled me in the finer points of trapping lobsters; and John Dennis, Cultural Director of the Center for the Aroostook Band of MicMacs. We had a lovely Irish boiled dinner together, and I plan to use some of what I learned from him in the next

N. A. Granger

book. I'd also like to thank Nancy Sferra, Director of Science and Stewardship at the Nature Conservancy Maine Field Office, for information about Crystal Bog.

Finally, as with my previous book, *Death in a Dacron Sail* is fiction and Pequod is an imaginary place, living only in my mind. Some of the places mentioned *are* real, for example, various cities and Crystal Bog. Some of the recurring characters have the last names of people with whom I grew up in Plymouth, as a tip of the hat to the wonderful memories I have of those years.

Stay tuned for the third volume in the Rhe Brewster Mystery series, *Death by Pumpkin*. I'll leave you thinking about that!

Made in the USA
Middletown, DE
09 May 2015